no Brief affair

a beyond courtship novel

RYAN TAYLOR &
JOSHUA HARWOOD

WAINSCOTT PRESS

NO BRIEF AFFAIR (BEYOND COURTSHIP BOOK ONE)

Revised Edition

ISBN: 978-1-7907-4814-3

Cover by Cate Ashwood Designs.

BOOKS BY RYAN TAYLOR & JOSHUA HARWOOD

Macadam Universe

No Brief Affair (Beyond Courtship Book One)

Legally Bound (Beyond Courtship Book Two)

The Chrismukkah Crisis: A Holiday Romance

What He Really Needs

Too Close to the Flame

Bethesda Barracudas Hockey

Nice Catching You

The New Next One

Fire in the Ice

Ice Angels

Ice Devils

STAY IN TOUCH WITH RYAN AND JOSH

Never miss the latest news, promo, or freebie. Subscribe to our Newsletter.

Check out our Website for complete details about all our books and audiobooks. You can also contact us there.

Join our Facebook group, Ryan & Josh's Room.

Like us on Facebook.

Follow us on Instagram.

Follow us on Twitter.

Follow us on TikTok.

Follow us on Amazon.

Follow us on BookBub.

Follow us on Goodreads.

ACKNOWLEDGMENTS

Steven Clark, Jerome Clarke, Charles Cohen, Gail Lambert, and Emily Muddle gave a lot of time to this project and made extraordinary contributions to our work. You are wonderful people and we are very grateful for you.

Very importantly, we thank *you*—our reader—for choosing this book. Sharing our stories with others is a high privilege, and we appreciate your support. We hope you enjoy *No Brief Affair*.

CONTENTS

STAY IN TOUCH WITH RYAN AND JOSH

Never miss the latest news, promos, or freebies. Subscribe to our Newsletter.

Check out our Website for complete details about all our books and audiobooks. You can also contact us there.

Join our Facebook group, Ryan & Josh's Room.

Like us on Facebook.

Follow us on Instagram.

Follow us on Twitter.

Follow us on TikTok.

Follow us on Amazon.

Follow us on BookBub.

Follow us on Goodreads.

DEFINITIONS

This book has X-Ray enabled. Most names, places, and unusual words or phrases are defined there. Simply touch the word in question, and if material in X-Ray is associated with that word, a window will pop up with the information. The list below contains a few of the terms used in the book that might be most unfamiliar to the average reader.

UNY School of Law: A highly ranked law school at the fictional University of New York in Syracuse.

1L: A first-year law student. ("He's a 1L.") Or something associated with 1Ls. ("That's a 1L class.")

R&W: Research and Writing. R&W teaches 1Ls how to do legal research and write persuasively for legal audiences. Unlike most classes, R&W lasts for both semesters of the first year.

SBA: Student Bar Association. A school organization for law students.

Torts: The 1L class focusing on noncriminal acts and omissions that harm others.

Civ Pro: Civil Procedure. The 1L class focusing on the rules courts follow in civil lawsuits.

Property: The 1L class focusing on the ownership of real and personal property.

Con Law: Constitutional Law. The 1L class focusing on the law pertaining to the U.S. Constitution. This class emphasizes U.S. Supreme Court decisions.

Study Group: A small group of students who meet to review material covered in class. Traditionally, each member of a group creates an outline covering one of the 1L classes, so everyone in the group has an outline for each class at exam time.

Bar Review: Drinks at a local bar sponsored by the SBA. Bar Review is usually on Thursday evenings and generally includes a free drink or two, paid for out of students' SBA dues.

Reading Days: The days between the end of classes and the beginning of exams.

Law Review: Scholarly legal journals at law schools, edited and administered by the students who rank at the top of their 1L class. Being "on law review" is a high honor for law students and can help them obtain prestigious jobs or clerkships after graduation.

PART I

1

University of New York School of Law, Syracuse

Liam

I was late! It wasn't like me, but ever since I got upstate the weather had been fucking hot and humid and that had really slowed me down. Not to mention, I was nervous as hell and wondering if I should've gone to law school at all. I was pretty sure almost anything else would have been a better choice. Dogcatcher sounded good, right about then.

I hoped the sweat creeping down my back wasn't a bad omen. I probably stunk since I ran all the way from my apartment, and I hoped my whole law school career wouldn't stink, too.

Ah, piss-fuck-shit, the doors were already closed. I pulled on one of them, which of course just had to screech open and make a big noise, and the heat from inside blasted me in the face. *Isn't anything air conditioned up here?* Right after the heat came the smell—musty, like my grandma's attic.

On the positive side, I was glad to see that things hadn't started yet. A ton of people were crowded into a space that looked like a church hall. Full of round tables surrounded by folding chairs, the room had a ceiling that was too low, and cheap windows let in yellowish light.

Just inside the door, a tired-looking, wrinkled guy sat at a long table. "You're late," he groused in a smoky voice. "That doesn't work around here, as you'll soon learn." The silly half-moon glasses perched at the end of his nose, along with the permanent sneer etched into the lines around his mouth, seemed calculated to help him look down on people.

Idiot! In three years, I'll be a lawyer making pretty good money, and you'll still be sitting here getting off on intimidating kids starting law school.

"Name, please."

"Macadam. Liam Sean Macadam."

The man traced a bony finger down a list and tapped an empty space. "All right, Mr. Macadam. Sign the matriculation book right here."

After I signed, he started handing me things. "Here are your name badge and key card. There's a twenty-five-dollar fine if you lose the key card. Here is your class schedule. You're in Section Blue."

He tucked his chin and squinted his eyes, peering at me over those preposterous glasses. "Now listen closely, Mr. Macadam, since you apparently have a timeliness issue. Tomorrow morning, you have an appointment in this very room at 8:15 sharp to have your student ID made. Don't miss the appointment, or you won't be able to have your ID made until next week. That would mean you couldn't go to the bookstore until next week, which would cause you major problems."

"Thank you, sir," I said. "I'll be here for sure, but I already bought my books online."

He sniffed like I'd taken a shit on the floor. "I see. Well, we're all out of orientation schedules, so find someone else to share theirs. The dean is going to start any minute, so you'd better get in there."

Great! How the hell was I supposed to know when to be where over the next few days without a schedule? At least it gave me a little satisfaction to realize that the supercilious, condescending bastard couldn't count. All he had to do was look up how many people paid the admissions deposit and make that many copies of the goddamned schedule—problem solved.

I'd barely stepped into the main part of the room when the kind of *dudebro* I despise rushed over to me like we were long-lost friends, holding out his hand for a *dudebro handshake.* Bleach-blond hair fluffed up with salt spray, loud wrinkled clothes, and fluorescent white teeth. *Spare me.*

"Man, I'm glad I wasn't the only one running late," he said. "I've been here like thirty seconds. Check out all the sweet women going to law school!"

I barely suppressed a groan. Dudebro... dudebro handshake... straight. It was a good thing for him that he was, because I wouldn't have fucked him if he was the last man on earth. He started yammering on about something, and I couldn't have cared less what he had to say.

Stepping around Dudebro, I surveyed the room. There were a few cute guys, but they were all my age or younger, which excited me like a flat tire in the rain. Then I saw him —*holy shit! Hot, hot, hot guy alert!*—and he was looking at me, too. OMFG, I hoped like hell I didn't look as sweaty as I felt.

I'd caught this total knockout of a guy red-handed, totally checking me out. He was a few years older than me and had that shy, mature look that really got me going. A blue Lacoste shirt made his eyes pop from across the room, and I started walking toward him.

I was halfway there when the microphone blared to life. "Attention everyone, please find a seat. We need to get started so you have time for lunch before your first Research and Writing classes."

Mr. Blue Eyes sat down, and lucky for me there was an empty chair right next to his. I trucked it so I could get there before someone else claimed the seat, almost flooring some poor girl along the way and making her squeal. So much for fitting in quietly, but I made it. *Yes! High five to the checking-out-hot-guys gods.*

I smelled him as I sank into my seat, and my dick twitched. A citrusy cologne paired with his own musk to create a sensation that went straight to my privates. Pheromones, gotta love 'em.

He was speaking to someone across the table, and I needed to get his attention since I figured I had about an hour to check him out and gauge his interest. The schedule—Mr. Hot Stuff had a fucking schedule! I leaned in close so he'd realize I was talking to him. "Man, did you grab a schedule? Can I see it? They were all gone when I got here."

I sounded okay, a little high-pitched but okay. He turned in his chair and blushed pink as soon as he saw me. After a few blinks, he smiled—*OMG, erection-worthy dimples*—and looked me up and down—*thank God I took time to get properly dressed.* Then he hesitated—*maybe 'cause he knew I'd busted him checking me out?*—and licked his lips—*bring it on, man.* He put on a shy smile as he fixed me in a neutral but friendly gaze, and the minute he opened his beautiful mouth I knew I was already under his skin.

"Y-yes, I h-have one. H-here."

You've got him stuttering already! I breathed in slowly

while I looked him over. He was even more handsome than I'd thought from across the room. Ultra-fair skin, clear blue eyes, and luscious, pink lips just begging to be kissed. He was slender, but not skinny, and shorter than me. There were just enough laugh lines around his eyes to make me want to trace every single one of them with my tongue.

"I'm J-John Lawrence." He extended his hand and I took it, holding on long enough to watch his cheeks turn rosy. *John Lawrence*, I thought, looking at his nametag for the whole thing, *John William Lawrence.* Awesome name, and I was already inside him: Liam—Wil*liam*.

He wiggled around in his chair. "I-I'm just getting started here. I guess you are, too, but at least you look the part." His lips blanched as he pressed them together for a few seconds. "I-I mean, you look really good." He blinked a few times while his blush went scarlet. "Uh... y-you look like you belong...." With that, he closed his eyes and swallowed hard. "*God*, don't you think it's *hot* in here? D-did I say I'm John? Who are you?"

This incredibly sexy, apparently crazy man was interested in me. At least, I hoped it was me and not just heat stroke. I thought I'd better keep it together if I wanted to stand a chance with him. It's easy to spook older guys. Deciding that it was better to show some cool and leave him wondering about me, I put on my best killer smile.

"Hey John, I'm Liam Macadam. Nice shirt." I took the schedule he offered and only barely resisted grabbing his hand again. Someone up front began speaking in a ridiculous monotone, but I concentrated on checking John out and trying to keep my dick from becoming too obviously involved. After things got started, he turned his head up front and didn't look back at me. That is, unless you counted the two hundred times he glanced sideways when he thought I wasn't looking. He'd mastered the trick of looking at a guy and then looking away a millisecond later, as if no one would notice his head whipping around at light speed.

After we endured ninety minutes of welcomes, rules, and introductions, as well as an overdone description of how our lives were about to change, the session mercifully ended. I needed to leave John wondering about me, so I pushed back my chair, stood up, and enjoyed one last look before I took his schedule and walked away. Taking the schedule was key because in my quickly-hatched scheme, I needed an excuse to talk to him when I saw him later. That would be right after lunch, something I knew because his name badge said he was in Section Blue, same as me.

John

I WENT to the student center food court for lunch and thought about that Liam guy all the way over there. How rude he'd turned out to be. I'd been nice and there was no reason for him to act like a jerk, but he barely even looked at me for the whole orientation. When it was over, he took my schedule and walked away without even saying goodbye. Be that as it may, I have to confess that all conscious thought was suspended as I watched him saunter across the room. You could have stood a crystal goblet on top of his perfect ass.

He was beautiful, in a very masculine way. His face was gorgeous, like a Roman statue, and his chocolate-brown eyes matched the color of his perfectly messy hair. The shirt he'd worn showed off a great physique, muscular but not muscle-bound. *Damn it!* I hated to admit it, but he was the kind of man I'd fantasized about my whole life.

While I ate a mediocre club sandwich, I tried to call my so-called partner, Thorne. Of course, there was no answer, so I sent a quick text.

JOHN: *Hi, how are things?*

I ate half my sandwich while waiting for him to respond.

THORNE: *Still trying to get them to listen to me.*
JOHN: *Coming home for dinner? I'll make something good.*
THORNE: *No, I'll be here late. Probably won't see you until the weekend.*
JOHN: *Couldn't you please come home? It's a big day here and I don't feel like being alone.*
THORNE: *Every day's a big day for me. Don't you need to do homework or something?*

I felt like crying and hated that he still had that power over me.

JOHN: *I'm not going to beg you. See you later.*

Things were frightful between us. I'd had more than enough and our sixteen-year relationship was over, something I needed to tell him—not that he would mind. I wasn't getting any younger and couldn't afford to waste more time hoping things might improve when they were only getting worse.

Thorne had always been controlling, manipulative, and passive-aggressive. His verbal abuse had worsened over the years, and he became increasingly remote. His emotional unavailability escalated into virtual abandonment, and the abuse became constant. If he still loved me in any sense, it was the best disguised secret of the century.

We lived in Wisconsin before law school, and I'd been surprised when he moved to New York with me since I was certain he was having an affair. Nothing got any better after the June move; only the location of the misery changed. By late July, he'd taken an apartment near his work, saying his hours were too long and the drive home too far. ("Thirty minutes is too far?"—"You're not the one who has to drive it.") He said he would be home every weekend, which was only the latest promise he'd ignored.

Enough of Thorne. I needed to think about law school. After teaching college for twelve years at Northstar University, I was disgusted with the administration there and decided to use my sabbatical year to try something else. I'd thought about going to law school for years, and now I would. If I didn't like it, I could always go back to Northstar, where I conducted most of the choirs and taught music history.

I was nervous, as I'm sure everyone was, but I was also self-conscious. Older than the other students—almost twenty years older than most of them—I wondered how they would react to having an old man in class. It was going to be very different sitting at a desk again, listening to someone else talk at the front of the room.

Thinking about law school made me think about Liam again. I'd first noticed him while I looked around for a place to sit. He was incredibly eye-catching, but while I admired his cock-of-the-walk smile, I'd noticed he was talking to some guy who looked like a jerk. I thought Liam was probably the same because he was simply too good-looking not to be in love with himself.

When the orientation session began, I took the first seat I saw. I was speaking to a girl across from me when someone slid into the chair next to mine and asked if he could see my schedule. When I turned around, my heart jumped into my throat. It was the same gorgeous guy who'd caught me checking him out like an old troll. He wore a grin you could drive a truck through, and I could barely force out a sound.

Eventually, I managed to introduce myself, and when we shook, his grip was firm, but his hand was so soft and warm that I wanted to keep it. He sat there staring at me silently, and after a moment I felt feverish. Muttering like a deranged man, I groped for something to say and stuttered my way through some stupid remarks. Mortification reached critical mass as I embarrassed myself more with every sentence, and amusement crept across his face.

He was grinning again by the time he told me his name, and what an awesome grin it was. It could have melted the polar icecap, and I wondered how many more teeth he had than usual. For a wild second, I imagined he scooted his chair closer and sniffed me.

Jesus! Didn't you stop fantasizing about straight guys back in college?

It really didn't matter because I doubted I'd see him again for at least a year. The law school had three 1L sections, each of which had all of its classes together for both semesters. Liam would most likely be in a different section, so I wouldn't have to worry about him.

Liam

I LIVED in on-campus housing for graduate students. My apartment was small but all mine, and I liked it. The furnishings were mostly from Ikea, but Mom had insisted on providing a few nice touches, like the sofa with down cushions and a mattress that made me want to stay in bed all day.

During the lunch break, I went back there to have a couple

sandwiches and enjoy the air conditioning. Of course, I thought about John. He was drop-dead gorgeous and a little zany, prime material for a hookup. Or who knew? Maybe he was the guy who'd make law school unforgettable.

The last couple years I'd been through a hard time, losing a cousin, a boyfriend, and my dad, all pretty close together. After that emotional hat trick, I was in bad shape for a while. In fact, I was still protecting myself and hadn't dated anyone for over a year. I'd only had two hookups in all that time, the minimum necessary to maintain sanity.

Yet here I was allowing myself to think all kinds of thoughts about John William Lawrence. Was I ready to dive back into the water, or just fooling myself? I thought maybe I should play it safe and try for friendship with him, but he woke up something inside me and we'd have to see.

After a quick jerk-off—John *really* got under my skin—I headed back to the law school for our first R&W class. In the basement, I walked into a stuffy room with green walls, exposed pipes, and desks that looked like they were borrowed from an elementary school. I didn't give a shit, though, because the room wasn't important. What mattered was that Mr. John William Lawrence was already there.

John

I WAS the first person to arrive for class. While the others came in, I took out my phone to read the news, but that guy Liam kept invading my thoughts. Why was I fixated on such a jerk? He was obviously only concerned about himself, and thinking about him only made me more nervous than I already was. Besides, he was a thief. I would have made a copy of the schedule for him if he'd only asked.

Still, I couldn't stop thinking about how he looked at me with those damned brown eyes and that heart-stopping smile. *Mental sigh.* Oh well, sexy dickheads were a dime a dozen, and I wouldn't have time to worry about one this year. I had more important things to do than make a fool of myself by chasing a straight man close to twenty years younger than me.

The classroom door's shrill creak caused me to look up, and I was flabbergasted to see none other than Liam Macadam—not that I remembered his name—walk into the room. *He could not be in this class with me, could he?*

Liam looked right at me, immediately hypnotizing me with his devil eyes, and my breath caught in my throat. I hated to admit it, but he didn't look like a devil at all. Liam was pure sex on legs, and a shock ricocheted to the tips of my toes. He'd changed shirts, and the fresh one showed off his body even better than the first one had.

As he swaggered across the room toward me, I couldn't force my head to look down. I hoped he would sit at one of the desks along the way even as I prayed he would come and sit next to me. The Doppler effect of his echoing footsteps made me dizzy, and for the second time that day, he claimed the seat right next to mine and turned on one of his incandescent smiles.

"Hey John! I'm Liam, from this morning, remember? I took your schedule, sorry, but I made a copy so here's yours back." He paused, and I got the impression that he was nervous. "What do you think? You like everything so far? I'm a little worried about this class because I hear we have the hardest prof of all."

Liam was talking fast, and my resistance was slipping. Irresistible brown eyes threatened to suck in my soul if I didn't look away, but I just couldn't. He really was the devil, but he was the sexiest devil there ever was, a devil disguised as an angel whose looks invited eye-fucking for days. *Maybe the devil will make deviled John.*

No! It hit me like a ton of bricks—Liam was more than gorgeous, sexy, and evil. My notoriously accurate gaydar kicked in, and I was sure of it—he was gay. Not many men had ever looked at me the way he did, hopeful and hungry, as if I were something to be devoured. *Oh, how I wish he would devour me.*

Pathetically, I stammered at him again. "H-Hi Liam, I remember you. Thanks for bringing my schedule back."

Liam

The first thing I saw when I walked into that classroom was John, turning his head toward the door. We locked eyes, and I walked across the room to sit at the desk next to him. He never looked down, the deer in the headlights thing, I think. As I got closer, I smelled his cologne again, but there was more man-smell this time and my shorts got a little tighter.

I gave him back his schedule and tried to make conversation, but he just watched me with his dreamy blue eyes. I kept wishing he'd say something—just be friendly, you know? He looked even hotter than he had before, which only made me more jittery. It was so bad I got afraid I might start panting. Before, I'd thought I only wanted to take him to my new apartment and have my way with him, but sitting next to John again, I realized that I actually wanted him to like me. *Maybe we can be friends* and *lovers?*

I had to get him to say something, but my brain just wasn't turning over. When another whiff of him wafted my way, I went with what I had. "I really like your cologne. What is it?" *Smooth, Liam.*

The dimples creasing his cheeks made my stomach quiver.

"Thank you. It's Citron Summer by Belle Eau. I like it this time of year."

"It's nice." *What the fuck? You're crashing and burning.*

He spread his lips into a smile and gave me something I could work with: "You look comfortable, considering how hot it is outside."

"Yeah? I have an apartment on campus, so I was able to go up there and enjoy the air conditioning for an hour while I ate lunch."

"Lucky devil," he said, his smile broadening as he totally checked me out again, head to toe. His dimples deepened as his eyes sparkled, but just when he opened his mouth to say something else, Professor James walked in.

She introduced herself and made us all take turns saying our names and what brought us to law school. After that, she handed out the syllabus and sent around a seating chart for us to sign. Where we sat the first day was where we'd be sitting all semester.

I had a horrible thought that John might move rather than sit with me, but he didn't. He just wrote his name down and handed me the chart. My fingers brushed his when I took it from him—an accident, I swear—and I almost yelped, it felt so good. Quickly scrawling my name in the spot right next to his, I passed the paper along before he had second thoughts.

2

Liam

After class, John and I both sat there pretending to pack our bags. When we'd stretched that out as far as it could go, everyone else was gone and one of us had to do something. I was debating between 'see ya later' and 'you wanna see my apartment?' when John looked at me and smiled. "Where are you from, Liam?"

Fuck, where was *I from? Oh yeah.* "Long Island, growing up. Undergrad at Columbia, graduated last May. How about you?"

His bashful grin totally gave me a semi. "I grew up in North Carolina, but I've lived everywhere. I was a college professor, and you go where the work is. Most recently, I lived in Wisconsin and taught at Northstar University."

Wow. "That's a good school and you were a prof there? Why are you here, then?"

Moaning softly with desire, I traced his cheekbone with my fingertips. Well, to be honest, not really, but I wanted to.

In actuality, John rolled his eyes. "Long story. Basically I wanted to try something new. I have a year off, and since I always considered going to law school, here I am."

"Way cool." I winked. "I'm glad you're here."

Big, long pause while his smile faded. *Shit, what have you done, Liam? Gotta save!* It was time for desperate measures, so I took a deep breath and wiped my brow for effect. "You wanna go get something cold to drink?"

He glanced at the floor. "Well, I have to go home soon...."

Say yes! Say yes! Say yes!

He looked up and wiped his brow, too. "It *is* awfully hot. Why not?"

Hallelujah! The heavens opened up, the chains fell away, the birds sang, and all was right with the world. John was smiling again, and my innards relaxed.

"You have someplace in mind?" he asked. "I live in town, so I don't know this area yet."

"There's a cool bar just off campus with happy hour specials and tapas." *It's early and shouldn't be crowded yet, so I'll have you all to myself.*

His dimples were at least a mile deep. "Sounds great. Lead the way, Liam Macadam. I'm right behind you."

Hopefully I'll be behind you *soon, John Lawrence.*

John

Liam took full possession of my senses. I knew I was playing with fire, but he comforted me. It sounded crazy, but he made me feel safe amid the stress of starting law school. And his smile, the one with those thousand teeth and maddeningly lickable red lips, made my breath hitch.

I probably shouldn't have said anything engaging after class, but I wanted to hear him talk some more. When he winked at me, I realized again how much older I was, but when he asked if I wanted to get something to drink, a thrill zipped up my spine. Thus, I found myself at a college bar, eating tapas and drinking gin with the hottest guy who'd ever flirted with me.

Under Liam's spell, I realized I needed to mention Thorne just to get it out there. I didn't want to mislead Liam, and also wanted to communicate that Thorne didn't matter. "Did you move here with anyone, Liam?"

"No, just me." He cocked his head. "You?"

I took a deep breath. "Yes, actually. My partner moved here with me."

He blinked a couple of times and licked his lips. "What's your partner's name?"

"Thorne, as in thistle."

He snickered. "You're gay then?"

That made me snort. "Yes, of course, in all my fabulous glory."

"That's really cool because I am too." He grinned, but then a flicker of worry crossed his eyes. "Is it serious with Thorne?"

"Not anymore. He's a lying, cheating son of a bitch, and it's over." *And would you lean across the table and kiss me, please?*

He smiled again. "You couldn't be a rose if you hadn't had a thorn, right?"

Certain that I was blushing redder than any rose, I recovered enough to ask Liam if he had a boyfriend in the picture. Sadness, or perhaps pain, crossed his face. I wasn't sure which, but he quickly came around. "Nah. Used to be, but he was a fucking bastard, too."

We laughed and fell into the best conversation I'd had in a long time.

"What did you teach at Northstar?" he asked.

I'd been wondering how my classmates might react to a musician in law school, and this would be my first test. "Music."

"Really?" He leaned into the table. "What kind?"

I took a sip of my drink. "Choral music, music history, and music theory."

Liam's eyes sparkled as he wiggled in his chair. "Awesome. I love music."

I managed to keep from chuckling and braced myself. I'd heard this from young people before. Rap, heavy metal, and pop were about the extent of it. "What kind of music do you like?"

"All kinds." His eyes twinkled. "I've played cello since I was six, and I was in an orchestra all through college."

All rightey, then. This gorgeous guy just gets better and better. "What are some of your favorites?" That was always one of my questions for people.

He scratched his chin while he thought. "Best oldies, The Beatles. Best Classical, Brahms." He took a breath and pressed his lips together. "Something really cool, Foo Fighters. Kind of new, Adam Lambert." He snickered. "When I feel down, The Cure."

I nodded, impressed by the variety. "Interesting list. You really do like a little of everything."

He put an elbow on the table and propped his chin on his hand. "Your turn."

"Gosh, that's really hard...." I took a breath while I tried to decide. "Classical would be Bach and Mozart. Choral, anything from the Renaissance." I couldn't let him think I only liked Classical, because that wasn't true. "Michael Jackson, Gloria Estefan. Completely agree about Adam Lambert." I grinned. "Backstreet Boys."

He burst out laughing. "Backstreet Boys? I didn't see that coming."

Before he could dig into that, I asked about his time at Columbia and learned that he'd done a triple major in English, history, and politics, and he also competed on the swim team. He talked about his mother and two sisters but didn't mention his dad.

When he asked about my teaching career, I talked too much and ended up listing all the reasons I was frustrated to the point of quitting. *Don't scare him away before he finishes his drink.*

We sat there exchanging stories and information about ourselves for over two hours. Well, two hours and forty-five minutes, and three G&Ts, to be honest. I finally told him I had to go home, that my dog Theo needed to go outside. *Liar! There's a doggie door.*

"Guess Thorne will be home soon, eh?" He looked a little concerned.

"Actually, he's not coming home tonight, thank God. But I have that R&W assignment to do for tomorrow." *Please notice I said 'thank God' and read into that.*

The waitress came and took our credit cards, and while we waited for her to come back, Liam opened his eyes wide. "I've got an idea. How about we meet up for dinner in a couple hours, and we could work on that assignment together?"

It was very tempting, but if I didn't control myself, I'd wind up in bed with him before the night was over. *Would that be so bad? It's not like you aren't desperate for a man to touch you.*

"I can't do that," I said. "I'm sorry. I promised my nephew to talk on the phone before he goes to bed." *Come on, John, that lie was as transparent as the glass your gin was in. Not to mention lame, so very lame.*

Liam seemed disappointed but he wasn't deterred. "I

understand. How about tomorrow then? Study and get dinner tomorrow?"

His eyes brimmed with such hope that I could almost smell it. "Okay. I'd love to have dinner with you." *I can't resist you, so there.*

"Awesome! I'm stoked," he said, with a brilliant grin I could have looked at forever.

I was thrilled—and scared to death—that he liked me. I was far too old for him. "I had a great time this afternoon, Liam. Thanks for making time for this."

"I had a lot of fun, too." He looked like he wanted to swallow me whole, and I so much wished that he would. "Glad we connected."

"Me too. You've made today wonderful."

The waitress came back, and after we signed the receipts, Liam walked me to my car where we exchanged numbers—or as he said, digits.

"See you tomorrow, John. Have a good night."

Last chance. He'll probably take pity and do you. "I'll be here. Take care."

Liam

After seeing John off, I went back to my apartment to chill. I watched the news and drank a Widmer Upheaval, an outstanding IPA from Oregon. After the news, I made a couple cheeseburgers with some frozen fries, and accompanied my meal with another Upheaval. Yep, I love beer, but I'm a connoisseur. I like beer-art, not beer-sewage.

After I ate, I couldn't avoid the R&W assignment anymore. Professor James had given us guidelines that she said were the backbones of good legal writing, along with a set of facts about a burglary. We had to write a three-page argument about why the accused was guilty or not, our choice. By nine forty-five, I was almost finished but had some doubts about whether I was interpreting a fact or two correctly, and decided that was a good reason to hit John up.

LIAM: Hey john, its liam, wassup

Thirty seconds.

JOHN: Hi Liam! Working on this damn assignment. Bet you're all done.
LIAM: Kinda sorta but not sure im reading a couple these facts right, can I call u
JOHN: Sure. I'm shaky about one or two myself.
LIAM: K gr8 thx, calling

Talking to John helped clarify things. After we discussed our work, we went personal, and John said Thorne-the-Shit sure enough didn't come home and he was glad of it. He'd said the same thing earlier, and I was getting the vibe that Mr. Lawrence wanted to be Mr. Available. I hoped it was Mr. Available-for-Liam.

For the record, it is amazing how much I hated that asswipe Thorne already, partly because he existed at all, and also because John seemed sad when he talked about him. He deserved better.

We talked about our dinners, and he told me he'd had a salad with some tuna on top. I called him a health nut, he called me a trashy eater, and we laughed about that. He was so much fun to joke and laugh with. Anyway, that gave me an opening to remind him we were having dinner together the next night, and my heart skipped a beat when he said how much he was looking forward to it. Emboldened, I decided to put another idea out there. "I have a suggestion."

"Okay."

State the facts. "It helped me a lot to talk this assignment through, and you said it helped you?"

"Absolutely. My paper is going to be a lot better now."

Make your argument, simply but convincingly. "Mine too. Since we both feel that way, how about we work together on our assignments? Two heads better than one and all that?"

He didn't hesitate. "Sounds like a good thing to do. Let's give it a try and see how it goes."

It's decided in your favor. Wow, you didn't even have to tell him what you told him. We wrapped up the call pretty soon after that, and I thought we were gonna be friends if nothing else. *Please, let it be something else.* I finished up my paper and had time to watch Steven Colbert and enjoy one more Upheaval before bed.

I couldn't stop thinking about John. He was so hot he lit me up like a bonfire, and I hoped we could be something really special for each other. It was obvious that we both needed it. He seemed awfully jittery for a guy with a partner, even a shitty one, and I figured Thorne-the-Douchebucket must not put out much in the way of boyfriend duties. What a shame, because I would have taken such excellent care of John. Walking might be a problem for him some days, but he sure as fuck wouldn't be wound up tight as a spring.

Since I couldn't keep John out of my head, I couldn't keep my dick out of my hand. Ordinarily I watched porn when I jerked off, but not that night. My feelings about him were too special, and memories of him were all I needed. One toe-curling orgasm later, I fell into a deep sleep that was ornamented with exciting visions about what could be.

John

"That isn't right. Give me the damned book!" Liam and I were standing in the stacks at the law library. He was so close that I could feel his body heat, which made me a little giddy.

Laughing playfully, he held on tightly to the book. "No! It's mine. And I *am* right."

A tug-of-war followed, both of us chortling so hard I was surprised a librarian didn't come over to tell us to be quiet.

Liam suddenly went silent, a wicked grin on his face. "Have it your way. Take a look."

He turned loose, and I was pulling so hard I started to fall. Moving quickly, he caught me before I hit the floor, and I fell into his bulky arms. He tightened them around me, and both of us started laughing again. I hadn't been held like that in— *Shit! I'm getting hard!* He tightened his grip a little more, and his warm breath brushed against my ear.

I started twisting around. "Turn me loose! Let me go!"

He released me, and when I looked at him, there was a befuddled expression on his face. We finished our assignment, but the merriment was gone. Later, before we parted ways, his expression grew serious. "I'm sorry I made you uncomfortable in there."

I smiled and put a hand on his arm. "Don't apologize. I just got a little panicky, and I'm the one who's sorry."

When I got home, my sister Susan called to see how things were going, and of course I talked about Liam. Never a Thorne fan, she was excited to hear about someone new. "I'm so happy you're finally talking about somebody else, John. You've got to kick Thorne's cheating butt out on the street, once and for all."

"I know, and I'm going to, but...." I sighed into the phone.

"But what?"

"That doesn't mean I'm ready to move on, especially with Liam."

She grunted her disapproval. "Why? You obviously like him."

"I do, so much that it terrifies me. I'm afraid of being hurt. There's a big age difference, so getting hurt's a lot more likely."

"Why?"

The conversation was giving me a headache, so I went into the kitchen for a glass of wine. "I think what I need is a friend."

A loud scoff came across the connection. "Who says that friend can't be a boyfriend?"

"Sue, a quick hookup would ruin that with Liam. Things would get too awkward." I poured a glass of Chardonnay and took a big gulp.

"Who said anything about a quick hookup? Just get to know him and see what happens." She used her *John's being difficult* voice. Sue was three years younger than me, but always played the role of big sister.

Why did she have to make so much damned sense? Couldn't she just tell me that Liam sounded dangerous and I should run for my life? "I hear you. Maybe, with Thorne out of the picture, something could happen between Liam and me."

I drained my glass and poured more wine while Sue stayed quiet. After another sip, I had to say something. "He'll move on to other conquests. Liam is twenty-two, and I remember what I was like at that age, restless and trying to figure out what I wanted."

Another sip of wine. She still didn't say a word.

"Look, why would Liam be interested in anything more than a hookup with someone my age? For that matter, why would he be interested in hooking up with someone my age at all?"

"Stop putting yourself down," she snapped. "That's

Thorne in your head. Beauty is in the eye of the beholder, you know that. Just because you aren't interested in men who are older than you doesn't mean others can't be."

"I know," I said, or did I moan?

"See where things go, hardhead. You don't need to jump into bed with him right away, just keep seeing him."

"But—"

She huffed. "Tell me that spending time with a nice man wouldn't do wonders for how you feel."

"I told you I'm afraid, Sue." I paused, frustrated with myself. "I don't want to hurt Liam, either. I haven't even thrown Thorne out yet, and I shouldn't use Liam to help me get over that asshole. I don't want to bounce into a weird rebound thing that could leave Liam and me both hurting. Maybe what I need is some space to get myself together."

"John, you have a lot of excuses." Can someone sound exasperated and kind at the same time? "Maybe you do need space, but you've had an awful lot of that over the last few years, if you ask me. I think what you need is company, from a decent man who cares about you."

"Yes, but I—"

"There's no perfect way to move on, but I think you should forget all that psychobabble about rebounds and age differences. Follow your heart because you'll never know what feels right until you're open to something."

The next few days were wonderful and horrible at the same time. Between class, studying, and hanging out, Liam and I spent most of our days together. We got along really well, and it was obvious that he liked me. My infatuation with him grew by the day, and he was so attractive that I was constantly in some state of arousal. Spending time with Liam was the most fun I'd had in years.

The horrible part, in retrospect, was all in my head, and I

had Thorne to thank for it. He's the one who instilled so much paranoia and distrust in me. Worried that I'd come up lacking with any man, and concerned about our age difference, I was afraid Liam would hurt me once he realized I was too old for him. A few times, I even suspected he was leading me on, that it was some kind of demented sport. I didn't truly believe that was the case, but thanks to Thorne and his emotional abuse, it floated across my mind a few times.

Damn Thorne for the things he had done to me.

Liam

"I love studying with you."

John was so handsome in a green polo and khaki shorts. His cologne had a floral note that kept tickling my nose, among other interested body parts, and as the library heated up, a clean-sweat smell joined the cologne. We were sitting so close together that our arms touched while we read an assignment.

He looked up at me with a beautiful smile on his face. "I love studying with you, too." His elbow pushed into my arm. "Want to get some lunch soon?"

After a few minutes, he had to go to the restroom, and he left a lot of space between us when he came back and sat down. I needed to establish contact again. "You ready for lunch?"

He sat there like he didn't hear me.

I raised my voice, not angry, but loud enough that he couldn't ignore me. "John?"

He looked over, a little cross. "What?"

I smiled. "Ready for lunch?"

He shook his head. "I'm not hungry. You go on."

It took ten minutes of wooing to convince him to go with me. Just like that, though, he was really friendly for the rest of the afternoon. Something similar happened every day. I didn't understand his moodiness and figured he was just being an artiste.

We spent a lot of time together, and I got to liking him a ton. He was amazing when he wasn't being temperamental, not to mention that just looking at him made me chubby. Sometimes, I sat next to him with a full-blown hardon that was getting harder and harder to hide. I checked him out every now and then—maybe a hundred times an hour—and saw the same thing happening to him, more than once, which made his moodiness even more confusing.

We shared meals and went to another couple happy hours, but he wouldn't hang out in my apartment and didn't invite me to his place. After Saturday's class, we were finished until Monday, when the real schedule with all the other classes would start. We'd been joking around all morning, and he was leaning his whole body against me. It was all I could do to keep from laying one on him right there.

I had a great idea when we finished up our research. "Go to lunch with me? My treat. We need to celebrate making it through the first few days." I wanted to go to lunch with him so much I was rocking in my chair.

He lost his smile and shook his head. "I'm sorry but I'm really tired. I wouldn't be good company."

All the charm I could muster couldn't get him to change his mind, so I went home. I hated his mixed signals. Even after he turned me down for lunch, he kept touching me, and I could tell he wanted to hang out. My diagnosis was that John was very insecure after spending years with that douchebag, shithead partner of his. I hoped he didn't think I was too young to understand anything about him, because I wasn't.

My worst fear was that he thought I was only out to bag him. He even made a few comments that sort of pissed me off, wondering why I wanted to hang out with an 'old guy' instead of finding 'hot guys' my own age. A couple times I almost told him that I wasn't into guys my age, hot or otherwise, and I probably should have. The only reason I didn't was my fear that it would scare him even more, and make him think I really did only want to get him into bed.

I spent most of the weekend in my apartment. Saturday night, I went to a building mixer and met some people, law students and grad students in other fields. When the mixer was winding down, a guy named Hank and his girlfriend invited me to their apartment for a nightcap.

Talking about the first few days, Hank pretty much summed up my feelings. "What a fucked-up mess we've signed on for, law school. This ain't nobody's idea of fun."

You said it, dude. Except for John. He was fun even if he was so locked up it might take me months to break down his defenses. I had time.

3

John

On Sunday morning, I woke up thinking about Liam. The bed was warm and cozy, and I decided to relax for a while before getting up to start the day. Beginning with orientation on Wednesday, it had been a rough week, so I felt justified in resting a little while longer.

I was also hard as a rock and couldn't stop fantasizing about Liam and his amazing body, thinking about how it would feel to kiss him, which of course led to thoughts about him touching me, me touching him, and how he would taste. Before long I was at the edge, trying to hold back a little longer. I wasn't quite ready for it to be over. Then I remembered the electric moment when I almost fell and he caught me in his big, beefy arms, and that was all it took. Greatly relieved, I slept a little longer before getting up to make tea.

As tempted as I was to call Liam and see how he was doing, I couldn't. I was too conflicted. My erratic behavior had probably frustrated the hell out of him all week. Regardless of how much I liked him, I was trying to keep some distance between us.

The thought of being hurt again weighed heavily on my heart, and law school added to my anxiety in a big way. I was deeply insecure about my new adventure. Although I'd done well in my previous degree programs, I had no idea what to expect from law school, and the first few days had been brutal.

My sad conclusion was that I needed to nip things in the bud with Liam before crushes and fantasies went any further, and I decided to talk to him and explain that I didn't have time for a social life. It would be the best thing for both of us. He could go play with guys his own age, and I could get my life in order.

Liam

One more day to get my ass in gear before real hell started the next day, so I took a shower and made a big breakfast of eggs, pancakes, bacon, hash browns, orange juice, and coffee. While I ate, I reconsidered my John Theory and decided that if I wanted him to feel less threatened, I needed to back off a little. He had to get used to the idea of being close to me, and some subtle backpedaling might actually push things along in the long run.

After working a couple hours, I decided to text him and see how he was doing. Surely that wouldn't be too pushy.

LIAM: How's it going?

No reply after an hour.

LIAM: Get all the reading done?

No reply after thirty-two minutes. *Fuck. Is he ignoring me on purpose?*

LIAM: Did u read mohr v williams? I'm a lil confused

My phone buzzed. *Finally!*

JOHN: It's a little confusing.

No shit! Still, at least he'd responded.

LIAM: How did an operation improving one ear impair hearing on other ear?

Seven minutes.

JOHN: Not sure, but she didn't consent to surgery on her left ear.
LIAM: But how did it impair her hearing?
JOHN: Not specified. I have to go.
Fucking hell!
LIAM: Ok c u tomorrow

No answer. *Goddammit.* I shouldn't have texted him at all because that was one of the most unsatisfying experiences I'd ever had. Maybe Thorne the shitweasel was there and they were fighting.

John

I WAS READING cases for Torts and Property when my phone dinged. Thorne hadn't come home for the weekend, and I thought maybe he was letting me know he was alive. Instead, it was Liam.

Deciding it was time to put my plan into action, I ignored the message and got back to work. I didn't think about Liam at all, except for the fifty times I did. *Liam texted! Wonder what he's doing? What he's wearing? Text him back.*

After a while, the phone dinged again. *Answer it, you know you want to. Don't be so rude—just say hi.*

No way. I had to protect myself and deal with my life. *Wonder where he is? He's waiting for you to text back. You know you want to.*

I couldn't buy into it. Liam needed to be screwing around with another young guy, not texting me, so I picked up my phone, went upstairs, and put it in my sock drawer. Uneasily, I went back downstairs to read. *What the hell are you doing? He's such a nice guy, and he's so hot. Bet he looks really good hanging out in gym shorts or whatever, so stop being an ass.*

I went back upstairs to get my phone. Liam, of course, had texted again.

LIAM: Did u read mohr v williams? i'm a lil confused

All right, I would text him back so I wouldn't be an ass, but that was all. No change of plan.

JOHN: It's a little confusing.

There. Vague and meaningless.

LIAM: How did an operation improving one ear impair hearing on other?

One more text wouldn't hurt.

JOHN: Not sure but she didn't consent to surgery on left ear.
LIAM: But how did it impair her hearing?

Enough. *No, don't stop! Go for it! I'll bet he smells really good. Wonder what his mouth tastes like?*

JOHN: Not specified. I have to go.
LIAM: Ok c u tomorrow

I turned the phone off and went back to my reading. Actually, I *tried* to read but couldn't stop thinking about Liam. I had to tell him my decision the next day because this madness had to end, for both of us.

The next morning, I got to school a little early, nervous about seeing Liam. I'd decided to talk to him after class. As politely as possible, I'd drop the news and emphasize that it wasn't him, that I liked him. The problem was my own nervousness about needing to get off to a good start.

Dear God, I don't want to do it. I want Liam in my life. As I walked down the hall, there he was, coming toward me. He looked good in gray shorts that showed off his muscular thighs and big bulge, with a skintight, light green T-shirt. The whole package was gilded by one of those dazzling smiles that showed off his red lips and thousand beautiful teeth. I ignored his greeting and walked by with barely a nod.

There was a seating chart by the door of the lecture hall, and I almost choked when I saw my seat. Liam was right beside me. *Of course.* The chart was in alphabetical order, and I'm an L and he's an M. My blood pressure rose, and my head twanged with the beginnings of a headache.

I went into total stress overload when someone said that all 1L classes had seats assigned in alphabetical order. If I had to sit next to Liam in every class, every day, I would either make a fool of myself or die of horniness within a week. My heart galloped as I walked into the room, and I decided to tell Liam as soon as he got there. After class, we could request different seats.

Liam

My head spun while I wondered what the hell had just happened. I was on my way to Torts when I saw John coming down the hall. "Hey wassup," I said, taking in his tight khaki shorts and pink Polo shirt, and enjoying the small gust of cedarwood that wafted my way. He looked at me out of the corners of his eyes and walked right on by. *What the fuck? What's his problem that he had to be so rude?* He was probably nervous, but there was no need to treat me like that.

A crowd of people blocked the door to the classroom. "What's going on?" I asked some crazy-looking chick standing right in front of me.

"We have assigned seats. We will in every class this semester. My friend who's a 2L said we have to sit in alphabetical order."

Sure enough, I got to the door and there was a seating chart, standing on an easel. Each box on it contained someone's student ID photo, with the person's name printed boldly underneath. I already knew it was alphabetical, so I looked about halfway back and found my ugly mug at seat 5G. A thrill buzzed around my stomach when I saw who was in 5F—wait for it—John Lawrence!

As I made my way back to the fifth row, I barely noticed the lofty room with its dark wood paneling. John was sitting in the middle of the row and did not look happy to see me coming. I picked my way along and practically had to climb over him to get to my seat.

"Hey man," I said, as cheerfully as I could. *Your voice is way too high-pitched.*

He'd pinched his eyebrows tightly together, and where his mouth should have been was a deep frown instead. "Hi."

I scooched closer to him, loving his cologne. "How ya doing today? Get all the reading done?"

He turned, and for a second I thought he would smile and say something nice, but one look told me that whatever was coming wasn't good.

"Liam, we're apparently going to be sitting together in every class this semester, so we need to get on the same page about some things."

He didn't sound hostile, but his tone certainly wasn't friendly. I gulped as my heart began to thud. "Okay, what's on your mind?"

He pursed his lips tightly for a few seconds before letting out a hefty sigh. "You're a nice guy, but we can't keep hanging out." His chest caved in, causing his shoulders to stoop, and he looked at the floor. "It's me, not you. You're driving me crazy."

Thoughts struck like lightening. Driving him crazy? *That's a good thing, right?* For a wild second, I thought maybe he was gonna ask me out and had a weird way of going about it, but those were desperate thoughts for a desperate man. He looked up, and it was clear that a date wasn't at all what he had in mind. His eyes were wet, but his mouth was set and hard.

"You're young, and I know you have a lot on your mind." He winced, I was sure of it. "I understand that, but I'm here to learn the law."

"Me too, man." My breath was hot in my lungs, and my voice came out raspy and way too high.

His eyes were dull, like they weren't focusing well. "You

shouldn't act like we're buddies because it's a waste of time." Slowly, he shook his head while his eyes got wet. "I'm *so* much older than you are, Liam, and I'm really not here to be anybody's buddy. I'm sorry if I gave you the wrong impression last week, but I have to do well this year and don't have any time to waste."

My face got hot and I could imagine all too well how red it was. "What the fuck? Waste your time? John, I like you. And I know you like me, don't try to deny it."

His smile looked more like a grimace. "Please understand. I don't *dislike* you. I don't know you, so how could I?" He stared at his hands and his face got splotchy. "We are so different. I'm older and you're... well, you're what you are."

Oh shit-fuck, this is bad. It was like my heart stopped and I needed a defibrillator. For a terrible second, I was afraid I might cry. *Why is he doing this? Did I fuck something up that bad?* "What are you talking about?" My voice got a little loud, but I couldn't help it. "It only makes sense for us to try to make all this as pleasant as we can. Why can't we be friends?"

The space between his eyes narrowed even more. "Pleasant?" He flared his nostrils and raised his voice. "*Pleasant?* Liam, every time I try to concentrate, you're distracting me. How is that supposed to be pleasant?" He glared at me. "Is it *pleasant* when I ignore you? You're messing up my time here already!"

My heart was about to shoot right out of my chest. I needed to stop this now before either one of us said any more, so I held up my hands. "Calm down, man. You're talking really loud and people are looking."

Unfazed, he was almost yelling. "How can I calm down when I'm constantly thinking about you? Or about what I can say when you talk to me?" He looked at the ceiling and shook his head. "*Calm down?* How is that possible when I've got to focus on school, my partner, and my dog, and you're constantly on my mind? You don't calm me down, Liam. You make me the polar opposite of calm!"

His partner and his dog? Constantly thinking about me? I wish I'd been listening with different ears because I would have understood. No such luck, though, because I was already at DEFCON 1. *I insisted on talking to him? I was messing up his time?* No! What I was doing was getting really pissed at the arrogant windbag.

"Hold on," I said, and I was yelling too. "I'm messing up your life? Like you said, you don't even know me, so how can I fuck up your pathetic life? If you can't study and make time for your so-called *partner*, that's on you, you bedbug. It's your sad life, not mine, so don't you dare try to put your fucking problems on me." I bit my lip and tried to pull it back a notch. "I'm not trying to bother you, you conceited asshole. If you want me to leave you alone, you can be abso-*fuckin*-lutely certain that's what I'll goddamn do! Go ahead and try all this bullshit alone, and let's see how you do with that." I stopped to breathe and wipe some slobber off my lip. "Jesus Christ, who the *fuck* do you think you are anyway? What is *wrong* with you?"

John's face was so flushed I was afraid he might stroke out. "You just don't get it, do you? I'm in a tight spot with very few choices. One decision I *can* make is to do what I have to do, and if that pisses you—"

"Come on, boys, cool it down." I recognized the voice, a guy named Michael I'd met at the mixer. "Shake hands and let it go. Everybody's on edge today."

Professor Zimmermann walked into the room just then, took the seating chart off the easel, and put it down beside the lectern.

"Good morning, ladies and gentlemen, and welcome to Torts. I assume you've all read the cases, so let's start with

Vosburg v. Putney." He glanced down at the seating chart and looked up again. "Ms. Hopper, please give us the facts of the case." He was looking at a girl at the end of the third row, and I was so glad it was her. Right then, I'd have fainted if he called on me.

I'd never been so motherfucking mad in my life. How dare John talk to me like that, let alone humiliate me by yelling it all out in public? What a self-absorbed ass he was, acting like God almighty and making me feel like something he scraped off the bottom of his ugly damned shoe.

I was hurt and my pride was wounded, and on top of that, he'd embarrassed both of us before we had a chance to get to know anyone. That probably took care of any hope for a social life for the next three years, since everybody probably thought I was some kind of deranged stalker. Leave John Buttwipe Lawrence alone? You'd better believe it. I'd shat better than him down the toilet.

John

I KNELT in front of the toilet in a one-seater bathroom on the sixth floor of the law library and threw up everything in my stomach. It was the only one-seater I knew of in the law school, and I'd barely made it there after class before the retching started.

Things hadn't gone remotely the way I'd planned, and I was deeply embarrassed by the scene I'd made. Liam—that beautiful, warm, sexy man—had fought hard not to cry. What in the hell had I done?

I'd hurt him, and he was absolutely furious. It was a wonder he hadn't hit me, but I knew he was far too fine a person for that. Someday, I would apologize. It wouldn't fix things, but at least maybe he would know I was sorry for humiliating him.

What a dreadful way to start a second career. I'd thought the age difference between my classmates and me might be problematic before, but I had undoubtedly just made it fatal. After my performance, they all probably thought I was an insane old coot. Maybe Thorne was right, and I really was crazy.

4

Liam

The first two weeks of class crawled by. I struggled to keep up, unsurprising since my mind was about as shiny as tarnished silver, with lots of things battling for space up there. By the end of the second week I wondered if I'd make it. Law school sucked most of my strength away, leaving me feeling like I was only one day away from failure. Whatever energy law school didn't claim was spent worrying about other nagging things, like the funny noise my car had started making, Mom after me to come home for a weekend, the dwindling balance in my bank account, and the shitty mess my apartment had become. Every surface was stacked high in the 350-square-foot mansion for which I paid the University of New York $1,150.00 a month.

I was obsessing about everything, especially that idiot, John Lawrence. After our stupid fight, I went to the profs claiming extenuating circumstances in the form of his hostility and unprovoked attack on me. I requested moves to other parts of the lecture halls, but no dice with any of them.

Professor Zimmermann, who taught Torts, summed things up pretty maddeningly. "You're an adult, Mr. Macadam, and you're going to be a lawyer. I appreciate your situation, but you can't start off here like this. You'll be settling disputes, or trying to, for your entire career, and you will do much better if you learn right now to manage things in your own life."

I sat in his office, bobbing my knee up and down, frustrated that he wasn't getting it. "Professor, I—"

He didn't want to hear it. "Regard this as your first field test and rectify the situation. Mr. Lawrence seems reasonable, and I suspect he had a severe case of first-day nerves. Anyone who has ever been to law school can understand that. Try to work things out, and let me know if anything changes for the worse."

Fuck that. John, reasonable? He ranted like a lunatic baying at the moon and treated me like a stupid child. He got me so worked up I acted like a raging bull, certainly not doing my own image any good. He hated me, wanted nothing to do with me, considered sitting with me intolerable, and didn't want to exchange a single word. Every time I saw him, all the hurt and humiliation washed over me again.

Was I so delusional that I didn't see he hated me all along? *No!*—he liked me, goddammit, I was sure of it. He was moody, but why the hell, when we had so much fun together, did he decide overnight that I was human salmonella?

JOHN

THE FIRST WEEK of class was abysmal. With a B.A., two master's degrees, and a Ph.D., I had a lot of experience being a student, and if it was so hard for me to keep up, God only knows how everybody else did it. Only one explanation made sense, and it added to my depression: age was catching up with me. Toward the end of the week, to my immense relief, I finally noticed the first signs of adjustment and tried to adopt a more positive outlook.

The second week, school got a little better. I got the work done, met a few people, and did well when called on in class, but the personal misery, heavy during the first week, snowballed during the second. I missed Liam terribly, and my home life was worse than ever. I hadn't seen Thorne since before classes started and was so lonesome that I actually missed him.

Only sheer willpower got me out of bed in the morning and saw me through the day. My gut was twisted with guilt over how I'd treated Liam, and it hurt to face him. We still sat together in every class. I hadn't asked to switch seats because I couldn't bring myself to break that last connection with him.

Every day was the same. He looked at me with those soulful brown eyes brimming with hurt, which morphed into anger, which gave way to tears that threatened to mar his perfect face. I wanted to hold him, to beg for forgiveness and try to make it all better, but I didn't even have the balls to try. Instead, I looked away, pretended to focus on something else, and hoped he didn't notice the tears in my own eyes.

I was going to have to talk to him soon, to apologize. There was no telling how he would react, but I'd never be able to live with myself if I didn't try to make things right. It was too much to hope that he'd ever be interested in me again, and my behavior had been so egregious that he might not even talk to me, but I had to make an attempt.

One night when Thorne actually came home, I had the reckless idea to seduce him and show him what he was missing. We went to bed and I watched him undress in the pale light, wondering how I could still find him physically attractive after all the hurt he'd dealt my way. He got into bed without looking at me, and when I scooted over to kiss him, I met an elbow.

"I'm tired. Later, okay?" He reached for a book.

No big surprise, since he'd been uninterested for years. That night was to be no different, and I huffed as loudly as I could. So much for showing him what he was missing—he wasn't missing me at all.

"Fuck you, too," I said as I rolled to the side, incredibly frustrated in every way.

"Don't be that way." His voice had the edge I hated.

"What way?"

He looked at me like you might a dead rat you found on the kitchen floor. "That pissy way you get when you don't like something I say or do. I'm in no mood to deal with it tonight."

I jumped up and grabbed my robe off the chair by the bed. "You're in no mood for a lot of things, at least not with me. You shit!" I marched over to the door and turned back around. "I'll give you your privacy so you can call your boyfriend and jerk off." Slamming the door shut behind me, I stomped down the stairs.

Liam

I hurt so much that I'd gone to a counselor in student health and talked things through. He said that avoiding John as much as possible was the best thing for my own well-being. It hurt, but I had to put it behind me. John was a shitpouch, and whatever his problem was, it wasn't really me. He was bad news for sure, but whatever else he was, he was irresistible, and although I'm ashamed to admit it, I would've still sucked his dick in a heartbeat.

Thankfully, I'd gone to that mixer and met a few people

before the fight, and they had still been nice to me. I also hung out with my best friend, Jessica Daley. I'd known her since freshman year undergrad, and we'd seen each other through all kinds of nonsense over the years. Blonde, built, and smart, men flocked to her like bees to honey.

She listened to me rant about the fight and promised things would be okay, that life would go on and I'd find the right guy. Jess was the only one in Syracuse who knew the real reason it hit me so hard, that I was struggling to get my life back on track after suffering a crippling loss. Three losses, actually.

My dad died on Flag Day after my junior year of college, and my would-be boyfriend broke up with me a month later, saying he couldn't be around someone who was so depressed. Then, last January, only a few months later, my cousin Dan died. He was a year younger than me, and in school he'd been one of the Mighty Trio of Best Friends, along with a guy named Ben Roth. We all lived close to each other in Suffolk County and were together all the time. Since I had two sisters and no brothers, Dan was more like a brother than a cousin.

The idiot went out with two friends one night, and the designated driver started drinking. The fucking assholes didn't call an Uber when it was time to leave, and ten minutes later the driver crossed the line and hit another car head on. Miraculously, no one in the other car suffered worse than a broken leg, but Dan and his buddies were killed.

After losing the three most important men in my life, I drew into myself. I didn't hang out with friends much, and I stopped dating. It seemed a lot safer keeping to myself, and relying on my right hand was preferable to putting my heart back out there. Only one of the three men I lost was my boyfriend, but he'd hurt me badly, destroying my trust and putting a big dent in my self-esteem. My dad and cousin left painful holes in the same injured heart that wouldn't heal.

Of course, just when I was getting a fresh start, John the Fucker tore the massive scab away and left me bleeding on the floor. *Why did he do it? I liked him so much.* Whatever the cause had been, I felt like fucking shit and was trying hard not to climb back down into that pit where I'd lived for a while.

John

One Friday night, I sprawled on the new leather sofa in the living room and watched moonlight dance across the glass collectibles scattered around the room. The house we'd rented was nice. It was small compared to our house in Wisconsin, but was otherwise perfect. Built in the 1940s, it had been excellently maintained. High ceilings and hardwood floors graced the interior, which included beautiful built-ins and other details. The appliances in the kitchen were new, and several floor-to-ceiling windows in the living room overlooked a spacious back yard.

I turned on the television and began flipping through channels, finally settling on an infomercial while I thought about law school. There was no real way to know how classes were going because only R&W had any graded assignments. All my other grades would be determined by comprehensive final exams in December. I hoped I would do well because I couldn't stomach the idea of returning to Northstar.

As the television droned on, I thought about Liam. I decided to speak to him on Monday when I got to class, to ask him if we could talk. Better still, I'd offer to buy him coffee, and we could get away from the law school.

I wondered what he was doing right then, whether he was sleeping, studying, or maybe taking care of himself before he went to sleep. That was certainly a hot thought.

The leather was warm underneath me and I fantasized about Liam's muscular, hairy legs, his irresistible smile and rosy cheeks, and his intoxicating scent that made me high every day. I hesitated as my hand moved down my body, but how could a little fantasy hurt? Despite everything, thinking about Liam made me feel better, and my thoughts focused on the bulge in his shorts and how it would feel to writhe under his touch, with his body heavy on top of me. I gradually picked up the pace until heat surged out of me in a rush of bitter pleasure. *I have to talk to him,* I thought, as I drifted away to sleep.

That night, I dreamed of sunshine and Liam Macadam.

LIAM

WHILE I FRETTED about my fucked-up life over Saturday morning coffee, I decided to get my shit together, and to start clearing my head by cleaning up my space. My phone chimed while I was washing dishes and feeling sorry for myself.

JESSICA: Sick of reading. Lunch?
LIAM: Sure, what'd u have in mind?
JESSICA: New place downtown supposed to be really good, finn's pub, microbrews and burgers.
LIAM: Im there, u know I love beer and burgers

We rode together and ordered a flight of beers as soon as we got there. Jess talked about the study group she and her new friend Emily were starting on Tuesday night, and she said they'd found a couple other willing dorks.

"We want to create some ground rules, agree on goals, and divide up the outlines for finals. Then we can go out for a few drinks to cement our partnership. You still in?"

I nodded, glad it was actually happening. "Definitely. With all this shit they're trying to cram into our heads, I need all the help I can get." I paused to drink. "The group? I know it's you, Emily, and me, but who else?"

"Definitely Michael Lawton, and possibly Lauren Wilby and Chris James. Emily's firming that up."

"Cool," I said, about the group, as well as the arrival of two amazing burgers and another flight. "I got to know Michael a little at the mixer. Did you know he was a rugby player in undergrad? He's a handsome, musclebound boy, just your type."

"Believe me, I have taken note."

Over lunch, we talked about people we knew from undergrad.

"Did you hear that Kyle Corbin got a job at a different brokerage in Philly?" Jess asked. "Probably got caught stealing from the old one."

Kyle was a short-term boyfriend and roommate of mine at Columbia, and I struggled to swallow before I laughed. "He was always a liar, but I never thought he was a thief."

She rolled her eyes. "Nothing I ever heard about Kyle would surprise me. He's the lowest of the low."

"C'mon, Jess," I said. "I know you never liked him, and he's sure as hell no angel, but he's not *that* bad."

Her expression was harsh. "He's a total shit and I hope I never see him again."

We'd been eating in silence for a while when she dropped a bomb. "What really happened with you and John Lawrence?"

"Don't wanna talk about it, sorry," I mumbled around a mouthful of fries.

"Oh, c'mon, hon. We've been friends a long time, and you've been depressed ever since that fight with John. I just want to know how you're feeling, considering... well, you know. I don't want that to happen again."

I took another bite of burger and watched her while I chewed.

"Talk to me, Liam. I see how you look at him."

"Pff!" I pushed down anger that threatened to boil over. "That's interesting since I don't look at him at all."

"I call bullshit," she shot back. "I see you looking, and I see your face when you do." She smiled and put a hand on mine. "I also see him looking back with his tragic, puppy-dog eyes."

I told her about my visit to the counselor and what we'd decided, but I needed to get some things off my chest and she was a safe person to do it with. I told her the whole sad story, including my continued fascination with John. I ended with my latest theory, that he probably did have a bad case of nerves, like Professor Zimmermann said, and took it out on me. "I'm the one who escalated things and took it personally. If I'd only stayed calm, he would have gotten over it and things would be fine."

She stared at me. "You really like him."

"*Liked*—past tense."

She rolled her eyes and sighed. "Honey, look up your ass and find your brain. You just talked about him for twenty-five minutes—*twenty-five minutes*, do you realize that? And you were smiling for once, animated. You told me what happened and talked all about how he hurt and humiliated you, the anger you've been carrying around ever since."

She took a sip of water, and I couldn't think of anything to say.

"But then—and this is the thing—*then* you rationalized and basically excused his shitty behavior. You said that *you* were wrong to take it personally instead of that *he* was wrong to act like that." She smiled and took my hand, giving it a hard squeeze. "Like it or not, hon, and whatever you want to call it, you didn't just *have* it bad for John. You *still do*."

I opened my mouth to say something, but she held up a hand to stop me. "Tell you something else. I've talked to him a couple of times—*not about you!*—and he seems to be a nice guy, all things considered. He even asked me about you, how you were getting along, and all I said was that he should talk to you since you two sit together all day long."

I took a minute to finish my beer so I wouldn't snap at her. "Big motherfucking deal. None of that has anything to do with me."

She ignored what I said. "I have a question."

I nodded my head and held out my hand, palm side up.

"He must be, what, about forty? I know you like older men, but that much older?"

"Jess," I snarled, "I don't give a fuck how old he is because it's not my problem. Besides, you know goddamn well that I've always liked older guys. I'm just not attracted to guys our age. I'll fuck younger dudes if I have to, but I can't imagine anything serious with a guy who's still trying to figure out if he likes boxers or briefs. I'll never forget what it was like when Kyle and I were together and he'd barely learned how to tie his shoes."

"You don't have to explain it to me. I love you, and I've always understood. Besides, John *is* pretty hot... for an older guy." She stuck out her tongue at me, and I threw a napkin at her nose.

Sporting a wicked grin, she kept talking. "Now that I think about it, you two would be really cute together, a real power couple." She looked off over my shoulder for a moment and got a weird grin on her face. "Try to relax," she said, glancing back at me. "Leave things to me for a couple of days and I'll think of some way to get a truce between you two."

I sat bolt upright, gripping the edge of the table. “No, Jess, *NO*! No, and hell no, and *fuck* no! Stay out of it!”

“Don’t know what you’re talking about.” She tossed her goddamned hair at me. What a bitch she could be, as I’d told her a hundred times through the years.

“*Please* don’t stir anything up.” I sounded pitiful. “There’s only so much I can stand.”

She grinned but wouldn’t meet my eyes. “I promise I wouldn’t do anything to hurt you. But what good’s a girlfriend if you can’t worry about what she might do?”

I flopped against the back of the booth. “*God!* I’m so glad I’m gay and don’t have to put up with women just to get laid.”

She giggled. “Relax. I have a big mouth, but you know I’ve always got your back. What could I possibly do, anyway?”

“Promise me you’ll stay out of it?”

She nodded, looking very pleased with herself. “I’m good for whatever you need, hon. Eat your pie.”

A knot of anxiety materialized in my belly. She hadn’t really promised to stay out of things, but surely she wouldn’t try to interfere in this mess. *Would she?* I trusted her, but she was never any good at minding her own business.

But wow. What if things *did* improve with John and me? Maybe we’d have a chance. I was sure he still liked me; I saw how he looked at me every day. *Holy Jesus, you are pathetic!* The fantasies had already started, and I was getting chubby. What a tragic excuse for a man I’d become.

“Liam, why are you smiling?”

I ignored her and ate my pie. I was not smiling. Definitely. Not too much, anyway.

John

Liam was already there when I got to Torts on Monday, and I took a deep breath. "Good morning, Liam. How's it going?"

As soon as I started to speak, he picked up his backpack and started rummaging through it, pretending not to hear me. I spoke louder. "Liam?"

He took his time putting his pack down before looking up at me with wet, sultry eyes. "Mm." It was a grunt.

I tried to smile but was so nervous I wasn't sure it worked. "I really need to talk to you." He looked at me again, and his lips were pursed, his eyes wetter than before. "Liam, please talk to me."

He folded his arms and sighed. "Hmm?"

I was close to hyperventilating. "Please let me buy you a coffee after class? Give me fifteen minutes?"

"Not a good idea."

"Please? I want to apologize, try to explain. I was wrong, Liam." My eyes were watering and were going to overflow any second.

His face softened, but he kept his arms folded. "Maybe Wednesday? I have an appointment today."

I nodded. "Okay. Wednesday? Coffee?"

"Mm." He nodded. The response was infinitesimal, but it was a start.

Okay. You're in for a very long haul but maybe you can thaw the Cold War.

Liam bolted as soon as class was over, and Emily Williams caught me on my way out of the room. She was a striking young woman with flaming red hair and gray eyes, and I liked her. We'd talked a couple of times, and I had lunch with her and a few other people last Friday. She seemed to be a straightforward person who didn't thrive on drama. Today, characteristically, she came right to the point and asked if I'd joined a study group yet. When I told her I hadn't, she asked me to join one she was starting the following evening.

I wanted to join a group, but after my disastrous argument with Liam, I'd had no invitations and didn't feel comfortable looking for one. Emily's offer was an opportunity, and although I wondered who else was in the group, it seemed rude to ask.

She must have read my mind. "It will be you, me, Chris, Jessica, and maybe Michael or Lauren. We won't be sure until tomorrow." I guessed the Jessica she referred to was Jessica Daley. She was thick with Liam, but I'd talked to her and she seemed friendly. *Surely nobody smart enough to get into law school would also be stupid enough to try to put Liam and me in a study group together.*

"Thanks, Emily. I'd love to."

"Great. 7:30 tomorrow night in my apartment, 506 Johnson."

My phone buzzed as I walked down the hall toward the law library.

THORNE: Hey, how's your day?
JOHN: Fine so far, yours?
THORNE: Busy.

Now there was a surprise. Busy was his default descriptor for every day.

JOHN: Are you still coming home tonight? Thought I'd make Cajun shrimp for dinner. Don't be late.
THORNE: That's why I was texting. Can't come home so no trouble for me.

A bolt of anger flashed behind my eyes. He knew I was going to cook dinner tonight and had even hinted for the shrimp. I'd planned to stuff him with food he loved and then talk to him about a joint strategy to end things between us. I couldn't take it anymore.

> *JOHN: Don't worry. There won't be much more trouble for you at all.*
> *THORNE: What does that mean, drama queen?*

I shoved the phone back into my pocket without responding, just as I saw Liam and Jessica Daley walking down the hall, heads together like gossiping schoolgirls. They were probably laughing at me, wondering why Crazy John wanted to buy Liam coffee.

5

Liam

As I pulled on some jeans for the study group meeting, I thought about John's invitation to coffee the next day. I'd go for fifteen minutes, if he still wanted to. It might be interesting to hear what he had to say, but I'd be sure to keep my distance, since it would be like having coffee with a scorpion. I'd been thinking since my lunch with Jess, and there was no way I was ever letting John into my life again. His brand of assholery was the last thing I needed to deal with.

That decided, I left for the meeting. Emily lived in my building, so I took the elevator up to her apartment on the fifth floor. Jess opened the door and invited me in, and—*whoa!* I immediately smelled a trace of the delicious cologne John had worn to class earlier. Sure enough, there he sat on the sofa, looking my way, his eyes as wide as full moons. My pulse pounded in my ears as my chest tightened. I was *so* out of there. "Gotta go."

I turned back toward the door, but before I could take even

one step, someone grabbed me from behind. I twisted my head around to see Michael, the rugby guy with huge muscles, looking unamused. He was a nice guy, but a brute by any standard. "Easy dude, not so fast. At least have a drink. I brought Tanqueray and lots of tonic."

"Back off, Michael, I gotta go. This is false imprisonment."

He strengthened his grip and barked more orders. "After a drink, dude, not before." He swiveled me around like a rag doll and walked me forward.

You could see white all around John's eyes, and his voice came out choked. "It's okay because I have to go. Just got a message from Thorne."

Michael's voice was a little menacing. "*Nobody's* going *anywhere* till you've tried my gin and tonic. Tanq's goddamned expensive and I bought it especially for tonight, so *everybody* sit the hell down!"

He shoved me onto the sofa. *Oh no he didn't!* That fuckwad pushed me down right next to John, like I didn't have to sit beside him enough already.

John was up like a rocket. "Sorry, Michael, it was a nice gesture, but I really do have to go."

Michael narrowed his eyes and took a step forward, blocking John's path. He stood in front of him with his arms crossed, scowling. "Sit your ass back down on that motherfuckin' couch and drink my gin, you stubborn sonavobitch."

Dumbfounded, John sank back down. Michael stepped back and speared John and me with a don't-fuck-with-me stare. "Like I told you boys weeks ago in class, shake hands and at least *pretend* to be adults. You're not five years old, for Christ's sake. You don't have to be best friends, but you need to get along. You sit together, and now you're going to be partners in this group. Shake!"

Partners? Jess had a coughing fit when he said that. *Fuck me, they're in cahoots!* Other people were nodding, and everyone was watching John and me. *Piss-fuck-shit, they're all in cahoots.*

"Liam?" Michael squinted at me and then nodded toward John.

Taking the path of least resistance, I stuck my hand in John's face. "Sorry for the radio silence. Maybe I acted like an asshole." I attempted my own don't-fuck-with-me stare, but I think it looked more like please-just-say-it-back-so-he'll-shut-up.

"Hey," was all he said, grabbing my hand for about a tenth of a second before dropping it like it was covered with Ebola.

I hated the fucking bastard for humiliating me again, but damn if his hand didn't feel good. My thoughts ran wild. *Keep touching me. Why do you have to be so fucking sexy?* Followed immediately by *Jessica is dead to me now. And soon dead for real.*

John

I WILL KILL MICHAEL LAWTON, and Emily Williams, too.

They could not possibly think this was a good idea. I almost had a panic attack, angry because I felt rooked by Emily, insulted by the way Liam turned on his heels when he walked in, and furious at Michael for being such a bully. Worse, I was afraid someone might realize how thrilled I was to be sitting on the sofa beside Liam with nothing between us. He smelled like petrichor and warm leather, and I barely resisted stroking the perfect stubble on his face. The way he kept looking at me from the side made me giddy.

Does he really think I won't notice? Wonder if he's seen me looking at him, too?

I felt a stirring below and would have died on the spot if anyone else had seen. To keep things down, I called to mind some of my worst meetings with the music department chair at Northstar.

Liam leaned close, and I almost fainted when his warm breath gusted across my ear. He spoke so softly I could hardly hear him. "I don't like this anymore than you do, but just chill. It'll be over soon."

"Not soon enough," I snarled, if you can snarl through a whisper.

"I know." He brushed my side with his elbow, just barely, but it was enough to ratchet down my anxiety.

Emily brought in appetizers, and Michael made more drinks. As we talked about the group, I relaxed more and realized that Michael was making my drinks strong.

Jessica took the floor. "Emily and I have been talking about the presentations we're going to do every week, and we've decided it would be best to work in twos. So, me and Michael, Lauren and Emily, John and Liam."

"We need to rethink that," I blurted out.

Jessica smiled sweetly. "It's already settled, John. You two will just have to make the best of it."

Liam shrugged. "Whatever."

"Yeah," I said, stealing a quick glance of him. His lips were quirked up, ever so slightly.

Emily looked as if butter wouldn't melt in her mouth, and Michael proved that his voice didn't always have to be loud and gruff. "Guys, it's time to bury the hatchet. Give each other a *real* handshake this time. Your sorry asses aren't going anyplace until you do."

I'd had enough. "Michael, this—"

Michael threw a look in my direction that silenced me. No

one had looked at me like that since my father died. "If this group is gonna work, you two have an awful lot to do together. If you don't shake and make nice, I'm going to get some superglue and stick your hands together for good."

Neither Liam nor I moved, and Michael sighed. "Go on, surely one of you has a set of balls."

Liam turned toward me and licked his lips, and a weird look in his eyes told me I could make of it what I would. For an instant, I thought he was about to kiss me, and when he held out his hand, I took it.

A spark of magic tingled its way up my arm and the tension in my stomach dissolved. *Oh... I have Liam's hand in mine. I've been so stupid. Maybe it isn't too late.* "Liam, I'm very sorry I treated you so badly. You didn't deserve it at all. Please forgive me." My voice was breathy and desperate.

We weren't shaking anymore, but we still had each other's hands. His eyes were soft and bright. "I accept, and I'm sorry for whatever I did to freak you out."

We both nodded, and I stared at the most beautiful man I'd ever seen. I don't know how long we held onto each other's hands and gazed into each other's eyes, but it was nowhere near long enough.

Liam moved a little, and for a terrible second I thought he was letting go, but he pulled my hand deeper into his own and covered it with his other hand. My head swam and I vaguely heard applause.

Michael chuckled. "Okay guys, that's enough. I'm really glad to see this, but anything else you have to get a room for."

Everyone laughed while Jessica and Emily exchanged a smug look. Lauren, who had been quiet until then, piped up. "I knew it and I told you all so. Go for it, guys—our first law school romance!"

More chuckles and applause. Liam and I eventually let go of each other, but things had definitely changed.

"Okay?" I asked, looking into his eyes.

"Yeah." He nodded. "Oh yeah."

The rest of the meeting passed quickly, and when it was over, Liam got waylaid in the kitchen. Lauren came over and gave me a not-so-subtle talking to about taking advantage of this opportunity to be happy. I stalled for time, hoping Liam would head out so I could grab him for a few minutes. My heart was still beating like a drum, and my mind was alive with crazily inappropriate thoughts about him. At the same time, I realized that if we were to stand a chance of fixing things, I shouldn't crawl into his bed that same night, tempting as it was to try.

He finally broke free and walked my way. "John, did you drive?"

"Yes, but after Michael's drinks, I think I'll call an Uber to go home."

"Talk to me while you wait?"

We went down to the lobby, a small, musty-smelling room with mailboxes on every wall. I noticed he didn't invite me to his apartment and figured he must have felt the same as I did about avoiding temptation.

"Wanna talk about what happened up there?" he asked.

"I'd really like that," I said, enjoying the first warmth in my chest since the day of the fight.

He nodded while he showed me a bashful smile. "Coffee? Place just across the street."

"Let's go."

Liam

We ordered our drinks and found a seat after we picked them up. I couldn't quite believe how things had turned on a dime. It was amazing that all those people realized what was going on and cared enough to do something to help John and me. "I don't want any more weirdness between us," I said. "We've both apologized and accepted, so how about we just move on?"

He exhaled, and his smile lines emphasized the light reflecting off his eyes—those deep, Lake-Placid-blue eyes that looked so hopeful. "It wasn't your fault, Liam. I was a total jerk. You did nothing but be good to me, and I'm sorry I hurt you."

"You already apologized. We're okay, John."

"Thank you. I'd like to move on, too." He fiddled with his watch. "Isn't there anything you'd like to say? Or know? We really should clear the air."

My mind was still in awe, but he was right. "I know we'll be good working together, but can I ask a question?" *Wonder what he looks like when he's sleeping?*

He nodded. "Considering my shitty behavior, you've earned the right to ask whatever questions you want."

"Would you tell me why I spooked you so much?" *Bet his hair gets all kerflooey at night.*

His smile faltered a little but he still looked happy. "I've been with Thorne for a long time and have to get out of that relationship. I didn't want to end up in a rebound situation that would hurt you and me both, and I was scared."

I nodded. "Anything else?" *Bet he's so beautiful when he comes. Wonder what kinds of sounds he makes?*

He looked down into his hot chocolate for a few seconds and then back at me. "Well, since I'm being honest... you take my breath away, but I was afraid I'm too old for you, that you'd get tired of me. I hate to say it, but I was a little afraid of getting played, so I decided I should stop things for both our sakes." A muscle twitched under his right eye. "Please try not to be offended."

"We're moving on, remember?" I wanted to reach across the table and take his hand, but I held off. "Thanks for your honesty. Can I return the favor?"

"Please."

I traced the rim of my cup with my forefinger while I gathered my thoughts. "I really, *really* liked you by the end of that first day and you need to know something. I've always liked guys who were older than me, so your age isn't an issue at all. It's the opposite of an issue, it's a benefit." *Mental om.* "I'm not into sugar daddies or anything like that. That's weird to me. I just want someone to care about, who cares about me. And it's guys older than me that... that turn me on."

His smile broadened into a big, wide grin. "Good to know." He nodded and took another sip of his chocolate. "I really liked you right away, too. I was stupid to let my fears control me."

"No, you were just human."

I took a sip of my coffee, and he leaned forward across the table. "You're incredible," he said. "Mind, body, and, as far as I can tell, spirit.

"I'm so attracted to your mind, too," I said. "I mean, you're beautiful, and that turns me on a lot, but I've never been interested in looks alone." He'd laid a hand on the table, and I pushed my fingertips against his. "Don't sell yourself short thinking you have so little to offer that I'd play you, even if I did operate like that, which I absolutely *do not*. You picked up on something real between us, something we both felt."

He played with his napkin until I got afraid I'd done something wrong. "I made an assumption," he finally said. "Then I overreacted and behaved stupidly, and I think you're right about picking up on something real. That's why I got so scared." He turned up his lips into a quizzical smile. "Question?"

I hooked an eyebrow.

He looked down again while a purplish blush worked its way up his throat into his cheeks. "Do you still like me that way? You have feelings for me?"

I snickered, nodding fast. "I do. Dammit, John, after what happened up at Emily's, it's pretty clear we both do."

"How serious are you about what you feel?" he asked.

"Serious as in, you kinda broke my heart and I can't get you outta my head. Serious as in, this could lead to something really special and I wanna see if it does." I held my breath for a second. "How serious are you?"

He smiled and looked a little sheepish. "Serious as in, I broke my own heart when I broke yours. Serious as in, you had me when you sat next to me that first day. And serious as in, I don't want to ever hurt you again, and I think this could lead to something special, too."

I relaxed for the first time in weeks, and we both sat beaming at each other for a while. *Suck it up, Liam, and ask!*

"How...."

He raised his eyebrows and turned his head to the side.

"How would you feel about dating me?"

"You'd give me that chance after what I did?"

I sat still, waiting for an answer, and he met my eyes. "I'd love to date you, Liam. Dating sounds great."

"Okay, then." *Thank God!* "When do you want to start?"

He laughed, sounding a little giddy. "Officially? How about now?" No sooner had he said it than a cloud passed over his face. "No, wait. I haven't formally gotten rid of Thorne yet, but I'm going to do it right away. That's not a line, I swear."

"I believe you." He was so beautiful when he got earnest about something.

He furrowed his brows just enough to make him look a little worried. "Would you be okay with hanging out and studying together this week, and going out this weekend?" Another shadow passed over his face. "Please be honest. I don't want to make you feel like I'm taking advantage. I'm fine with it if you want to wait until I tell Thorne."

I put my hand over his, but remained quiet.

"I promise, Liam, things are dead between him and me, and they are not coming back to life."

I chuckled. "You had me at, 'how about now?' You're on, for everything you said about this week, and the weekend." I traced one of the blue veins on his wrist for a moment before looking at him again. "Listen, whatever with the prick-thorn. I don't care about him one way or the other. I care about you."

He grinned, catching his lower lip with his teeth. We finished our drinks, and he said he felt fine to drive. Outside, I took his hand and walked him to his car.

"I feel really good about this, Liam," he said, once his car door was open. "I can't wait to see where things go."

I kissed his forehead. "See you in class in the morning?"

"I'll be there."

When John started to get into the car, I called his name. "You're an idiot, you know?"

He turned, his eyes wide and his mouth hanging open. I couldn't hide my smile, and after a few beats, he laughed. "What?

"We're weeks behind where we coulda been, so you get to buy dinner on Saturday." I started chuckling. "Dimwit!"

"You dolt!" he said, laughing some more. "If you hadn't been so damned pushy...."

"Numbskull!"

"Dunderhead!"

"Moron!"

"Lamebrain!"

We guffawed for a moment, and then it was all simmering heat as we stared as each other. John took a slow step forward, and never looked away from my eyes. Leaning in, he brushed his lips against mine. The touch was light and sweet, leaving a frisson of desire in the wake of all the merriment. "Night, sexy. See you in Torts."

I watched him drive away and stood there considering my luck. After laughing like a madman, I whooped in joy and sang all the way back to my apartment.

6

A Week Later

Liam

THINGS WERE SO MUCH BETTER IN MY HEAD. A LOT OF THE stress I'd been feeling was gone, and I had an awesome boyfriend. Well, we hadn't actually said that word yet, but when you're dating a guy, he's your boyfriend, right? I needed to clarify that with the boyfriend.

It was eleven at night and I was in bed, thinking about John. I knew I shouldn't text him since it was late and he might be in bed too, but *damn*—what a hot thought that was.

LIAM: U still up?
JOHN: Yes, civ pro's a bitch. In bed reading.
LIAM: Im wide awake 2, fuck this, might go 4 pancakes
JOHN: Sounds good. Have some for me.
LIAM: What u wearing hot stuff?

JOHN: Liam Macadam, are you getting fresh with me?
LIAM: U bet I am, cause all ive got right now r fantasies about u laying in ur bed
JOHN: Me too. And I know it's hard. Really. ;)
Fucking yes! That was the sexiest we'd gotten up till then.
LIAM: Well john lawrence r u getting fresh with me too?
JOHN: If you'll let me. What are you wearing?
LIAM: I asked u first
JOHN: Okay, bad boy. PJ bottoms and a t-shirt.
LIAM: Ooooh, anything under those PJ bottoms?
JOHN: Probably not. :p
LIAM: It's hard to think about that ;)
JOHN: Turnabout is fair play. What are you wearing?
LIAM:Boxers
JOHN: And?
LIAM: That's all and i might take them off because it's very ~hard~ to wear them right now
JOHN: OMG please stop!
LIAM: Wanna join? ;)
JOHN: Of course I do, but let's wait just a little while longer?
LIAM: OK babe
JOHN: Thank you for being patient with me.
LIAM: I'll wait as long as u need to... might explode but the timing has to be right for both of us
JOHN: This won't go on forever, I promise.
LIAM: Somersaults!!!!! so how about pancakes?
JOHN: I have to pass because I didn't finish this reading earlier.
LIAM: Ok i understand :(

JOHN: And I might not have much self-control if I saw you right now.

I wanted to say he didn't need to have any self-control, but I'd just promised him to wait as long as he needed.

LIAM: Maybe instead of pancakes ill entertain lewd visions of u in ur PJs if u know what i mean
JOHN: You'd better. I can promise I'll be having lewd visions of you having a hard time in your boxers.
LIAM: Ur killing me
JOHN: Sorry. I'll make it up to you soon.
LIAM: Holding u to that :)
JOHN: I'm counting on it. Sorry but I have to read now. Coffee before class?
LIAM: I'll be there, probably still having a hard time ;)
JOHN: Goodnight bad boy. <3
LIAM: Goodnight babe

I meant it, I'd wait however long it took, but now that we'd broached the subject, I could tease him just to make sure it stayed on his mind. He wanted it too, and all good things would come in time. *Har, har!* I lay in bed and thought all kinds of lewd things about John. As you might imagine, I felt much better afterward and was barely able to clean up before I fell asleep.

John

On Saturday, Liam and I had gone to dinner, with plans to see a new Chris Pine movie later. While we ate, we talked about Thorne. Three times that week, he'd promised to come home the next day, but he'd never shown up. I was desperate to end things with Thorne, and told Liam I'd decided to have the locks changed and send Thorne a break-up text.

Liam's expression was dubious. "You should do what you want, but I'm not sure you'd be happy if you did that."

"Why? I'd be rid of his sorry ass."

He reached across the table and squeezed my hand. "You're a wonderful person with a huge heart, and I'm afraid you'd feel bad about yourself for a long time. You guys have been together for sixteen years, and you loved each other a lot of that time, didn't you? You'll feel a lot better if you tell him in person."

I was so discouraged. "You're right, but I have to get it done." Suddenly, I had an idea. "How about this? If he doesn't come home again next week, will you go with me to find him on Saturday? If he won't come to me, I'll go to him."

"You mean, tell him together?"

Liam looked a little apprehensive, so I smiled and shook my head. "No, you don't need to be with me when I tell him. Just take me to find him? You could get a drink or something, and I'll make it short and sweet."

"You've got it." He showed me that million-dollar smile. "A hunt-his-ass-down date next weekend unless you see him before then. Afterward, we'll do something to celebrate."

"Absolutely."

Liam cocked his head and looked at me. "I have a question. There's no wrong answer."

I nodded for him to go on.

"Is that why you're holding off on things with us? You'd feel like you were betraying him if we really kissed, or something?"

I snickered. "Or *something*?"

"Whatever. You know...." His cheeks turned bubble-gum pink. "Is that it, though?" he asked.

I took a bite of the cheesecake we were sharing while I

thought about it. "No, that's not it. I'm just being careful. I want to be sure we do things the right way, so we don't set ourselves up for failure. I want...." I was flexing my toes nervously inside my shoes. "I want a lot more than kissing.... I want you so much it hurts, but can we hold off just a little longer?"

He showed me a sweet, closed-mouth smile. "No pressure. Whenever you're ready." Liam broke into a snarky grin. "If I explode first, I might ask you to help clean up the mess."

When we stopped laughing, he looked at his watch. "We have to haul ass. I'm glad we already got our tickets—the show starts in fifteen minutes."

Liam

I knew John loved ice cream, and after the movie I surprised him with a visit to Syracuse's best old-fashioned ice cream parlor. While we ate, I got a massive hard-on because I couldn't tear my eyes away from his pink tongue making love to his waffle cone of vanilla pistachio. During a pause in conversation, he got a far-away look in his eyes.

"What is it?" I asked. "Anything wrong?"

He shook his head, smiling. "Not at all. I was just thinking how I've been waiting for you all my life."

John kept looking at me like I was Santa Claus, as if he wasn't sure I was real. His teal sweater brought out the rosiness in his pale skin, and his sweet, dusty cologne had been driving me crazy all night. He held my hand with the most amazingly long, lanky fingers, and I could see why he must have been a good pianist.

His plump lips slayed me, and for a while I couldn't think about anything but nibbling at them, licking and sucking on them, and getting my tongue between them. I finally had to stop looking because I got afraid I might spunk my pants right there in public.

John

It floored me that Liam remembered from some random conversation that I loved ice cream. After all our years together, Thorne always seemed surprised when I asked him to take me out to get some on my birthday. Liam was showing me what it felt like to be with someone who really cared.

After ice cream, we went for a drive by Onondaga Lake. Later, at my house, I wanted to invite him in, but the sexual tension was palpable, and I wasn't quite ready to pull that trigger. He walked me to the door, and I had to turn my back on him to unlock it. When I turned around to say goodnight, he was holding a gorgeous red rose.

"This beautiful flower is for the most amazing man I know," he said, handing it to me with one of his huge smiles. "He's so gorgeous he makes the poor rose look plain by comparison."

I took the flower. "Wow, you're a magician, too?"

His bashful grin made my stomach flip. "Nah, I just believe in being prepared."

He moved his head forward, and I closed the distance. At last, we shared a real kiss, chaste but very hot. I leaned into him, and he brushed my cheeks with his fingertips while he kissed me. He licked my lips but didn't try to push his tongue into my mouth, which, for some reason, turned me on more than if he had. When we pulled apart, the way he looked at me told me he'd felt my hardness against his leg, and I had sure felt his. *Good to know my boyfriend's packing.*

He walked to his car and turned back around. “Lunch tomorrow, then study?”

“Come here at noon. I’ll cook.”

“I’ll be here.” He winked. “Sleep well, gorgeous prince.”

I watched him drive away, wishing I’d asked him to stay. *One more week, Liam. I’m going to get Thorne out of here and beg you to make love to me.*

7

Liam

John made quiche and salad for lunch, and we spent the afternoon cuddling by the fire while we studied. He let me give him real kisses and we shared some electrifying caresses—he even brushed his hand over my dick once—but the couple times my hands got near his, he quickly moved out of the way. When we were both hard as rocks, I was in trouble. It was either leave right then or hit him over the head and drag him to my cave, so I claimed exhaustion and went home.

I jerked off and felt a little better, but I wasn't in the mood to be alone, so I ordered pizza and called Jess to come over and share.

After the pizza came, she nibbled at one slice for about five minutes before she said anything. "Liam, do you realize next weekend is Falderal?"

"What?" I was so lost in my thoughts that I'd almost forgotten she was there.

She rolled her eyes. "Next weekend is Falderal, the fall

festival on campus."

"What's that got to do with anything?" My brain was still at John's house, I guess.

"The SBA's Falderal party is Friday night. You can get drunk and raise hell if you want."

"Dunno," I mumbled.

She squinted her eyes and swallowed. "Wait a minute. Liam Macadam skip a party with free beer? *Puh-leez!*"

"I was kinda thinking it might be a quiet night alone."

She turned her lips into a wry smile. "Quiet and alone with yourself, or quiet and alone with John?"

I scoffed at her. "Am I that fucking transparent?"

She snorted. "It's okay, you're dating. You're really hung up on him, and—*news flash!*—he's crazy about you, too."

"I just wanna be with him all the time," I whined. "I thought I'd ask him over to watch a movie." I used to make fun of people who said things like that.

"Invite him to go to the party with you."

"Invite John? To the party?"

She rolled her eyes again and cocked her head to the side, her blonde hair catching the light. "Why not? He's your boyfriend. Who else would you take to a party?"

"Jess, it's... of course I want to take him. I'm not sure it'll be a good weekend, is all. He's dumping that sicko next Saturday."

"All right!" She held up her hand for a high five. "What great news! All the more reason it'll do him good to let off some steam." I stayed quiet, and she tilted her head again. "At least ask him. He needs to be around people."

I gave a grunt of frustration. "What he *needs* is to get laid. By me."

"What? You two still haven't...?" She shook her head. "Liam, you've made out, right? What are you waiting for? Take that man to bed and put both of you out of your misery."

"Jess—"

"I don't care what the circumstances are, you have *got* to move things along. You know he'll be willing."

"I don't want to be an insensitive jerk and pressure him. I like him a whole lot. *Fuck,* I think I'm fall...."

Her mouth opened. "Were you about to say what I think you were?" she asked, after a moment.

I put my hands over my face and groaned. When I pulled them away and managed to look at her, she was smiling at me. "Liam, what you almost said is totally cool. We're besties and it's just between us. If it turns out to be true, nobody will be happier for you than me."

I stayed quiet.

She arched her eyebrows "Hey Liam?"

"Hey what?"

"Take him to the party. Insist. He'll have a good time, and it'll be the perfect night to seduce him."

She was right, at least about him needing to have fun—*not* about intentionally setting out to get him into bed. I was going to honor my promise to wait, however long it took.

"I'll ask him." I changed the subject before she could say anything else. We talked about our families, and I asked if she was going home to Watertown for Thanksgiving.

"Thanksgiving with my eighty-year-old grandma, yes sir. What about you? Home to Wainscott?"

I shrugged. "Still up in the air. Mom wants me to come, but I'm not sure I want to drive anyplace with all that fucking traffic. It's too early to decide."

"If you don't go home, you're coming with me. You cannot spend Thanksgiving alone."

"It's too far off to make plans."

She finally finished her one slice and wiped her fingers on a napkin. "You're the one who brought it up. Are you thinking of spending the holiday with a certain handsome former professor?"

"Maybe. I dunno."

"Just remember my invitation."

"Thank you. I'll remember."

John

After lunch and a wonderful, happy afternoon, Liam went home. We'd made out, and both of us eventually got hard as tree trunks. I could tell he was frustrated, and he left soon after that. I really hoped that I hadn't scared him off for good. What the hell was I waiting for, anyway? I was head over heels about him.

The truth, astounding and scary, was that I was falling in love with Liam. I probably already had. It was very quick, and I couldn't explain it, but I didn't need to. I knew how I felt.

After chastising myself for being so difficult, I sat down to edit a paper for R&W. I couldn't concentrate, and had barely decided to call him when my phone rang.

Liam didn't even say hello. "Will you please go to a party with me on Friday?"

"Party? What party?"

"The SBA Falderal party. You've seen the posters."

My stomach tightened. "I guess I have."

"Sure, you have. John, would you do me the honor of being my date?"

I grimaced. "What would I do at a party with a bunch of kids? I'd be a downer. You know I'll be worried about going to find Thorne the next day."

"*Excuse me?* Did you say *kids*? Don't you mean your *classmates*? The ones who are in law school with you, all in the same boat? People who like you?" He snickered and made me smile. "John, everyone would be happy if you came, and you can get to know them better. We'll leave after a little while if you aren't having fun."

"Well...."

"Please! You're my boyfriend, and I wanna show you off, hot stuff. Besides, it would do you good to get your mind off Turdface for a little while."

I laughed. "You're right about that, and I'd like to show you off, too."

"Great, then! Let's plan to go for a little while."

I squeezed my eyes shut so hard they hurt. "I'll be nervous. I can't help being self-conscious about my age, and I haven't been to a college party for years."

"John, you're a fucking expert at negative self-talk. I'm not gonna tell you about that again, I'll just spank your ass."

Oh my God! Liam, spanking my ass?! That sounded so ridiculously hot that I started getting hard. Why not go to the party? I paid my SBA dues, like everyone else, and I was crazy about my phenomenal boyfriend.

"You're right," I said. "I shouldn't do that to myself. You're also right that I should put in an appearance at the party."

"You'll go with me, then?"

He sounded so excited that I laughed a little. "I would be thrilled to go to the party with you."

"Yes! It's a date. I'm gonna hold you to it."

LIAM

I'D HAVE FOUND something else for us to do if I hadn't convinced John to go to the party, but hanging out with the law school student body would be good for both of us. Maybe it would convince him once and for all that I was serious about him and couldn't care fucking less how old he was. I was getting into bed when my phone chirped, and I hoped he wasn't already trying to change his mind.

JOHN: *You asleep yet?*
LIAM: *Nope*
JOHN: *I just went to bed but need to say something.*
LIAM: *Anything*
JOHN: *I care about you so much. In case you have any doubts about how I feel.*
LIAM: *That makes me so happy, Punkin... I care a lot about you, too!*

A minute passed.

JOHN: *What's this Punkin thing?*
I'd been wondering if he would notice that.
LIAM: *I really really like u, and ur my Punkin... unless u object I guess*
JOHN: *It's really sweet actually. I want to be your Punkin.*
LIAM: *Good then because u already r*
JOHN: <3 *Have breakfast with me in the morning.*
LIAM: *Sure. Sam's cup, 8:00?*
JOHN: *It's a plan. Guess I'd better go because I need my beauty sleep to impress my incredibly handsome boyfriend.*
LIAM: *C u at 8 Punkin*

I was barely between the covers when the phone rang, John again. I grinned as I thumbed the button to answer. "Hey, what's up?"

"Feeling lonely and missing you. I wanted to hear your voice."

Closing my eyes, I imagined John lying in his bed. "Glad to hear yours, too. Lately, I'm always lonely when I'm not with you."

"Could we talk a while?" His voice was a little thick, and I figured he must be getting sleepy.

"Let's talk forever."

We gabbed, and eventually both of us started yawning. The pauses between sentences got longer. Neither of us wanted to hang up, and John fell asleep before too long. I put my phone on speaker and closed my eyes, luxuriating in the sound of his breath.

"I'm falling in love with you, John Lawrence," I whispered.

IT WAS a busy week and I was really stoked about the coming weekend, which promised to be momentous. John was going to the party with me, *and* he was ending things with Thorne. He said they represented two sides of the same coin. Going to the party was his declaration of independence, and breaking up with Thorne was his declaration of victory.

Thursday after class, John and Jess went shopping for something new to wear to the party. They invited me along, but I let them have the time together, happy they were becoming friends because both of them were so important to me.

I didn't feel like studying so I went to Bar Review. The place turned out to be a dump and hardly anyone I knew was there, so I hid at a corner table and texted with my little sister, Siobhan. I finished my two free drinks and went home, but when I got there, I was still not in any frickin' mood to read. I flipped through channels for a little while before reaching for my phone.

LIAM: Hey good lookin
JOHN: Hi sexy, what's up?
LIAM: N/m, got home a little while ago from bar review which sucked big time and now I have to do the property reading
JOHN: Me too. I am NOT in the mood.
LIAM: How was shopping
JOHN: We had a great time. Found outfits for tomorrow.
LIAM: Cool, send me a pic?
JOHN: No. You have to wait so you can be properly impressed.
LIAM: Seems like im waiting for lotsa things these days ;) j/k-------not!

I hoped that wasn't too much.

JOHN: I won't keep you waiting much longer, I promise. I know I keep saying that, but I mean it.
LIAM: Told u id wait as long as u need
JOHN: ~I~ can't wait much longer. You won't be the only one exploding! ;)
LIAM: That sounds hot... let's explode together :)
JOHN: Very, very soon. I promise.
LIAM: Im not going anywhere
JOHN: xoxo <3 I hate to go but I've got to finish reading. Breakfast tomorrow morning?
LIAM: Sams at 8?
JOHN: Can't wait.

8

Friday Morning, October 7

John

The phone dinged while I was drying off after my shower.

THORNE: I won't be home this weekend. Got invited to a golf tourney in TX so I'm going there. I'll be back late Sunday and will definitely come home Monday night, I promise. Maybe shrimp?

I made two quick decisions. First, if he didn't come home on Monday, I would be as cold as he was and do what I'd thought about before, have the locks changed and send him a break-up text. Second, I was tired of torturing an extraordinary man who wanted me as much as I did him. If he was still game after the party, I was his.

After daydreaming for a few minutes, I realized I was running late and had to rush to get dressed and take care of Theo. Liam was already at Sam's when I got there, and he stood up when I walked to the table. I took his hands. "Sorry I'm late."

He smiled and gave me a quick kiss on the cheek. "Four minutes late? Shut up! I'm happy you're here!"

We sat down, and I put my hand on his, on top of the table. "You're unbelievable, in the best possible way." I interlaced our fingers. "Something I now see very clearly is that you don't keep a good man waiting." I wiggled my eyebrows, hoping he got the message.

Liam

We'd flirted a lot by then, but something felt different that morning and I went with it. "Do all 40-year-olds have time issues?" I asked, with my best I-wanna-suck-your-dick smile.

He lifted my hand off the table and touched it to his lips. "I can't answer that, but I can tell you that *this* 40 is *very* concerned because he's making a certain awesome 22 wait."

I was a little confused. Was he talking about being late for meeting me at Sam's, or waiting for sex? "Rest easy," I said, "because this 22 is totally cool with you."

His dimples unfolded into a beautiful grin, and my dick definitely noticed.

We sat staring at each other until Sam interrupted, wearing a little smirk. He looked harried, with his cook's hat slightly askew.

"What's up, Sam?" I asked. "You seem stressed today."

He grunted and shook his head. “Two servers out with a bad cold. It’s a good thing that new cook I hired has a lot of experience so I can wait tables. What’s for breakfast, gentlemen?”

“Banana pancakes, scrambled eggs, bacon, and coffee,” I answered.

John hesitated a few seconds. “Mushroom omelet, bacon, and tea.”

Sam walked away, and I smiled at John. “What’s up? Something’s different this morning.”

He regarded me from under his eyelashes, wearing an enigmatic smile. “What’s different?”

“You are. Your voice, the way you’re looking at me. Being so touchy-feely in public.”

He cocked his head. “What? I can’t be happy to see you?”

“Oh *hell* yeah, you can. I want you to be happy to see me. I *need* you to be.”

“I need you too, sweetheart. I’m stupid for keeping you waiting so long. It’s going to end, much sooner than you may think.” His expression turned impish. “If you’re still interested, that is.”

My voice was a hoarse whisper. “Right here on this table, right now, if you want.”

He hesitated, and when he spoke, his voice was breathy too. “I needed you last night when I... took care of myself... with a toy.” *Jesus God!* I gasped as all my blood ran south, but John wasn’t finished. “And I needed you this morning when I jacked off in the shower and painted the tile in there.” He was cherry-red by then, and I was about to jizz my pants.

I leaned in very close. “I needed you when I shot over my head onto the wall last night, and when I ruined my sheets early this morning.”

John closed his eyes and moaned softly.

"*Fuck*," I whined. "Let's go home right now. Please."

"Not right this second, but *very* soon." He met my eyes. "Do you trust me? I'm done keeping both of us waiting."

"I trust you." I felt a little desperate. "Even if I might lose my mind." I tried to relax but had to ask, "Did you really... last night... a toy?"

"Yes, and I pretended it was you."

I gasped again. What was I supposed to do with that? I plotted a quick path to the bathroom in case I shot a huge wad in my pants, something that seemed imminent. Fortunately, the food came before I had to reply, and by the time Sam left, I'd recovered enough to pull my tongue back inside my mouth.

John

Things were definitely hot between Liam and me, and the morning classes rolled right on by. Since there were no Friday afternoon classes, I'd planned to go home and take a nap so I wouldn't konk out at the party like a senior citizen. After the morning at Sam's, I was seriously considering asking Liam to join me.

Calmer heads prevailed. "Lunch, hot stuff?"

I hope he's still calling me that after tonight. "You've got it, stud muffin."

He drove us to a pizza place near campus, the kind of restaurant that doesn't look great but serves the best pie in town out of a brick oven. While we waited for our meal, I asked a question. "What should I expect at this party, Liam?"

"Hmm...?" He arched his eyebrows and shook his head. "To be endlessly hit on and therefore driven fucking crazy by all the choices you'll have to make."

I pulled my best horror face. "Liam! I don't like 22s that

way."

His expression morphed into a silly frown. "Not *any* 22s?"

I tried for a fetching smile, hoping I remembered how. "Well, there may be just *one* 22 I like that way."

His eyes were wide. "Only one?"

I nodded. "Only one."

"Cool." He grinned. "Hang with me, and I'll protect you from the hoi polloi."

After a lunch of delicious pizza and endless flirting, he drove me to my car. "I'll be there to pick you up at eight thirty."

"I'll be ready," I promised.

"Wait, you have a little sauce... right here." He brushed my lips lightly with his. "Such sweet sauce.... See you at 8:30, hot stuff."

Liam

I STARTED down John's street at 8:10, just early enough to show I was stoked about our date. My heart thumped like a bass drum, my breath came quick, and I was sweating a little. After the morning, I was so worked up that I'd had to take matters in hand in the shower like I was sixteen all over again. If tonight was the night, as John kept implying, I didn't want to risk an explosion the first time he touched me.

The porch light was on, and my hand trembled as I rang the bell. Theo, John's dog, started barking, and I heard John tell him to be quiet. Footsteps approached, the door opened, and —*oh my God!*—there he stood, looking so good my eyes almost popped out of my head.

"Liam! Come in. You look amazing."

I threw my arms around him as soon as he closed the door. He smelled incredible, musky and powdery, and things started firming up below as soon as the fragrance hit my nose. He pressed himself against me hard, nuzzling my throat and planting a couple kisses there, not letting go until I was rock-hard and struggling for breath.

When he turned me loose and stared blatantly at the bulge in my jeans, I was damn proud. He needed to know how he affected me, and I was glad to see him sporting wood, too. I licked my lips and remembered I'd brought him a gift.

"I know how much you like these. I was walking by that bakery and thought of you." I handed him a bag of shortbread cookies I'd gone to buy that afternoon.

"You're so sweet. Thank you." He kissed my cheek and left it tingling. I wanted to grab him again but kneeled down by the dog instead.

"Hey, puggy boy! How's Theo?" I scratched behind his ears while he took quick, wheezy breaths. *It's okay, boy, I'm breathing hard, too.*

When I stood back up, I caught another whiff of John's cologne. The beguiling, sexy fragrance finished me off, and I was a man completely lost to lust. God help me if John wanted to wait longer than tonight. *Or help him!* I leaned in close and took a deep breath before speaking softly. "Your cologne is making me hard."

He laughed, a gentle, mellifluous sound. "Thank you, handsome, but you already were." His eyes twinkled and his grin was wicked. "I'm wearing Dark Night, and I was a little afraid you'd think it was too much."

"Are you kidding? I want to smell that at my wedding."

Oh, holy Jesus and Mother Mary! What the fuck had I just said? I tried to chuckle and was glad when John smiled. What a thing to say when we hadn't even *done it* yet.

Be careful, Liam. You don't want tonight to be the end of the most beautiful thing that never happened.

9

Liam

I kept sneaking looks at John all the way to the party, and damn if he didn't look incredible. He must have painted those jeans onto his ass, and his blue sweater brought out the color in his eyes. My dick had developed a mind of its own by then, and all I could think about was holding John and making love to him.

He seemed surprised when I insisted that he stay in his seat until I came around to open his door. Being a gentleman made me feel good, and I could tell he was impressed.

After I took his hand and helped him out of the car, I gave him a kiss on the cheek. "Listen, this is gonna be fun. Stick with me. I know you're feeling a little awkward, but I promise I won't disrespect you, and I won't let anyone else disrespect you, either. I won't leave you alone, and I'll take care of my man."

He swallowed hard and smiled. "Thank you. You're the best."

When we got to the door, I asked if he was okay and he said he was. I squeezed his hand. "Great, let's get drinks, then."

It was a bigger crowd and smaller room than I expected, and people were every-*fucking*-where. I led us to the bar, where I claimed two primo craft beers and handed one to my beautiful boyfriend.

We found some people from our section standing on the sidelines, and I noticed a few pointed looks at our joined hands, John's and mine. Come on—how could anyone in our section not have known by then? Jess had me believing they were placing bets on us in Vegas. John was pretty quiet at first, but soon relaxed and joined in the conversation.

"Hey, man." Michael and Jess came up behind me, and he yelled in my ear. "Looks like things are going great between you two."

I couldn't hold off a big grin. "Things are awesome, dude. Thanks for your shitty, but invaluable, help with that."

"No problem. Glad it worked out."

Jess kissed me on the cheek. "How's my bestie?"

"Great thanks." I nodded toward John. "Look at my man!" *Check out his ass*, I mouthed.

She snickered. "He was hoping you'd like those jeans."

"Like them?" I gave a little growl of appreciation. "I fucking love them!"

She looked me over. "You look great, too. New shirt?"

I nodded, noticing how her blue dress brought out the color in her eyes, even in the dim light of the party.

"Anything new on the... you know... dragging him to your cave thing?"

My breath caught. "Chill! He's kinda nervous, and I don't want him to hear you."

She snickered at me. "I'm sure you can think of a way to calm his nerves, Casanova."

I needed to stop that line of conversation and noticed my beer was empty, so I leaned toward John. "Going to get us a couple more beers. Don't move, and I'll be right back, 'kay?"

He brushed up my side with a finger. "Promise?"

I sucked in breath. I was in such bad shape that his fingertip on my side had given me a semi. "On a stack of Bibles."

His dimples popped, and his happy smile would've guaranteed my return even if a swarm of giant wild African wasps flew in and set up camp between us. I spoke to people on my way to the bar and was glad to see everyone relaxing. It was about time we all kicked back and forgot about law school for a night.

"So, dude, you and Lawrence?" A guy named Greg practically stepped on me, leering as only a drunk can. He was in another section but lived in my building.

"Dating," I said, hoping he'd let it go.

"Awwwwww, I get it," he said, and looked a little disappointed. "Good luck, my man."

While I waited in line at the bar, I glanced back toward John, who was watching me. As soon as I got the drinks, I scurried back to him and his perky ass as quickly as I could. "Sorry it took so long." I handed him his beer.

"It's okay." He leaned close to my ear. "People were asking about us and I said you're my boyfriend. I hope that's okay."

I grinned and kissed his forehead. "That's what I am, right?"

He took my hand. "Without a doubt. You're the most amazing boyfriend ever."

The party grew louder and we mixed around some, enjoying getting to know people. John kept giving me these flushed, hungry looks that made my heart flip. My sister Vonnie would say I was in trooouuuble! John Lawrence was taking my heart down for the count.

John

My nerves let go and I wondered why I'd been so afraid. Everyone was nice except for one drunk jerk named Greg who came up while Liam was gone to get beer and asked me if I'd always been a cradle robber. What a shit.

Liam was irresistible in black jeans that left nothing to the imagination, and a burgundy button-up shirt made him look like the regal prince he was. I'd expected him to get bored with babysitting me and want to spread his wings a little, but he seemed very happy staying by my side.

After a while, I looked at my watch and was surprised to see we'd been there for over two hours. People were still arriving, and it was extremely hot inside with so many people packed into a ridiculously small space. I leaned close to Liam because there was no hope he would hear me unless I yelled in his ear. "How about getting another couple of drinks and going outside for a while?"

"You read my mind. Come with me." He started moving toward the bar, pulling me along. Clearly, he'd navigated college parties a lot more recently than I had, because he seemed unfazed by the heat and crowd, and we arrived at the bar surprisingly quickly. Picking up two beers, he handed one to me and expertly led us to the door. I sighed with relief as we stepped outside. The air was much cooler, and the noise receded as we walked away from the building.

He grazed my lips with his. "How's it going? You having a good time?"

"An amazing time. It's nice talking to people. You've been an angel the way you've stayed beside me."

He glanced at me with an odd expression. "I told you I wouldn't leave you alone."

"Yes, you did." I took a moment deciding what to say. "It's nice to see that there are actually men in the world who keep their word."

He squinted his eyes. "What the hell kinda shitty dudes have you been hanging out with, anyway?"

His smile was puckish, and the words were funny, but they hit home. I wondered the same thing and swallowed hard. "Obviously none who compare with you, Liam."

His widened eyes, the blush, the toothy smile and twinkling eyes—they warmed my heart. I couldn't wait to get back home. As long as I had anything to do with it, the wait was definitely over.

Liam

I didn't know how to react when John seemed surprised that I was being good to him, so I went for humor. I wanted to be the best man for him that I could be, and was glad he noticed, but it pissed me off a little, too. Thorne was not a good guy, that much was obvious, but what the fuck kind of dumbass, dickweed, twatwaffle would treat a partner so badly that they'd actually be surprised when somebody else only did what they said they would?

Unable to say any of that to John, I asked what kind of dudes he was used to hanging out with. His answer nearly put me on the ground. His words, along with his enthusiastic, proud smile, made electricity crackle up my spine. "Let's find someplace to sit," I managed to say.

He pointed at a table with four chairs around it, well to the side of the courtyard. "Over there? It's out of the traffic."

We sat down, and the play of the moonlight on John's face brought out his beauty. After a while, I got up the nerve to say what was on my mind. "You know how I feel about you?"

"I have a definite idea." His eyes twinkled as he gave me a beautiful smile.

"The thing is, I want to show you in every way. I said I'll wait, but—"

Two beer bottles slammed hard onto the table, and John and I both jumped as if we'd been shot. I was out of my seat like a rocket. "What the hell?"

Strong hands clamped my arms in place. "Easy, big fella." It was Michael and Jess, both of them grinning like Cheshire cats.

The shadows around us made Michael look even bigger than he was. "Sorry I scared you, dude," he said. "Thought you guys might like the brews."

"Thank you," John said. "It's really nice of you, but next time, could you try not to give us heart failure?"

Jess smirked at us. "We've been standing here for a while. You guys had no idea." She raised her eyebrows and looked at me. "Sounded hot, though."

"Jess!" I snapped.

Michael's chuckle started deep in his chest. "Boys, everybody's glad to see you two together, especially since we've watched it simmer since the first day we were all here."

"Watched what simmer?" John asked.

Jess huffed, and Michael laughed. "Hey, man, please don't insult us by maintaining verbal denial in the face of visual confirmation." John and I chuckled along with them. "Seriously, it's great. Enjoy yourselves!"

"It's *awe-some*!" Jess sang. "I'm going to expect a full report later, Liam, so take notes."

John

I WAS tired of sitting and asked Liam if he'd like to take a walk. We started down a path that curved around behind the building. People were back there, but not a lot, and some of them were camouflaged behind the trees. It was darker as we got farther from the front of the building, and smells of autumn and weed were thick in the air. The evening had cooled off quite a bit, and Liam put an arm around my shoulder.

Someone yelled, and he dropped his arm as we both turned in her direction. Realizing there was nothing to be alarmed about, we were turning back when our eyes met. His were deep and hungry, and my heart began pounding. Liam's face was strong and kind, and his cheekbones seemed even more prominent in the dim, shadowy light. When he licked his lips, I felt desperate to be in his arms.

"John, I really wanna do something, but I'm kind of afraid."

I realized I'd been holding my breath and slowly let it go. "So afraid that you don't want to do it?"

"No. I really want to." He moved closer and dragged his tongue across his lips again.

I swallowed hard. "You'd better do it, then."

Liam's fingers were soft under my chin as he tilted my head upward. He took another small step forward, and I smiled as he moved his hand behind my head and caressed my hair. I took another tiny step forward, and my arms went around him as his warm, soft lips softly brushed against mine. My breath caught when he licked at my lower lip.

"I've been lost in your eyes all night," he said, pulling me even closer with his free arm, and I shivered despite the warmth of his body.

"Me too." My voice was little more than a whisper.

He touched his lips to mine again and nibbled at me for a few seconds. When he brushed his tongue between my lips, I opened for him and he moaned softly. I relished the sensation of our tongues sliding together. He moved his hand from behind my head down my back, and I relaxed into his stout embrace.

I caressed his back and deepened the kiss. Soon my tongue was in his sweet, beery mouth, and I enjoyed the heady taste. I whimpered, wondering briefly how long I could stay on my feet. When I ground my throbbing cock into his, he moaned again and pushed back, igniting lustful sparks that further weakened my knees.

It wasn't our first kiss, but it was definitely the life-changing one. Time stopped until our lips separated, and even then we held onto each other for a while. Both of us were panting, and Liam nuzzled my throat, his tongue leaving tiny trails of moisture that felt cold in the chilly air. I was in total sensory overload.

"That was awesome, John," he murmured in my ear. "You're *everything*."

I whispered back. "After all this time, I finally know what it feels like to be swept off my feet."

Just then, a male voice called out. "Woo hoo! Guess you guys finally got over that fight!"

Liam looked at me and grinned. "Wanna get outta here?"

10

Liam

I got completely drunk on John at the party. When we walked around the back of the building, I knew that going for the kind of kiss I needed might scare him, but I also knew that if I didn't, I'd regret it for a long time.

On the way home, I was nervous, wondering what would happen next. I wanted more of that kiss—no, I wanted a helluva lot *more* than that kiss, and it was clear that John did, too. I'd been with guys my age who never got as hard as that cock I felt pushing into mine. He'd been insinuating all day that the wait was over, but if he changed his mind, I had to be prepared to roll with it. We both needed to get laid, but it wouldn't do either of us any good if he wasn't ready and regretted it in the morning.

Before I knew it, we were at his house, getting out of the car. He looked a little nervous and I wasn't sure what he expected, but if he asked me inside—whatever happened—he was going to know exactly how I felt about him before I left. I'd never fallen in love before, and I couldn't keep it a secret.

"This has been such a great time," I said, when we reached the door.

"It has been." He reached into his pocket for a key. Everything was quiet except the click of the lock, and he kept his back turned long enough that I wondered if I should take the hint.

"Well, maybe I'd better be—"

He whirled around, his brow wrinkled and his eyes as round as the sun on a bright day. "Please don't say going. Come inside with me?"

"I'd love to if... if you want me to."

"Of course I want you to."

He opened the door and we stepped inside. Theo was waiting, panting away. John kneeled down to greet him, and when he stood back up the little dog looked expectantly at me. I bent over to give him a pat on the head and he woofed happily before bouncing away. I think he told me to take good care of his dad. *No worries, Theo.*

John closed the door, and we settled on the sofa after he got us some water from the fridge. The moonlight coming in through the windows made the whole room sparkle. Even John's house was happy tonight.

He laid his head against my shoulder, and I put my arm around him. "How are you, Punkin?"

"Never better," he said, moving his fingers back and forth against the front of my shirt.

We sat like that for a while until I found the balls to say what I needed to. My breath came hard, and my heart, which was bouncing off my ribs, was making a concerted effort to blast right on through. "I need to tell you something. I have to say it, and I guess.... *shit*!" I took the deepest breath I could and looked into his sparkling sapphire eyes. "I've never felt this way about anyone before. You're.... Well, I'm... I might be...."

He cocked his head. "You might be...?"

I blew out my cheeks and plunged ahead. "I'm in love with you, John."

His eyebrows unkinked and he touched his fingers to his parted lips. I held my breath as I watched his mouth twitch, and a big smile took over his face. "Liam... sweetheart, I love you, too."

We sat facing each other, and magic filled the air. Our lips met, and we held on tight. First one of us deepened the kiss, then the other. I might say we explored each other's mouths, but I think we were exploring souls. Our bodies melted into each other, and who knows how long we sat there making out. Finally, I pulled away and looked at him, giving him one last chance to back out if he wanted to.

"You know what I wanna do, but I promised I'd wait as long as you needed—"

"I don't want to wait anymore." His voice was thick. "Please stay with me."

His hand trembled as he stroked my cheek with the pad of his thumb. I went in for some more mouth hockey—championship mouth hockey.

Now that we knew what was coming, neither of us was shy anymore. I palmed his solid cock through his pants while I licked and sucked at his throat, enjoying his salty taste and the needy sounds he made. He ground into my hand while he squeezed the bulge in my pants, making me see sparks.

"Take me to bed, Liam?" he pleaded.

"Yeah," I finally said. "Oh yeah!"

John stood, held out his hand, and led me upstairs. He stopped in front of the first door down the hall. "This is the guest room."

"It is?" I heard the disappointment in my own voice. "I have to stay in there?"

His eyes shone. "I'm going in with you. The guest room doesn't have any ghosts."

A lamp sat on a chest of drawers, casting just enough light to see by. That was no problem because all I wanted to see was John. He showed me a bashful grin and licked his lips, his need palpable. I launched myself at him, backing him up hard against the wall and pushing my knee between his legs. He grabbed my ass with both hands and ground his desperate cock into mine.

"I need you so much." I was barely able to whisper.

He was panting. "Take what you need."

Didn't have to tell me twice. John threw his head back and moaned while I sucked at his throat. Then we shared a filthy kiss while I tugged at his sweater, our lips parting only long enough for me to pull it over his head. Determined to feel his bare skin, I fumbled with the buttons on his shirt, but when I finally got it off, I found a T-shirt underneath.

I pulled back and complained loudly. "Fuck, it's like getting into a chastity belt or something."

He kissed me softly before pulling the T-shirt over his head, and my mouth fell open. *Oh shit!* His chest was perfectly smooth, the kind of smooth you don't get by shaving. His pecs were small but defined, and his stomach was tight. His taut pink nipples stood out against ivory flesh, and I had to give each one a kiss.

He worked on my shirt, and finally we were skin to skin. I groaned my approval. I had some hair on my chest and when it scraped against him, the sensation made me shiver with delight. Shit, I'd thought I was as hard as I could get but realized I was mistaken when the swelling grew painful. John's hot, sweaty chest against mine fanned the fire inside me, and I bit into the tender skin at the base of his throat.

"Yes!" he gasped.

I unbuttoned his jeans and slid my hand inside. His underwear was wet and sticky, and his cock was throbbing. He groaned as I squeezed, and he pushed into my hand while he fumbled with the button on my jeans. I whimpered like a baby when his warm hand encircled my cock.

With one hand still holding his dick, I pulled him from the wall. I turned us around and walked him backward, my tongue still in his mouth. "Lie down," I said, when we reached the bed. "Wanna taste you."

I spent a minute taking off the rest of my clothes and then got on my knees at the foot of the bed to finish undressing John. After I tugged his boxer briefs over his feet, I looked at him and almost stopped breathing.

Oh. My. God.

There he was at last, completely naked, just for me. How many times had I fantasized about it? As if reading my mind, he spread his legs on either side of me, and the view almost made me come.

His pubes were painstakingly manicured, and his cock was as beautiful as the rest of him. He was cut, about six inches, rigid and dripping with need. His precum leaked in a thin thread down toward his belly. I bent over to lick it up, salty-sweet and delicious, and enjoyed his choked moan when I tickled the underside of his dick with my fingernails.

I went down on him, and he rewarded me with one of the most helpless and beautiful whimper-groans ever. The sound was incredibly sexy, and combined with the view and his earthy scent, it fanned my arousal into blast-furnace mode.

John

I HADN'T BEEN SO TURNED on since I was a teenager. When Liam first began toying with me, I tried to maintain some shred of dignity and remain quiet, but once his mouth engulfed me, whatever "dignity" was left simply evaporated. I became a writhing, whining mess.

His tongue and throat were magic. Slowly, he prodded me toward ecstasy, sucking and licking my cock and balls like candy. His rhythm constantly changed, so I couldn't anticipate what would be next. It nearly drove me out of my mind.

Completely at his mercy, speaking some unknown tongue, I was close to passing out. My entire existence seemed to be inside his mouth, and I wondered if I'd ever really had a blow job before. Thinking was too difficult right then, though, so I just lay back and felt, doing all I was capable of at the moment, squirming and begging.

Liam

I WAS ALWAYS proud of my fellatic skills, and I pulled out all the stops that night. John was obviously starved for sexual release. His excitement was such a powerful aphrodisiac that I couldn't keep my spare hand off my own dick while I worshipped his. He moaned and groaned, in between a steady mix of babble and real words.

"Fuck, Liam... incredible. Abagoood ubarb. Omigod odgabaaaarv don't stop, don't stop, don't stop, pleeeeeease!"

Whatever. He was communicating just fine. He loved what I was doing, didn't want me to stop, and was out of his mind with pleasure. He twisted and flailed around while he tangled one hand in my hair. His precum became richer and muskier, and it was looking like I just might succeed at giving my boyfriend the most shattering orgasm of his life.

"*Fuck*—really close!" His hand tightened in my hair as he gasped and panted. "Oh please! Please, please...."

His body tensed and jerked, and his amazingly hard cock swelled until the skin was smooth as glass. He yelled out, and his upper body lifted off the bed as hot cum furiously jetted out into my mouth. I didn't want to miss a drop, so I clamped my lips down and swallowed as fast as I could.

John

When the big spurts subsided, my bones turned to jelly and I flopped backward onto the bed, helpless. Liam continued suckling me gently, bringing me down into a numb bliss. Eventually I heard him chuckle, and with a Herculean effort, I spoke. "Thank you." *Eloquent, John.*

"The pleasure was all mine."

My attempted chuckle sounded like a grunt. "Obviously not true."

He got up on the bed and wrapped his arm across my stomach. After a moment, I turned so I could get to him and played with the hair around his nipples before licking one and giving it a soft nibble.

He sucked in a sharp breath. "Oh! Careful!"

I grinned up at him while I gave the other nipple a pinch and played with the first one a little more. A glance at his cock confirmed that he was enjoying the attention. "You like having your nipples played with."

"Anything you want—*ouch*!"

I'd nipped at the one nipple again, at the same time as I pinched the other.

"Get up here!" he squawked, and I shimmied up the bed to kiss his mouth.

He started moaning when I went to his throat and reached down to take his very hard, extremely sticky cock in my fist. I gave him a couple of firm squeezes.

"Feels so good!" He brushed my cheek with his fingertips and angled my face up to meet his eyes. "Could I fuck you? Are you up for that? I want to so bad I can't even think about anything else."

His words hit my libido like a bomb, and I desperately needed him again. It had been *so* long. "I want it too!"

He gave me another smutty kiss. "You have condoms and lube?"

"Nightstand drawer. I put some there just in case."

He laughed softly, and I caught sight of his cock as he reached over me to open the drawer. It was huge—turgid and purple, heavily dripping precum. I reached out a finger to trace the beautiful veins adorning his girth, and when some of his precum smeared onto my finger, I licked it off.

With the lube and condoms in hand, he shifted his position so he could get at me, and I spread my legs farther apart and bent my knees. As his slick fingers gently massaged around my hole, I lost control of my mouth again and begged him to get on with it. When he slipped a finger inside me, I yelled out my delight.

Liam

I used lots of lube and was as gentle as I could be. I didn't want to hurt John, but he kept rearing up into my hand, and seeing how much he needed me made me more frantic than I already was. It must have been a long time for him, and my fever rose at breakneck speed. I *had* to make him mine. He bucked when my fingers found his swollen prostate, yelling so loud that I thought the neighbors must have heard.

After a couple of minutes, he got real mouthy. "Enough, I'm ready!" He huffed for good measure. "Fuck me now! Here, give me that condom."

"Bossy," I replied, grinning and handing him the condom. He ripped it open and unrolled it down my cock. After drizzling on a lot of lube, he looked at me with frenzied eyes, and I couldn't wait another minute. "On your back okay? I wanna see your eyes."

I hoisted his legs onto my shoulders and lined myself up. He gasped hard when I pushed, and I got nowhere. I went easy because a guy hurt me the one time I ever tried to bottom, and I'd made it a point to be really considerate going in ever since.

"*Please.*" He begged for it, sounding desperate. "It's been forever. I need you so much!"

I kissed him while I pushed again. *Fuck! He isn't opening up at all.* I looked into his feral eyes. "You're way tight. I gotta push harder, but I don't wanna hurt you."

He nodded his head wildly. "Just get inside me. I'll try to relax more."

When I pushed again, his stubborn muscles gave way. The head of my cock popped inside and—*oh shit*—I felt slapped. His eyes flew open, bright and panicky. He was so tight that, for a second, I didn't know if I could take it. "You all right?" I asked.

He panted like a wild animal. "Yes. Just go slow, okay?" He closed his eyes and swallowed. "You're really big."

Way to make me feel awesome! I waited until he opened his eyes again. "I'll go as slow as I can." An excruciating minute went by while I kissed him, with the head of my dick just inside his ass. I wiggled slightly and then pushed again, and we both groaned while I worked my way inside. Just when I thought I was going to lose it and involuntarily shove the rest of the way in, our hips met.

"Fuck!" he yelled. "Yes!"

I began rocking, slowly at first and then a little faster. John was crooning, and I could tell he was enjoying it as much as I was. "You're huge. Feels so good."

I was still dazzled by how tight he was. "You're squeezing my dick off."

His eyes were wild, his hair wet with sweat. *Yes! He is* all *into this.*

He never looked away as he twisted underneath me, and I grunted while I picked up speed. Over a couple minutes, I went from rocking, to pumping, to snapping my hips into him like a piston. He threw his head back, moaning and speaking gibberish again, and I took his cock in hand and jerked him in rhythm to our thrusts. His moans turned into wails of ecstasy.

John

Liam fucked like a god. He was flushed and sweaty, his eyes fiery and full of lust. His kisses made me burn with desire, and the way he jerked me in rhythm to his fucking had me screaming with delight.

Between grunts and groans, he whispered the most wonderful things to me. "You're so beautiful, John.... Love you.... Need you so much.... Wanna be inside you forever."

No one had ever said things like that to me before. The emotions were so powerful, and tears ran down my cheeks while I gave myself to him. He slammed into me over and over, pounding against my prostate like a battering ram, and I begged him to never stop.

Liam

John's eyes were fierce, and he watched me like I was Superman. He met every thrust for as long as he could, but I soon had him pinned and he couldn't move. His face was florid, his hair was plastered to his forehead, and he unashamedly demanded more. His ass was getting tighter, not looser, his muscles squeezing me so hard I almost became incoherent.

"Come for me, John. Come for me?"

"Yeah, so close."

"Unnh!"

"Gonna come!" I heard one of us yell, or was it both of us? A massive bolt of electricity kicked me in the nuts as John erupted in my hand, twisting and bucking like a bull.

"Fucking hell!" I yelled. My muscles all contracted at once and everything went dark. Somehow, I was still thrusting while I came harder than I could ever remember. My asshole spasmed, propelling shards of pleasure through my gut. My back arched, and my head thrust back as if someone had clocked me.

After a moment, I couldn't hold myself up anymore and collapsed on top of John. His pleasure was wet and sticky between us, and our tongues played lazily inside each other's mouths. I was still hard despite being totally empty, and my cock remained buried deep inside him.

After twenty-two years, I'd finally experienced life, the real thing. Making love with John wasn't a one-night-stand, get-each-other-off-and-go-home kind of thing. Instead, it was the magic you make with somebody you love, your bodies expressing things that words can't.

I eventually managed to get myself into the bathroom where I got rid of the condom, wet a washcloth, and cleaned myself up. After I rinsed the cloth, I took it back into the bedroom, where John still lay just as I'd left him.

He opened his eyes and smiled at me, speaking in a low voice. "I've never felt this good before."

"It was incredible," I said. "I love you, John." I was grinning like a fool.

"I love you, too." He chewed his lip. "You're the best I've ever had, by far. You're magnificent, and that's the truth."

I sat on the edge of the bed and cleaned him up. He could barely move, and I got up the nerve to ask a question that was on my mind. "Will you tell me something? It doesn't change anything, and I don't care, but—"

"Anything."

"You'd done this before, right? Bottoming? I mean, you're so tight, and you were wild."

He laughed so hard I couldn't help joining in. I lay down beside him, and he brushed his lips against mine, still chuckling. *Goddamn!* He was even more beautiful when he laughed, and I wanted to keep him at it so I could watch him forever.

"Yes, I've done it before," he finally said. "It's what I like, what I need, being the bottom." He took a breath and sighed sadly. "I've not been fucked for such a long time."

I wasn't sure I really wanted to know. "How long?"

"Four years."

My brain tripped over itself. *Four years?* Since I started college? It took me a minute to speak. "But you and Thorne...."

"I told you it's been dead forever. *Totally* dead. Our—*activities*—slowed down to oral and hand jobs, then to nothing. There was nothing for such a long time."

"So you... what? Jerked yourself off for four years?" I struggled to get my mind around what he'd said.

"Yes. And used my toys."

Shit! John wouldn't have had any trouble finding someone,

he was way too attractive. He looked ashamed. Oh, *hell* no! "That fucking moron is so stupid. How could he resist?" I was angry, but forced my voice down so that John wouldn't think I was upset with him. "John.... What an evil thing he did to you."

He brushed my side with his fingertips. "You're so sweet, and believe me, you just helped me make up for a lot of lost time." We lay in silence for a moment before he spoke again. "Please, let's not talk about him anymore. Tonight's about us."

"Okay, but know this. As long as you want me, you will never have to suffer like that again. I promise."

Dimples!—big, juicy, gorgeous ones. "I'm holding you to that."

"You'd better," I said, and kissed him again.

When we came up for air, he asked if I wanted to spoon. I wrapped my arms around him, certain that I'd never felt so happy. Things got quiet, and before long, John's breathing slowed down. His warm body felt so good pushed back against my belly, and I lay there thinking about us, fucking like rabbits. The intensity of our feeling had been laid raw in a way that was totally new to me.

Why I was in love with John was no mystery at all, but I was the luckiest bastard on God's green earth that he felt the same about me.

11

Liam

For a minute I didn't know where I was and then it all came back. I'd turned over in the night and taken most of the covers with me, and when I flipped back around to rearrange them, I was in awe.

There he was, John Lawrence—naked, lying very close to me, and absolutely gorgeous. His hair was mussed, the cutest case of bedhead you ever saw, and he grumbled a little in his sleep when I moved. I leaned up on one arm to watch him, and when I wrapped myself around him a few moments later, his sigh of contentment told me he was waking up.

"Good morning," he said, his voice very sleepy.

"Morning, beautiful." I sounded pretty groggy myself.

He turned around to face me, looking serious. "I really want to do something, but I'm a little nervous about it."

Funny guy. We both smiled. "So nervous you don't wanna do it?" I asked.

"Oh, I'm going to do it."

He put his hand on my cheek and gave me goosebumps when his fingertips brushed over my left ear. I pulled him against me as his hand slid to the back of my neck, where he made circles with his fingertips while he touched his lips to mine. That was all it took to ignite a blaze that turned my morning wood into iron. He pushed his dick against mine and moaned as I deepened the kiss.

When we broke for breath, his eyes were bright. "Are you okay with all this?" he asked.

"So far past okay. I'm outta-my-fuckin'-mind happy." The deep contentment I felt had me moaning as he cuddled into me.

After two earth-moving blowjobs, we fell back asleep for another hour and woke up hungry. After a shower to wash off the dried sweat and cum, John asked if I'd walk Theo around the block, and when the little pug and I got back, unmistakable smells of bacon and pancakes filled the house. John was wearing pajama bottoms and a Toronto Maple Leafs T-shirt, standing in his cheery blue and yellow kitchen. The light streaming in through the windows highlighted his translucent, perfect skin. "I didn't know what you were in the mood for, so I'm making a little of everything. How do eggs, bacon, sausage, pancakes, and waffles sound?"

I put my hands on his waist and leaned in for a kiss. "Sounds like heaven. Those are all the things I like best."

He fawned over me, serving me and repeatedly insisting that I have just a little more. He made me blush when he told me how handsome I was, and how lucky he was that I loved him.

When we'd finished eating, I thought about going home but really didn't want to. "I know we have work to do for Monday, but how about a drive in the country this afternoon? We can be lazy and stop whenever we see something interesting."

He leaned over the table and touched my hand. "Sounds great to me."

We stopped at my place long enough for me to change clothes. John seemed unsure of what to do when we got to my building and asked if he should stay in the car.

"Come in with me, please? I'm *so* proud to be with you." I traced his lips with my thumb. "If anyone sees me doing the walk of shame, I want no doubt about who else was involved."

John

The bad dream woke me, and as I lay in the dark in Liam's arms, I thought about what I should say to Thorne on Monday. Should I voice my suspicions, or simply talk about what I knew to be fact—his unhappiness, restlessness, avoidance, cruelty, and constructive desertion? That was quite a list, so I decided to stick with facts he couldn't plausibly deny.

The more I thought, the more restless I became, and after a while Liam started moving around, too. "What's the matter, babe? Why aren't you sleeping?" He planted a few kisses on my throat, making me groan from the luxury of feeling loved. "Maybe I didn't wear you out enough?"

"Mm. You wore me out just fine." I thought about saying nothing was wrong, but I wasn't going to lie to him. That was not the relationship I wanted. "Just thinking about what I'll say to Thorne. No biggie, it's just on my mind."

"It *is* a biggie," he said, suddenly wide awake. "You guys were together for what? Sixteen years? And for a bunch of them, he treated you like shit, hurt you worse than I can probably imagine. John, that's a biggie."

I blew out a hard sigh. "It's tempting to play it down. Self-defense, I guess." Liam remained quiet, so I went on. "What the hell should I say to him?"

He pushed my hair back and gave me a kiss on my forehead. "I'll be glad to talk about that tomorrow. Right now, I want you to try to settle down and get some more sleep." He rubbed his hand on my chest, comforting me. "You're not in this alone, so please try to kick that shitweasel out of your head for tonight. You need your rest so you can do what you gotta do."

THE LIGHT IRRITATED me at first, and I looked at the clock out of morbid curiosity. 9:50. Liam was facing away from me, so I scooted closer and kissed him on the cheek. "Wake up, sleepyhead."

No movement, no response. I spoke a little louder. "Liam? Wake up sweetheart." I trailed little kisses down the side of his neck before licking his ear lobe.

He wiggled but didn't turn over. "John?" His voice was very thick. "Why are you awake again?"

I stretched out and wrapped my leg around him. "It's almost ten. Want to get Sunday started?"

He turned over, yawning, and kissed me as if we'd been apart for a year. "There's only one way I wanna start this day."

An hour later, while we ate omelets, I asked him what he wanted to do for the rest of the day. He gave a little sigh, followed by a groan. "Don't want to, but I need to read some cases. Maybe we could chill later this afternoon?"

"Only if you let me make you dinner," I said. "Meanwhile, I need to read some, too."

He nodded and narrowed his eyes. "Dammit! I don't have my books here."

My teacup was halfway to my mouth. "It's all right, use mine. I read the cases already. All I need to do is skim through them again to check my briefs, and I can do that on my iPad. Or we can go get your books, if you'd rather."

He winked at me. "Your books are fine, but tonight, *I* cook for *you*."

We made a nest in front of the fireplace and studied together. Several hours and a few cups of coffee later, Liam sat up and stretched. "What would you like for dinner?"

He was serious—he wants to cook for you! "Whatever you feel like making. I like anything."

He snickered and tapped my foot with his. "Give me a hint?"

"Hmm...." I had no idea what his cooking skills were like. "Can you make spaghetti with meat sauce?"

He grinned and stood up. "You've got it." Holding out a hand, he helped me off the floor. "Just need to go shopping first."

The spaghetti turned out to be delicious, and after I ate two helpings and a salad, we did the dishes together. He sang to me while we worked, and his voice, though off-key, was so sweet I couldn't stop smiling.

We took Theo out for a walk, and when we came back inside Liam looked at me and smiled. "I really hate to go home, but I guess I should give you some space."

Wait, what? "You're going home?" I sounded as disappointed as I felt.

"Don't want to overstay my welcome." He hugged me before pulling back. "Tomorrow's Monday, and if I've done my job right this weekend, you should be pretty worn out."

My hand went to my stomach, which felt a lot tighter than it had a moment before. "Do what you want, but don't leave because you think I want you to go. I don't."

He played with his hands for a moment. "I'd love to stay, but I really don't want to intrude. You have a big day tomorrow."

I took a deep breath, trying to get my stomach to unclench. "I know what's happening tomorrow and I've thought it through. We talked about it over dinner, remember? I'm going to tell Thorne what he's done and how I feel, and then send him on his way." I shrugged. "Or maybe go on my own way, I suppose."

Liam, looking surprised, cupped my face in his soft hands. "If you need a place to go, you've got it with me." He grinned again, making my heart *ka-thump*. "As long as you bring Theo, that is. *Please* don't leave Theo for that asswipe."

I snorted at his apt description of Thorne. "Theo's with me, no matter what."

12

John

Class inched by. My mind certainly wasn't on Torts, and I kept obsessing about what might happen with Thorne later. Liam took my hand after a while, and when class finally ended, we decided to go to lunch.

"Where are we headed?" he asked, as we walked down the hall.

"Emperor Wok? It's quick, delicious, and has booths." A little privacy would be good since I wanted more of his feedback on what I should say to Thorne. We walked the ten minutes to the restaurant. Thankfully there was no line, and we ordered kung pao chicken, and beef with broccoli.

When the waiter left, I went over what would happen later, my plan to stick with facts, and my talking points. I swore that if Thorne didn't show up, I would call an after-hours locksmith to change the locks and send him a breakup text.

Liam nodded. "That would be good. I know I said differently before, but things have changed a lot, and I don't just mean us. He's been avoiding you for weeks—lying, saying he'd come home then not showing, ignoring your calls. The sonovabitch knows something's up and doesn't want to face the music."

I munched my crispy spring roll and tried to control my nerves. "Can you think of anything else I should say?"

"Let's see." He got quiet while he finished his hot and sour soup. "Don't forget how the shitbag thorn-in-the-ass is flagrantly cheating on you and has been for years."

That tickled me so much I struggled to keep a bite of food in my mouth. "Maybe I'll call him that, but I don't have absolute evidence of his cheating, and I don't want to get sidetracked arguing about it. Wouldn't it be better to support my decision with things he can't deny? That might make him mad, but he won't get far trying to deny facts. And certainly not by trying to tell me how to feel."

The entrees came, and we changed topics, discussing ideas for the future. Liam wanted to go somewhere together over Christmas vacation.

"Maybe Colorado?" I said. "We could hole up there and ski a little if we feel like it." I knew he liked to ski, and we both loved winter.

He nodded eagerly. "Sounds like a plan."

We sat in silence for a while after the waiter cleared the table, both of us thinking about the coming confrontation with Thorne.

Liam

Jess and Emily stopped us as we left Property.

"How was the weekend, guys?" Jess asked. "Liam, I didn't see you around the building even once."

I would eventually tell her some of what had happened, but wasn't ready to talk about it in front of Emily. "I was busy all weekend."

Emily and Jess exchanged conspiratorial glances, and Jess rolled her eyes. "I was at the party, and what I didn't see, I've heard. Then there's today? I can't remember ever seeing either one of you look so happy, let alone strutting all over the place hand-in-hand like lovebirds."

Pinpricks of red appeared on John's face, and I realized we needed to get away. "We *are* really happy, and we partially have both of you to thank for it. Let's all get together soon, but right now John's gotta be someplace and I'm his ride." I looked at him. "Ready, babe?"

"Ready as I'm going to be." He tried to smile, but his nerves were stepping up and it looked a little like a scowl. We must have left Jess and Emily wondering what was going on.

In the car, John said he felt like he was going to the dentist, that he dreaded the experience but knew he'd feel a lot better afterward. As we neared his house, I asked if we should stop at the market.

He shook his head, looking a little perplexed. "No, why?"

"You cooking dinner?"

He barked out a bitter laugh. "I've cooked my last meal for Thorne. I don't want to prolong things tonight."

Butterflies in my belly told me that I was getting nervous too. "You know I'm gonna be right by my phone?"

He gave me a tight smile. "I know, and I'll call as soon as one of us leaves the house."

"Are you sure he'll show up?"

He shrugged and held up his palms. "As sure as I can be. When he texted earlier, I told him I had something very important to tell him, and he asked if I'm sick. I almost said I was sick of him. He promised to be here by seven o'clock."

My stomach was starting to ache, and I kept trying to think of some way I could help. “I’m worried, John. I could stay.”

He slowly shook his head. “That’s sweet, but I need to do this on my own.” He turned in his seat, the expression on his face serious. “The breakup should have nothing to do with you. It’s something Thorne has caused, and he doesn’t need any wiggle room to blame anyone else.”

There was obviously nothing I could do but be available. “Okay. Call me anytime, even if you just need a word of encouragement or a breather?”

One of my hands rested on the console, and John was drawing on it with his finger. “I promise.”

I knew I should be quiet, but I couldn’t let it go. “If I don’t hear from you by eight thirty, I’m calling. If you don’t answer, I’ll be at your door as fast as I can get my ass there.”

“You can call anytime. I’ll just tell him I have to take the call, something he’s said to me a million times.” He closed his hand around my thumb and smiled. “You have the right to call your boyfriend anytime, you know, and I’d much rather you call than make yourself sick imagining the worst.”

I had a great idea. “Hey, listen. This might sound silly but I’m frickin’ serious because Thorne could get violent or something. We need a code word. *Chattels?* He won’t know what that means.”

John tittered. “And of course I can work it seamlessly into any conversation.”

“Chattels it is, then,” I declared. “I’m *so* fucking serious. Please promise you’ll remember.”

“I promise, Liam. I will say *chattels* if I need you for any reason. I’ll even text it if I have to.”

After we walked Theo around the block, John asked me to stay for a while, and I couldn’t agree fast enough. I kept worrying that Thorne, asshole that he was, might try to do something to John. You know, one of those I-don't-want-you-but-no-one-else-can-have-you-either things that nutjobs do.

We drank iced tea and talked about Long Island for a while, and when John said he'd never been, I promised to take him. That afternoon, I realized even more what an amazing man he was, because although he must have been a lot more nervous than I was, he wasn't the one sitting there sweating, biting his nails, bouncing his knee, and constantly shifting around. He was tense but calm.

I put off looking at my watch as long as I could, but finally gave in. "Babe, I really should get going. I don't want to, but what if he finds me here? It's almost six and he could be early."

Disappointment passed over John's face, followed closely by dread. "I really don't think he'll be here until after seven. He's never been early for anything in his life." He paused to take a deep breath. "I guess you're right, though. Or you could just stay until he gets here, and when he comes in, we can be talking about chattels."

Hyped up, we laughed our asses off. When the hoopla died down, John's smile made my heart skip a beat, just like it had the first time I saw him. He must've felt it too because when I leaned in for a kiss, he closed his eyes and moaned.

John. Was. *Everything*. But if I really loved him, I had to get out of his hair and let him do what he had to do.

John

"Before you know it, I'll be calling to say it's done." I wasn't sure who I was trying harder to convince, Liam or me. "And you *will* come back over, right?"

"An army couldn't stop me. Walk me out?" Liam put his arm around my shoulders, and when we got to the door, he kissed me, surprisingly chastely. “That’s for luck,” he said. Then he kissed me again, licked my lips, and caught my lower lip between his teeth. “And that’s for courage.” Finally, he put his arms around me and squeezed tight. We kissed again and there it was—passion, desire, and emotion. “And that’s for my amazing boyfriend, who I love unbelievably much.”

He busied himself with his jacket while I caught my breath. When he turned back around, his face was etched with worry lines. “Chattels?”

I nodded, smiling as bravely as I could. “I remember.”

“I’ll be waiting, John.”

“I’ll call you. Please try not to worry.”

With a killer grin, he was gone. I would be forever grateful to Liam for keeping me company that afternoon, and for being so good to me through the whole thing.

Liam

I DROVE HOME, part of me regretting that I hadn’t insisted on staying. I could have hidden upstairs or something. That would have been a terrible idea, though, for lots of reasons, like sending a message that I didn’t trust John to be smart and take care of himself.

One thing was clear. I couldn’t just sit in my apartment, hoping Douchenozzle Thornprick didn’t go berserk and hurt John, which was my worst dread. I threw a change of clothes into my duffel and made sure I had my books and laptop. If John didn’t feel like me staying over, no harm done.

I drove to the coffeeshop near his house, where I checked my phone for the hundredth time to be sure the ringer was on and the phone was fully charged. The wait was on.

John

I WENT UPSTAIRS to pack a bag while I mentally reviewed what I was going to say. Packing was necessary because I needed to be ready in case I had to get the hell out for whatever reason. Maybe Thorne would insist on keeping the house, or I would need to run for safety. He had never been violent with me before, but he was prickly and had a temper, so better safe than sorry. Liam would have been proud of me for thinking so clearly.

It occurred to me that if I needed to leave, I should go to a hotel instead of imposing on Liam, but who was I kidding? Laughing at myself, I zipped the bag and took it out to my car. I also took my books, messenger bag, and computer, along with a couple of Theo's favorite toys. After locking it all in the trunk, I went back inside and sat on the sofa cuddling with the dog. I'd just thought about turning on the news when a car pulled into the driveway, followed by footsteps and a key rattling in the lock.

Thorne was inside before I knew it, taking off his coat and then fiddling with his phone. I stood and walked to the edge of the entryway, and he slowly turned around.

"John, how're you doing?" *Way too much effort to sound friendly.*

"Okay, thanks. You?"

He closed his eyes and shook his head. "Rough day, but I promised to come home. What's to eat?"

"No, sorry."

He opened his eyes and glared at me. "I thought you'd have cooked since it's dinnertime. Get me some chips and salsa."

Is he kidding? No, he isn't. This is how you lived for sixteen years. "I have to go pee, so help yourself. I'll be right back."

Hell would freeze over before I fetched him a snack, and

I felt a little skittish and really did need to pee. I left him frowning, and while I used the toilet, I heard him rummaging around downstairs. I washed my hands and checked myself in the mirror. *You can't let this misery go on any longer. You're drowning, and this is your chance to claw your way to the surface. Get out of this hell and make a good life with Liam.*

Downstairs, I found Thorne in the living room. He was sitting on a chair, probably so there was no chance he'd have to sit next to me. I took a seat on the sofa. "Thank you for coming home tonight. I have to talk to you about something serious."

"You said that before." He squinted at me. "You didn't go and get sick, did you?"

Leave it to him to make getting sick something I would *do*, as if intentionally. I swallowed hard and took a deep breath. "We've both been unhappy for a long time." He raised his eyebrows and frowned slightly. I went on. "Sixteen years ago, I fell in love with you and all I wanted to do was spend my life with you."

Some of the color drained out of his face and he cocked his head. "Me too. I thought you were the best."

"And now?"

He pressed his lips together for a few seconds. "Sixteen years is a long time, and we've both changed, but I loved you, Johnny."

I held up my hand and sounded eerily calm. "Did you notice we're both speaking in the past tense?"

He munched some chips, stalling for time. "I didn't, but now that you say it—"

"Thorne, you and I were good for a while. There were always issues, but we had some great times. Remember that trip to Myrtle Beach?"

I waited while he crunched more chips and took a sip of his

beer. When he looked up, I went on. "As you said, things have changed over the last few years."

"I still love you," he said, but his smile didn't reach his eyes.

"*You don't!*" I swallowed and regained my bearings. "You haven't loved me for a long time. Somewhere along the way, you decided I was excess baggage—someone holding you back, or something like that."

He put the bowl of chips down on a table. "That isn't—"

I couldn't let him get started. "Look at the facts. You have ignored me, made me look like a fool in front of other people, talked to me like I'm an idiot—"

He shook his head like a wet dog. "Christ! You're being a crazy drama queen again. Stop it."

A flash of anger had me raising my voice. "No, *you* stop! You've done your best to make me feel defective, like a sick person. You called me crazy for years."

"*I said stop!*" he yelled. "Someday you'll go too far. I've been damn good to you and you know it. You say I treated you like a crazy person? Well, somewhere along the way, you became one. I haven't treated you like a precious little princess? Ha!" He stood up, yelling even louder. "Who else would have moved all over the country, played second fiddle to the 'professor'"— (he actually used air quotes)—"and put up with your damn nagging and wheedling? Not to mention your nymphomania."

"Thorne, I'm not a woman! I'm not a princess, and I'm not a nymphomaniac. I'm all man and I'm proud of that." I tensed my shaking hands to get them under control.

"I *know* you're not a damn woman, believe me. You're not a princess, but you're sure as hell no prince, either." He was so mad he was spitting every time he pronounced a 'P.' Shaking his head, he watched me for a moment while he calmed down. "You're right that it's been pretty miserable the last few years. If you just didn't want so much from me. I can't give it all."

I noticed a chip that must have fallen to the floor when he set the bowl down, and it was all I could do not to pick it up. Instead, I forced myself to meet his eyes. "What have I wanted that was so unreasonable?"

"I've begged you to go to a doctor."

"I've *been* to a doctor." I wondered if he cared so little he'd forgotten. "The last two years we lived in Wisconsin, I went to see a psychologist. You *know* that." He shrugged and sat back down. "You know he said I had situational depression and that is not grounds for calling anybody crazy. He also said that needing affection from a partner was not an unreasonable expectation."

He shook his head and popped another chip into his mouth. "Just be quiet. You're not a lawyer and you never will be. You're way too 'creative.'" He used air quotes again and I wondered when he'd started that unattractive behavior. "All your smug talk isn't going to work with me."

Not wanting to let him sidetrack me, I went on to the next item on my list. "We haven't had sex for four years, yet I haven't noticed any frustration on your part." That was as close to talking about affairs as I was going to get; I would stick with what I knew for sure.

"Fuck you, John."

"That's what I've been trying to get you to do for years now, *Thorne*, but you're no longer interested."

He stood back up, raising his voice again. "Why the hell would I *want* to fuck you? You've driven me almost as crazy as you are. I can't think. I just need to be away from you. It's all too confusing."

He took a step forward and I stood, wanting to show him he couldn't intimidate me any longer. I spoke softly, clearly, and slowly. "This is over. I can't do it anymore. We're done. You said you want to be away from me, and you've got it."

"You damn fool." He took another quick step toward me and slapped my face, hard. My reflexes kicked in, and I stepped around behind the sofa. He took another step but thankfully stayed on the other side of the furniture.

"You're pathetic!" he yelled. "What will you do with me gone? I'll tell you what. You'll have nothing, you'll be nothing, and you'll go completely off your rocker. They'll have to come in and peel you up off the floor just to get you to the loony bin."

"Get out!" I was yelling too by then. "You're done here."

He had the audacity to look shocked and hurt and then tried to smile. "Johnny, come on, I'm sorry. I didn't mean it. Just don't make me mad like that."

An odd combination of empowerment, humiliation, and anger washed over me as I glared into his eyes. "Get the hell out!"

I tried not to run as I went upstairs and into the guest room, where I locked the door behind me. When I reached for my phone to call Liam, it wasn't in my pocket. *Shit, it must have fallen out when I sat down.* Suddenly, Thorne was on the other side of the door, pounding on it and rattling the handle. *Chattels!*

"John," he yelled, rattling harder. "Open this goddamned door and talk to me. I have to tell you something."

"You've told me plenty. Just go."

"Fine, stay in there and I'll talk through the door." He rattled again and hit the door so hard I was afraid it might break.

Jesus Christ! What kind of horror show have you opened up? If he knocked in the door I had nowhere to go, and the bathroom door in the guest room didn't even have a lock. Thorne could kill me before Liam called at eight thirty. How the fuck had I lost my phone, anyway? *Chattels!*

Things were quiet for a moment until Thorne spoke, more softly this time. "You're right. There's been a lot going on with me, and it hasn't been your fault. I was in denial, I guess. I tried to make myself believe it would all work itself out."

Was he trying to get sympathy from me now? Way too little, way too late. At least he sounded calmer, but I was not falling for his shenanigans even one more time. "Go away."

"You deserve an explanation first." He paused briefly. "The truth is that I *don't* love you anymore. I'm sorry, but I don't."

I rolled my eyes and threw my arms in the air. "I already figured that out for myself. Is that all you have to say?"

"Okay, here it is." He cleared his throat. "I'm in love with a woman."

That certainly stopped me dead in my mental tracks. "Don't try to bullshit me, Thorne. In all the years we've been together you never said a word about being bisexual. Try something else."

"I didn't know." He sounded more reasonable than he had all night. "Maybe I wasn't bi until the last few years, or maybe you never suspected because you never thought to look." He took a noisy breath and groaned as he exhaled. "What I *do* know is that when we were in cold-as-hell Wisconsin, I got really frustrated with you, with us. Christy, a woman from work—you remember her—she sensed something was wrong and asked me to lunch one day to talk. Within a week, I was sleeping with her and wasn't able to stop."

In a flash, random things from over the last several years came together, and I realized Thorne was being honest for once in his shameful life. "What a shit move, even for you." *Breathe, John.* "Are you still with her?"

"No, it ended when she found out I was moving to New York with you."

Shaken and a little dizzy, I sat down on the edge of the bed and struggled to make sense of this new reality. "Nice of you to tell me all this."

"I should've told you a long time ago."

"No fucking shit."

He made a pitiful sound. *He couldn't possibly be shedding a tear?* "It's what's right for me, John. I can't deny myself a life anymore."

For a few heartbeats, I couldn't speak. "That's rich. You can't deny *yourself* a life? What kind of pathetic excuse for a life have you given me all these years?"

He ignored my question. "You'll be just fine. I have to move on."

"So move on. I deserve a happy life, too, and I'm going to do my best to find one. Maybe I already have."

"Whatever that means, you deserve to be happy." His voice was tenderer than it had been in months. "Give me fifteen minutes to get a few things together. Maybe next week you can go study somewhere else one night, and I'll come back for the rest of my stuff."

"Is it safe for me to come out and take Theo for a walk, or are you going to beat me up some more?"

"It's safe, I promise. I never hit you before, and I'll always regret doing it tonight."

I couldn't help but scoff. "Step back. Go into the master bedroom, you prick."

When he told me he was out of the hallway, I hesitantly opened the door and hightailed it toward the stairs.

"I'm only going to take personal things and clothes." I looked over my shoulder, and he was standing in the bedroom door.

"Fine. Just let me know what furniture you'll want so I can plan."

"You know what?" He waved his arm around like a king bestowing a privilege upon a serf. "You can have it all."

"I'll be outside with the dog. Hopefully you'll be gone when I get back." I needed to get Theo out of the house in case Thorne wanted to pack him, too. That was silly, though. Thorne didn't care about anything but Thorne, and a dog would only attract attention he wanted for himself. I almost made it outside before he yelled out again.

"You'll always have a place in my heart, John."

I patted Theo on the head. "Come on, sweet dog. Let's get out of here." I realized too late that I'd forgotten to find my phone.

Fifteen minutes later, Theo and I turned the corner toward home, and I was relieved to see that Thorne's car was gone. Everything was quiet inside the house. I hung Theo's leash and my coat back on the rack and noticed a piece of paper on the hall table. "Johnny, thanks for all the memories and I never meant to hurt you." *Fuck you very much, Thorne. Glad to see the back of you.*

My phone was on the sofa cushion. Emotion welled up and I started crying as I grabbed it, feeling free and very much needing to see my boyfriend. He answered the call before the end of the first ring.

"Babe?" Liam's sweet voice was thick with tension.

"*Not* chattels. I'm safe, but I need you."

"Thank God." He heaved a sigh of relief. "There in five."

13

Six Weeks Later

John

Liam changed my life. With him, I found more love, joy, and satisfaction than I'd ever thought possible. I wasn't used to being with a man who respected and valued me, but I was enjoying every minute of the adjustment.

With Thorne out of my life, my head was much clearer, and even Theo was calmer. It's amazing how sensitive dogs are to the environment around them. Theo had always been wary of Thorne, but he'd already adopted Liam as a second dad. The only odd thing was that Thorne still hadn't come to get the rest of his things, and I got tired of looking at them.

One weekend, Liam asked me to go to a wedding with him in Buffalo. He and Jess had planned to go for months, since the groom was someone they'd known at Columbia, and they thought it would be nice to go as two couples—Jess and Michael, Liam and me. Unfortunately, Michael's dad got sick and his mom needed Michael at home that weekend, so he couldn't go. I had a surprise to arrange, so I told Liam and Jess to go together and have fun.

After they left on Friday, I went shopping and picked out new bedroom furniture. Thorne and I had bought the existing furniture at the same store only a few months earlier, so they gave me an excellent trade-in allowance on it and agreed to deliver the new furniture the next afternoon.

I went home and packed all of Thorne's things into boxes, which I stacked in the guest room. By the time Liam got back on Sunday afternoon, I'd put all of his things and mine into the new furniture in the master bedroom. I told him I was horny, which was true, and he led me upstairs. The guest room was full of boxes, and he turned around, looking confused.

I took his hand again. "Not in there, sweetie. We've been promoted. Let's go into the master bedroom."

I led him in and he looked around, still confused. "What gives? This is new."

"Remember when I told you a while ago that we used the guest room because this room had ghosts? Well, I performed an exorcism and now we have a new room to enjoy."

"Oh, wow!" He gave me a quick kiss. "It's great. This stuff is beautiful."

"Your things are in these two drawers and hanging in the closet." *Say it. Don't get upset if he doesn't think it's time.* "There are lots of empty drawers, and plenty of room in the closet for when you think it's time to move in." He raised his eyebrows, and I forged ahead. "Which is now, in my opinion. I want to live with you officially, Liam."

His grin was blinding. "If you're ready, babe, I am. Why don't we start moving the little stuff as we come and go, and we'll deal with the bigger things on Christmas break?" He looked around the room again. "This looks fantastic!" He picked me up and twirled me around before putting me down on the bed and kissing me again. "You know what?"

I saw mischief in his eyes. "What, bad boy?"

"We have a new bed to christen."

"What are you waiting for? Let's make this *our* room."

Liam

Just when we started to forget about him, Thorne tried to prick our bubble. One night, he called John and said he wanted to come and get his belongings. He also asked for some things from the house besides his personal stuff, and I loved it when John reminded the jerk about his 'you can have it all' proclamation. Nevertheless, wanting to be completely through with the god-forsaken bramble, John told him to come and get it, but that he'd have to make an appointment since the locks had been changed and our hours at home were unpredictable. He also demanded a list of what Thorne was going to take before he'd let him in.

John had barely hung up when I took his hand. "When's he coming?"

"Saturday afternoon, assuming he sends me a list before then." He beamed at me. "We'll be rid of him for good!"

I smiled as I nodded my head, but John and I had to get something straight right then. "Babe, I absolutely do not want you here when he shows up."

John looked confused. "I have to be. I don't want him to take anything that isn't on the list."

I moved my head to catch John's eyes head-on. "I'll be here."

He pursed his lips. "I still don't see—"

"I've never tried to tell you what to do, but this one time I am!" John closed his mouth and listened to me. "When that asswipe hit you, that was it. He will have absolutely zero chance to ever touch you again."

John sighed. "That's sweet, but I can't—"

I lost my smile. "It's more than sweet. It is the way it's gonna be, and I'm not budging on this. I love you and I'll do whatever I have to do to protect you."

He still didn't look convinced. "What if a fight broke out between you two? That would be horrible."

"I'll get Michael to be here with me. You and Jess can go to a movie or something."

The beginnings of a smile played across John's softening face. "I actually would much rather not see him."

"You don't have to. Look, with me and Michael, it'll be two against one. Michael's a huge guy, and I'm kinda ripped for a swimmer dude. Me and Michael together could put a bad hurt on somebody."

THORNE SENT JOHN A LIST, and on Saturday afternoon, John and Jess went shopping. Michael and I watched TV and ate sandwiches while we waited for the big event. Thorne finally showed up and was surprised when Michael and I answered the door.

He got uber pissed when he realized John wasn't there. "He always was a sniveling coward. What is it, he knows he blew it and can't face me without begging for another chance?"

There it was. It didn't take the shitface thirty seconds to set me off. I was ready to blow anyway, and I grabbed him and slammed him against the wall. Michael pinned one shoulder while I pinned the other, and I felt a ripple of satisfaction when a shadow of fear crossed Thorne's face.

I was breathing hard and had to concentrate to talk. “You prick, you’re the fucking coward. You treated John like shit for years and then hit him just because you could. If you ever touch him again, you’re a dead man.” I let up on his shoulder so I could shove it into the wall again, and loved the way he winced when I did it.

Michael was no happier than I was. “John’s one of the best men I know, you dumbass farthole. Fess up. Was it a power thing or plain old stupidity that you treated him the way you did, hurting him for so long and then hitting him like he was nothing?”

Thorne stuck out his chin, since he couldn’t move anything else, and looked back and forth between Michael and me. “Which one of you is Johnny’s new fuck? Or is he doing both of you?”

Michael spat in his face. Big old loogie, just hanging there.

Thorne tried to move, and I grabbed his hand and bent the wrist back so far he grimaced. “You say another word about John and we’ll throw you back out the door like the piece of trash you are, snatch queen.”

Michael was so close to Thorne that their noses were touching, and his voice was a menacing growl. “You ever touch John again and you’ll have some big worries, dude. I will hunt you down and you *will* suffer. Believe me, you don’t want to try me.” I’d never seen Michael like that, but I knew one thing—I never wanted to get on his bad side.

Thorne’s lips trembled, and his eyes darted around like a cornered animal’s. “Don’t freak out, guys.” He looked at me. “I’m guessing you’re the boyfriend. You’ll get tired of crazy John soon enough, but don’t worry. I don’t plan to have any more contact with your new piece of ass. Just let me get my things and get out of here.”

We turned him loose. He wiped the spit off his face, shook

himself out a little bit, and sneered at us again, causing Michael to body-check him into the wall at the foot of the stairs. "Watch yourself, fuckwad."

"Get your shit and make it quick," I told him. "You've got thirty minutes and then you're out the door, whether you've got everything you want or not."

He didn't say anything, just took the steps two at a time. Michael and I were right behind him and looked over his shoulder the whole half hour he was there. Michael was awesome, the way he kept talking shit just to keep Thorne uneasy.

It was thirty minutes later before Thorne said anything else, and his voice was shaky. "Tell John I'm not impressed with his goon squad."

Michael got deep into Thorne's personal space. "Get the fuck out before I change my mind and rearrange your ugly face right now, just for the fun of it."

Thorne picked up the last box and trotted down the stairs with us hot on his heels. We managed to lock the door after him before we broke into a loud guffaw. After a bit, Michael asked if we were gonna tell John everything that had happened.

"We've got to," I answered. "He has a right to know, and if we don't tell him and that asshole makes stuff up, John wouldn't know what was what."

"Did you see his stupid face?" Michael asked, still laughing. "I think he might've shit himself."

"He stunk bad enough." I tried to calm down because my abs were getting sore, but we kept setting each other off. "Tell you what, I hope it's the last time I *ever* see his face."

We all went for pizza when John and Jess got home, and Michael and I gave them a blow by blow. John listened to every word, smiling sadly and shaking his head.

Back home alone, we were drinking water in the kitchen

when John said he owed me some special gratitude. He gave me one of his delicious, smutty kisses, pushed me against the counter, and dropped to his knees. My heart pumped with excitement because besides being the world's most awesome boyfriend, John gave the best head I ever had.

A few minutes later, I was holding onto the counter behind me for dear life, grunting and thrashing around while my cock exploded in John's mouth. Desperate gulps competed with my cries, and when the squirting finally eased off, John rubbed my belly, encouraging me to ride it through. He kept sucking lightly, and I finally had to push him off. "Sensitive, sensitive."

He looked up at me with the most angelic face, a drizzle of cum running down his chin. "Thanks for feeding me so well. That was an excellent dessert."

Mom and I talked most days and she'd heard about John since the first day of school. She could tell how much I liked him, and she supported my new romance. Her reaction when I told her we were in love was so positive that I almost cried.

She called one day and didn't spend any time beating around the bush. "Honey, Thanksgiving is in two weeks and I really want you to come home for the weekend."

"I'm not sure that'll work out this year. I—"

"Why not? I haven't seen you since we moved you up to Syracuse in August." She was using her Determined Mom tone, and I suspected I wouldn't win this one.

"Mom, I don't...." I really wanted to spend the holiday with John.

"Both your sisters will be here, and we haven't all been together since July when we were in Maine." She paused for a couple seconds. "Have you made plans to go somewhere else?"

"No, but—"

"Ah, it's John, then."

No one could ever accuse Andie Macadam of being slow on the uptake. "It's our first Thanksgiving, and I really want to spend it together."

"I understand, Liam." A timer went off in the background, and I heard her moving around. She must have been cooking something. "Bring him along, honey."

"John can come?"

"Liam Macadam!" She scoffed, and then changed to the Incredulous Mom tone. "Since when could you not bring someone home? Let alone the man you love?"

Of course, she was right. "That's actually a really good idea. One day, John told me he'd never been to Long Island and would like to go."

"The perfect opportunity, then. Besides, I'm eager to meet him. He must be really something."

I took a breath and wondered if he would go. "How about this? I'll come if I can talk him into coming with."

"That's exciting. You know we'll have a great time. When do you think you'll—"

"Whoa, Mom!" I needed to slow the train down. "We'll have to see if he's willing to go. If not, I'll stay here with him."

She chuckled. "Son, you can do anything you set your mind to, so convincing John shouldn't be a problem. Would you like me to call him?"

"Maybe that would...." *What? Are you ten years old again?* "I don't think you should do that. Tell you what, let me talk to him, and I'll tell you if I need reinforcements."

I promised to call the next day and let her know, and after we hung up, I spent a moment thinking about how lucky I was. Mom always had my back, and even though she drove me frickin' crazy sometimes, we were totally cool with each other. I told her I was gay when I was fourteen, and her response was that we had to have a family party to make the announcement, which we did, that very night. My dad and sisters were also great about it from day one, and now that I realize what so many gay teens go through, I'm more grateful for my family than ever.

That night at dinner, I asked John to go home with me for the holiday. He was understandably nervous about meeting the family, afraid they might be weird about our age difference. After I explained that they already knew and didn't care, he agreed to go.

Being self-conscious about our ages was something he had to get over for his own good. I didn't care how old he was; what mattered was that he loved me, and I loved him. He treated me better than any guy I'd ever dated, and he never made me feel like he was pulling rank because he was older, which some other guys had done. We shared the same sexual appetite, which was fantastic, but I wanted a guy to love me for lots of reasons besides my dick. It had always been hard to find men who interested me, who challenged me intellectually, and John did all that in spades.

14

Tuesday, November 22
Two Days Before Thanksgiving

John

Civ Pro, our final class before the break, was finally over. On our way out of the room, we talked with some friends about what everyone was doing with the precious days off. I was still wary about meeting Liam's family, but his enthusiasm was contagious, and I was excited about the opportunity. One of the many things I loved about him was that he made *anything* fun.

On our way to the library to print out two cases we had to read over the break, we ran into Professor Zimmermann from Torts. Everyone's favorite, he was smiling and talking about his holiday.

"My wife and I are leaving for Florida this evening. What are you both doing?"

Liam grinned and squeezed my hand. "We're going to spend the weekend with my family in Wainscott."

Zimmerman cocked his head. "On Long Island? It's beautiful there. We have friends in Amagansett."

"Amagansett's great. I run there sometimes."

"Well...." Professor Zimmerman narrowed his eyes and smiled. "Am I to assume, in light of all the evidence, that things are going well between you two?"

"More than well," I said, returning his smile.

Liam raised our hands up in front of us. "Quite excellently, in fact. I keep meaning to thank you for the best advice anyone's ever given me."

Zimmerman's phone buzzed, and after a quick look he stuffed it in his pocket. "I'm glad someone took my advice for once, Mr. Macadam. I can't say I knew exactly what was happening, but I'm happy to see everything worked out. It's not always easy to find someone who cares about you."

"Thank you, Professor," I said.

He nodded. "One more thing—and call me Bob out of class, by the way—one more thing, your classmates are certainly excited for you and I am too, so let me know if I can ever help you. You can always call me at home. I don't believe in standing on ceremony with my students."

"That really means a lot, sir, more than you know," Liam said, giving him the drive-a-truck-through-it smile.

I put out my hand for a shake. "It really does, Bob, and we'll remember that. Have a good holiday, and safe travels."

"You too. Try not to think about this place."

On the way down the hall, I asked Liam what advice Zimmermann had given him, and he said he'd tell me later. We turned a corner and the library entrance was on our right, faced by a utility closet on the other side. Liam hesitated, looked at the closet door, and then tested it. It was unlocked, and he glanced inside before closing it again.

"You up for some fun?" His eyes were wide. I knew that look.

"What did you have in mind, bad boy?"

His sultry expression left no doubt. "I've always wanted to make out in a janitor's closet."

Heat crept up the side of my neck and my cheeks started burning. "Liam, it's unlocked."

"That's why we can go in." His face was already ruddy with arousal, and he leaned in toward me, going for the close. "There's a push-button lock on the inside of the door. We'll be okay."

I never could tell him no about anything, and I had to admit it was a turn on. We looked up and down the hall to be sure the coast was clear, and after Liam pulled the door open and we scooted inside, he locked us in. His hand caressed the back of my neck and he pulled me toward him in the dark.

"You're dangerous," I whispered. "We could get in so much trouble."

He snickered, and licked my Cupid's bow. "What for? Looking for something to clean up a mess?"

I rolled my eyes in the dark. "What mess would that be?"

"Just wait a few minutes. There'll be a big mess to clean up."

I laughed out loud and quickly clamped my hands over my mouth.

He urged my hands away and kissed my upper lip. "You're so sexy," he whispered, and started nibbling at the lower one. "I want you so much right now."

Sneaking a hand under my shirt, Liam began rubbing my belly. His fingertips grazed my nipples, which made me whimper with delight. He skimmed his other hand down my back and squeezed my ass, something he knew always got me going. My cock was already throbbing in my pants.

The need, like the testosterone, was heavy in the air, and soon we were both making noise. I caught myself. "Got to keep it down," I whispered, before going back to his lips. I was humping into him and already had one of my hands down his pants, sticky with his precum. Both of us tried to be as quiet as possible as I squatted to pull his pants and underwear down his thighs.

He sighed with relief when his cock jumped free. I stood back up and closed a hand around it, giving him a couple of solid pumps. He groaned as he finished undoing my pants, then knelt long enough to get them down to my knees. After he stood up, we leaned our foreheads together. His breath blew hot and fast across my face and I whined softly as he played with my dick.

"Put our hands together," he whispered, and I shivered as our cocks pressed against each other, inside the warm sleeve we made with our hands. We each started pumping, fucking our joined fists, the wonderful friction between dicks and hands quickly taking us both to the edge. We came hard, groaning as quietly as we could. Leaning against each other for support, we couldn't help laughing when we finally caught our breath.

"Told you there'd be a big mess." He playfully bit the end of my nose.

"Aw! That hurt!" I snickered again. "How are we going to get ourselves decent enough to go out there again?"

He rummaged around in the dark. "I saw some paper towels on one of these shelves... here we go." He handed me a bunch. "Let's clean up the best we can. I'm sure we both have cum stains on our pants, but we'll just get out of here and print the cases at home."

We mopped up as best we could and got our pants back in

place. Liam turned the knob, carefully peeked outside, and opened the door. I almost jumped out of my skin when he closed it behind us—there stood Michael. He'd been hidden by the door.

"Christ, fellas, I almost ran into that door!" He grinned, no doubt taking in our sheepish expressions. "Not gonna ask," he said. "Not gonna ask, but I can well imagine." He tried to look stern. "Get a room, you two. You want to get thrown out of school for indecent behavior?"

Liam

After the Janitor's Closet Escapade, John and I went home and decided to read the two cases for next Monday so we wouldn't have to do any schoolwork on our trip.

I thought about how much better my life was than when I got to Syracuse in August, mostly because of John. It's amazing how when your heart is full of love, the holes in it become more bearable. They don't go away, but the love puts them into perspective. I would never forget Dad or my cousin, Dan, or stop wishing they were still with us, but with John in my life I didn't feel like I was lost in a cave.

When I finished reading, I went into the kitchen to start dinner. We were having a beef stir-fry, and looking at the ingredients made me remember how much I liked Szechuan beef. I used to make it a lot, so I took stock of what we had. The only two things missing were bean paste and Szechuan peppercorns, two things I figured would be okay to leave out. I'd just add a little cayenne to make up for the peppercorns.

As I put on the rice, I remembered what Mom had said on the phone when I asked if it was cool for John and me to stay in my room together. "You don't have to ask, Liam. I'd already planned on it. You're in love so of course you want to stay together, and that's no problem for me. I want you to be happy."

While the rice cooked, I mixed the beef with some seasonings and put it in the fridge to marinate while I cut up the other ingredients. When I'd talked to my big sister Cait, she said that as long as John treated me well, she didn't care about anything else. My baby sister Vonnie told me that if John was as gorgeous as the pictures she'd seen, she'd be hella jealous. Near the end of the conversation, she got serious and asked if I was sure I loved him.

"As sure as I've ever been of anything. I'm crazy in love with John."

"Then I've got your back, big bro. I can't wait to meet the man who's won Liam Macadam's heart."

After I plated up our dinner, I called John to the kitchen and he ate like a starving man. I've always loved the way he eats. He doesn't sacrifice good manners, but he sure takes no prisoners. I wondered if he realized that watching a hot guy enjoying his food was a huge turn on for me, especially if I was the cook. I'd never told him because I didn't want to make him self-conscious about it.

After finishing two servings, he looked around and his eyes got very wide. "Oh my God, I'm so sorry. I ate all of it. Did you get enough?"

"I got plenty." I couldn't hide my goofy grin.

He looked at me through squinted eyes, underneath a wrinkled forehead. "Are you sure?"

"I'm full, and I'm really glad you enjoyed it so much. If I can make you that happy with something quick, I'm gonna start cooking big meals."

Wednesday Morning, November 23

John

Emily's family lived in Syracuse and had recently lost their dog. She offered to keep Theo while Liam and I were gone, saying they would enjoy having the little pug for the weekend. I was glad my baby boy would be well looked-after, and we dropped him off before getting on I-81, and then headed to Long Island by way of Pennsylvania. I was dubious of the route, but Liam showed me on a map that it really was the quickest way.

We both relaxed and Liam cranked up some Abba, a mutual guilty pleasure. A couple of weeks earlier, we'd been surprised to discover that we both had a thing for the group, and Liam said that if we ever had a wedding, we had to play Abba. I agreed, thrilled with the possibilities I was imagining. We sang along as he drove, happy to be getting away from Syracuse for a few days.

After the singalong, we told stories about our families and holiday traditions. Liam eventually got serious and told me more about his heartbreaks of the last few years and his resulting depression. He told me about uncontrollable crying jags, days when he couldn't eat, and others when he hurt so badly he could barely get out of bed because of what he vividly called ragged holes in his heart.

He also told me about his ex-boyfriend leaving him because the bastard couldn't stand to be with someone who was sad. I hated the son of a bitch for hurting my sweet Liam that way. It boggled my mind that anyone could do that to another human being, especially one they supposedly cared about. "Did you love the guy?" I asked.

He sighed so heavily I thought the car may have slowed

down. "No, but I liked him better than anyone I'd dated before. I thought he cared about me." He shrugged and his frown deepened. "It hurt like hell when I realized he'd never really liked me at all. If he had, he couldn't have done that to me. There were some other things, too."

Steeling myself, I asked what he meant by other things. He shook his head.

"Please tell me. Get it out." I reached over and took his free hand.

He pursed his lips and took a deep breath. "He was five years older than me, and looking back, I don't remember him ever mentioning anything about me that he liked except my age and looks." Liam's skin had gone pale and his eyes were vacant, something I'd never seen before. "He never talked about any ways I made him feel good. He said I was a prize—his word—and that he was happy his friends were so jealous of him for having a hot young boyfriend. Again, his words. I admit it felt good the first few times he said it, but soon it got really weird. I guess I wanted affection instead of words."

"Of course you did." My eyes were misty, but this wasn't about me and I was determined not to cry. "He was an asshole and had no right to treat you like that."

Traffic had gotten heavier and Liam took his hand back. "I know you're right."

"You are the kindest, sweetest man I have ever known, Liam Macadam." I reached over to brush a finger against his cheek. "He was right about one thing, that you're incredibly hot, but you are *so* much more than a guy who's hot, or gorgeous, or young."

"I—"

"Tell you something else. No one has ever turned me on the way you do, but if all you could offer were your good looks and age, I'd probably still be horny for you, but I sure wouldn't love you for it. I love you because of *all* you are."

He glanced at me and his eyes were full of tears. "You really think what you said? All of it?"

"Every word. I love you more than I've ever loved anybody, and you should never doubt your worth, to me or anyone else."

He smiled and took my hand again. "I love you, John. I'm so lucky I found you."

After that, we rode in silence for a while—not awkward silence, but the comfortable kind that doesn't come easily.

Liam

We stopped in Stroudsburg, Pennsylvania for a restroom, gas, and drinks. I called Mom to let her know we were about three hours out.

"I can't wait to see you, honey. John's really coming, then?"

"He is, Mom, and we're having an amazing drive. He loves me even more than I thought." I knew I sounded like a teenager with a bad crush, but I didn't care.

"I'm so pleased for you. You deserve to be happy, especially after all that's happened."

We ended the call when John came back from using the facilities. After we got back on the road, some Bach piece he liked was on the radio and he told me all about it. It was really cool, and I caught a glimpse of why he was such a good teacher. He knew just the right things to say to help me hear the music instead of letting it go by. Afterward, I asked a few questions and he told me more about Bach and his times, and some of the things that made his music so special.

"You're really good at this stuff, John. Can you see yourself ever going back to teaching?"

He grunted. “Not at Northstar, for sure. If law school doesn’t work out, I’ll find something else to do, and if it happens to be teaching, I’d be open to that.” He took my hand and squeezed hard. “I don’t know exactly where my life is headed, but as long as you’re in it, everything will be great. I’m trusting the future to take care of itself.”

15

John

Liam called his mom to tell her we were less than thirty minutes out. He said we were off the Expressway and would be coming straight to the house.

After he hung up, he gave me a quick look. "How are you doing, babe?"

"I'm fine. So glad to be with you."

"Nervous? You seem a little nervous."

I wagged my head back and forth. "A little, but who wouldn't be nervous about meeting the family? Will they think it's too soon?"

"They don't think that. You're the man I love. They know that and want to meet you."

"I'm good, then," I said. "I want to make the best impression I can and show them how much I love you, and that I'm not some weirdo who's only after you for your hot ass."

He snorted. Drawing his eyebrows together, he looked at me from under hooded eyes. "You do like my hot ass, though.

Right?" He followed that with his million-dollar smile. I poked my hand into his side, getting the ticklish spot I'd found a few nights earlier and making him screech. "Stop! You'll make me wreck!"

"I like every part of you, stud muffin, hot ass and all."

His face grew serious. "About my family and you. They're curious, of course, but they know all about us, including the age difference you worry about so much. They're cool with it. They're all glad I'm happy, and they'll like you. You're gonna like them, too. I know all of you, and I'm sure of it."

I loved the ardent expression on his face. "I trust you. Admit it, though—you'd be a little nervous if you were meeting my family. What I feel reminds me of how musical performance can be, when a little case of nerves can actually help you focus and do your best."

He smiled and changed the subject, pointing out some things as he drove. Anything was fun with Liam, even driving by the biggest Chevy dealer in New York.

Liam

John was right when he said I'd be nervous if we were going to meet his family. Hell, I'd have probably been a wreck and begging him to turn the car around. He sat up a little straighter when we started down Arboretum Drive toward Mom's house, and I reached for his hand. He remarked about how beautiful it was there, and how much he liked the house. It was nice, for sure, but houses are only as good as the people inside them, and this one was full of a lot of love.

Neither of my sisters' cars were there, which was good since John could meet Mom all by herself. The wind hit me head-on when I got out of the car, and we walked around to the side door, the one to the mud room. Everything was quiet when we walked inside.

"Mom!" I called out. "Mom? We're here." Still quiet. I knew she was home because we'd talked not thirty minutes before, so I led John into the kitchen, where something in the oven smelled great. Spice, earthiness, the definite smell of brown sugar… it had to be pumpkin pie, which *was* Thanksgiving.

"She's baking your pie, Punkin." I couldn't resist saying it, and he rolled his eyes while he grinned at me. Walking out to the hall that led to the front of the house, I called for Mom again.

"Coming, Liam." Her footsteps sounded on the stairs, and I hurried back into the kitchen and grabbed John's hand. He didn't have to do this alone.

I'd no sooner gotten to him than she was in the kitchen door, still as petite and beautiful as ever, with a smile that was pure sunshine. "Oh, Liam," she said, closing the distance between us and giving me a crushing hug. She was small in stature but surprisingly strong, and I reveled in the smells of jasmine and nutmeg. "Honey, I'm so glad to see you."

"I'm glad to see you too, Mom," I squeaked.

She let me loose and turned toward John. "You must be John," she said, beaming at him. "I'm Andrea Macadam. Please call me Andie, everyone does."

"I'm John, Andie," he said, and they shook hands. "I'm happy to meet you. I can see where Liam gets his killer looks."

Smiling at the flattery, she let his hand go and told him how much she'd heard about him. "You are welcome here, John, and I want you to make this your home over the next few days."

"Thank you," he said, "I'll do that." He took my hand again. "There's something I need to get out there right away. I love your son very much, Andie, and I hope you're okay with that."

Mom is a frank woman who doesn't abide bullshit, and her smile broadened. "That's what I needed to hear. As long as you love Liam, I have no problem with you." She picked a kitchen towel up from the counter and hung it on its hook. "Thanks for saying so, by the way. A lot of people wouldn't care what the mom thinks."

She took his arm and asked if he wanted to see her autumn garden, saying she needed to gather some herbs. I followed along behind, thrilled by the warmth I already sensed between them. They were the two people I loved most in the world, and they needed to love each other.

When we were back inside, Mom sent us upstairs to settle in before dinner. My room was pretty big, and I had a private bath. John admired the dusky lavender accent wall, and immediately inspected the photo collage over my desk. We unpacked while we danced with no music, me poorly and John slightly less so, and ended up holding onto each other and smooching while we swayed back and forth.

He suggested we take showers to freshen up and then rest a bit before going downstairs to hang with the fam.

I waggled my eyebrows. "Waste water, or shower together?"

He took a T-shirt out of the suitcase and tossed it to me. "Silly question, but would your mom mind?"

"She won't know, but I wouldn't care if she did. Obviously, she has no problem with us staying together, and c'mon—there's only one bed in here. She knows how I feel about you and sure as hell doesn't think one of us will be sleeping on the floor."

"She doesn't?" he asked, all deadpan. He handed me a whole stack of T-shirts.

"Trust me, Mom has survived all the times my sisters brought boyfriends home." I chuckled at a memory. "Shit, this one time, Cait and her guy-of-the-weekend kept us awake all night. Vonnie and I went downstairs, made hot chocolate, and laughed our asses off."

He groaned. "All the more reason I think we need to be as quiet as possible, okay?"

"Good with me, Punkin." I leaned in to steal a kiss. "I don't want to keep everyone awake either, but I *do* want to make sweet love to you all night. I think both can be accomplished."

We finished unpacking and got into a steamy shower. He blessed my throat and neck with little kisses, fleeting as shooting stars. A sword fight followed that ended with us moaning and panting as quietly as we could. Wordlessly, we staggered back to the bed and fell in, immediately going to our default position, John as my little spoon. The bed was firm, the comforter was warm, and the next thing I knew someone was pounding on the door.

"Liam? Liam, are you in there?" *Shit-fuck!* This was hardly the ideal moment for lil sis to make her appearance.

"It's Vonnie," I told John. "Go 'way, Vonnie!" I yelled. "Come back in five minutes." Of course, she took that as an invitation and opened the door. *Note to self, lock the door the rest of the weekend.*

"Coming in guys, back off each other."

"What the fuck?" I asked, as John and I both jerked upright. "We're asleep. At least give us a couple minutes to wake up."

"You're awake now, brother." She quickly crossed the hooked rug and stuck her hand out to John, who looked like he was about to throw up. Somehow, he managed to smile and take her hand.

"I'm Liam's sister, Siobhan. I've been excited to meet you."

"Hi, Siobhan, I'm John. I've heard a lot about you. Would you please give us a couple of minutes to get dressed?"

She tossed her auburn hair back. "Only because you asked nicely, *unlike* my brother. I'll be back in exactly five minutes." She left, and I flopped down on my back.

"Got to get dressed," John said, moving to get out of bed.

"Wait," I said, wrapping my arms around him and rubbing his stomach. "Don't you dare break this peace for Vonnie."

He lay back down, and I immediately took advantage by kissing him, deep, wet, and slow. After a couple minutes of that, I hesitantly agreed to get dressed and we dragged ourselves out of bed. John walked to the dresser while I locked the door. No sooner had we buttoned up our shirts than Vonnie was at the door again, banging on it when it wouldn't open.

"It's been five minutes, lovebirds, so open this door right now!"

"Yeah, yeah," I grumbled, loud enough for her to hear, as I walked to the door and unlocked it. She bounced in, and this time we hugged and greeted each other properly. She looked great, but my heart hitched when I saw her. She reminded me so much of Dad, with her auburn hair, ivory skin, and blue eyes.

She gave John a hug too, and after a little chitchat about the traffic and her med school applications, she came right to the point. "I like you already, John." She got that devilish little-sister expression on her face and looked at him sideways. "That's good, because as I'm sure you're aware, my brother's in love with you, and therefore you need my approval."

John grinned, showing his dimples in all their glory. "I love him, too, Vonnie. He's an incredible man."

"Well, you'll get to know him eventually and we'll revisit that adjective then." We all laughed. "You're both so lucky," she said. "I'd be glad to find some guy who's decent enough to go out with twice, but look at you two."

John

Downstairs, in the TV room, we found Andie talking to another beautiful young woman. She was tall and svelte, and I figured she had to be the older sister. It was unnerving how much she and Liam looked alike. With the same bone structure and their brown hair and eyes, they could have been twins. She even had exactly the same big smile that he did—wide, white, and happy.

After giving her brother a hug, she gave me one too. "John, welcome. I'm Caitlin, Liam's older sister, but please call me Cait."

We all chatted until a timer went off in the kitchen and Andie stood up. "Dinner's going to be another two hours, so everybody into the kitchen for snacks."

We sat around the kitchen table and feasted on a platter of crisp, buttery snickerdoodles. The conversation was about what you'd expect from a family reunited after a few months apart, but they managed to include me. The talk eventually turned to the menu for Thanksgiving dinner the next day, and what we were contributing.

Andie put a hand on my arm. "John, we should explain. In our family, we follow my mother's tradition of everyone cooking something for the meal, so the kids each make a side dish. Whenever boyfriends have been here…." She looked between Liam and me. "It's okay to use that word with you two, right?"

He put an arm around my shoulder. "It's fine, Mom, it's what we are."

"It *is* fine," I threw in. "Liam's my bae."

For some reason, his sisters found that hilarious, and Liam

jumped in to defend me. "Hey, John's my bae, too, and you two fuckers know that, so chill."

"Language, Liam, please." Andie glared at him, but it was obviously contrived.

He grinned wickedly as he reached for another cookie. "Dammit, I'm so fucking sorry, Mom."

Even Andie had to laugh. "All right, back to what I was saying. Whenever boyfriends are here for holidays, they work with their significant other on a joint contribution."

"That sounds great," I said. "Liam and I like cooking together."

Another timer sounded, and Andie stood to turn it off. "Fine then. We have ninety minutes until dinner, so off to the market, all of you. Get what you need and tonight the kitchen's yours."

The siblings all groaned, but I noticed they were groaning through those ubiquitous Macadam grins. Liam and I went upstairs for our coats, and he asked how I was holding up.

"Fantastic. Your family's great, and they're making me feel very welcome."

"I'm glad." He cupped my cheeks in his hands, momentarily stealing my breath away.

"They're all beautiful, too. I said it before, it's obvious that you come by your smashing looks and winning personality naturally."

He dug into my ribs and chuckled happily. "If you're trying to *soften* me up for tonight, you're gonna be sorely disappointed."

I leaned in close and brushed my hand across what was indeed a very promising bulge. "I'm counting on that."

He grinned and handed me my coat. "What are we gonna make? Any ideas?"

"I have one, but if it's wrong or doesn't sound good, please say so. My mother made the best broccoli casserole in the world, really good for holidays. Would that work?"

"Sounds perfect." He zipped up my coat for me. "We'll tell everyone it's your mom's recipe, and it'll be a way she can be part of this weekend. You know the recipe by heart?"

A cascade of memories made me smile. "Absolutely. I've made it a lot through the years."

Vonnie chose that moment to yell from downstairs. "Not *now* guys. Surely you can wait until tonight. We need to go."

John

Liam decided we should take Andie's Volvo because it was big enough to carry the four of us plus groceries. He drove and Vonnie called shotgun, so Cait and I shared the spacious backseat. It was cold and I was glad there were heater fans back there.

"Where are we going out tonight, brother?" Cait asked Liam, as soon as we were on our way.

"Out?" I asked.

"After we finish cooking on Thanksgiving Eve, we go out for a few drinks," Vonnie explained. "Boyfriends invited, of course."

"I'm in," I said. I should have listened to Liam and stopped worrying two weeks ago.

"You're definitely cool, John," Cait said. "I like you, and I'm the best judge of character in the family. Ask anybody."

"Except me," Vonnie said, turning around and shaking her head. "I'm the best judge, and you're definitely in with us. Just don't do anything stupid."

"Whoa, there, girls." Liam said, glancing at Cait in the rearview mirror. "Do I get an opinion?"

"No!" his sisters said in unison.

Cait grinned. "We already know how you feel and we're agreeing with you."

"My sisters are smarter than I thought," he said. "We'll go to The Green Lantern."

Cait scrunched her face. "We went there last year."

"I think we could do better," Vonnie agreed. "John, you're the new one. You pick."

"Me? I've never been here before and I'm with Liam."

"Green Lantern it is, then," Liam said. "They have the best beers and I'm glad we all agree."

I was quickly catching on that Liam had the three women in his family wrapped around his little finger. They kidded and chided him to no end, but they ultimately seemed to agree that it was his world.

It took a little while to get in and out of the market, one of those upscale places that had everything and charged twice the going rate for it. Liam and I quickly found everything we needed for the casserole. Of course, it being the night before Thanksgiving, everyone in Wainscott was there, and the checkout line was so long that it was dinnertime when we left. Liam pushed the speed limit getting us back home, much to the contrived consternation of his sisters.

Liam

We all pitched in to clean up as soon as dinner was over, and then the cooking began. Mom sat and talked to us, drinking a glass of wine and offering advice as needed. Soon the broccoli casserole smelled like a million bucks, and when it was done I sneaked a taste.

"That's for tomorrow," John said, nudging my hand with his.

"Screw you! This is the best broccoli I ever tasted. You guys are outta luck." Everyone laughed when I took another bite.

"Enough, Liam," Mom said, getting up to move the cooling casserole out of the way. "You can have all you want tomorrow."

"Aw fuck, I want it now," I stage-whispered to John.

Of course, Mom scolded me. "I heard that, Liam Macadam. Language!"

"Sorry, Mom. I can be such an asshole."

John

The Green Lantern was a real English-style pub. It had the same pint glasses I remembered from visits to London, and things like Scotch eggs, Walker's crisps, and fruit machines—even if they did only dispense fruit-flavored gum. Vonnie proved to be the darts champion, and Liam introduced me to some delicious beer. Cait seemed to spend most of her time flirting with various guys.

Vonnie was excited because she'd turned twenty-one the month before and was able to order her own beer. A couple of pints later, she took a trip to the bathroom, leaving Liam and me alone, since Cait was at another table with some guys she knew from high school.

Liam signaled the waitress for two more drinks. "You having fun?" he asked me.

"A ball. Thank you so much for bringing me here. Not just to the pub, but home with you in general."

He tapped my ankle with his foot. "You're my man. You think I'd have come without you?"

The waitress delivered our beers and asked if we wanted anything else. It was getting late, so I asked for the check.

"Coming right up," she said, and winked at us. "You two are adorable together."

Liam took a sip of his beer and ran a finger over the top of my hand. "You're healing my heart, John."

A tingle of contentment warmed my stomach. "You're healing mine, too. You're the man I wish I'd met years and years ago."

He showed me a wry grin. "Good thing we waited, though. Till after I was born and all."

I sneered at him, and he stuck out his tongue at me before leaning in for a kiss. Instead of meeting his lips, I slapped the top of his hand and a hand-slapping fight ensued, both of us laughing like the happiest men in the world.

16

John

It was chilly in the room and barely light outside, so I did my business and crawled back into Liam's arms as quickly as possible.

"Cold...." He grumbled. "Why'd you get up?"

"Had to pee. It's early, go back to sleep."

"Wish I coulda aimed it for you," he whispered, chuckling sweetly.

When I woke again, he was snoring in my ear. I loved his sweet little buzz, quiet and reassuring. The smell of bacon and coffee made my stomach rumble.

"Wake up," I said, turning over. When there was no response, I caressed his cheek and brushed his throat with a few wet smooches. He moved, smacking kisses into the air.

"Come on, Liam, wake up. I smell breakfast. Shouldn't we go down?"

His voice was croaky. "In a while. Mom makes a breakfast

buffet on holidays, so give her time to finish." He rubbed my tummy and growled. "I *really* wanna do something...."

I snorted. "But you're so nervous you're not going to?"

"Um, yeah. No!" He gave me one of his special good morning kisses, which he immediately followed up with a few more.

Liam

All available evidence suggested that John needed me as much as I did him, but he called time after a couple minutes. "We have to stop, or you know what's going to happen."

Feeling the fever, I didn't want to stop. "Would that be bad? We can make it quick."

John squeezed my cock and showed me a salacious grin. "As tempting as that is, let's go get breakfast." He traced his fingers through the hair on my chest. "I'll be up for any fantasy you might have later."

I blinked a few times, wondering if I'd just heard correctly. "*Any* fantasy?"

He nodded slowly, still wearing that tantalizing smile. "*Any* fantasy."

The play of the morning light in his eyes and hair convinced me. "With that promise on the record then, counselor, let's go eat." *Hmm, which fantasy should I choose? Do I have to choose only one?*

While I was considering, John threw off the covers and slapped my ass. "We should take a shower before we go down." I didn't move, and he elbowed me in the ribs. "We might not be so fresh."

Remembering the night before, I tittered. "You're probably right. We'll be quick."

A few minutes later, we walked downstairs wearing flannel pajama bottoms and long-sleeved thermals. Mom was in the dining room, reading the newspaper and drinking coffee. There was a lot of food on the table, and smells of bacon and cinnamon filled the air.

"Good morning," she said. "Right on time."

I kissed Mom on the cheek and followed John over to the big bay window where he stood, looking out. He glanced back at Mom. "The view of the garden is beautiful from here, Andie. I can't believe how much color the flowers still have in November."

"Thank you. A lot of it has been growing for years, so it's a matter of maintenance. If it were warmer, we could go out there and sit for a while." She took a sip of coffee and smiled. "You'll just have to come back another time for that."

"I'd like to," he said. We walked over to the table and sat down.

Mom held her hands out over the table. "Dig in, both of you. There's enough to feed an army."

Vonnie breezed into the room right behind us. After one look at her narrow eyes, I knew she was up to no good. "What's new boys?"

"Hi Vonnie," John said, oblivious. "Sleep well?"

She flashed a wicked smirk. "I slept okay, no thanks to you two."

Shit! Her room was right next to mine and she never could keep her mouth shut about anything. John went a little pale, and my cheeks started burning. "I'm sorry, was the TV too loud?" I asked.

"The TV?" She rubbed her chin, feigning confusion. "That's what they're calling it now?"

She had no decency at all. The heat in my face increased by several degrees.

"Morning, Mom," she said, granting a temporary reprieve. "Everything smells great."

Mom was always thrilled when people liked her food, and when John asked her to teach him how to make the cinnamon rolls, she agreed right away. I was amazed because she never gave that recipe to anybody.

Vonnie babbled on about her med school chances, and Cait came down after a little while. She poured a cup of coffee, all she ever had for breakfast.

"So, how are the beautiful, *very* boisterous boys today?" Her expression made her look like the demoness she was.

Fuck!—had we really been that loud? My cheeks were on fire again, and I thought I might just die. When Mom chuckled, I was *sure* I'd die. I groaned and my eyes started watering. I looked at John, who was amazingly calm.

Faster than I could process, he put down his knife and fork and reached over to cup my face in his palms. One hand moved behind my head and his gentle fingertips brushed the back of my neck. He leaned in and gave me a sweet, tender kiss. Someone gasped, but I was beyond caring.

When he had me completely breathless, John broke the kiss, turned, and smiled at everyone else. All of them sat still, their faces impossible to read.

"I love this man so much," he said. "He's my treasure." He smiled at me again, tweaked my nose lightly, and took my hand and kissed it before looking back at them. "You're all great, and I know you're trying to be funny. I usually like funny, but right now you're embarrassing Liam—hurting him, I think. Please stop. If we really disturbed anyone, I'm sorry. I promise we'll be a lot more careful." His dimples were on display, but his eyes were dead serious.

My breath stopped while I waited for somebody to say

something, and Mom finally did. Looking squarely at my boyfriend, she smiled. "I like you more and more, John. Thank you for reminding us that there's a fine line between teasing and causing pain. For being brave enough to take care of Liam in what has to be an intimidating situation." Shifting her gaze to me, she said, "I apologize for contributing to the boorishness, honey."

I nodded, and her smile broadened into a grin. "I hope you realize that this one's the real deal," she said, nodding toward John. "You'd better treat him well. There are a lot of jerks out there, but not so many Prince Charmings."

"Thanks Mom." I cleared my throat. "I'm giving it everything I've got."

JOHN

AFTER BREAKFAST, Andie shooed us away so she could cook, and Cait and Vonnie asked if I wanted to go for a walk around the neighborhood. I did, but I needed to talk to Liam first. I hoped he wasn't going to tell me that I'd embarrassed him more than his family had.

He wanted to talk, too. "Sounds like fun, girls, but in a little while. John and I need to get ready for the day first." He raised his eyebrows at me. "Let's go get dressed."

Taking my hand, he practically dragged me up the stairs to his room. The lock clicked as soon as he closed the door. His eyes were unreadable but his lips were twitching into a smile. "Get on the bed."

I did as he said, and he was on top of me in a flash, wearing a sin-inspiring grin. We talked between gentle kisses.

"Nobody has ever done anything like that for me before,

John. Ever." He chewed his lip for a few seconds while he regarded me out of bright, glossy eyes. "Dammit! You're *bold*, John Lawrence! You took a *stand* for me."

I couldn't hold in a chuckle. "Did you see their faces? They were so stunned I don't think any of them could move."

"You were brilliant!" We chortled for a long minute before he kissed me again. "Once Mom processed what happened, how brave you are and how much you love me, her face changed. You're in with her solid. You know that, right?"

"If so, it's only because I love my Sugar Plum so much."

"I love you t—wait, wait! Did you say Sugar Plum?" He glanced away, then back at me. "*Sugar Plum*...? You called me fucking *Sugar Plum*!" His jaw went slack.

"Liam," I said, laughing at his hilarious reaction, "it just popped into my head. Sugar Plum... you know what they are?"

He shook his head, still wide-eyed.

"They're boiled sugar candies," I said. "Pure sugar, the sweetest candy of all." I licked his lips and gave him a peck. "Your lips are so sweet. You're *definitely* a Sugar Plum." I snickered again, almost able to see the wheels spinning in his head.

Finally, he smiled. "Dammit John, that's so sweet.... Har, har, har!"

I rolled my eyes and stayed quiet.

"Seriously, it really is sweet. It feels like you. I mean, it's *honest* coming from you." He took a deep breath and sighed. "I'll be damned. I guess I'm your Sugar Plum, then, whenever you want. Which by the way is forever, I hope."

Liam

We made out and both of us got worked up. John rubbed my belly, gradually going lower and lower until he swept his fingertips under the waistband of my pants, barely grazing the head of my very interested dick. He licked and sucked at my throat, and without warning, stuck his hand all the way under my pants and squeezed my cock.

I gasped at the urgent need that punched me in the gut. "Fuck, John, I've gotta have you. Now!"

We went into a frenzy that involved almost no foreplay. I didn't want to hurt him, but within a couple minutes, I had him pinned against the mattress, giving him everything I had. Both of us grunted like animals, the need to be quiet intensifying the physical sensations. It seemed as if we'd just gotten into high gear when we exploded together.

Afterward, I lay there holding my spent lover, breathing in the sharp smells of sweat and cum while I thought about how things had changed. We weren't just boyfriends anymore, but that meant I didn't know what our status was, or what I was going to do about it.

After another quick shower, I put on black jeans and a gray sweater over a white T-shirt, and John was gorgeous in dark blue jeans and an emerald green turtleneck. Before we went downstairs to rejoin the family, I pulled him into a bearhug. "Just so you know for sure, I'm yours, three-hundred-percent. Got it?"

He smoothed circles on my sweater over my pecs. "I'm yours, too, Liam. Totally and always."

"So...." I was a little nervous, brushing my fingertips up and down his sides while I stalled for time. "Boyfriends-plus, or what? What are we?"

He moved a hand up to stroke the side of my neck. "Way past boyfriends. You're my everything."

A long kiss later, we let go and found Mom downstairs in the kitchen. The room smelled like Thanksgiving—spice, sugar, turkey, veggies. She gave us both big hugs, and John asked if she needed any help.

"No, thank you. I'm almost finished for a while. Why don't you two go into the TV room? The girls have a pitcher of Bloodies in there."

"That's where we'll be," I said. "Don't work too hard."

Cait and Vonnie were slouched on the furniture, sipping their drinks and ignoring a parade on TV. "Well if it isn't the long-lost boys," Cait said through a big smile. "Bloody?"

Without waiting for an answer, she got up and poured one for each of us. I sat on the recliner and John took a place beside Vonnie on the couch. Cait was sprawled across an easy chair. They all chatted while we nursed our drinks, and I was struck by how well he was already fitting in.

Before long, Vonnie sat up straight and put her hand on John's knee. "I apologize for what happened earlier. I was way out of line." She hesitated before going on. "I've never witnessed a declaration of love like you laid down for Liam this morning. All the family around, not knowing how anyone would react, embarrassed by two crazy sisters? I'd never have the balls to do something like you did."

Cait leaned forward in her chair, looking between John and me. "John, you impressed the hell out of me. If I had any doubt about how much you love my brother, it's gone. You're both great guys, so stay focused on making each other happy."

John

The wind made it hard to close the door behind us. Snow was expected later that day, but the siblings told me it never amounted to much on Long Island. They led me through a traditional-style, upper-middle-class neighborhood, with houses on the larger side. Each home was unique, and all the yards were big. The Macadam house had a lot of land away from the street, and I suspected the other houses did as well.

It was fun listening to Liam and his sisters talk about their memories of growing up there. After a few minutes, Liam squeezed my hand and pulled me to a stop in front of a three-story brick building that appeared to have been built in the 1950s. Extremely well-kempt, it was striking in an all-American way. He grimaced. "Here it is, my elementary school."

I peered at him dubiously, making him snicker. "Looks kind of staid to have produced a bad boy like you."

Cait chimed in, wearing a snarky smile. "Oh my God, John, you have no idea. He was a wild thing, always into something. He even got Vonnie and me into trouble sometimes, purely by association."

"I plead not guilty," Liam declared solemnly. "You know me better than that, John." He looked at me and batted his eyelashes—I swear, he batted his eyelashes at me.

"Yes, I *do* know you." I couldn't resist giving his lips a little warming up. "Bad boy!" He yelped when I slapped his ass.

It had begun snowing, and they said we'd go back home a different way so I could see the rest of the neighborhood. We turned the corner from the school onto a commercial street with beautiful little shops and a gallery, all closed.

Cait pointed out one of the stores. "That bakery's great. Pastries all around tomorrow."

We soon turned another corner and were back in the residential neighborhood. The walk home took us down streets with houses that were even larger than the ones I saw on the way to the school. All of them, like those I'd seen earlier, were original in their design, some of them more contemporary than their counterparts near the Macadam house. A few of the residents had installed modernistic sculptures on their lawns. The entire neighborhood was gorgeous, but this was obviously the posher side.

Liam tugged at my hand again, holding me back and looking me directly in the eye. "We should go to a hotel tonight."

"Okaaaaaay.... Did somebody complain again?"

He shook his head, looking serious. "Nobody complained. They might, though, with the things I'm gonna do to you tonight."

My heart took off at the thought. "Whatever you think is best, but you get to explain it to your mom."

Vonnie and Cait called for us to get moving, so I pulled on Liam's hand and we quickly caught up. When we got home, he was in the house first and I followed behind his sisters.

"Hey Mom!" he yelled. "We're back. What's for lunch?"

Andie came into the foyer, wiping her hands on a towel. "I have a veggie tray ready. That should tide us over until dinner. We're eating at 6:30 and it's a big meal."

Liam

We munched through Mom's veggie tray, and when the platter was bare, John and the girls excused themselves. The lemonade we drank was making itself known, and although I needed to go too, I got up to help Mom clear the table. Her eyes sparkled at me over a warm smile. "Are you having fun, Liam?"

"A fantastic time! It's great to be home. And I'm glad you all like John, because he really likes you." I thought I'd hint for a little advice. "Mom, don't get too excited, but I think he's the one. I'm afraid to hit him with that yet because he might think it's too early, and I sure as hell don't want to run him off again. I'm pretty sure, though."

She put down the platter she was carrying and engulfed me in a hug. "That's wonderful, honey. I'm thrilled to see you so happy." Turning me loose, she straightened the neck of my sweater. "You two make me think of your father and me in the early times. Your dad was valiant, like John. There wasn't anything either one of us wouldn't have done for the other."

"If you ask me, it stayed that way till the...." My thoughts stuttered, but reality was what it was. "It stayed that way till the end."

She put a hand to her chest. "It certainly did." Her eyes got a little misty, and then she swallowed hard and smiled again. "John's obviously in love with you, but I think you're right to leave that discussion for its own time. Enjoy the weekend and get through the end of the semester first. You'll have an opportunity to talk things through on your vacation."

"You're right." I took a breath and blew it out through narrow lips. "There's something else I wanted to ask you."

She held up a finger and peeked into one of the ovens. Satisfied with what she saw, she turned toward me again and nodded.

"Maybe John and I should go to a hotel, tonight at least." *Fuck*, my face was on fire, yet again. "I mean... with this morning and all, today is really special. We don't want to make anyone uncomfortable... but, um... uh... you know...." I was starting to hyperventilate. Talking to Mom about sex, even indirectly, was hard.

She put a finger across my lips. "Shh, it's okay. I understand."

Flames were licking my cheeks, and she patted my arms.

"Relax, son. I'm not a dinosaur. Your dad and I were in love, too. We had times when—"

"Oh, my God!" I shook my hands in the air, trying to clear away the words. "Gross! *Stop!*"

Her voice was low-pitched, and I loved it when she laughed. "Why don't you and John move downstairs to the bedroom down the hall there, behind the kitchen. The one that was probably a maid's room back in the day?"

"We could do that?"

"Of course," she said, waving me off. "I should've put you in there to begin with. It's easily as large as your room and has its own bathroom. It even has that little seating alcove."

My chest loosened. "That'd be awesome. Thanks."

"Move down here this afternoon. You'll have all the privacy you need, and we'll all still be together."

"Thanks, Mom. You're the best." I kissed her cheek.

She snickered and nodded toward the door. "Go on, get out of here and go tell John. I need to tend to the rolls."

She called after me before I got out of the room. "Liam, you've become the young man I always knew you would be. You're strong and determined, so much like your father." I turned to face her and was surprised to see tears on her cheeks. "I'm proud of you, and your dad would be, too. He loved you, Liam. One of the last things he told me was to watch what a great man you were going to become."

Fuck!—now I was crying, too. "I wish he was here, Mom. But you know what? He *is*, in our hearts."

John

Liam and I moved downstairs to a bright, cheery room with early American furniture and a king-sized bed. Three walls were covered with pale yellow wallpaper, and the windows diffused the light beautifully, giving the room a soft, buttery feel. We showered and dressed for dinner, and I was glad we'd decided to wear ties when their Uncle Zach arrived decked out in a full suit.

Andie had invited several people, and I enjoyed meeting everyone. In a private moment, Liam's Aunt Alex, Andie's sister, confided that everyone had been worried about Liam after his triple whammy, as she called it. She said she'd even wondered if going to a hospital for a few days might help him get a handle on things, and I remembered him telling me the same thing.

"Now he's made a one-eighty," she said. "You've made a huge difference in his life."

I couldn't let her give me the credit. "He's a strong man, Alex. All I've done is fall in love with him."

She held my arm and leaned close. "You're old enough to know how much being in love can help a person. I'm excited for both of you."

At dinner, Andie put Liam and me beside each other, to her right, and I sat between him and a friendly older woman who lived nearby. The conversation was easy, and I admired Andie's beautiful mahogany table, set with fine china, crystal, and silver. There was enough food to feed the entire neighborhood, so much that the sideboard was burdened with the overflow.

We all ate too much and socialized for another hour or two after dinner. Once the guests had gone, Liam made Andie sit at the table while the rest of us put away the leftovers. She wouldn't let us do more than straighten the kitchen, saying she'd hired a cleaning service to come in the next day.

When we finished, Liam and I excused ourselves. We cuddled up on the bed after we changed out of our dressy clothes, and thanks to the turkey's magic, he soon fell asleep. I watched him for a little while, so handsome and relaxed, and wondered what the future would bring. I'd never felt about anyone the way I did about Liam, and it was already difficult to imagine a future without him.

17

Liam

The rest of the weekend flew by. We Macadams enjoyed visiting museums and historical sites, and so did John. Mom insisted on giving him a local tour on Friday, and after we drove around the Hamptons, we ended up at the Montauk Lighthouse. John enjoyed it a lot, which only made my family like him more.

On Saturday, we went Christmas shopping. After the first round, I insisted that Mom take John with her because I wanted to shop for him. I bought a sapphire blue cashmere sweater that would make his eyes gleam even more than they already did, and also found a pair of shearling slippers for his birthday, December 16th.

I needed something for Mom and went into a swanky jewelry store. Nothing caught my eye for her, but a white gold Celtic knot ring captured my attention right away. It was perfect for John's hand, and I suddenly knew exactly what I needed to do at Christmas. That stunning, elegant ring was the perfect symbol of our love, and if John wasn't ready to take it, I'd hold onto it for another try. I gulped, handed over my credit card, and left the store a few minutes later with a small light blue box and the conviction that Liam Macadam had done exactly the right thing for once.

By the time the weekend was over, John was part of the family. My mother and sisters loved him, and the feeling was mutual. On Saturday night, Cait and Vonnie monopolized him to the extent that I complained—all in good fun, of course. When we headed back to Syracuse on Sunday morning, I loved John even more than I had when we left, and that's really saying something.

The coming two weeks promised to be hectic. One more week of classes would be followed by three reading days, and then the big exams that would determine our first-semester grades. Those grades were important because they were our first measure of how we would do in law school. They were also half of the grades that would determine who made Law Review at the end of the year.

As soon as we got home, we needed to finish our outlines for the study group—John's on Torts and mine on Civ Pro. The next weekend was reading weekend, and John had to meet his sister in Washington, DC to attend a memorial service for someone they grew up with. He asked me to go along, but I needed to finish packing up my apartment on Saturday so we could move the rest of my stuff to the house. I was under time pressure because if I wasn't out of my apartment by December 20th, I'd be liable for another semester's rent.

John

I WAS sorry when the weekend was over, but happy to have found a place in a new family. Liam and I were going to my sister's in North Carolina for Christmas, and I hoped he would feel the same way about them. After the holiday, we would make the trip to Colorado that we'd planned earlier in the fall.

Before any of that, we had to survive exams. I was confident we'd both do okay. Liam was brilliant, and I knew I could hold my own, so the real question was whether we'd do well or finish with so-so grades. What an obnoxious system it was, when a single exam at the end of a class was your one and only grade, your legacy for the course, whether deserved or not. What bullshit law school could be.

In the car, we listened to music for a while and I thought back on some of the things I'd learned about my boyfriend over the weekend. He had three women who adored him, and the feelings were entirely mutual. All the Macadams were ardent about being there for each other, and after the time with his family, I understood how he came by his determined outlook about things.

I helped Andie heat up some leftovers on Friday evening, and we talked about Liam. When I told her what an inspiration he was for me and how I envied his ability to keep going no matter what difficulty he faced, she smiled. "Our Liam, always so tenacious. That's why good things come to him, you know, because he won't let up until they do."

I grinned as I finished washing lettuce. "You certainly hit that nail on the head."

She nodded happily while she handed me the salad spinner. "When he was a young boy, he was such a scrawny little thing that I worried about him. Even Vonnie was bigger than he was for a while. We'd go on family outings and he could barely keep up, but he would never let his father or me pick him up, or even carry things for him. He might be gasping for air, but he was determined to make it on his own, or not at all."

"That sounds just like him." I snickered as I spun the lettuce. "I *love* that about him."

"I do too." She took a dish out of the microwave and set it on the counter. "Another example, when he was in Little League. He'd grown by then, but he wasn't very good at catching balls, and his teammates gave him a terrible time. We went to every game and always praised him, but he really wanted to get better."

I began tearing the dried lettuce into the salad bowl. "How did he do it?"

"His dad and I both spent a lot of time throwing balls so he could practice catching. His grandfather was still alive then, and he would come over and toss balls, too."

I glanced over at Andie. She had the same brown hair and eyes that Liam did, and her bearing was absolutely regal. "That was so cool of you all."

She snorted. "The thing was, he wore us out. He wouldn't give up, and he'd run around chasing balls until we were all exhausted. Of course, it paid off, and he became so good the coach finally put him on first base."

"Wow, those guys really have to know how to catch," I said, reaching for a serrated knife to slice tomatoes. "That's exactly how he is with schoolwork. I get fed up with things and go do something else—or simply give up—but Liam never stops until he gets it."

"I'm sure." She stopped grating cheese long enough to smile at me. "You've fallen in love with one of the two most determined people I've ever known. Liam's father, Mark, was the other."

Liam

John and I worked hard all that week finishing up our

classes. Our first exam, in Property, was scheduled for the next Monday at noon. We would finish prepping for it before John left for Washington on Saturday morning, so we could spend some time relaxing after he got back on Sunday.

Friday was the first reading day, and our study group kept us busy all day long. That night we went out to dinner. We laughed our asses off when we arrived back home to find Theo looking cross, with part of the Property outline in his mouth, like he was telling us we had to study more. We tried, but soon realized that some things were more important than school, so we went to bed and sated our hunger for each other before falling into an exhausted sleep.

We were up extra early on Saturday morning so we could drive out to Hancock Airport. John's flight was at 8:50, and we needed time to stop for breakfast along the way. It was an emotional farewell before he went through security.

After saying goodbye, I went back to the house and played with Theo for a few minutes before we went to my apartment. Along the way, John called to let me know he'd landed safely in DC. He promised to call back later, after the memorial service.

At the apartment, I put on some music and started packing things into boxes. Michael and Jess eventually showed up to help, and it didn't take the three of us long to blow through most of the packing. I ordered pizza for lunch, and we fretted about exams and talked about the coming holiday break while we ate. By the time we finished, we were due at a study group meeting, so we walked over to the law school to meet the others.

John called just before five o'clock, and after everyone yelled out greetings, I excused myself to talk to him. He said the service had been beautiful and he thought their friend would've liked it. He and Susan had gone for a long walk afterward to clear their heads.

"I miss you so much," he said. "Wish I could hold you right now."

"Me too." I thought about how warm he would be in my arms. "I'd cheer you up after that service."

"I'd let you." He snickered, and I imagined how his dimples were creasing his cheeks. "After all, you're my Sugar Plum."

"And you're my Punkin." I closed my eyes and could almost feel his lips on mine. "I'm sorry I didn't go with you."

"It's okay, I understand. Please tell me you got all the packing done." His voice was a little sad, but I'd make it up to him the next day.

"Jess and Michael were lifesavers. I need to put in another hour tonight packing clothes, but that's it. All we'll have to do next weekend is move what's left, and then we'll be free."

He moaned, probably anticipating the luxury. "I can't wait for us to be together for a few weeks with no schoolwork to do."

"It will be awesome. Oh, just so you know, Theo and I are gonna sleep at the apartment tonight. We'd both be too lonely at the house."

"That's cool." He sounded wistful again. "How is Theo?"

"He misses you but we're doing great together."

"Aw, I miss him, too. I can't wait to get back to both my boys."

I was glad he missed me but didn't want him to be sad, so I tried to sound upbeat. "Ditto. We can't wait for you to get home."

Emily stepped out of the meeting to tell me they were almost ready for my presentation. I told her I'd be another couple minutes, and when I went back to John, he sounded better. "Susan and I are going to a play at the Kennedy Center tonight, and out to dinner after that, so it'll be pretty late when we get in."

"Sounds like fun. Will you call me when you get back?"

"Absolutely. I'll want to hear all about how you're finished packing."

"Believe me, I can't wait to tell you that." I chuckled. "I might even have to cheer you up long distance, if you know what I mean."

"Mm." I imagined his eyes opening wide the way they did when I talked about sex. "I'd definitely be *up* for that."

"You've got it then."

He hesitated. "I know you have to get back to the meeting, so I'll let you go. Remember, it'll be late, but I'll definitely call tonight."

"I'll be waiting. I love you, John. Have a good evening."

After the study group meeting ended, I went home and decided to watch TV for a while before I packed my clothes. When the phone rang, I grabbed at it, thinking it was John, but it turned out to be Kyle Corbin, my friend from Columbia that Jess hated so much.

Kyle and I had been boyfriends for about three disastrous weeks during my freshman year, but once we realized it wasn't meant to be, we became good friends and were roommates during my second year. Everything was strictly platonic, and we had lots of fun. Kyle was two years ahead of me, so he graduated at the end of my second year. He got a job as a stockbroker in Philadelphia and we only saw each other periodically after that, but we texted and talked every now and then.

"Guess what, man?" he said, after we shot the shit for a couple minutes.

"What?"

"I'm in Syracuse. I was on a plane to Montreal, where my mom lives, but there's too much snow there. They diverted us here for the night. Think I could crash with you?"

I looked around at all the boxes and grimaced, but Kyle was a friend and I was sure he'd seen worse. "You're welcome to the sofa, but fair warning, it's surrounded by boxes. I'm moving in with my boyfriend and I'm packing up my place."

He was quiet for a few seconds. "Maybe I should get a hotel room? I don't want to get in the way with you and your guy."

"Nah, it's cool. He's out of town today and I'd enjoy having company, actually."

"Oh, wow! You're sure it's not too much trouble?"

I scoffed at him. "Fuck, Kyle, you're always trouble."

"Fuck you too, man."

We both laughed. "Nah, it's fine, seriously," I said. "John will be back tomorrow, but I'm free tonight. We can hang and maybe have a few beers, it'll be fun. Where are you?"

"I'm still at the airport. Give me your address and I'll take a cab."

"Save your money. I'll come pick you up, it isn't far. We can grab dinner if you're hungry." It would do me good to get away from the boxes for a while.

We ate at a pub near campus and caught up on things. I talked a lot about John and how much I loved him. When I told Kyle about the ring I'd bought the week before, he watched me long enough that I had to look away.

"Are you sure you're ready to propose?" he finally asked. "You haven't known him long."

I couldn't hold back a big grin. "I'm *so* ready. You've heard of instalove? I used to be cynical about it, but it's for real. You just have to meet the right guy."

He didn't say anything, so I talked about law school. After we finished eating, I had another beer and Kyle had a couple. He livened up again and told me a few stories about weird clients of his that had me laughing hard.

Eventually I had to go to the bathroom, and when I got back, Kyle leaned across the table. "I appreciate you picking me up. Dinner's been great." He looked at me in a way he hadn't for years. "I wish we saw each other more."

He's drunk. You know how weird he gets when he's drunk. "What if you, John, and I got together for a weekend soon?"

He gave me another odd look before nodding. "I'd like that."

"All right, we'll make it happen." It was time to get us home. "What time's your flight tomorrow?"

"Soonest I could get was 1:30, but I'll take off earlier if your man's coming home before then."

I was glad he hadn't said 6:30 in the morning. "No, that's perfect. John's flight gets in at one o'clock, so I'll take you to the airport when I go pick him up."

He nodded, looking happier than he had for the last hour. "That'd be great. What do you think about heading home? I'm beat."

I stood up and pulled on my jacket. "I was thinking the same thing. Let's fly."

When we got to my apartment, Kyle said the drive had given him some energy, and asked if I had any beer.

I pulled my head back and rolled my eyes. "Are you kidding?"

He made his selection from my well-stocked fridge and we returned to the living room, where I sat on the sofa while he plopped down on a chair. He went back to the kitchen a couple times for more beer, and was soon quite drunk. I have to admit I was feeling no pain. I considered calling John to introduce them, but remembered that he'd promised to call when he got in. He and Susan were going to dinner after the play, and I knew how it was to catch up with sisters.

After a while, Theo needed to go outside, and Kyle came with us. It had started raining, so we wasted no time getting back upstairs. I toweled off the dog while Kyle got another beer from the fridge.

I declined and sat down on the sofa, and Kyle surprised me when he did too. It felt like the sofa was shrinking while we talked, and I became increasingly uncomfortable. An alarm started ringing in my mind, but I decided it was my imagination, that I was just drunk. Kyle and I were friends and that's all we'd ever be, and I knew he understood by then how I felt about John.

Still, something about the look in his eyes had been bothering me since before we left the restaurant. Maybe I'd have reacted sooner if I had been sober, but as it was I ended up scooting as close as I could get to the sofa's arm, and—*fuck all!*—Kyle moved with me. I told him I was going to bed, and that was when he grabbed my head and kissed me.

I jumped up off the sofa, yelling, "What the fuck? That isn't cool. You know I have a guy."

He waved me off. "Not a big deal, man. Just being friendly."

Sheer force of will helped me lower my voice. "It may not be a big deal to you, but it's huge to me."

"I just meant that you look really good, and I thought since you were alone tonight, maybe we could help each other out. It's cool if you don't want to."

I couldn't believe my ears. "I *definitely* do not want to, Kyle." I took two deep breaths and counted to ten. "Look, John is the best thing that's ever happened to me, and I love him more than anything. I'm gonna propose to him at Christmas. You *know* that!"

He started shaking his head, waving his hand in the air again. "No, you've got it all wrong. I didn't mean...."

The clamor in my head receded, and I felt really sad. "You've been a good friend, Kyle, but that's it. If you can't deal with that, call a cab and go to a hotel. Otherwise, it's time for both of us to go to bed. Alone."

"I'm sorry." At least he tried to look sheepish. "Do you want me to go?"

After another deep breath, I relaxed my eyebrows. "If we're clear that nothing is happening here tonight except us sleeping in different rooms, I guess it's okay. Just back off. Pillows and blankets are in the boxes outside the bathroom." I turned to go brush my teeth.

"We're cool, then?"

I glanced around, and he still had a look I didn't like—kind of hungry instead of embarrassed. "Well, I'm certainly on alert," I said. "I thought more of you than that, but I know you're drunk. Let's just try to forget about it."

When I got to the bathroom, I felt a little nauseous about having another guy's lips on mine. I sure as hell hadn't kissed him back, but I felt dirty nonetheless, so I scrubbed my lips and brushed my teeth. Whatever Kyle was playing at, I hated to see him act that way. He'd sure made me a lot less enthusiastic about seeing him in the future.

I discovered there was no lock on the door in my bedroom. *Shit!* Hoping that Kyle was finished being an asshole for the night, I got into bed and picked up a book. I figured I'd read until John called. It turned out that I'd drunk too much beer to focus, so I lay back and thought about my boyfriend's beautiful face.

Suddenly, I was sitting up in a panic. I'd fallen asleep, and was just taking a deep breath when there was a knock on the door. *What now?*

"Yeah?"

"You awake?"

"Unfortunately."

"Can I come in?"

I closed my eyes and shook my head. "Depends on why you want to. Can I trust you?" *No, you cannot trust that fucker!*

"Yeah."

Bullshit. Be careful. I tried to relax my stomach. "Okay, but make it quick. I'm tired."

Kyle came in and apologized for making noise. He said he'd been trying to get to the bathroom without turning on the light and had tripped over some boxes.

"It's okay. Let's get back to bed."

He didn't move. *I told you to be careful. Throw his ass out of here.* After too long, he looked at the floor and started talking. "I owe you an explanation about earlier. The truth is that I never really stopped having feelings for you. I kept it to myself, though, and we've been good friends for years now." He looked up. "I just want to tell you not to worry. I won't drink around you again, just to be sure nothing like that repeats."

I rubbed my forehead, speechless. "I had no idea, Kyle," I finally said. "You must remember that you and I went nowhere as a couple. It's amazing we even managed to stay friends."

He stepped toward the bed, and though I instinctively tried to move back, the headboard stopped me.

His face was red and his eyes were full of tears. "I... I've been feeling bad about myself lately."

He sat down on the edge of the mattress, and I should've pushed him off right then. Call me a stupid fuckup, because I certainly was.

"I'm really lonely," he said, "and it's always somebody else who's lucky with love. Listen, if you and I were to do something—"

That snapped me out of it. "Shut up! Get the fuck off my bed and get out of here!"

He shook his head, and I noticed the beginnings of a smile on his lips, "Liam.... No one knows I'm here, and I'll be gone tomorrow. Nothing would get back to your boyfriend, no way it could. Come on, man." He put a hand on my leg.

"Kyle, you are fucking certifiable!" I shoved him off the bed and jumped to my feet, breathing so hard snot flew out of my nose. "You just don't get it. It wouldn't matter if John knew or not, because *I* would know!" I put my hand over my mouth for a second or two, using every ounce of control I had not to hit him. "Dude, even if I were attracted to you—*and I'm not!*—I wouldn't do something like that to John. He and I are the real—"

"So you won't even consider—"

"Dammit, are you deaf?"

Kyle's eyes turned fierce. "Save it. That's enough, I get it. I'm going to bed, and I'll be gone in the morning."

"Good!"

The door slammed behind him and I reached for my phone. I didn't know why I hadn't heard from John, but I was calling him right then. *Oh, fucking shit!* I'd missed a call from him while I was asleep, and he'd texted after that. Hell, I must've been drunker than I thought.

JOHN: Hi sweetheart. I tried to call but you must be asleep. I guess you're worn out from working so hard. I'm going to bed now but wanted to say goodnight and I love you. I've missed you so much today and can't wait to see you tomorrow! No more trips alone, deal?

How had I not heard the phone ring? I looked at the clock—2:47 a.m., which meant John had called almost three hours earlier. I started to call him back but decided to text instead of waking him up. It would've been nice to get the bullshit with Kyle off my chest, but I thought it wouldn't be fair to wake John up for that.

LIAM: I miss you too babe and u have def got a deal on no more trips without each other! Sorry I was asleep before and didn't hear the phone... call me in the morning and I LOVE U!!!!!

I tried to get back to sleep, but between missing John, worrying about exams, and processing all the weird shit with Kyle, it took a while. I remember looking at my phone around five o'clock and wishing my boyfriend was cuddled up nice and warm against my belly.

18

Liam

I WOKE UP ANXIOUS, SENSING THAT SOMETHING WAS OFF. After a moment, I realized the light outside was too bright and grabbed my phone, which *of course* had died while I was asleep. Plugging it in, I opened my laptop and was shocked to see it was 11:42. That really sucked because I was sure John must have been trying to call. I hoped he wasn't too worried.

Kyle was still passed out on the sofa when I went to piss. So much for being gone in the morning. When I got back into the bedroom, I held down the phone's power button until it turned on, and sure enough, John had been burning it up. There were four missed calls, and he'd sent a text at 9:51.

> *JOHN: Hi sweetheart. What's going on? I've been trying to call you and now I'm getting worried. Please call me back. I have a surprise. <3*

The last missed call had been at 11:24. That was only

twenty minutes earlier, so he must have tried to call from the plane. I didn't know you could do that with a cell phone. I hit the button to call him back and got his voicemail, so I thumbed out a text.

> *LIAM: Im so sorry!!!!! My phone died and I just woke up... sorry 2 worry u but im fine, just didnt sleep well... got stuff 2 tell u... ill be waiting at the airport... I LOVE U, HANDSOME!* <3

After hitting send, I stomped out into the living room and started yelling. "Kyle, wake the fuck up! It's almost twelve o'clock, and I have to be at the airport before one. We're late, so get your ass in the shower."

He slowly opened his eyes. "Coffee?"

"Get your coffee at the airport. It's either get in the shower now or go without." I shrugged. "You oughta get in the shower 'cause you stink."

I hooked Theo up to his leash and told Kyle we'd be back in five minutes and to be out of the shower by then. I needed to clean up too.

Outside, Theo peed right away and began the search for a place to poop. I wanted to talk to John and reached for my phone before I remembered that it was still upstairs charging. Just thinking of him made me smile—he was coming home! We needed to study when he got back, but first things first. As soon as we got to the house, I was going to show that man in no uncertain terms exactly how much he was missed. Love first, then studying. Then more love.

Theo took his time, and when we finally got back upstairs, the clock said 12:03. John's plane was due at 1:00 and the fucking shower was still going. I walked to the bathroom door. "Goddammit, get your ass outta the shower, Kyle. If you're not ready in ten minutes, I'm leaving without you. I mean it." We didn't have to leave quite that soon, but he was obviously in slow gear. At least he turned off the shower.

I was in the kitchen drinking water when a key rattled in the front door, and John walked in. I ran into the living room and launched myself at him, wrapping him in my arms. "*John!* Thank God you're home!"

After kissing him, I backed up so he could get in the door. He threw his bag on a chair, said hi to Theo, and grabbed me for another hug. "I managed to get on an early flight." He turned me loose and held me by the shoulders. "Are you okay? I was worried."

Seeing him, knowing I could talk to him and get all the bullshit from the last twenty-four hours off my chest, had me close to tears. "I'm sorry. My phone died during the night. How did you get here?"

"I tried to call when we landed, but you still didn't answer so I took an Uber."

I gave him another quick peck on the mouth, but my grin was too big to turn it into a serious kiss. "That must have been right before I woke up. I tried to call you back."

His bright face and the smile lighting up his eyes were like warm sunshine. "Susan had called me, checking in to be sure we both made it home okay. By the time I told her to wait, you were gone." He cocked his head. "Are you sure everything is all right? I got off the phone right away and tried to call again, but you *still* didn't answer."

I nodded while I feasted my eyes on him. "Everything's fine. I was outside with Theo and my phone was still up here charging. Listen, I have to tell you—"

"It's okay, I'm just glad you're all right. Have you had lunch? I thought we could go to—"

"Liam, you got any shit I can put in my hair?"

John turned toward the voice, and his mouth dropped open. He took a couple steps back and his arms fell like dead weights. I turned and—*oh, fucking shit!*—there stood Kyle in the bathroom door, naked as the day he was born, dewy from his shower, trying half-heartedly to get his towel in the general area of his waist.

"Sorry dude, I didn't realize you had company." That would be Kyle, looking almost as surprised as John, but with a big smile on his face. The fucker swaggered over to me and wrapped an arm around my shoulder while he extended the other one toward John. John's face left no doubt about what he thought, and I desperately tried to shrug Kyle off me.

"Liam, what's going on?" That would be John. His voice was shaky, and I could already see hurt washing across his face.

"Babe, remember I told you I had something—" That would be me, trying to explain. But Kyle tightened his grip on my shoulder, kissed my cheek, and applied the coup de grâce.

"What's up sweet meat? Who's this?"

"Kyle! What the fuck are you doing?" I shoved him away so hard he nearly fell.

John's cheeks were washed out and even his lips had gone pale. His mouth was open, and he'd pulled his eyebrows so close together that he looked like he had a migraine.

"My God." He shook his head as tears welled up in his eyes. "Liam...." His voice was so weak I had to strain to hear him. "I can't believe you would do this to us."

No, no, no! "John, it's not what—"

He held up his hands, palms out, shaking his head violently. "Stop."

"No! This isn't—"

"Liam, do not even *try* to tell me it's not what it looks like." His voice broke. "I can see exactly what it is." He pressed a fist against his mouth and his shoulders shook.

"John, please...." His eyes softened, and I thought I was getting through. "I was just trying to tell you—"

Kyle interrupted, speaking to John. "Dude, you're early. We didn't expect you back yet. I'm Kyle." He stuck out his hand again.

"Shut up, Kyle, you fucking idiot!" I yelled.

John's face was drawn up again, and his breath was ragged. "Clearly, you didn't expect me."

I took a step forward, reaching out to him, when the first tears spilled from his eyes.

"No!" He pushed my hands away and made a choking sound. After he gasped a few breaths, he finally spoke. "Stay away from me...." His voice faltered and he took a second to recover. "I knew it was too good to be true."

"Don't *say* that." I hated the way his hands and lips were shaking, and he was so unsteady on his feet I was afraid he might fall.

"Tell me," he said, his voice barely a whisper, "were you playing me all along, or could you just not keep your dick in your pants for one night?" He shrugged. "Either way, I guess you made me your fool."

He started sobbing and my heart broke. For a horrible minute, all I could do was stare at him, but I finally got my feet in motion and stepped toward him again. "John," I begged, "please listen to me."

"No." His hands were unsteady, but he pushed me away again. "I actually thought you were different. I-I thought it was real." His voice caught in his throat again, and his warbling, whispery voice made me shudder. "I thought *we* were real. I even thought we might...." He sobbed again and folded in on himself, sagging back against the wall. He shook like he was freezing to death and wrapped his arms around himself.

John was scaring the hell out of me. I looked around desperately, trying to decide what to do, and caught a glimpse of Kyle. That son of a bitch was actually grinning, and I was just pulling back to hit him when John started talking again. My head snapped around in his direction.

"Don't worry, Liam, you don't have to fuck the pathetic old guy anymore." He swiped at the tears on his cheek. "I knew you were bad news the first time I saw you. What was I thinking?" At that, he stood up straight and waved his arms like he was telling people to stop singing. "You know what? It doesn't matter, because I'm done." He tossed a hand in Kyle's direction. "You can have this stupid shit, or anyone else you want."

I must have looked like a caught fish trying to breathe, the way my mouth was opening and closing. My jaws worked silently, trying to get something out, but Kyle spoke up again before I found my voice.

"Man, I just crashed here. I'm Kyle, Liam's old roommate from New York. You weren't here and we... it was nothing serious, we just helped each other out for old time's sake, and—"

"Kyle!" I yelled. "You're a goddamned liar! I'll slit your fucking throat!" I turned back toward John. "We didn't!" I shuddered at the hollow, wounded look in John's eyes, his trembling chin, and the way he clutched his stomach. "We didn't...." My voice cracked and I couldn't go on.

John looked back and forth between Kyle and me. "Spare me, both of you. I'll bet you crashed here, all right. Old time's sake? Was it as good as you remembered? How about you, Liam? Was it worth hurting me like this?"

"Dude, I—" For the life of me, I couldn't fathom why Kyle was still talking, or breathing for that matter. If I hadn't been so busy trying to calm John down, I would've gutted Kyle on the spot.

John obviously felt the same. Snapping to life, he took a swift step toward Kyle with murder in his eyes. "Shut up, you vapid whore, or I'll chop off your micropenis and shove it down your goddamned throat."

Kyle jerked back, looking slapped, and finally shut up. John turned back toward me again, and the fire was gone as quickly as it had appeared. "I loved you, Liam, I really did. With all my heart." He leaned against the wall again. "Dear God, what am I going to do?"

I tried to go to him, but as soon as I moved, the fire was back. "I told you to stay away from me."

Theo, who had been getting increasingly upset, was making pitiful sounds by then. John bent over to pick him up, and I took advantage of the moment and tried again. "Please, Punkin. Hear me out."

His voice was frigid. "No. And do not call me that ever again." He stood up and turned, Theo still in his arms, and walked toward the door.

"John!" I shrieked, as I ran around him to block his way. "Stop it! It's not like you think. Listen to me!"

His beautiful blue eyes were tragic, overflowing with tears and pain. The voice that came out of him was far worse than anything *The Exorcist* ever imagined. "Get out of my way. I can't be around you anymore."

It's hopeless. Whatever I said, he wasn't going to listen to me. Better to let him go, I thought, and talk to him in a couple hours. I dropped my head and stepped aside.

He clomped out the door while I stared at my heart on the floor and listened to the elevator doors close on my happiness. After a moment, I came to my senses and ran for the stairs, realizing I couldn't let him get away, but he was nowhere to be seen by the time I got to the lobby. I ran outside and around the building and then spent some time looking around the area, but John had vanished into thin air.

I thought about going to Jess's apartment for help, but

decided I'd rather go back to mine and beat the shit out of Kyle. When I got there, he was gone too, probably a good thing because at that point I really might have killed him. My brain was in free fall, trying to piece together exactly what had happened. Kyle always was a fucking liar and had a vengeful streak, and I guess he was getting even because I wouldn't fool around with him.

John thinks you fucked Kyle.

Why the hell hadn't I called John the night before to let him know what was going on? So what if I woke him up? There was no way I could've known what Kyle would do when John got there, but if I'd kept John in the loop, he would have at least been prepared to deal with it for what it was.

Shoulda, coulda, woulda—Jesus, I'd fucked up so bad. John's heart was in pieces and it shouldn't have been because the only thing I'd done wrong was be one really stupid fuckwad. Jess was right. Deep down, I'd known Kyle was bad news for years, and I couldn't believe I'd even given him the opportunity to pull something like this.

John thinks you fucked Kyle.

How could I explain things to John? I collected my thoughts and tried to call him. Voicemail. I considered driving to the house, but since I was afraid that would infuriate him even more, I texted and begged him to see me. Knowing I could use some support, I also tried to call Jess but only got her voicemail. *Where the hell could she be on a Sunday?*

I texted and called John all afternoon, but he never answered. Finally, I wrote an email and decided that if I didn't hear from him by seven o'clock, I'd drive to the house and do whatever I had to do to get him to see reason.

John thinks you fucked Kyle.

About six thirty, somebody knocked on the door. I ran to it, convinced that John was back, but it was Jess. She marched in as hard as John had marched out, and her splotchy face, flared nostrils, and hard mouth announced that more trouble had arrived.

"You are a much more stupid asshole than I ever suspected, Liam." She didn't even yell. It was just a simple, declarative sentence.

"You know something?"

"You're damned right I do, and it stinks to high heaven." She looked at me like I was a cockroach. "*You* stink to high heaven."

"Jess, listen—"

She slowly shook her head. "No. You sit your ass down and listen to me."

I must have waited too long because she snapped, "Now!"

I sat. At least her subsequent tirade answered some questions. I hadn't found John downstairs because he didn't leave the building right away. Instead, he'd gone to her apartment and told her everything.

"Is he still there?" I asked, standing. "Take me to him."

She put a hand on my shoulder and pushed me back down. "No, he isn't there, and if you want to have any chance of ever redeeming this shitshow, you need to give him some space. He almost blocked you when you kept calling, but I talked him into waiting a day or two, to make sure of his feelings. I drove him and Theo home and stayed with them for a few hours. He's broken, Liam."

I whined in frustration. "I didn't do anything wrong."

Apparently, she'd taken look-of-death lessons from John that afternoon. "You need to drop that line and start telling the truth. John might be able to forgive you if you confess, but you're only going to make him madder by lying." She glared at me until sweat broke out on my brow. "How could you cheat on him, Liam? That's *so* not you, and I know you love him."

"I did not cheat on him. *Please* listen to me."

Her sigh could have been a wind blowing through the Arctic Cordillera. "He caught you red-handed, in this apartment, with a naked man who was all over you. Who unambiguously stated that you'd hooked up. Is that or is that not what happened?"

She stood there with her arms folded while I considered how to respond. What she said was technically correct, as far as events went, but everything Kyle had said was a damned lie. She huffed mightily before I could say anything. "Well? Answer the question." Jess would make a good prosecutor.

"No. I mean... well.... Yes, Kyle stayed here, but there was no sex. And don't cross-examine me like that."

"Kyle?" She looked confused, then horrified. "Oh, my God —not Kyle *Corbin*!"

I hung my head, unable to say anything.

Her nose curled, as if she smelled something rotten. "For God's sake, Liam, what was that asshole doing here? And why would you fuck *him*, of all people? I thought you got that idiot out of your system freshman year."

"We didn't *do* anything. You know I wouldn't fuck him." It was my turn to huff. "I wouldn't cheat."

"Kyle's a piece of shit. He isn't good enough to tie John's shoes."

"Jess, I *know* that. I didn't...."

She unfolded her arms and shook her head. "You've got to admit, the only clearer evidence would have been for John to walk in while your dick was up Kyle's ass."

I wanted to rage and scream at her, but I didn't have the strength. "Please, Jess. How long have you known me? In all that time, have I ever cheated on anybody even once?"

She passed a few seconds appraising me before her face

relaxed a bit. “No, but look at this through anybody else’s eyes. What would you think?”

“Jess?”

She tilted her head.

“You know Kyle—you hate him for how he is. He was being his lying, shitty self, trying to make trouble between John and me.” My voice caught and I had to swallow. “I didn’t touch Kyle. He came on to me last night and got really pissed when I turned him down. I almost threw his ass out then, and I obviously should have. You were right all along. I should have ditched him a long time ago.”

“Oh, Liam,” she mumbled, puffing out her cheeks and rolling her shoulders. “This is a terrible mess. I took John home and got him to lie down. He couldn’t stop crying, and Theo? God, he’s so traumatized he won’t leave John’s side, and he wouldn’t stop whining, either.” She shuddered and wrapped her arms around herself. “They just laid there crying together, the most pitiful thing I ever saw. John asked me to stay a while, and I spent the afternoon trying to be the friend he needed.”

“Thank you. I’m so glad he didn’t have to be alone. Now let’s go over there together.” I stood again, and she pushed me back down on the sofa.

“No. Think about the times you’ve been hurt. It won’t do you any good to go confront John now. You need to stay away until he’s ready to talk to you, to hear you.”

I closed my eyes and rubbed the back of my neck. “I can’t let—”

“You’ve got to stop texting and calling him. He gets upset all over again every time you do. You’re only making things worse.”

I opened my eyes and was glad to see her looking a little friendlier. “But I—”

She took my hands, a sad smile on her lips. “John’s humiliated and angry. He's talking about how much he loved you and how he'd started thinking about the future. Now he thinks you were never serious about him, that you played him all along."

This was insane. I'd heard about someone seeing red before and always thought it was a metaphor, but how wrong I was. A cloud of red flashed across my vision, and I yelled, "He knows that's complete bullshit and you fucking do too!"

Emphasizing just how bad this clusterfuck was, Jess broke down crying, something I'd seen only once before in all our years as friends. John had to be in terrible shape to upset her so much. She sat down, and after a moment she was able to talk again. "You're right, I've known you a long time and you've never cheated. You're honest, and I know how much you love John." She inspected her nails for a few seconds. "Still, the evidence looks bad and you know it, but I'm inclined to believe you."

"I'm—"

"But if you got scared or something, tell him that."

A tear ran down my cheek, and then another. "I didn't get scared. I love John and I've got no doubts about that."

She pressed her lips together so hard they went white. "You swear you're telling me the truth?" She put a hand on my arm. "You know how bad things were with him and Thorne. I'm sure you would have realized how sensitive he'd be to cheating."

It was all I could stand, and I jerked my arm free and beat my fists on my thighs. "I'm telling you the fucking truth!" I lost it and violent sobs overtook me. Jess wrapped her arms around me and made soothing sounds while she rubbed her hands across my back.

When I eventually got myself together, she sat back and spoke gently. "Look at me, Liam." I was busy wiping my face, and she repeated herself. I looked up, and for the first time since she came in, there was genuine kindness in my friend's eyes. "My heart hurts for both of you. Whatever happened, you're in as much pain as John is."

I broke down again. I couldn't even sit upright and had to put out an arm against the sofa's back to support myself.

"Hang on," she said, getting up. After a moment, she came back with a box of tissues from beside my bed and sat down on the couch with me. "I'm sorry that I called you a liar. You've been my bestie forever, and you've seen me through thick and thin. The best advice I can give you is this: tell John the whole, unadulterated truth. He's upset, and things look bad, but he's also smart and he loves you."

"I will."

"I don't believe you cheated on him, but you've got to think of a way to convince him of that."

I was still mopping tears and snot off my face. "How am I supposed to prove a negative?"

"You don't have to prove it, you just have to get through to him. I think reasonable doubt would be enough."

"I'll try."

"I'll do my best to help both of you," she said. "I can't guarantee anything, but I promise to do everything I can."

For the first time in hours, I felt a sliver of hope. "Thank you."

"I'll encourage him to talk to you, and to do his best to keep an open mind."

Another strangled sob escaped my throat, and she took me in her arms. "You realize it may take a while to work this out?"

"I've got the rest of my life."

She nodded. "Do not lie to that man, whatever you do. People as hurt as he is already expect the worst, and they have a nose for bullshit that would put any bloodhound to shame. I don't think he'd be able to forgive being jerked around."

"I've got nothing to hide, but will it be enough?"

Jess squeezed my hands and exhaled loudly before standing up. "Is that John's bag on the chair? He asked me to bring it back to him, and when I take it, I'll try to get him to talk to you. Meanwhile, please leave him alone, for both your sakes. Let him tell you when he's ready to talk."

She took the bag and left. I tried to let John alone like she'd said, but I couldn't help myself. When I hadn't heard from him by eleven o'clock, I tried to call. Voicemail again. A few minutes later, he texted me.

> *JOHN: Stop it and leave me alone. I can't think about anything right now except what I saw. I'll try to get to where I can talk to you, but please leave me alone for now or I'll never get there.*

At least he left the door open a little, and I decided I'd better listen to Jess and give him space. For the rest of that awful night I cursed fate and prayed for John to come to his senses.

John

How could he do that to me?

Liam kept texting and calling, and I thought I'd die every single time. It was so tempting to answer the phone. I needed comfort badly, and craved the safety of his arms, but he was the reason I needed comfort to begin with.

I'm in hell.

The Liam I missed was the Liam I thought I'd known—the one I'd fallen in love with and wanted to spend the rest of my life beside. I wanted *my* Liam back, but apparently he never really existed. I lay on the bed in the dark, shaking and crying.

After Jess left, I knew I had to get up and take care of Theo. I wasn't sure if he'd had anything to eat all day. He was so traumatized by the whole ugly show at Liam's that he didn't act hungry, but I wanted to have food available for him. When I got up, I barely made it downstairs. Theo went outside through the doggie door while I poured some food into his bowl, but he didn't eat when he came back in.

I put a cup of soup into the microwave and managed to take two bites before I almost vomited on the floor and threw it away. Somehow, I made it back upstairs and into bed. Theo stayed right by my side, and we had to sit down on a step twice before we made it back to the bedroom. I lay there for hours, thinking about how Thorne cheated on me for years, and how Liam—knowing how much Thorne had hurt me—did the same thing.

Is that all I'm worth? What is it about me that attracts men like that?

Liam's smell was all over the bed, and when I couldn't stand it anymore, I went back downstairs and spent the rest of the night weeping on the sofa.

I wondered how I'd live through exams all week, having to sit next to Liam for hours on end, every day. By morning, I had a plan. When we'd talked to him at Thanksgiving, Professor Zimmerman said we could call him at home, and at eight o'clock, I looked up his number in the law school directory.

19

Liam

I didn't see John all week. He wasn't in any of the exams and didn't show up for study group meetings. I walked the halls and haunted the law library hoping to run into him, but he was nowhere to be found.

Only superhuman restraint kept me from walking up and ringing the doorbell the hundred times I drove by the house. I kept hearing Jess tell me to give him time, and although it went against my instincts, I knew I was hardly objective. Once, when his car wasn't there, I got out and walked around back where the tall windows were. Theo scurried over, woofing and licking the glass.

Judging by the cold shoulder I got from people, they'd heard something. Not many would look me in the eye, and when they did, something between contempt and pity stared back at me. I tried to pump Jess for information, but no dice. She said she wouldn't talk about it, but promised she was keeping her word to me. She assured me that John was fine physically, but she got testy when I asked her to give him a message.

"You've got to understand the position I'm in. I'm friends with both of you. I promised you I would try to help, and I am, but I also warned you that things could take a while. John told you he was trying to get to where he could talk to you, and I really hope he does, but I will not carry messages between you two."

"Please."

The set of her jaw was as unyielding as her words. "No, I will not."

"It's the only—"

"*Damn it,* Liam. *No.* I will not be put in the position of trying to say words for either one of you. What if I got something wrong? What if I even got an *inflection* wrong? I've been telling you to give him time and that's what you're going to have to do. When he talks to you, you can tell him whatever you want."

I was so lovesick and worried about John that I couldn't eat and slept very little. It was a wonder I was able to sit still through the tests. His birthday was on the 16th, and I left a card in his student mailbox, along with the slippers I'd bought for him. The next day, the card and slippers were gone but he hadn't replied to the letter I'd enclosed with the card.

Jess stayed in touch, and Michael came around every day to check on me. He told me stories and tried to keep my spirits up. Late Friday night he showed up, and as soon as we sat down with a beer, he got serious right away.

"How long are you going to wait, Liam?"

"For?"

"To go after your man, dude."

I immediately teared up. With all the crying I was doing, I

probably needed to drink extra water to stay hydrated. "Jess keeps saying I need to give him time."

"Yeah, she does." He eyeballed me for a moment. "What do *you* think? I mean, you can either leave John alone, hoping he might come around, or you can actually do something."

"Like...?"

"Go see him, at least say your piece. It's been a week now and I know what I'd do. And it needs to be done soon, because things aren't getting any better." He paused as if he was trying to emphasize something. "What if something else came along?"

That scared me. "What are you trying to say?" I had to force out the words.

He looked around, although we were alone. "Nothing that Jess is ever to hear, you understand? I need you to swear."

You've gotta be kidding me! "I swear. *Please* tell me!"

"I can't say much, but he's thinking...."

"Michael! *Fuck!*"

He pursed his lips for a second before he spoke. "He's considering other options."

The hair stood up on the back of my neck. "What do you mean? Other guys?"

"No, but he feels like he won't be able to move on here."

My voice was a bare whisper. "He doesn't have to."

Michael took another furtive look around the room. "I've already said more than I should've. Jess would have my head, and John would cut off my balls." He drained his beer and gave me a pleading look. "Just go see him and try to make things right." Michael put down his beer bottle and took hold of my shoulders. "Don't wait. Go right away. Yell through the door if you have to."

I was pretty freaked out by then. "I will. Thank you."

"Dude, Jess's advice is total bullshit at this point. The worst thing you can do is leave John alone. You hear me?"

I nodded and swiped at the tears running down my cheek again.

"Okay." He stood up. "I'm sorry, but I have to go. I'll drop by tomorrow."

"Please."

He fixed me in a hard stare. "Go see John. Don't wait."

First thing the next morning, I got up and drove straight to the house, but John wasn't there. I gave in to temptation and used my key to go in, but got no satisfaction. Even Theo was gone. There were just a bunch of memories that tore me up more than I already was. I found myself upstairs in the closet, smelling John's clothes and cologne bottles. I went back home feeling worse than ever.

Michael came over before long, looking a little frantic. "Did you go over there last night like I told you to?"

"I went first thing this morning. He wasn't there."

"*Fuck*! I told you.... You stupid ass!" He scrubbed his hands across his face. "Sorry. I... I wish you'd gone last night."

"Why didn't you tell me to go last night?"

His nostrils flared. "I *did*! I told you to go right away, not to wait. *Damn*!"

"Is he back home now?"

Michael closed his eyes and tilted his head back while he let out a long breath. "He's gone out of town. Won't be back until Tuesday night."

"Are you telling me it's too late?" I broke down yet again, and Michael held me while I cried.

"I'm not saying it's too late. Shit, I don't know if it is or isn't anymore, but I do know that this is killing you." He patted my back. "I don't know exactly what happened, but I'm a hundred percent certain that you and John love each other. You need each other."

"I know we fucking do!" I choked on the words. "And now I've listened to Jess and maybe thrown it all out the window."

He squeezed my upper arm. "Buddy, I'm a guy too. I know we screw up sometimes. We think with the wrong head, or we're stupid, or both." He sighed heavily. "*Usually* both. Dude, I really care about you and John. Would you talk to me? Tell me what really happened? I won't repeat anything you say, you've got my word."

It felt good to get it out, and when I finished talking, he sat staring at me. "You poor bastard. You really didn't cheat on him."

"No, I didn't."

"Oh, man." He slowly shook his head. "I'll do everything I possibly can to get John to talk to you, I promise. I want to see both of you climb out of this hell."

Hot tears of relief ran down my cheeks. Somebody, finally, absolutely believed me.

Michael came by every day that weekend to keep me company but didn't have anything else to say about John. On Monday afternoon, he brought Theo along and said Jess had been dog-sitting but was out getting a haircut. I had fun playing with the little dog. He was always a sweet boy and was the closest connection I had to John right then.

Later, Jess showed up. She brought some boxes of my things from John's house and said he asked her to pack them up because he couldn't face it. I was a little confused, but since I couldn't tell her I knew he was out of town, I just tried to enjoy her company.

She was back on Tuesday night, looking grim. Michael showed up a little while later and they shared a look of despair.

I actually saw him nod his head. They obviously knew something but by then I didn't even ask. What was the use? They wouldn't tell me anything, and I needed the few friends I had left.

After a little while, Jess said she was tired and had to leave, but Michael stayed. I told him I was going to go see John right away, but he said he'd picked him up at the airport and John was exhausted from his trip—that I should wait until the next morning so John could focus on what I had to say. It was against my better judgment, but I realized that waking John up probably wouldn't help my cause any.

I couldn't sleep, so I occupied myself with planning what I wanted to say to John. In a moment of clarity, I realized that he might not see me at all. He might run from the door, so even if I yelled through it, I couldn't be sure he'd hear me. I sat down and wrote a letter to stuff under the door if he wouldn't let me in.

First thing the next morning, I drove over to the house to try to make John listen to me, once and for all. His car wasn't in the driveway, but I rang the bell several times. Theo woofed on the other side of the door, and I thought about using my key. The garage door was closed, though, and I worried that John might have put his car in there and was actually at home. If he was ignoring me, it would upset him if I went in, so I decided to get some coffee and come back in an hour.

Coffee. *Go back.* Lunch. *Go back.* A walk. *Go back.* Goddammit! I worked up the balls to go peek through the cracks around the garage door. It was empty inside, so I walked back to the house, used my key to go in, and got a good dose of pug love. I'd considered the possibility that John wouldn't open the door, but it hadn't occurred to me that he'd be gone by eight thirty in the morning and stay gone all day.

I decided to leave the letter I wrote on the sofa where he

always sat. In it, I'd written down everything that had happened, sworn to my innocence, and talked about how much I loved him. I begged him to call me and told him I'd meet him anywhere if he'd see me. I also left his Christmas gift, the sapphire blue cashmere sweater, hoping I'd get to see him wear it someday.

I walked through the house one more time and was glad to see the slippers I gave him on the floor by our bed. He was using them—that meant something, right? After a few minutes, I walked back downstairs, told Theo goodbye, and left.

From there I went to the student health center because I couldn't sleep or eat, and my stomach and head were killing me. I ended up crying so much the doctor gave me a bottle of tranquilizers and told me to go home and celebrate the holidays with my family. She said to come back in January so she could hook me up with a therapist. *Great.*

I had no word from John all day. Jess and Michael had both left town, but I was determined to stay until I heard from John. I tried to stay busy but mostly ate cookies and ice cream, and binged on Netflix. I checked my email about midnight and was overjoyed to find a message from John.

Dear Liam,
I told you I would try to get to a place where I could talk to you. I'm not there yet, but I'm working on it. Tomorrow, I'm going to North Carolina for Christmas and I'll be in touch from there. Thank you for the beautiful sweater and slippers. Take care of yourself.
John

I went back over the email a hundred times. It was hard to read anything positive or negative into it, but I finally decided it leaned very slightly positive. Knowing John wouldn't be in Syracuse, I decided to drive home the next morning.

Friday, December 23

On the first part of the flight to Asheville, I fretted about my new job, and worried about how I could get the move done in time. Only Michael, Jess, and my sister knew about it so far, and I'd sworn Michael and Jess to secrecy because I wanted to tell Liam myself.

I spent the rest of the flight thinking about Liam. I still loved him; I was sure of that. On Wednesday, I'd gone to see a therapist, and he'd helped me admit that Liam probably still loved me. The therapist had pointed out that cheating does not necessarily mean there's no love. Especially in someone in their early twenties, it could have been the result of Liam being nervous about the feelings we had for each other.

I wasn't sure what I was going to do, but I would talk to Liam before I left the United States. The short trip to North Carolina would give me the space I needed to know what I wanted to say, and to be absolutely certain I really wanted to leave Syracuse.

Liam

When I got to Wainscott, I found a subdued mom and sisters waiting for me. John had been in touch to tell them how much he'd enjoyed meeting them, and he also gave them a pretty good idea of why we weren't together anymore.

I paid the price for not telling them right away because they heard his side first. They grilled me for every detail. Mom and Cait definitely came down on my side after I explained what happened. Both of them believed me and told me to stay the course. They knew some of John's history with Thorne, and said what Jess had, that he was hypersensitive about the idea of cheating. They felt sure that he would come around because of how much he loved me.

Vonnie was different, though, which surprised me because of how close we'd always been. In all fairness, she'd had several horrible experiences with men, but it hurt me deeply when she questioned me repeatedly about whether or not I'd cheated. She said she believed me, but followed that up with a harangue about how I'd have ruined my life if I had, and that if I had, she might try to convert to lesbianism. She said if I couldn't keep it in my pants despite how much she knew I loved John, there was no hope for men at all.

The next morning, Cait and I were sitting on the sofa by the fire after I'd had another crying jag. She talked me down, and then we sat quietly for a bit before she looked at me strangely. "Liam, I've been through this with men before. They're usually cowards and won't talk to you, so you don't know whether to believe them or not. I know you're telling the truth about what happened, but have you really done *everything you could* to try to talk to John?"

"That's all I've fucking done for two weeks, dammit, try to talk to him." My voice was far angrier than I intended. "He won't see me, he won't answer his fucking phone. He disappeared from school like he found an invisibility cloak or something." I took a breath and managed to pull it back a notch. "All I've done is try. He said he'll be in touch, and I hope to God he will, but I honestly feel like giving up."

"If you love him, son, you can't give up." Mom stood at the bottom of the stairs, smiling at me. "John adores you, and you know that. I think Jessica was right that this might take a little while. People need time to process."

"Mom's right," Cait said, smoothing her hand over my back. "I think Jess was wrong to tell you to stay away from John, but it isn't too late. Forget her advice and text the hell out of the man. Call him a few times a day so he knows you're really trying to get in touch. Talk to him when you can. You *will* have to give him time, but I saw how much he loves you."

"Absolutely," Mom said. "You have so much determination inside you, and you have to keep trying. I know it's discouraging, but you can do it."

She walked across the room and sat on the sofa with us. I sat between her and Cait and cried my heart out, yet again. I was sick of crying. My eyes and nose were permanently red, and they were sore as hell, but the tears wouldn't stop. Later that day, I felt like I was coming down with something and went to my room to lie down. I didn't come out much after that, mostly because I felt sicker by the day.

They all came up to spend time with me, but I mostly listened to emo music and tried to get in touch with John. I must have texted and called a hundred times, and on Christmas Eve, I left a voicemail and sent him an email, as well as an e-card. In the email, I begged him to see or at least talk to me, and I told him again I'd meet him anywhere in the country.

Emotionally, I was in the worst shape of my life. Making things even more delightful, I'd managed to come down with a bad cold, and feeling sick as a dog did absolute wonders for my spirits. On Christmas morning, I went downstairs to open presents but that wore me out, and Mom had to bring me dinner on a tray because I felt too bad to leave my room. I ate a few bites and put the rest of it out in the hall because the smell made me throw up.

In retrospect, going home was a bad idea because John and I had been there only a few weeks earlier and were so happy then. When I was at the house that last time, I'd taken a couple of his T-shirts, and I could smell him on them. I wore one on Christmas Day, which I mostly spent looking at the ring I'd bought and dreaming about what might have been. I wore the ring that night, but the next morning I put it in the back of my desk drawer and left the house for a long walk. By the time I got back, I'd come down with a full-blown case of flu and spent the next couple days hoping I'd die. I did nothing but wallow in my misery and text John repeatedly.

Late on the 28th, I finally got a text back from him.

JOHN: You hurt me so much. I'm not sure I'll ever get over it, but I still care about you. I'm in NC at my sister's now and I may be crazy, but I'd like to talk. I'll call you soon.

He still loved me! We could fix things!

LIAM: Anytime! I'm SO glad to hear from u and I LOVE U SO MUCH. PLEASE CALL ME bc i don't think i can live without u... U wanna call now? Please!

A few minutes.

JOHN: There are people here but I promise I'll call in a day or two when they leave.

I waited, but he didn't call the next day or the day after that, December 30. I texted him that afternoon.

John

I WAS in Syracuse and the movers were at the house, packing up everything. It was all going into storage while I was away. Considering that I'd only be away for six months, it would cost less than buying all new things when I got back.

While I watched a man pack up my grandmother's china, making sure it was being done properly, my phone buzzed.

LIAM: Can you talk right now? I'll call.

The movers were there, and my sister and brother-in-law had come up to help. They were leaving the next morning, and I'd decided to call Liam as soon as they were gone. I needed privacy to talk to him because—against Sue's strong advice—I was going to arrange to meet him and hear what he had to say. Before I left the country, I needed to know if there was any possibility that we could work things out.

JOHN: In the middle of something. I will call soon.
Please be a little patient.
LIAM: OK. On pins and needles.

LIAM

JOHN PROMISED TO CALL, but at ten o'clock that night, he still hadn't. I couldn't stand it any longer, so I dialed his number. Straight to voicemail. *He's blocked me.*

It hit me between the eyes that he'd changed his mind and wasn't going to talk to me at all. I finally got it: I wasn't going to be able to turn things around. I loved John more than I'd ever loved anyone, but it wasn't enough. We were over.

I cried until I retched up bile and my head felt like it might explode. I was still sick with flu, unable to breathe and achy all over, so I took a double dose of flu medicine. Half an hour later, I added two of the tranquilizers I'd gotten from the doctor before I left Syracuse. Maybe if I was lucky, I'd fall asleep. Who knew? Maybe my flu would turn to pneumonia and I'd be dead before morning.

Sometime later, I woke up in a panic, sweated through, with my heart pounding and my mind racing on about John. I had to get back to sleep, so I took another double dose of flu medicine, since the first time had worked. I wondered why I hadn't thought to take some of the tranquilizers before, so I took a few of them as well.

After another hour, I was exhausted and manic instead of sleepy, I found half a bottle of liquid cold medicine in the hall closet and used it to swig down the rest of the tranquilizers. They were obviously useless, but I hoped they'd help eventually. If I didn't sleep, I would go crazy, and I was determined to make sleep happen.

20

Sunday, January 1

John

The Uber driver helped me get my luggage and Theo's under-seat pet carrier for the plane into his car. When I was in the backseat, I looked at the house one more time, and nodded at the driver. I couldn't stop the tears. So much had happened during the short time I lived in that house. The sad demise of a sixteen-year relationship, the ecstasy of finding the love of my life, and the crushing heartbreak of how that turned out.

I would always wonder why Liam changed his mind and didn't take my calls. Maybe it was for the best. If he didn't care enough to talk to me, we wouldn't have been able to work anything out, and it would have been the worst kind of folly to try.

Hopefully, the coming six months would be a turning point and I could begin to get my life in order.

Wainscott, NY

Liam

A loud, incessant beeping sound chopped through my head like an axe. Memories swirled fast and furious. John—beautiful and smiling, wrapped in my arms. Kisses that made me weak in the knees. His dimples, just for me, making me feel like the most important man in the world. The giddiness I felt when he walked into a room.

Darker memories followed. John—deeply hurt, walking out the door. An empty apartment and a gloomy house. Hardly being able to breathe, willing the phone to ring, and finally realizing it wasn't going to. Not getting to say goodbye.

Christ, that beeping was driving me bonkers and everything was dark. Had I died? I tried to hold out hope for heaven, but shouldn't I be able to see in heaven? I noticed my eyes felt gummy and struggled to open them. One eyelid slowly peeled its way up my eyeball, but light blinded me and I quickly closed the eye again. Slowly, I reopened it and couldn't see much of anything.

Shapes soon began to solidify out of the blur, and I could barely make out one of those monitors that traces heartbeats. Before long, I noticed that the beeping sounds matched up with the flashing lights on the monitor, which matched the pounding in my chest. *Fuck me! This sure as hell isn't heaven.* I managed to get my other eye open and looked around. *Piss-fuck-shit!* There was no mistaking a hospital.

"Do you know where you are?" The voice was kind and female.

My throat was sore and I struggled to speak. "In hell."

"You're at Wainscott Memorial Hospital, and you're very lucky to be alive."

Lucky? Who was this bitch anyway, to tell me I was lucky? Memories flooded my mind and misery piled up like snow in a blizzard. My life was totally in the shithouse and anyone who thought I was lucky to be there—well, I'd like to see them go through what I had over the last few weeks. They'd be in a padded cell by now, which was probably exactly where I was headed.

The woman said she was a nurse and that the doctor would be in soon. Mercifully, she then left me alone. A few minutes later, another woman clacked in, her noisy heels drilling right into the middle of my brain. She introduced herself as Dr. Girard, a psychiatrist. *Great. Padded cell, here I come.*

"Mr. Macadam, can you talk yet? They had to pump your stomach and there was a tube down your throat to help you breathe."

"I can talk." I was very uncomfortable and tried to turn on my side, but I was hooked up to too many tubes and couldn't move.

The psychiatrist leaned against the wall, staring at me. Eventually, she said something else. "I'm here to help, not judge. We found a great deal of medication in your system."

I closed my eyes and tried to remember. "Medication?"

"You took a lot of cold and flu medication, along with a heavy dose of a powerful tranquilizer. Did you want to die?"

She was one hard-faced woman, but I wasn't smiling, either. "I didn't consciously think that way at the time, but I guess I did. I didn't mean—"

"We have a bed for you upstairs. As soon as the doctor down here gives the okay, we'll transfer you to the psych ward. You're going to be fine. We'll get this worked out."

Her heels clacked down the hallway, and I began to cry. I'd cried more in the last few weeks than the rest of my life put together. Now I'd somehow managed to make things even worse than they'd already been. I hadn't planned on killing myself, but right then I wished I'd succeeded. I'd been through enough pain. John was gone and maybe dying would have been for the best. He was the greatest thing that ever happened to me, and I managed to break his heart without even doing anything wrong. *Fuck fate. Fuck me.*

I couldn't believe I'd listened to that fool Jessica when she told me to sit idly by while John convinced himself I'd betrayed him, while he got used to me not being around. Who knew—while he got used to fucking another guy? I remembered how he promised to call me but hadn't. He probably only said that in a moment of weakness, or to get back at me. That didn't really seem like John, but people do uncharacteristic things when they're hurt or afraid.

Another doctor came in and approved moving me to the psych ward. It sucked up there, but at least everyone else had problems, too. I had to go to a group where they made me tell my story that brought me there. Everyone looked sympathetic, and a few of them even cried along with me.

Mom and Cait visited later and I learned how Vonnie woke up during the night and heard me through the wall, breathing strangely. She went into my room, noticed I was turning blue, and woke everyone up screaming for help. As a result of all that, she was so traumatized she wouldn't come to see me, and Mom and Cait said I should give her time. Fuck her. Fuck giving anybody time. That was the worst idea the world ever came up with.

I couldn't sleep that night despite the pills they gave me and lay there thinking maybe I should just give up and let John be. Maybe it was a sign, that he hated me so much when I hadn't done anything wrong, when I'd only been true to him. What kind of life could we have had, anyway, if he was just looking for some reason to dump me? He must have been. I was sure he knew I loved him, so how could he believe I'd hurt him like that? Didn't he know me at all?

Him being so ready to believe it, that hurt a lot. Up until then, I hadn't thought about how he'd hurt me because I'd been too focused on how hurt he was. Yet despite all we meant to each other, at least all I'd *thought* we meant to each other, it took him one split second to decide I was a dishonest bastard who had screwed around on him. Well, fuck him! Although, apparently I wouldn't be doing that anymore.

Romance and me, we didn't seem to be cut out for each other. I decided I'd do better by working my ass off at school, getting a job that would keep me busy twenty-four seven, and having anonymous hookups when I needed to. No emotion, no obligation, no hurt. I fell asleep thinking that way.

The next morning, I woke up after a night of awful dreams and wondered if I'd have the guts to carry through with my new decision. It would be for the best, I was sure, because I needed to get John out of my head. I decided to call somebody from Columbia and meet them in New York the next weekend. Maybe I'd find someone to hook up with and start moving on.

I managed to convince a hesitant Dr. Girard to let Mom bring my phone when she came to visit. The phone was dead when she got there, and we talked while it charged. When it powered up—*oh my God!*—I had two voicemails, both from John! He'd tried to call the morning after I overdosed, the thirty-first and then again later that night. It was now the second of January, so it had been two days earlier when he called.

I played the first message and started crying as soon as I heard his voice.

Hi Liam. I promised I'd call and I'm sorry it's taken a few days. I guess you're busy, or maybe you've decided not to talk to me. What happened was terrible for both of us, but I have a little perspective now. I still love you. I need to hear what you have to say, and I need to talk to you, too.... Listen, I'm back in Syracuse and I'm only going to be around another day, so please call me as soon as you can. I really hope you will, but if you've changed your mind, okay, I guess. Well... call me, all right?

He'd started crying halfway through, which was a good sign, and he said he still loved me. Maybe we really could work everything out.

The second message was just after midnight.

Liam—Happy New Year! I didn't hear from you all day, so I guess that means you've decided to let things go. I'm disappointed, but maybe you're right.... Shit.... I'm leaving in the morning, so if you want to call me back before then, I'll be sure the ringer is turned up loud. I love you and I hope you call.

He said 'shit' because he'd started crying again. He wanted to talk to me! I immediately called him back and had an awful shock when a rude sound came on, followed by a recording telling me his number had been disconnected. What had he said? Only going to be around another day? He was leaving in the morning? That would have been yesterday morning, right? Yes, New Year's Day. *Jesus Christ!* Where in hell would he go that he had to disconnect his phone?

My brain was going a mile a minute, and I felt like myself again. What the *fuck* had I been thinking? Give up on John and me? Find somebody to hook up with? Holy shit! I really had lost my mind.

Two days later, Dr. Girard discharged me from the hospital

on the condition that I report to student health the minute I got back to Syracuse. *Right.*

I went home to pack while Mom tried to convince me to stay a few more days. *Right.*

Vonnie finally came out of her room to hug me and say she loved me, and Cait made me promise to visit her in Chicago for MLK weekend. *Right.*

Even Aunt Alex came over to see me. She tried to get me to come stay with her for a few days, saying she knew it must be painful for me to be at home right now. *Right.*

I loved them all but I just wasn't interested. I needed John and had to go find him, and as soon as I got back to Syracuse I drove straight to the house. His car wasn't in the driveway and everything was dark and quiet. There was no answer when I rang the bell.

I walked around back to look in through the windows and had another shock that went to the tips of my toes. The house was completely empty. Not a stick of furniture was left, not a picture on the wall, not even a piece of trash on the floor. I felt like someone shot a huge batch of novocaine right into my skull.

Monday, January 9

John didn't show up for class. He wasn't on the seating chart, and when I went to the registrar to ask about him, they said they couldn't divulge anything about other students. Jess and Michael took me to lunch, but she still wasn't talking, and I caught on quick that Michael was afraid to say anything. I'd lost my patience with both of them. "At least tell me where the fuck he is. Did he transfer to a different section?"

She glanced at Michael and then sighed. "Liam, hon, listen to me. John's gone. He won't be back, so you need to let him go and learn from this. I can tell you he's fine, physically, and he's trying to find a way to move on."

My throat tightened and my eyes stung. "Gone, as in... *gone*? Gone from where?"

Michael shook his head. "Gone, as in gone from here. Gone from law school and gone from Syracuse."

Jess put a hand on my arm and gave me a sad smile. "He loved you so much, Liam, but he was too hurt to stay. I tried to talk him out of leaving, but his mind was made up."

Every time I thought things couldn't get worse, they did. I broke down crying for the millionth time since it all started, causing her to move around to my side of the table and hold me while I blubbered. It didn't matter that we were in public because I couldn't have controlled myself if my life depended on it.

When I finally got it together, Jess eyed me curiously. "Liam, will you answer a question?"

I shrugged, figuring anything I said wouldn't matter. "Yeah."

"Why didn't you answer John's calls, or at least return them? He was really confused."

My heart started pounding. I hadn't told her and Michael about what happened in Wainscott, and I really didn't want to. "I... uh...."

Michael spoke up. "I don't get it either, man. I know you wanted back with him and he'd decided to hear you out, to meet—"

Jess cut him a look and he shut up. She turned back toward me. "He wanted to apologize to you. He'd thought about...."

She was obviously measuring her words carefully, and I'd had enough. "He thought about what, goddammit? Just spit it out."

She huffed. "He wanted to see if you could work things out.

He was going to put off leaving and meet you in person if you still wanted to, but when you didn't answer he took it as a sign." She paused and cocked her head. "Did you decide you didn't want to talk to him? And if you did, why are you so upset now?"

You've got to come clean. If you expect them to tell you anything, you need to be honest with them. I ordered us some dessert and told them everything that had happened. Michael was so concerned he slept in my apartment for the next week, and Jess stuck to me like glue during the day. I finally convinced them that I really hadn't tried to commit suicide, and they gave me a little space, although I could tell they kept a careful watch for a while.

Saturday, January 21

It was already dark outside, and the only light in my living room was from the lamp on my desk, where I was trying to read cases for Monday. I'd just decided to order pizza when the phone rang. Although I usually ignored unknown callers, I'd been answering them since I started looking for John. "Hello?"

Nothing but silence and a little static. It had been storming off and on, and my phone service was weird all day.

"Hello? Anyone there?" More static, then movement but no words. "Hello?"

Someone sighed before the connection ended.

I wondered if it had been John. I was determined to find him and get him back, but despite my excellent cyber-sleuthing skills, I'd so far come up with nothing. I emailed him every day, but it was like I was sending messages into a void. It seemed as if he'd disappeared from the face of the earth, and I realized I was in for a long haul. I would find John again someday, and if I had any luck left, I'd win him back.

PART II

21

CAMBRIDGE, UK

Two Months Later: Friday, March 16

John

He was down on one knee, holding up a ring, his brown eyes bright. "I'm so sorry, John. I never meant to hurt you. I really didn't do it."

"Don't say that. I caught you."

"I didn't cheat on you. I'm guilty of letting you leave without a fight, but I was true to you. I'm sorry the whole thing happened, that you were so hurt."

Thinking about it still caught my heart in a vise. "I'm still hurt. My life is as barren as new-fallen snow. My emotions are a frozen tundra. I have only my work."

He had to clear his throat, and even then, his voice was shaky. "I can't live without you, and I know you love me. Please, marry me and I'll spend the rest of my life making you happy."

I wanted that so badly, but wasn't it too late? I whimpered before I managed to get the words out. "I don't know."

"Why? What do you want from me?"

"I want you, *Liam. I need* you."

He was close to tears, his words full of despair. "I'm right here."

His eyes were powerful, but I tore my gaze away. "You hurt me so much. We can't be together. Why did you have to sleep with—"

"I didn't! Jess told you what he said!"

Liam knew? My chest constricted, the guilt causing me to shudder. "She didn't believe Kyle." I met his eyes again and shook my head. "It's been too long."

He sighed, stood up, and took me in his arms. His warm smell brought back so many memories. I tried to fight him, but my heart wasn't in it. He kissed me, one of his killer kisses. As he hugged me tightly, I savored the feel of his tongue in my mouth and the way his muscular arms held me. My arousal was obvious and his was, too. We ground together and electricity shot to the sky.

I WOKE sweaty and short of breath, with my heart beating a fast tattoo. The dream was so realistic. Liam, on one knee, begging me to marry him. My hesitancy, my guilt; the kiss, the fireworks. I'd had this dream over and over for weeks now.

Reaching for the water by my bed, I felt Theo stir and wondered if I would ever stop dreaming about Liam, if I would ever stop missing him so much. I screwed the cap back on the water bottle and looked at the clock—5:37 a.m. in Cambridge, which was 12:37 a.m. in Syracuse. I might find him still awake if I called.

I had been miserable last Christmas after it all happened. Liam was all I could think about: how much I loved him, what he'd done, and how badly I hurt. I felt I couldn't live through another relationship with a man who screwed around. I loved Liam, but I'd also loved Thorne once.

Despite all that, I eventually decided that I was being unfair. I should have listened to what Liam had to say before calling it quits. Whatever really happened, I still loved him, so I called him twice on New Year's Eve, but he neither answered nor returned my calls. It all played to my worst fears, and I convinced myself it was for the best to cut all ties. I left the country, disconnected my phone, and blocked his email address.

Not long after I got to Cambridge, Jess called and told me about Liam's overdose and how depressed he was. That explained why he hadn't returned my calls, and I felt awful about the pills, but she didn't think it had been a suicide attempt. She said it was the result of flu-induced confusion, and that he seemed to be on the mend.

I decided to call him. I had trouble getting through, but on the third try, his phone rang and he answered. The sound of his voice triggered a thousand memories along with a giant flow of tears, and I froze. He said hello a few times, but when all the hurt flooded back, I took the coward's way out and hung up.

He didn't call back, and I had no idea whether caller ID worked on international calls. After thinking about it, I decided to let sleeping dogs lie. We lived three thousand miles apart, and we both needed to get on with our lives. Some things just weren't meant to be.

Now, months later, on the tail end of the night, I knew all my decisions had been bad. I was wrong not to talk to Liam right after things happened, wrong to hang up on him after I learned about the overdose, and wrong not to contact him in all the time since. *Especially after Jess told you what that asshole Kyle said.*

On that cold March morning in Cambridge, I knew I had to

talk to Liam. I still loved him, and while Jessica wasn't very forthcoming, she said he still loved me. If he and I talked, maybe we could start to put things back together, or at least put them to rest.

Before I could back out, I grabbed my phone and found his name on my favorites list. Even after moving to another country and getting a new phone, I still had his number on my favorites. It rang four times before I heard the familiar voice telling me he wasn't available but would call back if I left my number. Hearing his voice had me in tears, and I hung up so he wouldn't hear me crying on his voicemail. After my choir's spring tour, perhaps I'd send him an email.

Liam

"Ladies and Gentlemen, welcome to London Heathrow Airport, where the local time is 17:04. The outside temperature is six degrees Celsius." I tuned out the rest of the speech, excited to be in London.

Jess never gave me the slightest hint about where John was. Michael almost did once, but he was too afraid of getting her mad at him, and my habitual internet stalking never turned up anything current about John. Every week, I'd sent him an email or an e-card to let him know I hadn't forgotten him, but he never replied.

Here's the thing, though—I'm nothing if not one extremely stubborn bastard, and when you love someone as much as I love John, you don't just wake up one day, throw up your hands, and say, "I'm tired of this, forget it." At last, as a result of my persistence, I had a secret no one else but Mom knew—I'd found him! A week earlier, I'd typed his name into Google and learned that he was a visiting music professor at St. Bartholomew's College in Cambridge, England.

I deliberated about how to handle the information and whether I should do anything that might antagonize him, but fuck that. I was only regurgitating Jess's idiotic advice from the weeks right after the catastrophe, advice I'm still convinced was the nail in the coffin. My idiocy and John's stubbornness had ruined both our lives, and I was worried about antagonizing him? *Bullshit!*

I had no goddamned clue what would happen when I saw John, but I knew one thing for sure, that he was going to listen to me at long last. I would stare into his dreamy eyes and tell him how much I still loved him, that I never cheated on him and never will, and that I wanted him back. If that didn't work, maybe I'd take him hostage and fuck some sense into him. Just kidding, I think. Mostly.

Customs didn't take long, and I took an Uber to King's Cross station. I made it onto the 7:58 train, and the ride to Cambridge was about ninety minutes. My plan was to stay there as long as it took to talk sense into John, or for him to have me arrested for stalking, whichever came first. I didn't have too much money, but if I ran out, I'd call Mom and beg.

John

The dream about Liam had me out of sorts all day. It was so realistic that I could still smell him and taste his tongue on mine hours later. If only I could know for sure what really happened that night in Syracuse. Jess told me about Kyle's recantation right after she ran into him, but she thought it was better to let Liam get on with his life. I wasn't so sure—with every passing day, I felt less certain that Liam would have cheated on me, and I became increasingly convinced that I needed to talk to him.

I taught my class in Renaissance Music and led a choir rehearsal. We were leaving for the Czech Republic the next day on our tour, and the choir was ready. It was an excellent ensemble that included both male and female students, all of university age. Some of the colleges in town used only little boys as sopranos and college men for all the lower voices, and using adult women allowed the St. Bart's choir to achieve a rich tone that was a little unusual in Cambridge.

After I finished teaching for the day, I did some last-minute shopping. Ten days of singing in the Czech Republic and Germany would be demanding, and I wouldn't have any time to shop for personal things. On the way home, I almost forgot to stop by the cleaner's shop to pick up my good suit. The choir wore robes for singing, but I needed to be properly dressed before and after concerts.

At home, Theo and I went out for an abbreviated version of our evening walk. The bus would leave for the airport at eight o'clock the next morning, and I still had things to do. After a quick dinner, I finished packing, and then I walked Theo over to our next-door neighbor's. She was a young chemistry professor who was going to take care of him while I was gone. We went over his routine and I made sure she had my correct contact information.

It was hard saying goodbye to my baby, and I was tempted to take him back home for the night, but the next morning would be hectic. Ever since that awful scene at Liam's apartment, Theo got very nervous when things weren't calm, and I didn't want to put him through any unnecessary chaos.

Later, I tried to watch television but couldn't concentrate because Liam was still on my mind. I really needed to talk to him, and before I knew it, I'd dialed his number again. Like that morning, the phone rang four times before going to voicemail, and I hung up without leaving a message. At least I got to hear his voice again, but I wondered if his not answering was a sign that I should leave him alone. Maybe he'd found someone else.

Liam

The train was almost to Cambridge when my phone rang, unknown caller. I didn't answer because no one except Mom knew where I was, and the last thing I needed was to talk to somebody from school who wanted to gab about nothing.

After London's magnificent King's Cross, the Cambridge station was unimpressive. I found a cab outside and the ride to my hotel took less than ten minutes. As we drove, I looked around, but it was hard to tell much in the dark. I could see the city was old, and some of the lighted buildings I glimpsed were striking, but it only made so much of an impression. I was a man on a mission, and I'd have time to look around if things went well the next day. Hopefully, I'd even have a tour guide.

The hotel was old, but clean and cheap, and had a certain charm. Once I was in my room, I couldn't relax due to continually wondering what John was doing and where he lived. For all I knew, I was two minutes from his front door, but there was no way to find out. Deciding a walk might calm me down, I went outside and started along the street. I could see my breath and pulled my coat tight.

Near the end of the block, I came to a pub that was still open, though not for long. The beer was delicious, and two pints brought my blood pressure back down into normal range. Just as well that the place wasn't open late because I sure didn't need to deal with a hangover the next morning. I didn't want John thinking I'd turned into a drunk.

John

The alarm went off at 5:30 a.m., and I poked at the snooze button with murderous intent. I thought of how much Liam hated alarms and snickered at the memory. Turning over, I flapped around with one hand looking for Theo's warm body before I remembered he was next door.

I hurried through my morning routine and took the time to make a real breakfast, although I regretted the calories. One of the noteworthy side-effects of being lovesick was having an appetite the size of a small country, and only a religious dedication to working out had kept me from putting on fifty pounds since I left America.

Carefully, I checked my suitcase, garment bag, and toiletries to be sure I wasn't forgetting anything. Satisfied that I hadn't, I took one last glance around and ventured out into the cold fog.

I arrived at the chapel about seven fifteen and immediately wished I'd gotten there earlier. Dominic, the tour manager, had a hundred last-minute questions, and my phone rang every other minute—numerous students, unavoidably detained, who would be there as soon as possible. *Unavoidably detained* meaning still being in bed, apparently, since a couple of them didn't even bother to get the gravel out of their throats before they called.

The bus driver—or, as he corrected me, coach captain—had trouble getting one of the luggage compartments open, and I had to charm him into working on it after he tried to convince me that we needed to leave some things behind. No sooner was that problem solved than the dean of the chapel showed up, wanting to say a prayer before we left, which was fine. He was also in a loquacious mood, which was not fine. Too much was going on for me to stop, so I tried to avoid him without being rude.

Eventually, Dominic called the roll to be certain everyone was aboard the bus—or coach. At 8:10, the dean came on and said an exceedingly long prayer, followed by a sentimental talk that no one was in the mood to hear. I began to wonder if we would ever get going when he abruptly said goodbye and left the bus. The driver immediately closed the door and the engine came to life.

Liam

I WOKE JUST BEFORE seven o'clock, stoked for the day. My plan was to get over to St. Bartholomew's by eight thirty. I had no idea when John might come in, but I was betting that, like all professors everywhere, he had a schedule hanging by his door with class times and office hours listed. That would at least give me an idea of when to find him. Google research told me that his office was in the chapel, which I figured should be easy to find.

After one cold motherfucker of a shower—apparently the plumbing was as old as the building—I ate breakfast at a small restaurant next door to the hotel. The waitress recommended something called a full English, which had a little of everything. I polished off every bite, even the beans. They seemed odd as part of breakfast but were abso-*fuckin*-lutely delicious. Outside, I pulled up a map of Cambridge on my phone so GPS could lead me to John. Since it was eight o'clock, I'd probably get over there a little earlier than I'd planned. All the better.

Cambridge was beautiful in the early morning light, and the mist gave things an impressionistic aura. The colleges were pretty much lined up in rows on either side of the street, and each one I passed looked older than the last. My overall impression was of walking through a place that was a cross between Windsor Castle and Westminster Abbey.

I finally saw the red and blue signs for St. Bartholomew's and took a sharp right down another murky street. The college was spread out behind a tall wrought iron fence on the right. Seeing John's school almost made me cry—in relief, because I'd found it, and in awe, because it was the most beautiful one yet. The buildings were dark stone, and the genuine Gothic architecture was magnificent.

Up ahead was a massive building with towers, which I figured must be the chapel. A large blue and white bus was parked out front, facing toward me, with a *Heathrow* destination sign in the front window. An old priest in an open overcoat stood on the sidewalk, waving at the people on the bus. The engine started just as I got there.

My eyes followed the direction of the priest's waves, and my heart stopped. Just turning away from a front window—there was John! I yelled his name, but he didn't have a chance of hearing because the engine was so loud as the bus pulled away. I took off after it like a rocket, waving my arms and screaming, but it picked up speed and pulled so far ahead I'd never be able to catch up.

I couldn't believe I'd made it all that way only to watch John leave for who-knew-where without even knowing I was there. I had no clue how long he'd be gone, but I guessed it could be a while if he was going to the airport. I ran down like a toy with dying batteries, and finally stumbled and fell, overcome by tears of frustration.

A gentle hand touched my shoulder. "What is wrong, my son?"

The old priest was there, looking concerned, and I wiped my eyes as I stood up. "Father, I've come so far, only to watch him drive away."

"Who? Dr. Lawrence? I heard you calling for John." He handed me a handkerchief. "The choir and Dr. Lawrence are on their way to Prague."

My heart plummeted. "Prague? The Czech Republic?"

"Yes. They just left for their spring concert tour."

I'd finished wiping my face and wasn't sure what to do with the handkerchief. Awkwardly, I gave it back to him and he stuffed it into his coat pocket.

"Prague? When will they be back?"

"In ten days."

Piss-fuck-shit! I had to be back in Syracuse then, but.... The world began vibrating around me as my mind processed the situation, and I considered another possibility. A few heartbeats later, I looked into kind gray eyes. "Their tour? I can't miss it, Father. Please help me find them."

"It's Dean Mann, not father. I'm Martin Mann, dean of the chapel. And you, my new young American friend, are over-excited." He put a hand on my elbow and steered me toward the chapel. "Come inside and let's talk. I expect you have quite the story to tell."

Soon I sat in a large, messy office with stone walls and a threadbare rug on the floor, drinking a mug of steaming tea and telling my story to a man I'd met only fifteen minutes earlier.

He sat in a wingback chair facing mine, next to what he called an electric fire, and listened intently. When I'd finished telling him what happened, he leaned forward and smiled. "Yours is the most moving story I've heard in a while, Liam. I love romance, and what you tell me calls to mind a time when I had to convince a young woman to forgive me. Alas, I must be honest and confess that, unlike yours, my transgression was real. Nonetheless, I followed my heart and convinced her to take a chance on me, and she eventually became my wife."

Sweating heavily, I was rocking my knee up and down so fast it was starting to hurt. I felt like I might jump out of my skin, and I didn't have time to listen to his tales if I was going to catch John. Still, he'd been patient with my story, and I couldn't be rude to him. "I need to find him, Dean Mann. I love him with all my heart."

He set his mug down on the table beside his chair, his eyes sparkling. "For what it's worth, knowing what I know now, I believe he still loves you. There's been a great sadness about Dr. Lawrence since he arrived here, and if there's one thing an old man can recognize in a young man, it is a lovesick heart." His smile was as electric as the fire. "Hope is alive, Liam."

I'd set my mug on a side table and was wringing my hands so hard I got afraid I'd break something, so I cut to the chase. "Will you help me?"

Without a word, he got up, walked around behind his desk, rummaged in a drawer, and left the room carrying some papers. I finished my tea and wondered what was happening. Three minutes later, I had a copy of the complete tour itinerary, including every hotel where they would stay, and telephone numbers to boot, including John's.

"Thank you so much." I hugged the itinerary like gold. "You won't let him know I'm coming?"

"You have my word." His eyes sparkled again, and I thought he was probably a handful when he was young. "Your candor has convinced me of your honorable intent, and I agree that a surprise is probably best." He paused and held up a finger. "One favor, though?"

I was so eager to get out of there that I had to pinch my

thigh to keep from groaning, but I was determined to be polite if it killed me, which I was beginning to think it might. "Yes?"

"Let me know how it goes, no matter what? I'm quite certain I'll hear of it from Dr. Lawrence, but I want to hear it from your perspective as well." He flashed a roguish smile. "An old man has to take his satisfaction where he can."

"I promise I will. Listen, sir, I have to go now, but I'll never forget you or your kindness."

"Godspeed, my son. Best of luck."

Back out on the sidewalk, I broke into a hard run. If I had to chase John across the whole goddamned European continent, that's exactly what I'd do. I was sick of the miserable desert my life had become, and I'd die before I gave up.

John

Loud voices erupted in the back of the bus. "Stop! Someone is chasing us!"

"Someone is running after us!"

"We need to stop!"

The coach captain glanced questioningly over his shoulder, and I had to make a decision.

Dominic looked at me and pointed at his watch. "No time."

The captain glanced around again, and I shook my head. "Keep going. Everyone is here, and we'll just have to live without anything we forgot."

The coach picked up speed and soon we were leaving Cambridge, getting on the M25. "The fog's clearing," the captain said, "so we should make good time."

I tried to read, but it was impossible on a bus full of over-energized college students. Instead, I fell into a conversation with Dominic, who sat next to me. He was a thirty-something-year-old man with the most beautiful brown eyes I'd seen since Liam Macadam's. Soon, he was shamelessly flirting with me, and I found myself, for the first time since leaving Liam's apartment that bleak December day, looking at another man with something akin to interest.

22

Liam

I ran all the way back to my hotel and checked out as quickly as possible. After making sure my passport was in my pocket, I asked the doorman to get me a taxi to Heathrow. He said an express bus would be much less expensive and about as fast, and that the one sitting in front of the hotel was leaving in ten minutes. I bought my ticket and climbed aboard.

A quick inventory told me that I had $203.00 in my wallet, along with £24.00. I used my phone to check my bank account and learned I had another $271.00 in my checking account and $429.00 left on my credit card. I'd figured that would be enough for England if I was careful, since I was kind of counting on John taking me in, even if he made me sleep in the laundry room or something.

With the change of plans, though, I was in trouble. The money I had wasn't nearly enough for more plane tickets and hotels, so I called Mom and filled her in. She knew what was at stake for me. With no hesitation, she gave me permission to use the emergency credit card she'd given me, and said she'd go to the bank that day and deposit $1,000.00 into my checking account that I could access from an ATM.

My head sagged back in relief. "You're the greatest. I'll pay you back, I promise."

"Just get your life back on track, son. That's all the repayment I need. Would it be okay if I send a family bulletin to Cait and Vonnie? They love you and—"

"No problem. I need all the support I can get."

"Call me if you need anything else. Be safe and get John back. Chase him as long as you need to."

My heart picked up speed at the thought. "I'll sure give it everything I've got. One thing, though. Think you could send bail money if I get arrested for stalking?"

"I'm your mother, remember? I'll send bail money *and* a lawyer."

We shared a laugh before I hung up. Two hours and fifteen minutes later—*goddamned traffic!*—I got off the bus at the British International terminal at Heathrow. From Dean Mann's schedule, I knew the choir was leaving at any moment, so I ran to the ticket counter. The clerk said she could get me on a flight to Prague ninety minutes later. I handed over Mom's credit card and traded my luggage for a ticket.

THE CAB RIDE into Prague didn't take long, and crossing the Moldau River had me breathless. When I was in orchestra, in college, we played a piece called *Die Moldau*. The music rushed back into my head, a perfect accompaniment to the real-life dazzling blue water that made me think of John's eyes.

Downtown Prague was just ahead, and I felt like we were driving into a sea of buildings with red roofs.

I half expected to find John waiting for me in the hotel lobby. He hadn't seen me in Cambridge, but I was a little afraid that Dean Mann might have had second thoughts and let John know I was coming. I'd just have to live with that risk. It wasn't like John could cancel the tour and hop on a plane to get away from me again. *Could he?*

The daily rate was shocking, but there was a room available and I once again handed over Mom's emergency credit card. I said I'd stay for three nights, the same number I knew John would be there. When I asked whether the St. Bartholomew's choir from England had arrived, the clerk told me they'd finished checking in a little while before.

My room wasn't large, but like the rest of the hotel, it was modern and posh. I figured those Cambridge colleges must have a lot of money to put their students up in such first-class digs. I sat on the throne while I considered my next move. After such a hectic day, I took my time and enjoyed the peace and quiet. Finally deciding that I shouldn't try to find John's room and confront him there, I washed my hands, found the tour itinerary, and lay down on the bed.

The schedule listed this as a free night when the choir members could do whatever they wanted. Their first concert was the following evening in a place called the Klementinum Mirror Chapel. They had a rehearsal there in the afternoon, followed by a group dinner at a nearby restaurant.

I figured the concert might be the best place to approach John because he couldn't just ignore me or make a scene. *Shit!* I was already way too antsy and really didn't want to wait another twenty-four hours. What I wanted was to go find him immediately, but my gut told me that even if I did find out where his room was, it would be a mistake to knock on the door. I wanted him open and listening to me, not feeling cornered.

The hotel had left some information about Prague on the dresser, and one of the brochures boasted that Prague had a fine nightlife. I decided to find a place to eat and then walk around the city, so I got into the shower to wash off my travel stink.

John

It had been quite a day, and the early start and travel had tired me out. I was glad Dominic had the foresight not to schedule a concert on the first night, and as I lay on the bed in my room, I decided to stay in and order room service. I needed to be fresh for our first concert the next day, and there would be plenty of time to see Prague.

Dominic had flirted throughout our flight and the spirit was contagious, although I can neither confirm nor deny that I may have joined in. He was certainly attractive enough, with his deep brown eyes and dark hair. He told me stories about crazy things that had happened on tours he led, and before I knew it, I was laughing like a man with no worries. Then I embarrassed myself.

"She actually fainted," he said, "bringing the concert to a complete halt amidst the screams of all the choir and a fair number of the audience. We later found out she was a strict fundamentalist and was so spooked by the icons in the cathedral that she thought demons were coming to take her away."

"Oh my God, Liam, that is absolutely hilarious!" *Wait, what the hell did I just say?*

"John, are you okay?"

Dominic leaned in, his eyebrows furrowed, and I collected my wits. "I'm fine. Sorry."

"For?"

"I called you by the wrong name. I apologize."

"You did? I didn't even notice." He put a hand on my arm. "You stopped talking and went pale."

I pulled my arm away. "Sorry, I'm tired."

He nodded. "We're about to land, so you can take it easy on the coach into town and have a nap when we get to the hotel."

On the bus, I thought about what had happened. How silly I was—it should have been no surprise that I found Dominic attractive. He looked a lot like Liam, and his voice was similar. He even had the same slightly off-key sense of humor. Leading Dominic on would not be an honorable thing to do. If I ever did get seriously interested in another man, it couldn't be because he reminded me of the guy who shattered my heart but still managed to hold onto it.

The hotel bed was very comfortable and I must have drifted off, because while figments of Liam and I were walking Theo, a shrill bell rang in my ear. I grabbed for the phone.

"You've never been to Prague before, right?" It was Dominic.

I put together that I was in a hotel, and I'd had another Liam dream. "No, I haven't."

"Then it's my duty, Dr. Lawrence, to take you to dinner and educate you about the city. Thirty minutes in the lobby?"

I really didn't want to mislead him, but we had to work together for the next week. He was only asking for dinner, after all, not a romp in the hay.

"Sure, but it's Dutch treat."

"We can argue about that when the time comes. See you downstairs. Be sure to bring a warm coat."

Thirty minutes later, showered and awake, I took the elevator to the lobby. As I stepped out, I stopped dead in my tracks, my heart taking off like a horse at the races. *There, going out the front door!* That man looked like... well, no, it couldn't be. He was wearing a knit cap, so I couldn't see his hair, but he was the right height and build, and the walk was unmistakable. *It's Liam!*

I started walking fast. *Why is he here?* I may have wanted to talk to Liam, but I wasn't about to be hunted. Halfway to the door, someone grabbed my arm and made me jump.

"Are you all right? You look as if you've seen a ghost."

I stopped and shook my head before I met Dominic's eyes. "I think I might have, actually. I thought I saw someone I knew going out the door, but it's impossible. It was my imagination."

Of course I thought I saw Liam. I'd been constantly thinking about him for days, and I'd just figured out how much Dominic resembled him. I'd thought I saw Liam before, especially right after the breakup.

"I guess I'm still ditzy from my nap," I said. "It actually looked a lot like you walking out the front door."

"Without you?" He winked at me. "Not a chance."

Liam

I FOUND a fun place for dinner near the hotel. It was casual, kind of like a split between a beer hall and a restaurant, and I had a few great beers with some excellent sausages and sauerkraut. The waiter talked me into having a slice of something called medovník for dessert. He said it meant honey cake, which made me imagine something dry and crumbly, but it was moist, rich, and abso-*fuckin*-lutely delicious. When I finished it, I had another beer to celebrate getting to Prague.

While I enjoyed my drink, people started singing. It wasn't beer hall music, though; it was more like the kind of singing John had put in my ears. A group of college-age kids sang something so beautiful I teared up, and the crowd roared their approval. A couple minutes later, I heard some of the kids talking about how they had to tell Dr. Lawrence about it, that he'd get a real kick out of their trading Byrd for beer.

My stomach fluttered. Maybe this trip would actually pay off, and John and I could get back together. Even if it didn't happen—even if I did have to drag my sorry tail back to Syracuse between my legs—at least I would have done something to try to get my life going again. That would count for a lot, either way.

John

"What's his name, John?"

Dominic was chewing slowly, watching me like a hawk.

"Excuse me, what's whose name?"

He swallowed and took a sip of his wine before gesturing with his fork. "The man who broke your heart."

I ate some asparagus to stall for time. "What do you mean?" I asked.

Dominic turned slightly in his chair but kept his focus on my face. "I've known a lot of men in my day, John. Had my heart broken too many times. There's only one thing that could make such a beautiful, brilliant man as you so melancholy."

I took a deep breath and sighed. "Liam."

He paused, a forkful of schnitzel halfway to his mouth. "What?"

"Liam. His name was Liam." I finished my wine and picked up the bottle to pour more. "It wasn't all his doing, Dominic. I—"

"That's the name you called me earlier."

I smiled again, though not as sadly. "You said you didn't notice."

"I was being polite. Tonight, I've decided to be honest."

"Honest about what?" I speared my last piece of duck.

"You." He put down his knife and fork, and a warm smile spread across his face. "I was enchanted after our first lunch in London in January, when we began planning the tour. My fascination has grown over the last few months. I think you're a delightfully attractive man, and I've had just enough wine to ask if there's any chance you feel similarly about me."

I took another sip of wine. "I think you're a witty, intelligent man, Dominic, and I really do have fun when we're together."

"But?" He chewed another bite of his schnitzel.

"But," I continued, "I still have feelings for Liam. It hasn't been long, and things ended badly. It's actually why I came to Cambridge. A friend was going on sabbatical, so I accepted an offer to fill his job there temporarily. Cambridge is a long way from New York and I needed the distance."

"Is there a future there?"

"In Cambridge?" I asked.

"In your feelings."

I laughed. "Obviously not in my feelings, silly. But I don't think I'm ready to see someone else. I don't know if I could be fair, to be honest, if I could give what was fair."

The waiter came to take our dessert orders, and we decided to split a piece of medovník. Dominic wagged his eyebrows at me when the waiter had gone. "What if I said I'm a gambling man, and I'm willing to take my chances? I think you just might be worth it."

Even his grin reminded me of Liam. My heart flipped and images of Liam, smiling and happy, filled my mind. Then I thought of him and another man, of his choosing to be with someone else—if he really did. *Jesus!* I had to do something to get out of my rut. "I think I would say I'm a long way from being able to make any promises, but I do think you're awfully cute."

"Mm-hmm," he said, chuckling. "And witty, remember?"

"And witty," I agreed, smiling.

He nodded. "So, what's the verdict?"

Go for it. "If you know I'm still in love with someone else and yet you're willing to try, maybe we could see what happens. But I repeat, no promises, and we would have to go slowly. *Very* slowly. Nothing but dating for a while, and possibly never anything more."

"Agreed. As I said, you're worth a gamble."

I grimaced, unsure that he'd understood. "When I say nothing but dating—"

"John, I've been there. I promise, I won't push for anything physical until you tell me you're ready." He smiled as he held up his glass of wine for a toast.

When we'd finished dessert, he asked if I'd rather take a walk or go back to the hotel.

"Back to the hotel, I think. We have a big day tomorrow."

We got into our winter gear and headed out into the weather. The wind snapped right through my coat, and I hoped the walk back to the hotel would go quickly.

Liam

I NEEDED to take a walk to get my digestion going. All that food and beer sloshing round in my belly needed to recognize each other, or it could turn into an unpleasant night. My breath condensed and evaporated into the frigid air, but this part of the city was beautiful, bathed in golden light reflecting off the icy cobblestone streets. I walked slowly, gazing into store windows and checking out cafes and bars. I thought about those singers in the restaurant, which made me think about the next day and confronting John.

From the tour itinerary, I knew the choir was going sightseeing in the morning to the Zizkov Television Tower, which was apparently a big deal. I'd looked it up and found it was in the hills near Prague and had an observation deck with spectacular views. I might like to go myself, but I didn't want to risk running into John while he was being a tourist. That would really seem like I was stalking him—which I wasn't, of course.

I decided to spend the morning shopping for a suit to wear to the concert. Before leaving the hotel, I'd gone online and bought a ticket. I had to think things through a little more, but my plan was to approach John afterward. I knew seeing me would be a shock and didn't want to ruin his concentration, so beforehand seemed unwise. Besides, I hoped to convince him to go someplace to talk, and approaching him after the concert would make that a lot more natural.

Surprisingly few people were out, and as I looked around, I stumbled over a loose cobblestone. Regaining my bearings, I looked ahead. About a block away, the sidewalk I was on merged with another one coming from a different direction. I heard a familiar voice and saw two men walking down the other sidewalk toward the spot where it joined with mine.

There it was again, that voice—it was John! I recognized him now, the one in the dark coat. I fought the temptation to call his name and break into a run. Instead, I watched him walk and luxuriated in the sound of his voice. It was a treat, a reward to keep me focused on my goal. I wondered who he was with, but just as I noticed that the other guy was walking awfully close to John, he reached over and took John's hand. John looked at him and shook his head.

Oh, *fuck* no! Absolutely, *no fucking way*! I'd considered the possibility that John might have another boyfriend, and I planned to stay calm if that was the case. Regardless of his situation, he needed to hear what really happened back in Syracuse. Besides, our love had been real, and real love doesn't just disappear. I would do anything I had to do, whatever it took, to get him back. Period.

But now, actually seeing him with someone else, my plan to stay cool flew out the window. I snapped and started running. Unable to control myself, I quickly crossed the block between us, and both men turned toward the sound of my approaching footsteps.

"John, it's really you!" Lame, I know, but I was operating solely on adrenaline.

His face blanched as he took a couple steps backward. He glanced away, then back at me, and acceptance gradually dawned. "Liam? What are you doing here?"

My heart pounded like a bass drum and I was bouncing at the knees. "I'm, um.... I'm.... *John*, how the hell are you? It's *so* good to see you."

He looked me up and down as if he couldn't believe I was really standing in front of him. "Why are you here? Did Jess say something?" His eyes darted around, and he swayed slightly. "Were you following me?"

"No, I—"

He shook his head hard. "I can't, I'm sorry. I'm too tired." He looked at the douche. "Come on, Dominic, we have to go."

John turned on his heels and started walking, really fast, but the shitbucket spent another few seconds staring at me before he turned away. By then, he was behind. He started after John, who had broken into a jog, while I tried to decide what to do.

Oh, hell no—he is not getting away from me again! I

stupidly let him walk away once before and it cost me our relationship. No way in fucking hell would I make the same mistake twice. I took off after them. "John, no! Stop!" I yelled.

His leather shoe soles slapped hard against the sidewalk as he picked up speed, and I was glad I'd worn casual shoes. "John, *please* stop." I started running.

He looked back and jogged faster, but I soon caught up and grabbed his arm, aware but not caring that I was committing battery. He glared at me and hissed, "Let me go!"

"Oh, *fuck* no! Not this time." Tears stung my eyes. "You stand there like a man and talk to me, John Lawrence."

The anger drained from his face. Was it longing that replaced it? He begged me, in a desperate whisper, "Liam, please. *Please* let me go." His eyes were too bright in the golden light, and I realized he was about to cry. "I can't do this."

Holding onto his arm, I shook my head.

He gave a groan of frustration. "I don't think I can do this."

I squeezed his arm. "Yes, you can, John. We *have* to."

"It almost killed me before. I can't do this here." He seemed close to hyperventilating.

I hated making him feel afraid, but when I thought about the hell of the last few months and how much I loved him, I shook my head furiously. "I'm sorry, but I can't let you go." My voice broke. "It almost killed me, too. I can't move on, my life won't start up again. At least talk to me, and if you still want me to leave, maybe I can finally let go."

He stood very still and didn't look away. After a moment, he closed his eyes and blew out a heavy breath. "All right." He looked at me again and we both swiped at the tears on our cheeks.

John's friend, fucking *Dominic* I guess, had caught up to us by then and stood there looking worried. I guess, in his eyes, John had either lost his mind or was being kidnapped. Relieved that John had said he'd talk to me, I stood my ground and harpooned Dominic with a death stare. After a few seconds, he averted his eyes. Apparently, my alpha-male instincts were working just fine.

John looked at him. "Dominic, this is Liam."

Dominic seemed flabbergasted. *Does he know who I am?* He nodded at me. "Liam."

John turned back toward me and actually smiled. "I noticed a coffeeshop back near the restaurant where we ate. Want to go there for a few minutes?"

I smiled back. "I do."

We started walking.

"Wait!" It was Dominic the Dickweed.

John turned around to face him. "I'm sorry, Dominic. Liam and I have to talk."

Dominic seemed dazed. "John, are you sure?"

I *hated* this shitnoodle of a guy. He probably sat down to pee, and, of course, he had one of those royal-family accents.

"I'll be fine," John told him. "Go back to the hotel."

"John, please," he said. This douchenozzle just wouldn't give up. "What's going on here? Is this the Liam you told me about? I didn't realize he was in Prague."

Aha! So he *did* know about me.

John nodded. "It's him, and I didn't know he was here, either."

"And you're *sure* you want to go with him?"

"I said I'm going, Dominic."

Take that, dickweasel!

"Dominic, will you *please* go back to the hotel? I'll see you on the bus in the morning." John had a hard edge to his voice I'd only heard once or twice, and I never wanted it aimed at me again.

FUCKIN-A!!! They weren't sharing a room. Maybe I was in time.

The shitwad nodded, not looking at all pleased. When John didn't move or speak again, the miserable rat finally turned and slunk away. John indicated that we should walk in the other direction. "Sorry about that," he said.

23

Liam

Welcome heat enveloped us when we opened the door to the coffeeshop, which was right out of the Old World. A dark-beamed ceiling presided over a room full of heavy, carved, dark wood furniture, and rough-hewn beige walls badly needed a coat of paint. Everything was well-worn, and the atmosphere was undeniably comfortable.

The shop wasn't crowded, and a waitress took our drink orders after she showed us to a corner table.

John, pale and a little sweaty, took the lead. "I'm really surprised to see you here. Are you visiting Prague? Were you following me? How did you know I was here?" The questions came out shotgun-style.

I had to be honest if there was any chance for us to find a way back. "Bear with me, and I'll tell you the story. Deal?"

He nodded, and his expression was guarded, but not unfriendly. "I'm here aren't I? I'm listening."

"I wasn't following you tonight, but I did follow you to Prague from Cambridge."

He narrowed his eyes. "Did Jess tell you I'm working there?"

"No, her mouth has a fucking seal as strong as Fort Knox. I know the two of you have kept up, but she's never breathed a word about where you were."

"Well, how did you know?" He was still squinting at me.

Deep breath, Liam. You have nothing to be ashamed of. "I told you back on the street that I haven't been able to let you go. I've looked for you on the internet. About a week ago, I finally found you and knew I had to go to Cambridge."

He frowned, and I choked up. "I'm broken John. I have been since you left, and I had to try to get you to listen to me. With all we had, if we've got to be apart, you need to know what really happened in Syracuse. To make your decisions based on the truth, not a bunch of lies." He glanced away, and I angled my head to maintain eye contact. "You said you wanted to talk in December, on those phone messages, remember? I didn't get them till days later, though. I was in the hospital."

His guarded expression faltered. "I know, and I'm so sorry about everything that happened. I should have listened to you back then, Liam, but I'm here now. Say what you need to say."

I nodded, fighting a lump in my throat and wishing my eyes would stop burning. "I could hardly move for a while. I've missed you so much, John. I couldn't let go, but I didn't have you, so there was nothing to hold onto. It's like we're still together except that...." *Shit, tears.* "Except that we're not."

I had to take a couple deep breaths before I could go on. "When you left, you took a big chunk of me with you. I'm not whole anymore." I swallowed hard, trying to get rid of the boulder in my throat. "But I was really happy for you when I saw you were at Cambridge. What a goddamned impressive gig. Congrats!" I was grinning now, so proud of my boyfriend. Or my.... *Damn*, so much for the grin.

"Thank you," he said, and smiled briefly before returning to neutral. "So, you went to Cambridge? Why didn't you just come to see me there?"

"I couldn't," I said. "I mean, not like you probably think.... Oh shit, I gotta get my breath...."

He nodded, and I took a few seconds to breathe. My ears buzzed and I could hear my pulse in them. The waitress appeared with our coffee, and we sipped our drinks for a moment before John raised his eyebrows.

I set my coffee on the table. "I couldn't come to see you because I only got to town late the night before you left. I had no idea where you lived or how to get in touch with you. I didn't know you were going on a tour, and I was walking up to the chapel early the next morning—well, I guess it was *this* morning." My heart was thudding so hard it was difficult to talk, and my fingers tingled like they were asleep. *"Jesus!"*

John smiled encouragingly. "Take it easy, Liam. We've got time."

"I got to the chapel literally just as the bus drove away. I saw you, but you didn't see me. I tried to run after the bus."

Something clicked. John's face changed. "Oh God." He leaned his head against his hand and blew out a hard sigh. "The kids were saying someone was chasing us, but we were running late and I told the driver not to stop. I'm sorry."

"I was at the end of my rope, but Dean Mann was there."

John looked up and smiled. "Ah, Dean Mann. Getting a little tottery, but a very nice person."

I nodded. "He's awesome. He took me in for tea and listened to my story. I guess one time he did wrong by his wife, and he got really nostalgic about that. He took pity on me and gave me your tour schedule." I was feeling a little better. My ears had stopped buzzing and my fingers weren't tingling as much. "I followed you to Heathrow. I was too late but got on another plane. I was gonna go to your concert tomorrow night and try to see you there."

He took a sip of his coffee. "Surely you can understand why I'm unnerved to find you here, following me. Running up to us on the street like that was scary, Liam. We didn't know who it was."

"I'm sorry I made you freak, but I'm desperate. You've gotta remember me well enough to know I'm not crazy or a criminal or anything. I just want to talk to you."

He relaxed his eyebrows and showed me a small smile. "I remember everything about you, in amazing detail. I've been thinking about you a lot lately. In fact, I tried to call you a couple of times over the last few days."

"You kidding me?" I remembered the phone ringing on the train.

John's smile broadened, and those dimples I'd always loved so much creased his cheeks. "Not at all. It's been awful for me too since what happened, but I felt that I had to protect myself. It was so soon after Thorne, and I just couldn't deal with it." He lost his smile and took a breath. "Let's get down to brass tacks."

A surge of fear arced up my spine.

"There's really only one question I have for you," he said.

Fuck!— I have one shot? I took a shallow breath and nodded. "Okay. What is it?"

"What the hell happened back in Syracuse?" His voice caught. "What did you do and why?" He turned his head to the side, and his eyes were hard. "Tell me the truth right now, or I'll never speak to you again. I'll get a restraining order against you."

It was easy to be a hundred percent honest because I had

nothing to hide, and I stared back at him without blinking. "I didn't cheat on you, John. Not ever. Not that day, not once in the whole time we were together. And not one time since."

He considered what I said for a few seconds before arching an eyebrow. "Fine. Start at the beginning and tell me what happened."

I wrung my hands and rocked my knee up and down. This time it was me who was close to hyperventilating, so I held up my hands and took a moment to collect myself.

"Try to calm down. I'm not going anywhere until I hear your story."

I nodded and looked into his eyes. "All right, here goes. You were gone to DC. The guy you saw, Kyle, he used to be my roommate at Columbia. Before that he was my so-called boyfriend for a few weeks during freshman year. We were awful together. Nothing remotely sexual ever happened after those few weeks five years ago. Anyway, he called on the Saturday night you were gone and said his flight to Canada was diverted to Syracuse for the night. Remember, I told you in a text that I had some things to tell you?"

John looked uncertain.

"Well, anyway, I believed Kyle then, about the plane I mean. In retrospect, who knows? He always was a goddamned liar, and I shouldn't have let my guard down. I picked him up at the airport and we had dinner and drinks. He got way too drunk, and when we got home, he made a pass at me. I turned him down flat, *in no uncertain terms*, and went to bed." I punctuated "no uncertain terms" by thumping on the table in rhythm to the words.

John had been staring into his coffee, but he looked at me again. "Why was he in your apartment at all?"

I nodded. "When he called, he asked if he could spend the

night. That's what I meant about letting my guard down. I should've just said there was no room."

"Where did he sleep?"

"On the sofa." I splayed my hands on the table and raised my eyebrows. "Think about it *really hard*. You might remember there was a blanket and pillow on the sofa. I folded the blanket after you left, so I know it was still there when you came in."

One of John's eyes twitched and I thought maybe there was a flash of recognition.

"He knew all about you, John, I swear. He knew what we meant to each other, and that we were exclusive. He knew we were moving in together. It was the first thing I told him, and I talked about you all night. I loved you so much and was so goddamned proud to be with you. I never even considered doing anything with him. Zero interest. I had you and couldn't wait for you to get back home." John was studying every fucking twitch of my muscles, and I took a breath and ventured on. "You said you'd call me when you got back to the hotel that night and I fell asleep waiting. I woke up a couple hours later and got your message, but you were asleep by then. *Remember*? I sent a text."

He nodded. "I remember."

"The next morning, I guess you were talking to Susan when I tried to call you back, but I didn't know that. I didn't know you got on an earlier plane. In fact, I was confused about how you called me from the plane you were supposed to be on with your cell phone."

He sipped at his coffee and kept his gaze steady.

"Back to the night before. Kyle woke me up once in the middle of the night and made another pass. I got furious at him, maybe said worse things than I should've. I guess I hurt his pride because he was awfully sulky when I woke him up on Sunday so we could get to the airport. So I could get to *you*,

John. Then you got there early—" My voice choked. "You were early, and I was so fucking glad to see you, and...." *Shit, more tears.* I'd been crying for three goddamned months.

"It's okay, Liam," John said, his voice gentle. "Please go on." He looked uneasy, and I thought I was getting through.

"You were there early, and before I could even kiss you right, that son of a bitch walked in and made it look like we'd been fucking. We hadn't, John! *We didn't do anything*! I was a hundred percent loyal to you." I put my hands flat on the table and cocked my head, still staring into his eyes. "Think about it. I'll bet you can remember seeing those blankets on the sofa."

Something changed in his eyes. I stayed quiet, and he skimmed his fingertips over my hand before resting his hand on top.

Oh... that feels so *good.*

There was a long pause, and after a moment, he licked his lips. "Liam?"

I was using my free hand to wipe up the tears and snot from around my nose.

"Liam?" he repeated.

I looked back at him, and he had the oddest expression on his face.

"I believe you. I believe everything you said." His eyes were wet, too. "God, what did I do?" A couple tears rolled down his cheeks.

"You believe me?" I said, not sure I'd heard correctly. "You believe that I was true to you?"

He nodded and smiled. It was a teary smile, but it was the most beautiful thing I'd seen since December.

He took a deep breath and sighed. "I have something to tell you, but please try not to hate me for it."

"I could never hate you."

"Three weeks ago, Jess told me she ran into Kyle at a party

in New York over Presidents' Day weekend, and that he told her what he'd done, how he'd lied. But she thought we shouldn't tell you, because you were finally starting to get on with your life. She said it was better to leave things alone instead of stirring everything up again."

Anger tore through me like cannon fire. Jess hadn't bothered to tell me any of this? *She* was supposed to be my best friend?

John went on as if he'd read my mind. "She decided not to tell you because she didn't want to open up all that misery again, and I went along with her. Neither one of us wanted you to be hurt, but that's no excuse, not for me anyway. It's been eating away at me, and that's why I tried to call you." Tears ran down his red cheeks. "I'm so sorry for everything. I should have listened to you in December."

"Y-you tried, remember?" I asked. "I just wasn't able to answer the phone."

"I should have kept trying, and I've had all that time since. I'm so ashamed."

I heard a moan before I realized it came from me. I was overwhelmed, and John took both my hands in his. "I'm sorry, Liam, so very sorry. I was such a fool back in Syracuse and ran away like a coward. I've caused us both so much pain." He wiped his eyes with his napkin. "I hope that someday you'll be able to forgive me."

I used my own napkin to wipe at the sweat on my forehead. *This is really it, the moment of truth.* "What's done is done. I still love you, and I forgive you. Can you possibly forgive me?"

He smiled and a few more tears trailed down his cheeks. "I'm not sure what you need my forgiveness for, but if there is anything, you've sure got it."

We talked a few minutes more, but too soon John said we

had to go. I didn't want to, and I don't think he did either, but he explained about his concert the next day.

I held my breath and finally forced myself to ask. "So, what now?"

He still had hold of my hand, and his smile made my stomach flutter. "I want to keep talking. If I give you my number, would you call me soon?" Then he laughed.

God, how I've missed his laugh.

He shook his head. "What the hell am I saying? We're in the same city, we can see each other. Where are you staying?"

"The same hotel you are, of course."

He snickered. "So that *was* you I saw leaving the hotel when I came down to go to dinner."

"You saw me?"

"I did, but I convinced myself I was imagining things."

Before we forgot, we exchanged numbers. I didn't tell him that Dean Mann had already given me his.

He grinned, looking shy. "Since we're walking in the same direction, Mr. Macadam, would you please see me back to my hotel?"

"My pleasure, Mr. Lawrence—I mean *Dr.* Lawrence. But there's one other thing I have to say before we go. It won't wait."

He nodded, and I looked him directly in the eyes. "I want you back, John William Lawrence. I said I felt like we were still together, except we're not." I paused for effect. "Well, I want to be. I still love you, and I want to be with you more than anything in the world."

He stared at me for a long few seconds, still smiling. "I still love you, too, Liam. It sounds wonderful, but can we talk about it tomorrow? I'm not opposed, I promise, but I think we could both use a little time to digest what's been said tonight. I promise we can talk about it in the morning. I won't disappear again."

I didn't need time to think about anything. It was *all* I'd thought about for three months, but I knew he had to move at his own pace. I could tell that he wanted to get back together too, so I wasn't going to push.

On the way back to the hotel, we talked about our families, and he smiled when I told him how Mom had made the trip to Prague possible. I guess Dean Mann was a good influence, because I found myself praying that all this wouldn't be too much for John to deal with in the light of day.

John

My heart leapt when Liam said he wanted me back. I wanted it, too, more than anything, but felt that he needed a little time away from me to deal with what I told him at the coffeeshop. We also needed to think about what it would look like and how it would work if we got back together. We lived on different continents, but as long as we still loved each other, I knew we could work it out. I don't know why I didn't just say that.

Back at the hotel, I held his hand in the elevator, and it felt so right to be with him again. I resisted the impulse to ask him into my room. It was too soon. He had shown the guts and fortitude to come find me, and we both deserved more than an instant hookup. We needed a chance to be sure of things before we brought sex into it again.

I'd been in my room for an hour, trying to control my racing thoughts and ignoring the note Dominic had slipped under my door asking me to call him when I got in. I thought it would be him when my phone rang, but it was Liam.

"Hey, did I wake you up?" His warm, fuzzy voice set off a torrent of memories.

"No, I'm not sleepy. I'm trying to think through all that happened tonight. What's up?"

"You asked me to call you soon. Is this too soon?"

We both laughed. Be honest or play demure? *This is not the time for games, John.* "It isn't too soon. Not at all."

"I've missed you, babe, more than I can tell you in a thousand years."

His voice, so warm and reassuring, had me standing with a hand over my heart. I sat down on the bed. "I've missed you too, Liam."

"Back at the coffeehouse, when I asked what now?"

"Yes?"

"What now, John? Can we try to recapture what we had?"

No games, remember? This is a very rare second chance. "I'd like that, but there are a couple of things we need to get out in the open first."

"Like?"

I don't want to know, but I have to. "Don't you have someone? You're an amazing man, and you've been single. Is there anyone else in your life?"

He didn't hesitate a single second. "No, there isn't. Not at all." His voice got thicker. "I told you I never even cheated on you after you left. No one could measure up to you, John. No one else had a chance."

Wow. Just wow.

"How about you?" He sounded apprehensive. "Is there anyone special in your life?"

I grunted a whine. "No. No one had a chance after you, either, Liam."

Three or four beats went by. "What about that douchetwat? Um... *Dominic*?"

I giggled. No one else ever made me giggle. "Why not tell me how you really feel, Liam?"

"Well?" he was undeterred. "What about him?"

"There's nothing between us," I said. "Maybe in one sentimental moment I thought there could be, but only because he reminded me of you."

A playfully loud voice came through the phone. "I beg your fucking pardon?"

"Sorry," I said, "but to answer your question, not Dominic, not anyone. I never cheated on you, either."

"Good. So there's nothing to stop us from reconnecting."

A huge smile took over my face. "No, nothing."

"Babe, is it okay if we make this call FaceTime?"

I hesitated. "I'm ready for bed. I-I don't look my best."

"Oh, John." His tone was reverent. "I've seen it, remember? It's when you look your *very* best. Hold on a minute."

A few seconds later, I could see him lying on his bed, and my heart missed a beat. He looked sexier than any human being had a right to look after flying across an ocean and then a continent. We talked for a while, just like before, about everything and nothing. Conversation was never difficult for us.

"Did you notice something?" he asked, after a few minutes.

"What?"

"We both said we never cheated even when we weren't together. I think neither one of us ever really felt like we weren't together. We were just estranged."

I couldn't argue with that. "You may be right."

"I think so." He swallowed loudly. "John, I have a question."

"Okay."

"Sorry, not sorry. Who is he?"

"Who is who?"

"Fucking Dominic. I saw him hold your hand." Liam was not amused.

"He's the tour manager. He works for the company in London that's managing our trip. And if you saw him take my hand the one and only time it has ever happened, you must have seen how quickly I dropped it. I'm not interested in him, Liam. I never was."

He closed his eyes and his face let go. "Okay, then. I feel better."

I sighed to keep from laughing. "I'm glad."

"Is it okay if I come to your concert tomorrow night? I always wanted to hear what you could do with a choir. I've heard *about* it, but never actually *heard* it."

I grinned at him. "I can leave you a ticket at the VIP window. I have access to a few good seats."

His face lit up with that mile-wide, heart-stopping grin. "That'd be *awesome*. The only tickets left were for crappy seats. Concert's at seven thirty?"

"It is. What are you going to do all day until then?"

His smile turned sly. "I have to go buy a suit, but if I have time, I might go see this television tower I've heard about. Or maybe go to church and thank God for answering my prayers. I think I owe Dean Mann that much. Oh, and then go hear the best concert in the world, conducted by the most talented and sexy director."

"Sounds like a good day," I said. "I might be at said television tower in the morning, just in case you didn't know." He laughed, and I flirted a little. "If you see me there, will you say hi?"

He rolled his eyes and scoffed. "Try and stop me."

We talked a few minutes more.

"John...?" He sounded a little nervous.

"Yes?"

He looked away, then back. "Would you let me take you out to dinner after the concert?"

Yes! I couldn't wait to go to dinner with him, but I must have waited too long to answer.

"I'm sorry," he said, a little defensive. "Too soon?"

"No, no... not at all. I'm just happy." I smiled into the phone camera. "I'd love to go to dinner with you."

He nodded, grinning again. "You've got it then. And in case my bus takes a wrong turn on the way to the television tower, or the tailor takes too long with the suit, where should I meet you after the concert?"

"Come backstage. I'll be receiving my public." I laughed too hard, but he got it and laughed along.

I lay back on my bed, staring into dreamy brown eyes I'd feared I would never see again.

"I can't wait to see you tomorrow, John. Thanks for saying yes to dinner."

This has to be a dream. Please, may I never wake up? "Thank you for inviting me. Liam, I...."

"Yeah?"

"I'm really glad you came to Prague."

We disconnected, and I got into bed. Sleep finally came, and as I had before, I dreamed of sunshine and Liam Macadam.

Liam

We were getting back together—I could feel it! In fact, we might've been back together already. I wasn't sure what John wanted to call things yet. We had to figure out what we both needed and be sure we saw to it. Another incredible high followed by another crash might finish both of us off for good, but I was convinced that if two people loved each other and wanted something badly enough, it could happen.

So, what was it I needed? I needed John to trust me, to be

willing to build a life with me. I needed him to pledge to be my exclusive boyfriend and try as hard as he could to pick up where we left off. I would do exactly the same, and I was prepared to transfer to a school in England if I had to.

I woke up a few hours later thinking about him. I had been dreaming about how incredibly aggressive he was when he got aroused. No one had ever come close to getting me so worked up and leaving me as fulfilled. He'd been sucking me off in the dream, but in reality, I'd been grinding into the mattress, which was now damp and sticky. It didn't take more than a few strokes to finish myself off, and after the best orgasm I'd had in three months, I cleaned up, went downstairs for an early breakfast, and then headed to the hotel gym to work out.

Fuck! I looked at my watch a second time, thinking it couldn't possibly be right, but there it was in black and white: 11:04. *Dammit!* I grabbed my phone off the nightstand.

<<*LIAM: Hey maestro!*

Couple of minutes. I hoped he didn't think I'd gotten cold feet, and that he hadn't either.

JOHN: Hey handsome, what's up?
LIAM: Guess jet lag caught up with me... after my morning workout I fell asleep and just woke up. Sorry I missed the chance to flirt with the sexiest american at the tv tower
JOHN: LOL. We're just leaving there. I wondered what happened to that awesome stud I thought I might see. I was a little afraid he changed his mind about things.

LIAM: NOT A FUCKING CHANCE IN HELL!!! I wanted to be sure we r still on for the concert and dinner tonight and also to wish u the best, best luck - ur so smart and talented, knock em dead!!!
JOHN: Haha! You don't know if I'm talented or not, but I guess you're about to find out. Thank you very much and I'm so excited about having dinner with you. About seeing you again.
JOHN: Strike 'excited.' I remember you used to get 'stoked' about things. I'm totally stoked about tonight.
LIAM: So glad bc I'm totally completely stoked about it too... btw I was lucky and got us reservations at a super place
JOHN: Tell me where?
LIAM: U will c soon enough
JOHN: Okay. I've got to run but please promise you'll come find me backstage after the concert? I won't forget to leave your ticket at VIP.
LIAM: Nothing could keep me away from you after the concert and thanks a lot for the ticket - im really totally completely awesomely stoked! About u. Oh, and the concert 2
JOHN: Me too. <3 See you then!

Those texts left me grinning from ear to ear. As for the dinner reservations, I needed to pull a rabbit out of my hat. I pulled up Google and found a list of Prague's best restaurants, and—reinforcing my conviction that this was all meant to be—the first place I called, the person who answered told me they were booked up for weeks but he'd just hung up with someone cancelling for later that night. He said since I was the first polite American he'd talked to in a long time, he'd put me down. *Keep thinking positive for me, Dean Mann.*

After a shower, I headed out to a department store the hotel concierge promised wouldn't let me down. He advised me to give the salesman a big tip when I asked for the super-fast turnaround. The store turned out to be exclusive, not just nice, and a no-nonsense saleswoman showed me a magnificent suit. I handed over the emergency credit card yet again, along with $100.00 American as a tip, and she told me I could pick up my beautiful new suit, with all the alterations done, at five o'clock that afternoon.

Leaving the department store, I stopped at an ATM and was relieved to see that Mom had made the deposit. I withdrew enough cash to pay for dinner that night. No way was I letting John pay, and I didn't want him thinking I was going into debt to buy dinner at a place like that.

It seemed like the ATM gave me a huge amount of money, but there were a lot of Czech korunas in a dollar. After a late lunch, I walked around until five o'clock, when I picked up my suit and headed back to the hotel. I called Mom to thank her for the money and give her a progress report.

"I'm sorry, but I'm putting a bad hurt on the credit card," I told her.

"Use it when you need to. Now tell me everything."

She listened to my story and was thrilled to hear things were going so well. "Please give John my love," she said, right before we hung up. "I'm proud of you, son. Stay after what you want."

I spent the hour before I left for the concert showering and struggling with my hair. I'd had no time to get it cut before leaving Syracuse, and it was just long enough to be difficult. After getting dressed, I looked in the mirror and hoped John liked the new suit as much as I did. I wasn't sure what all was gonna happen that evening, but whatever it was, I was ready.

24

John

The concert was exhilarating. That choir of forty students, some of the more talented young singers in Great Britain, brought the music to life and followed me perfectly. The audience's reaction was electric, finally resulting in not one, but two encores.

Since I knew where Liam would be sitting, I looked his way after a set of Bruckner motets. He was standing, his face red, clapping for all he was worth. He caught me looking and raised his arm for a few victory pumps. I got a little flustered, so I didn't look at him again until the end, when his enthusiasm was even less restrained.

Backstage, I gave the choir a glowing postconcert review before greeting the amazing number of people who were waiting to speak to me. Despite language issues, I understood their enthusiasm and gratitude. I couldn't keep my eyes away from someone familiar who was standing over to the side, giving me space to greet people while he stood there beaming. He looked absolutely stunning in a navy blue suit that fit him like a glove. My heart fluttered when I noticed a rose in his hand.

At last, everyone else was gone, and he walked over to me, a broad, eager smile lighting up his face. "You are amazing, Professor Lawrence. I don't know much about choral music, but I'm totally hooked." He licked his plump, red lips and held out the rose. "This is for you."

I took the rose and looked into those gorgeous chocolate brown eyes I'd missed so much. "Do you remember that night on my porch in Syracuse when you gave me one of these?"

He caught his lower lip with his teeth and then put on a shy smile. "I do, and just like then, the poor flower's beauty fades away compared to you."

We spent a moment smiling at each other, lost in memories, and I finally broke the silence. "Give me a few minutes to go to the restroom and take a couple of deep breaths, and I'll be ready to go. Meet me right here?"

"I won't move."

A few enthusiastic students lingered in the changing room, along with Dominic. While I chatted with the students, Dominic kept looking my way. He'd asked me that morning if everything was okay and I told him it was, but aside from logistical matters, we hadn't spoken since.

The students left, and he walked across the room to stand beside me. His smile was slight, but appeared genuine. "I don't suppose you're up for dinner again?"

I felt bad about Dominic, and I was glad that whatever went on between us didn't last even a day. "I'm sorry but I already have plans."

He nodded, still smiling. "Liam?"

I knew grinning would seem insensitive, but I couldn't stop myself. "Yes."

"I saw him in the audience, and waiting to speak to you afterward." He put a hand on my arm. "May I be frank? I see how you look at each other and your body language. Whatever happened in the past, you belong together. Don't cheat yourself out of that kind of happiness, John. I'd give anything to find it."

I wasn't sure what I expected him to say, but that wasn't it. "Thank you. For what it's worth, I meant what I said to you last night. You *are* attractive."

"And cute," he said, smiling. "And don't forget witty."

I snickered. "I definitely won't forget. Can we still be friends?"

He put a hand on my shoulder. "I'd be hurt if we weren't. Now get out of here and go have a good time."

Liam was right where I'd left him. He'd gotten reservations at a beautiful contemporary restaurant that smelled like money, and they seated us as soon as we arrived. Although it was late, they were busy, and we had a corner table with a beautiful view out onto a well-lit square. Conversation was easy. We were each trying to get the measure of the other after our time apart, but everything felt very natural.

After the appetizers were delivered, Liam became serious. "If you can tell me about something, it will mean a lot. But if you don't wanna talk about it, I'll understand."

"What's on your mind? I'll tell you anything you want to know, if I can."

His eyes dimmed a little. "After that day in Syracuse when everything went so wrong, what happened? How did you get away so quickly? You didn't take any exams, and when I went to your house early in January, it was empty."

I was chewing a bite of paté, and the memories flooded back so fast I had trouble swallowing. "After how everything went down, my heart wasn't just broken, Liam. It was smashed."

"Mine too." The grief that crossed his face made my heart lurch.

"I know it was. Actually, I did take my exams. I got in touch with Zimmerman, and he helped me arrange to take them at odd times in other rooms."

Liam shook his head. "So that's how you did it. I didn't figure you'd have skipped out on the tests." He snickered. "That also explains why Zimmerman's given me the cold shoulder ever since."

"I'd give anything if I could go back and change how I reacted." I took in his serious face, the deep furrow between his eyebrows, the warmth in his wary eyes. *This can't go anywhere if you aren't honest.* "I was still smarting after what happened with Thorne. History seemed to be repeating itself and I thought I needed to get away from you, so I thought I'd transfer to another law school. While I considered where I might go, my friend Mark—a conductor friend I knew from doctoral school —called."

Liam sat back in his chair. "And?"

"Mark was lucky enough to land a job in Cambridge right out of grad school. We were never best friends, but we liked each other and always respected each other's work. We only talked a few times a year after he moved overseas, and when he called that December, I assumed it was for our annual Christmas season chat."

Liam made a noise to show he was still listening. His eyes were serious but not angry.

"As it turned out, Mark was calling to see if I could recommend anyone for a job. He was going on a six-month sabbatical to take a temporary job in Australia, and he needed someone to fill in for him in Cambridge while he was gone. It hadn't been firmed up until early December, so he was trying to figure something out quickly."

Dinner came, and after the server left, we kept talking.

"It's amazing how that happened." He took a bite of his beef and nodded for me to go on.

Internally, I breathed a sigh of relief that he wasn't pulling into himself. "Yes, it was. I told Mark that I *did* have someone to recommend—me. I explained the situation and asked if there were any possibility that they would be interested in hiring me, and he said that if I wanted the gig, he'd make sure I got it. He told me it would be a relief to leave the choir in the hands of someone with similar techniques. I hopped on a plane to London the next day and had my interview at St. Bart's the day after that."

"And you got the job, of course." Liam, whose heart I'd trampled, actually looked proud of me. "You went over a long weekend, right, back on Tuesday? I remember Michael telling me you were gone. Jess dogsat Theo."

I nodded while I swallowed some wine. "Yes, that's right. And it was incredible luck, or so I thought at the time. I flew back to Syracuse with three weeks to withdraw from law school, pack up the house, and move Theo and me to the UK. I could never have done it without Jess and Michael's help, but I hope you don't hold anything against them. They tried their best to get me to talk to you, and when they knew I was moving, they tried especially hard to convince me to at least tell you what was going on."

"It's okay, they were good to me, too. They refused to get between us, and I really can't blame them. The fact that you and I didn't communicate with each other is on us."

"I decided to talk to you, maybe even stay—"

He held up a hand. "I know, babe. We've been over that."

His smile was blinding. "We're back together now, and that's what counts. Is there any more to the story?"

I shrugged. "That's pretty much it. I made it to Cambridge, and I've had a wonderful time there, doing my friend's job and living in his house. He's back next year, so I finish up at St. Bart's in June."

"And then?

I shook my head. "No plans yet."

The gleam in Liam's eyes convinced me that everything would be okay. "Can we work on those together, you think?"

I nodded, feeling very happy. "I'd like that a lot."

He put down his silverware to drink some wine. "Thanks for telling me all that. It helps put some pieces together, and I'll tell you anything you want to know, now or anytime."

Go ahead and ask. "One ultra-important question? Then I'll leave it be."

He nodded while he cut another bite of his beef tenderloin.

"Did you try to kill yourself?" My voice was shaky. I had to know, but I dreaded the answer if he said yes.

"No. My heart was broken, and I can't say I was very excited about being alive right then, but I didn't try to make myself die. I had an awful case of flu and got really confused in the middle of the night. I ended up taking way too much medicine."

My eyes blurred from tears. "I'm so glad to hear that."

"My therapist asked if I might have had a subconscious wish to die, and you know what? I probably did, to be honest. I sure as fuck didn't wanna live without you, but I didn't consciously try to kill myself."

"Thank God," I said, immensely relieved. "I'm so sorry for what I put you through."

"Enough," he said, reaching across the table to put a hand on mine. "We both made mistakes, and we both regret them.

An important part of forgiveness is moving on, so let's focus on that."

I nodded and took a deep breath. He was exquisite, even handsomer than he used to be. His jaw and cheekbones were more defined, and his face was stronger. He'd definitely spent a lot of time in the gym over the last few months, and if he got tired of the law, he could probably make a good living as a model.

I made a show of taking him in. "You look incredible, and I don't just mean the suit, although it *is* breathtaking on you. You've changed some. I assume you work out a lot."

He kept smiling, and I wondered if I'd be able to resist him later.

"I went to the gym a lot after you left to help with stress, and I started running again." He made a show of looking me over. "You look awesome. Beautiful as ever, and—*oh, fuck!*—is that a little gray I see at your temples? Just a hint?" He brushed it with his fingertips. "It looks really good on you." He took a breath and looked at my chest before meeting my eyes again. "I can see you're no stranger to the gym, either."

"You're still sweet, that's for sure." I winked at him. "Sugar Plum sweet." We both chuckled. "I work out to deal with stress, too. I haven't tried to build muscle, just stay in shape."

"You've certainly succeeded." He gave me a sultry stare from under his lush eyelashes. "When you're ready, I can't wait to get my hands on that shape."

Liam

At the hotel, I didn't want to let John go, and he agreed to a nightcap. The hotel bar was done up as a greenhouse, with tropical plants everywhere, which explained the heat and humidity. Instead of tables all lined up, they'd arranged alcoves divided by plants, so that customers had privacy. We sat on a sofa, surrounded by bromeliads and banana plants.

John looked around, impressed. "It's beautiful in here. The heat feels good."

"It *is* beautiful, but like the rose on your lapel, it's nothing compared to you."

He grinned and glanced down at the rug. "Like I said, you're still sweet, but enough of that. I appreciate it."

We both felt the magic. I put my hand gently behind his head, trailing my fingertips against the side of his throat along the way. His lips were soft and moist, but he pulled away after a few seconds.

"Are you *sure*, Liam? Can you put your heart in my hands again?"

"I'm damned sure. You've had my heart all along." Of course, the waitress chose that moment to appear, and we ordered quickly.

John looked at me for a moment before he reached for me and brushed his lips against mine. He moved to my throat and blessed it with small kisses, creating flashes of desire that ricocheted to my core. When I began squirming, he pulled back enough to look into my eyes. "I want it, Liam. I want it so much."

I shuddered when he put his hands on my cheeks and brushed gentle circles across my lips with his thumbs. Running a hand behind my head, he twirled my hair through his fingers, and I moaned as I leaned close enough to share his breath. It was heaven when I traced his lips with my tongue, then nibbled gently the way he always liked. I licked into his mouth but didn't push, and it was just enough to turn a sweet kiss into a serious one. We opened our mouths to each other, and I savored the moist heat and the play of our tongues. I had dreamed about this moment too many times to count.

When we finally stopped to breathe, I leaned my head against his shoulder. “I love you, Punkin,” I mumbled.

“I love you too,” he whispered back. “Thank you for coming to Prague.”

John

It felt like another of the dozens of dreams I’d had since I left Liam. Dinner together, ending with a magical kiss amid tropical plants in the middle of a European winter. He gently asked me to go to his room, but I managed to talk him down without offending him. It wasn’t that I didn’t want to—*God, how I wanted to!*—but we needed a little more time to reconnect without making it all about heat and need. The moments in the hotel bar had demonstrated that wouldn’t be a problem at all.

The next day, we walked around the city discovering the wonders of Prague. We overheard a tour guide in the Old Town Square point out the Astronomical Clock overhead, which she said had been there since 1410.

“Think about it,” Liam said, pointing up at the beautiful contraption. “That clock has been there for over 600 years. It has seen so much—so many changes, governments, and wars. The Habsburgs and the fucking Nazis.” He paused to grin at me, then looked back up at the clock. “Think about how many couples it has seen down in this square, all the romances, great and small. This clock is a sign for us, John. It has survived, and we have, too.”

Liam was right, it *was* a sign. In another six hundred years I wanted that clock to remember the romance of Liam and John, a romance that changed their lives and survived hardship, one that was genuine and worth fighting for. He pulled me close with an arm around my shoulder, and we walked on. That moment in the square, looking at the clock, was when I knew we'd make it.

That night's concert was at St. Vitus Cathedral, a majestic, eight-hundred-year-old building with outstanding acoustics, standing on a hill overlooking Prague. Liam said the choir sang even better than they had the night before. We went to a beer hall after the concert, and a lot of my students were there, too. They were quickly figuring out, if they hadn't already, that Dr. Lawrence was awfully sweet on this good-looking stranger who was crashing their tour.

On the walk back to the hotel, I wanted to discuss what was going to happen next, since the choir was leaving for Germany the next morning. When we stopped to admire another beautiful square glowing in the yellow light, I walked around in front of Liam and put my arms around his neck. "How much time do you have off from school?"

"Until next Monday."

"I know you may have other things to do, but how about staying with us for the rest of the tour? I don't want to let you go yet."

He leaned in for a quick kiss. "That's good, because I don't want to leave. Nothing is more important than being with you and getting us back on track."

I took his hand again and we walked on toward the hotel. "You could ride with us on the bus. I'll make you master of the robes to give you an official job, so you won't feel out of place."

"Is that okay?"

I rolled my eyes and kissed his nose. "I'm the choir director." His grin made my pants a little tighter. "Please say you'll do it."

His eyes lit up with joy. "I'd be thrilled, Dr. Lawrence. How much do I need to pay?"

"Just for your hotel rooms and the flight back to London from Berlin. Everything else is already paid for. Fair?"

His eyes sparkled like the Fourth of July. "You just missed a big financial opportunity because I'd pay anything to spend time with you."

25

Liam

The next morning, when everyone was on the bus, John formally introduced me and appointed me as Master of the Robes. I said it sounded very English, and everyone laughed and welcomed me. Even frickin' Dominic shook my hand. He was actually a nice guy, and I decided I couldn't fault him for having good taste in men.

Germany proved to be a beautiful country, full of history. We enjoyed seeing Dresden, risen from the ashes of the terrible firebombing it suffered during World War II. Its beauty shimmered in the unseasonably bright sunlight. The choir sang that night at the Frauenkirche, an octagonal sandstone church that was originally built in the eighteenth century. Destroyed in the 1945 bombing, it was painstakingly reconstructed after Germany reunited. The concert there left people in tears.

John took me to dinner afterward, and while we waited for our food, he held up his glass of wine and his dimples popped.

"I've been to Dresden a few times and have always thought it's an incredible city. Now I love it more than ever because it's another symbol for us. Something once destroyed can become beautiful again." We gazed into each other's eyes, and the love I saw in his was sacred. "To us," he said. "To our love's rebirth."

"To us," I answered, and we clinked glasses.

After taking a sip of wine, I studied him through the dim light. "You know, our relationship is already beautiful again."

Tears ran down his cheeks. "Y-yes, I.... It is."

Oh yeah, we're gonna be better than ever.

The next stop was Leipzig. The first concert there was in the Thomaskirche, a beautiful old twelfth-century building where the great composer J.S. Bach worked in the 1700s. The choir sang a big motet he wrote and absolutely rocked the place. The next night, they sang at the Gewandhaus Leipzig, the city's elegant concert hall. I was amazed by how many people were attending the concerts, but I guess that says a lot about European versus American culture. We value very different things.

From Leipzig, we went to Berlin. Although the hotel there was large, they didn't have even one extra room. A couple guys in the choir invited me to crash with them, but John stepped in. "No need to put these gentlemen out, Liam. The hotel gave me a suite, and there's a pull-out sofa. You're welcome to that."

The choir guys exchanged a look, smiled knowingly, and stepped aside.

The first night, John and I made out for a while. We kissed and held each other, and just when I was about ready to take him to bed, he sat up and looked at me. "Not quite yet."

The crimson dotting his cheeks, the sweat on his brow, and the hardness in his pants told me what he wanted, and it wasn't to go to bed alone. "John, don't you want—"

"You know I want it." He turned his lips up into the cutest

smile. "Let's just get things a little more re-established. It won't be long, I promise." He chuckled. "I'm not going to let you go back to America without a complete reunion."

With that, he left me frustrated on the sofa bed. It was torture to know he was in the other room, only a few feet away, but I couldn't touch him. More than anything, I wanted to take him in my arms and satisfy both our needs while we celebrated finding each other again, but I wasn't about to try to force him. As much as I wanted John, I was not that guy, and the time had to be right for both of us. History was repeating itself. I remembered being in exactly the same position last fall back in Syracuse.

The next day was a sightseeing marathon that included everything from Checkpoint Charlie to the Berlin Opera House. After a concert that night at the Berlin Cathedral, we went out to a bar for a while and had a great time, but there was still no action back at the hotel beyond hugs, kisses, and eager caresses that almost made me come in my pants.

Too soon, it was Saturday. The choir's final concert was that evening, and we would all fly back to London the next day. Originally, I was supposed to return to New York on Sunday, but I called the airline and put it off until later in the week. John and I had fun all day Saturday, knocking around the city on our own, but I was a little distracted because we needed to talk about our future.

We went for a walk after that night's concert, and I was trying to get up the nerve to broach the subject when he did it for me. "Liam, we fly back tomorrow."

"I know." The dim light from the streetlamps combined with the flicker of car lights to create moving shadows that emphasized the softness of John's face. He was so beautiful that I never wanted to go back to Syracuse.

Worry creased his brow. "What's going to happen to us?"

"What do you want to happen?" I held my breath.

He stopped walking, and we turned to each other.

"I don't want to let you go, ever again. I want to build a life together. You're *it* for me, Liam. You're all I ever want."

The relief was so powerful it made me shudder. I reached a hand toward his face and then stopped. We'd waited so long to get back here and I wanted to prolong the moment just a little longer. He smiled, and I moved again, gently tracing his cheekbone and brow before lingering on his upper lip. "John, you're it for me, too. We are going to have the *best* life."

We both laughed joyously. He grabbed me and squeezed with surprising strength, and when we'd quietened down, we stood there holding each other. John backed up just enough to look into my eyes, and the way the light played on the tears streaking his cheeks reminded me of the twinkling lights on a Christmas tree. "I'm so lucky you made this trip and hunted me down."

A few heartbeats passed as we enjoyed each other's closeness, and I finally said the only thing I could. "I really wanna do something, John. I really, *really* wanna... but I'm a little afraid."

He brushed my chin with his fingertips. "You'd better do it, then. Don't be afraid."

We stood still another second or two, and then we were on each other. On a busy sidewalk in Berlin, on a Saturday night, we kissed as if there would never be another day. He smelled like sweat and citrus cologne, and his hair was soft as I played my fingers through it. I pressed myself against him, and he melted into me. Damn the clothes that separated us!

Eventually, we pulled apart and stood panting. Our hands still rested on each other's arms.

"John?" I asked.

He raised his eyebrows, ever so slightly. "Hmm?"

"Wanna go back to the hotel now?" I whispered.

His nod was slow, and his eyes didn't budge from mine. "I do."

"Professor Lawrence? Liam?"

We started, surprised to find ourselves surrounded by a group of John's students. He blushed hard and nervously rubbed his swollen lips. "Hi," he said.

One of the young women spoke up. "That kiss was worthy of a serious romance movie."

One of the guys who helped me with the robes wore an especially big grin. "We've known there was something between you two, and that was *awesome*. If you don't have a history, I'm giving up my gay card."

Everyone chortled.

"Dr. Lawrence, you've been so sad since you came to St. Bart's," another woman said. "It's been wonderful to see you happy this week."

John's cheeks were bright orange in the glow of the street-lights. "Thanks for the good words, gang." He tittered nervously. "Liam and I have known each other for a while, and we are...." He glanced at me, smiling. "We're happy again."

"You should be more than happy," the guy said. "Don't ever stop loving each other like this."

John's cheeks were carmine by then, and his dimples were deeper than ever. "We appreciate all your good wishes. Thanks so much, you're all stupendous."

"Thanks guys," I chimed in. "Enjoy the rest of your night."

"You too," another of the guys said, "but I think that's a given."

John

The minutes on the street with Liam had been transformational. The kiss was everything it needed to be to cement our reunion, and it was now time to celebrate it. I always sweat during a concert and needed to freshen up. When we got back to the hotel, I took a very thorough shower, making sure I was squeaky clean everywhere. Afterward, I found Liam in the living room watching TV, and sat down beside him. "We need to make some plans about how this is going to work until I get back to the U.S."

He looked at me with wide eyes, and I noticed the pulse in one of the veins in his throat. "Yes, we do."

I stammered, "W-would you consider—"

He silenced me with a kiss. I was hard from the second our lips touched, and by the time we came up for air, I had tunnel vision. "Are you planning to sleep on the pull-out tonight?"

He froze. "Do you want me to?"

I shook my head, still breathing hard "No, I don't."

Devilish eyes flashed at me. "I must warn you, Punkin, if I sleep in your bed, I won't be honorable."

"I'm counting on that, Sugar Plum." My heart thudded against my ribs.

He dragged his tongue—that same tongue I wanted to lick me everywhere—across his lips and glanced at the door. "Are any of your choir kids nearby?"

I pursed my lips and shrugged. "Only most of them. On this floor, at least."

"Well, then, I guess we'll give 'em something to talk about."

He dug his fingers into my ribs, making me squawk, and tickled me while I laughed outrageously loud. Then he sat up, looking stern. "Get your ass into that bedroom right now, or I'm gonna spank it, hard."

Opportunity! I snickered and cocked my head playfully.

"I'll go into the bedroom only *if* you promise to spank my ass when we get there."

He dug his fingers into me again, and I jumped off the sofa and ran into the bedroom, with him right behind me.

Liam

We dove onto the bed and rolled around, still laughing. After a couple minutes, out of breath, we lay on our backs with our sides touching, and it hit me that I was in bed with John again. Emotion kicked me in the belly, and I rolled on top of him. I held on tight, not wanting to pull up even enough to kiss him.

He shuddered as a strangled sob escaped his throat, which was all it took for me to lose it. We stayed like that for a while, me on top of him, clinging to each other for dear life as we cried out the emotions. When our bawling stilled, I pulled up enough to kiss him, but just as my lips were about to touch his, he smiled. "I don't know how I lived all this time without you."

We got busy exploring each other's bodies, rediscovering nipples, chests, abs—whatever we could get to. John fumbled with my pants and soon his hand was inside. Heat seared its way through me as another man touched me for the first time in way too long.

"Have to taste you," he said, watching my eyes while he crawled down the bed. He shimmied my pants and underwear down, and I groaned loudly when I sprang free. Gripping me in two hands, he looked on in wonder. "Your cock is so beautiful."

I closed my eyes when he squeezed me, and after giving my dick a few pumps, he licked the head and began sucking. The pleasure was so intense I cried out. He slowly kissed his way down the shaft, and my moans and cries grew more intense by the second. Taking first one ball into his mouth, then the other, he sucked gently and caused me to buck up off the bed. “Yes, yes.... I love you, John!”

He went back to my dick, and I groaned and begged as he sucked me into a frenzy. His mouth was hot, and he kept moving his tongue around while he massaged me with the back of his throat. I was very noisy, unable to control myself as I thrashed around. Too soon, the inevitable was brewing, and just as I realized he needed to stop, he deepthroated me again.

“No, babe!” I yelled, too late, as spurt after boiling spurt cannoned into John’s mouth. His throat moved around the head of my cock while I wailed in relief. When the orgasm trailed off, it left me lying there with my eyes closed, unable to move.

John was still between my legs, drawing lazy circles on my thighs with his fingers. “You okay?”

“Mm.... Rrrrrr....” I cleared my throat and groaned a couple times before I managed to say anything. “I’m sorry.”

He crawled up beside me and started playing with my pecs. “Sorry? For what?”

“I came way too quick.” I grimaced. “I wanted to wait for you.”

He shook his head and kissed my nipple. “Liam, it was *so* good. You wouldn’t believe how many times I’ve dreamed about tasting you again.” He chuckled and pulled some of the hair around the other nipple. “And I remember that it doesn’t take you long to be ready for round two.”

He climbed on top of me and lowered his face toward mine. I gave him a proper thank you kiss and reveled in the tastes of John’s mouth and my pleasure—the taste of love.

He rolled to the side, and I snuggled into the crook of his shoulder. He held me while we basked in each other. A few minutes later, I was kissing my way up his throat when he turned on his side and ground his very hard dick into my hip.

I chuckled softly. "Is that a hint?"

"When you're ready. Just needed a little friction."

It had been so long and we both wanted to make it last. John was still fully clothed, and he'd only gotten my pants down to my knees. We got off the bed and undressed each other, and I took my time worshipping every bit of him I uncovered. After I pulled his boxer briefs over his feet, I stood up and kissed him hard, pushing my knee between his legs. The movement brushed his cock across my thigh, smearing it with precum.

I caressed his cheek with one hand while the other one explored its way down his front, tweaking his pink nipples along the way, and tickling across his belly with my fingernails. At last, I claimed my prize, and he gasped as I squeezed my fist around him, pumping lightly. He was rigid, and a quick glance told me his cock was as beautiful as ever. The skin on his shaft was pink and translucent. The head was an angry red, and precum stretched out in strings that clung to my hand when I moved it. He was a good six inches, maybe a little more, with a slight curve.

I nibbled at his chin. "You've grown, I see."

He giggled. "It's just the angle."

We got back on the bed, and when I climbed on top of him, I relished the warmth of being skin to skin. His cock was still in my hand.

He sucked in air when I stroked harder. "I need you, Liam," he whispered.

I waggled my eyebrows at him and laughed softly. "Oh, you're gonna get me, babe, but I wanna have some fun first."

We rolled around for a while, finding and loving various parts of the bodies we'd missed so much. John groaned like a wounded man when he gave up his first load to my mouth, and I practically had to pry his head off me to keep from feeding him again. I wanted to give him my load, but I needed to plant it deep inside him.

"On your belly," I said.

He kissed me—open-mouthed, sloppy, and hot—before turning over. I made love to his back and legs for a while, and then told him to get up on his knees but keep his head down on the bed. He knew what was coming but squealed with delight as my tongue started loosening him up.

Soon I had him mewling, and sticky ropes of precum hung between his cock and the bed. He was still on his knees, and I was alternating my tongue and fingers in his ass.

"Fuck!" He was so loud that I was sure some kids down the hall must have heard. "I'm ready. *Please.*"

I got to my knees and crawled up beside him, where I spent time kissing his back and glancing my fingers across his ears. I left a few marks on the side of his neck. He was whining nonstop by then, begging me to fuck him.

"Turn over," I whispered into his ear. "Neither one of us can wait any longer."

He flipped on his back and I used my fingers to explore his feverish hole just a little more, while he cursed and demanded that I fuck him, *right this minute*. I remembered how tight he was and didn't want to hurt him.

"I haven't had sex with anybody since you," he whined. "Can we not use a condom?"

A fresh wave of lust crashed into my gut, and what had been urgent need became white-hot desperation. "Yeah." I grunted. "No sex for me either."

He laughed, or maybe cried, or both. "Do it then! Fuck me!"

For some reason that was funny, and I snickered while I applied more lube to his quivering ass.

"Stop laughing!" *Indignant.* "I'm fucking *dying* up here!"

Pitiful. "Stop dicking around and shove your cock up my ass right now!" *Demanding.*

"Bossy, bossy. Always loved it." I spoke in rhythm to my fingers as I applied more lube, smiling while I tortured him. I had no self-control left by then, and after swirling a big glob of lube on my cock, I pulled John's legs over my shoulders. We both yelped when the head of my cock slid inside him.

It took us a couple minutes to work me all the way in. The sensations and emotions were so intense that we both whimpered and groaned nonstop. More than once, I wasn't sure whether it was sweat or tears running down my face.

"Harder! Faster!" was his mantra, and I was all on board with the program. I slammed him with everything I had, and the noise level increased to the point that I put a hand over his mouth for a couple seconds. Our lust was frantic as our bodies demanded release after so long apart.

"Like that.... Right there!" John pushed out words between gasps. "Again! Right there.... Please! Harder! Right there."

He started keening first, and as more heat blossomed in my gut and spread into my chest, I joined in. An almost painful tickling gripped the back of my cock and shot a detonation ray into my balls.

The scream was loud. Was it me or John? *Fuck*, it was both of us!

I blasted fiery lava deep inside his ass. He squeezed his eyes shut, and his butt spasmed around me while his thick white globs slapped across both of us. The combination of emotional and physical relief was so intense that I blacked out.

When I came back, John was snuggling into the crook of my shoulder, his leg thrown over mine. He cleared his throat. "I love you." A little snore cut off the last syllable, and I was right behind him.

An hour later, we were awake and going at it again. The

intense need we had for each other wouldn't be satisfied quickly, but we both seemed determined to make a good start. After another incredible climax, we held each other, exhausted and happy. Just when euphoria turned into sleep, I'm not sure, but I rested better than I had since the night before John left for DC.

John

The light woke me and I heard street noises from below. Liam had his brawny arms wrapped around me, and as I snuggled my way deeper into them, it all came back. Last night's walk, the raging lust, the sweating and grunting—and the *coming*. Such mind-bending coming.

I twitched a couple of muscles down below, and sure enough, we had done the deed, and we'd done it hard. In fact, if memory served, we'd done it a few times. Just before eight o'clock, I extricated myself from his grasp to make my way to the bathroom. He came up beside me, grinning. "We haven't crossed the streams for way too long."

When we finished, he pulled me into a powerful hug.

"I have morning breath," I said, averting my head.

"I don't care. I do too." His fingers caressed my hair and drew me in for an astonishing kiss. Neither of us was able to hide our arousal, and he guided me back to the bed.

Reality was slowly coming back, and I sighed. "I'm sorry, but I need to call Dominic to see if everything's okay. Can you wait five minutes? We don't have to be downstairs to catch the bus until noon, so we'll have plenty of time."

"*Shit!* Go ahead." He gave my cock a firm squeeze. "Don't take too long."

The covers were still warm when we climbed back under them, and I tapped Liam's impressive abs a few times. "You behave for a minute, bad boy."

"Maybe," he said, squeezing his junk through the comforter.

I checked in with Dominic as quickly as I could, relieved to learn that there had been no disasters in the night and everything was on schedule for today. The deadline to be on the bus was noon, and I told him I'd be down there about eleven fifteen.

"Enjoy your morning with Liam." He paused briefly. "May I ask a question?"

"Certainly."

Liam pulled back the covers, treating me to an astonishing view of his very urgent need. In response, I swelled to full mast.

"I've really enjoyed getting to know you better. Maybe we could all have drinks sometime, and you and Liam could share your story?"

"I'd like that, Dominic."

Liam reached over and started jerking me with one hand while he did himself with his other. It was a 3-D, hands-on peepshow.

Dominic kept talking. "Am I to assume this reunion will be permanent?"

"If I have anything to do with it, yes," I said. "Dominic, I have to go. See you in a few hours." I hung up and turned to Liam.

"Hi," he said, smiling innocently.

"Hi," I said, as I crawled back into his arms. His good looks and the raw animal lust I felt for him were overwhelming. "I love you, Liam Macadam. I never stopped, even when I tried."

"I love you too, John Lawrence, and I never tried to stop."

I rode him hard. He was lost in his lust, his head lolling

around while he mumbled and groaned, and I was every bit as far gone. I couldn't have stayed upright if I hadn't used my hands for balance. We came violently and fell back into slumber, not waking up until 10:40. Far too late for breakfast, we jumped into the shower so we could make it downstairs on time.

26

The Next Autumn

Liam

When we got back to Cambridge in March, John and I spent some time figuring out how to make it through the rest of the year until he could move back to America. We knew we were meant for each other and had to find a way to be together.

Later that week, I flew back to Syracuse, but we kept in touch every day. On weekends, John would stay up late and we'd sleep with Skype on, connecting us through the night. We had a lot of support from our families and friends, including our classmates at the law school, and John's students in Cambridge. Even Dominic seemed happy for us, and Dean Mann, a hopeless romantic, was ecstatic. He sent me an email saying the joy of helping us had added years to his life.

John moved back in June, and we lived in a little Manhattan studio through August while I worked as a summer clerk for a judge in the U.S. District Court. It was great experience and set me up for a first-class summer associateship the next June at one of the world's biggest law firms, McBurnie Richards, in New York City.

John wanted to go back to law school, and Professor Zimmermann and Dean Crawford helped him work it out. It meant he would have to go to summer school the next year, when I'd be busy with my associateship. We would have to figure out how to deal with that.

We moved back to Syracuse in August, into a nice little house near the school. It was our first real place together, and Theo loved it as much as we did because the doggie door let out into a spacious yard. The house was only about a thousand square feet, but it had just the space we needed, plus a heated garage we thought was the height of luxury. John had put a lot of furniture into storage when he left the country, including the bedroom furniture he'd bought for us, so we were all set for a great year.

We really enjoyed being together. John was busy with his classes, and I had an insane amount of work. No subjects were required in the second year so I was taking what I wanted, but the classes were just as difficult as before. In addition to taking a full class load, I volunteered every Friday at Legal Aid.

The autumn limped along, too warm for a long time. By late October, the leaves began to fall, and the weather finally cooled off. John and I most definitely did *not* cool off, however. We were both deeply grateful for what we had and were determined to enjoy it to the max.

Mom and my sisters were thrilled, and "John is home" was a glorious refrain I'd heard since the previous spring. Once, back in the summer, Mom asked when I was going to give him a ring so he couldn't get away again. She tried to make it sound like a joke, but I could tell it wasn't. Vonnie said I was as giddy as a pig rolling around in shit, and that she hadn't seen me so happy since last Thanksgiving, when John and I went home together.

As for John, he and I were having a blast. It was actually better that we weren't taking the same classes because it kept us fresh for our free time. We didn't see each other much during the day, but we sure enjoyed our evenings together. Even if we both had work to do, we could at least snuggle up together while we did it.

John

Liam and I were so much in love. My feelings were even more intense than they had been the first time around, heightened by those months when I thought I'd lost him. I enjoyed being in touch with his family again. Since I met them, I'd never quite gotten over the feeling that they were somehow my family, too. Over the summer, they all visited us in New York, one by one, and we had fun getting reacquainted. At the end of the summer, before school started, we enjoyed a week together at the Jersey Shore, in Avalon. By the time that was over, I felt thoroughly Macadam.

Michael and Jess were our best friends, both of them relieved not to be caught in the middle anymore. There had been a lot of awkwardness after Liam's trip to find me, especially between him and Jess. I was still in the UK, but apparently there were several loud arguments and a period of nonspeaking. Their many years as friends finally overcame the difficulties, and they found their way back to loving each other. Michael and I had a few issues because he felt like I'd ignored what he tried to tell me that awful December. I felt that he should have been a lot more forthcoming, but in the end, we were able to put the past behind us.

Jess and Michael had gotten engaged while we were gone, and Jess constantly harped on the same theme with me—that it was time for me to kick Liam's ass into making me an honest man. I told her I didn't want to kick his ass into anything, that it wasn't how we rolled, but she said it was only a figure of speech.

"Don't forget everything you learned the hard way, John. You just need to take the bull by the horns, like I did with Michael. Go buy Liam a ring, stick your tongue down his throat, and don't let him draw another breath until he says yes."

I shook my head, looking away. "I want to marry Liam, but the timing has to be right. Someday it will happen."

"Hey, hey!" She clapped her hands until I met her eyes again. "It needs to happen now. I'd put money on it going something like this. You'd say, 'Liam, darling, you know I love you more than life itself. I bought this beautiful ring for you, and I want you to wear it forever. Marry me and be my husband?'"

I couldn't help grinning at hearing my dream spoken out loud.

She went on. "Liam would say, 'Babe, you don't need to ask me twice. Yes, Yes, YES!!! Where do I sign?'"

We laughed, but I knew she was right. I wasn't sure exactly when the time to ask would be, and I wanted to be ready. I absolutely, completely, undoubtedly, and desperately wanted to marry that incredible boyfriend of mine.

One weekend, Jess needed a new suit for interviews, so we went shopping. We happened to walk by a jewelry store, and she took me in, *just to look*. Before long, I was hyper-focused on the most gorgeous men's Claddagh ring I had ever seen—white gold, perfect weight, looking for a stunning guy with an Irish name to wear it. I handed over the money and walked out of the store with that gorgeous symbol of my hoped-for future, and Jess held me while I cried on the sidewalk. I wasn't sure when I would ask Liam but doubted it would be long. We needed to seize the rights the State of New York had finally given our people.

Liam

One night I came home to John's homemade chili and cornbread, along with the news that he'd talked to Mom earlier. That was no surprise. Since we'd been reunited, they talked a lot more than she and I did.

"Andie wants us in Wainscott for Thanksgiving. She said your sisters will be home for the holiday. I told her it was fine with me, but you and I had to discuss it before we could make a final decision."

We sat down and I started on my chili. It was as good a time as any to tell him. "Let's do it, but on one condition."

He barely kept his smile close-mouthed. "Which is?"

"I get you all to myself for Christmas and New Year's. Just us."

"No objection, counselor." John put another ladle of chili in my bowl. "You want to go someplace?"

"I already... well, it was gonna be a surprise, and we can change it if you want, but I kinda already made us some reservations."

He opened his eyes wide, grinning like an excited kid. "Where?"

"Stowe, in Vermont. You know it? I rented us a cabin."

John was out of his seat and on me like glue. Real sticky glue. "I've always wanted to go to Stowe!" He gave me a quick peck. "Seriously? Our own cabin, and just the two of us?" Another kiss, this one longer and with a burst of heat. "I might not want to leave."

"Oh yeah, there's a hot tub, too," I said. Nothing wrong with a little oversell.

John's dimples blossomed and then flourished. "Liam, I'm totally there. Now get in the bedroom and lie down so I can blow you."

I laughed, but quickly discovered he meant business. Just that easily, our holiday plans were made. It would be nice to see my family at Thanksgiving, but I couldn't wait to have John all to myself for Christmas. I had some big plans in mind.

27

Liam

Going home again for Thanksgiving was exactly what John and I needed, and I knew it would be an awesome weekend with the family all together. It somehow made it all real, that John and I were together for good.

We took a few minutes moving our things inside, and on the last trip from the car I asked him to wait up. "John Lawrence, my most extraordinary boyfriend, I cannot tell you how happy I am to be here with you."

Dimples! "Maybe about as happy as I am to be here with you? And your mom is amazing. She makes me feel like this is my home, too."

Arms burdened, we leaned together for a quick peck and headed inside. Mom told us we had thirty minutes before lunch, so we went to unpack. In our room I took John in my arms. "We have a tradition at this point, remember?"

John grinned. "You want to take a shower like last time, bad boy?" He winked at me. "I do, too."

We lost no time shucking our clothes and getting under the water, where we lovingly washed each other. Of course, dicks got hard, hands got into it, panting and moaning joined the party, and John ended up braced against the shower wall while I fucked him from behind.

Knowing how bathrooms amplify sound, we tried to be quiet, which only heightened the excitement. John came so hard that I had to hold him up for a moment before he was able to rinse off.

That was precisely what I wanted to do for the rest of my life, take care of John and make him feel great. That's what made *me* feel great.

We got dressed and found Mom in the kitchen, with some chicken salad sandwiches and oatmeal cookies ready for lunch. We spent the rest of the day welcoming my sisters, meeting Cait's fiancé, Chris, and following our usual Thanksgiving Eve traditions. John and I made his mom's broccoli casserole again for our contribution to Thanksgiving dinner, and I insisted on returning to the Green Lantern for drinks that night.

Cait and Vonnie fawned over John like he was the prodigal son. Since they were monopolizing my boyfriend-slash-*please let him be more*, I had a chance to hang out with Chris, who turned out to be a great guy. He was an investment banker, and since I was taking Financial Transactions that semester, I was able to talk to him about his work.

Over beer, he smiled nervously. "Listen, man, I've got a sister and I know how it is. I love Cait and I'll do anything to make her happy. I swear to God, I won't ever cheat on her or disrespect her. She's everything to me, and I really hope you and I can be good friends."

He had me at *I'll do anything to make her happy*. It was how I felt about John, and I was stoked about how much Chris loved Cait. “Dude, you be good to my sister, and you and I are solid.” I thought for a sec. “Well, you gotta be good to my man, too. Deal?”

He grinned, obviously relieved. “Totally. Thanks, Liam. It means a lot.”

We stayed out for a few hours, having drinks and playing darts while we all caught up. Once, Chris and I had to go piss, and when we came back, John and the girls were over in a corner squealing and hugging about something.

It was a little sad that in just a couple short days we all had to go our separate ways again, but I pushed those thoughts away. We could spend time together whenever we wanted. In September, Cait and Chris had moved to New York from Chicago, so they weren't so far away, and Vonnie was in her first year of med school in Boston. Dammit, we were all growing up.

John

At the Green Lantern, I gave Liam some time to spend with Chris because I knew they hadn't met before. Liam loved his sister and he would feel better if he got to know her fiancé, and as a relative newcomer to the Macadam family, I was betting that Chris wanted a chance to bond with Cait's brother.

Vonnie and Cait were eager to spend time with me, so we moved to another table for a little while. Cait talked about adjusting to life in the City, and Vonnie told us about med school. We wound up discussing what had happened between Liam and me. They were both thrilled that their brother was, as they said, back to his old self.

Cait grinned at me and confided that she hoped Liam and I

would tie the knot before too long. "It would be so much fun! Think about it. We could even make it a double wedding, if you guys wanted to."

"Hell yes!" Vonnie added. "I could be the maid of honor and best woman at the same time."

Spending the rest of my life as Liam's husband was exactly what I wanted, but I didn't think I was ready to share that. So it was that I surprised the hell out of myself with what came out of my mouth. "I can't wait to marry him! Just between us, I'll probably be getting down on one knee before the year's out."

Liam

On Thanksgiving Day, John spent a lot of time helping Mom cook, but whenever he wasn't in the kitchen, he was right by my side. When he was with Mom, though, Vonnie and Cait had only one thing on their minds, when was I gonna pop the question?

"You can now, you know. It's legal in New York."

"What if he asks you? What'll you say?"

"Stop bugging me," I finally begged. "I wanna marry him, okay? So bad. Things will happen, but it *is* up to John and me, after all. Trust me, I've got a plan."

Vonnie had asked what I'd say if John proposed to me. Well, I'd say yes, of course, but I really didn't think that would happen. I had the idea that he was waiting for me to ask him, and he didn't have much longer to wait.

The guests had come and gone, and we were all stuffed. I needed to go up to my old room, alone, so I said I had to go to the bathroom and was gonna grab something to show Chris while I was up there. Once I got upstairs, I looked for what I was really after, the ring I'd bought for John last year. I'd hidden it behind a couple old trophies in a corner of my bookcase last January after I got out of the hospital.

Fuck!—it wasn't there! *Oh, shit-fuck!* I knew exactly where I'd left it because it was an old hiding place for porn. I started ransacking the room, figuring I must have stuck it someplace else despite my distinct memory otherwise. I really needed to find it. It was way too expensive for me to replace right then, but that wasn't even half the point. The ring was *perfect* for John, and I'd never find another one like it. Just when my frustration reached its peak, there were two soft knocks on the door. I figured it was John missing me, but Mom walked into the room.

"Having trouble finding it?" she asked.

"Finding what?"

She smiled, and I remembered what she told me one time, that part of being a mom is making things okay. "The ring you're looking for."

I was surprised, to say the least. "Do you know what happened to it?"

"Here." She gently placed the blue box in my palm. "It's gorgeous, Liam. I didn't mean to scare you, but last summer I was giving the room a going over before letting a guest sleep in here, and I found it. It's far too nice to leave on the back of a rickety bookcase, so I put it with my jewelry. I meant to tell you, but it slipped my mind." She raised her eyebrows. "When did you buy it, honey?"

"When we were here for Thanksgiving last year."

Taking the ring out of the box, I turned it over in my hand, and man—it was even nicer than I remembered. I looked at Mom. "Can you keep a secret?"

"You know I can."

I nodded at the door. "Close that, then."

28

Thursday, December 19

John

Exams passed in a flurry of activity. Liam and I spent as much time together as we could that week, but between my study group meetings and his studying with people who were in his classes, it proved to be much less time than we wanted. By Thursday, both of us were on edge. As we stood in the kitchen cleaning up after a mediocre dinner of frozen eggplant parm and salad, Liam cast me a wide-eyed glance, and the muscle under his left eye twitched.

"What is it?" I asked.

He shook his head and went back to drying a knife.

"Uh-uh. We don't do that to each other, remember?" He turned to return the knife to the rack on the wall. I tried again. "What's wrong, Liam?"

He turned back around, chomping on his lip, and eventually took a deep breath. "What are we gonna do next summer? I have the associateship at McBurnie, but you're supposed to still be up here going to summer school."

I crossed the floor and stood in front of him. "You know we said we'll figure something out. One possibility concerns Jess. She has her summer job here, but Michael just this week got that summer associateship at Cross and Barton in New York. Jess wants us to be roomies here. We'd go down to Manhattan on the weekends, or you two can come up here."

Liam jerked away. "We'd be apart five days a week." He raised his voice, but I knew it was panic speaking, not anger. "We already wasted too much time apart. Is that what you want, to be here five days a week without me?" His face was tight, and his frown reached from his hairline to his throat.

I shook my head. "You know it isn't, Liam. You're right, we *have* wasted too much time already."

He blew out a frustrated breath. "Why'd you say it then? What about Zimmermann's suggestion? Go to the summer session at NYU as a visiting student? Taking classes at NYU would be awesome. It might open more doors for you."

"Is that what you want me to do? It would be awesome there, but I don't even know if it's really possible. Zimmermann mentioned it, but he has nothing to do with NYU."

Liam scoffed, his face hard. "He has *connections* there, that's *why* he mentioned it." His voice was rising again, and a vein popped out on his forehead.

I took another step toward him. "I will see if it works, I promise. It would definitely be my first choice." I ran a hand across his cheek. "Please try to calm down, sweetheart. I promise we'll work something out to be together. There are lots of law schools in New York, or I'll just not take any classes next summer."

"Don't say that! You wouldn't get your degree with the rest of us then!" He scrubbed his face hard and more veins appeared. "Christ, this is gonna be one huge goddamned fucked-up mess if we aren't careful." He went back to the sink and started rinsing it out. "I could turn McBurnie down, get a job at one of the firms up here."

"Liam, no!" Now I was the one raising my voice. "I will *not* see you waste your talent that way. You'd be bored to death, working on shitty cases, and would pretty much shut yourself out of being able to get a BigLaw job after graduation." I closed my eyes while I took a deep breath to the count of five, and Liam seemed a little calmer when I looked at him again. "Please, let's work this out after Christmas, okay? We'll find a solution that makes us both happy, and I promise we'll be together." I kissed him on the cheek. "No being apart."

His face didn't relax and I could tell he had more to say. Finally, he sighed. "Okay. I'm sorry I got upset, but I just can't live without you again." He stretched his neck and shrugged his shoulders. "I have to go review tax law for tomorrow."

"You're staying home?" I asked.

"Yeah. I know you have your study group."

I picked up his hand and kissed it. "Only until ten o'clock. Then can I come home and study with you?"

"Please do. I'm gonna miss you a lot." He kissed me, and when I told him I'd let him know before I left for the study group meeting, he nodded. Walking out of the kitchen with his shoulders slumped, he left me wondering what the hell we *would* do next summer.

Liam

I FELT like a day-old dog turd run over by a semi. I shouldn't have gotten so upset about next summer. Hell, I shouldn't have brought it up at all with us both worn out from studying, but nobody understands how much I worry about it. I talked to Michael and he said I should just tell John what I want him to do, but that isn't how John and I operate, except I guess that's exactly what I did.

I meant what I said, though. We already wasted too much time being apart. I want to *live* with John, not have him off someplace away from me again. Michael said it's just a sore spot, but I say it's a scar that we need to use as a reminder. Michael said we can do anything for three more months, but I don't know if I can. Michael said maybe I should just let John decide and then go along with his decision, but it's a decision that affects me every bit as much as it does John. *Piss-fuck-shit! When did you start listening to Michael, anyway?*

At ten o'clock, my phone buzzed.

JOHN: Hey stud muffin, how are you?
LIAM: Sick of tax but OK, u?
JOHN: Tired! On my way home. Be there in 10 minutes tops. I love you and can't wait to hug your sexy bod and kiss your pouty lips. <3
LIAM: Bring it on babe! Im here waiting

I went to make hot chocolate and grilled cheese sandwiches, one of our favorite late-night snacks. When John got home, I met him at the door and hugged him like the treasure he was. "I'm really sorry I was so grouchy earlier."

He gave me a kiss before he took off his coat. "I'd worry if you weren't concerned about it, but since when can we not find solutions to challenges? We got over that hump."

I nodded and took his hand. "Come with me. I've got a special treat ready."

We sat at the kitchen table to eat our snack. *Time to tell the truth. Being forthright is better than everybody being hurt.* "I'm gonna be honest and say that unless you really what to be up here next summer, in which case I'll have to figure out how to deal, I want us to be together in New York. I want you to be there, no matter what."

He took a big sip of his hot chocolate. "That's what I want, too, Liam, and I promise we'll make it happen, but can I ask a favor?"

I nodded and stole a chocolatey kiss before he could say anything else.

"Can we just agree that we'll be together in New York next summer, and then table this discussion until January? We'll have a solution in place long before the semester's over."

I wanted things solved right that minute, but I had to be a realist and accept that it was as solved as it could get until we knew more. "Okay." I smiled at him, remembering what was going to happen over Christmas. "Let's enjoy our break."

He nodded, and it was his turn to steal a chocolatey kiss.

"John?"

"Yep?"

"Your Crim Law exam is at nine o'clock, like my Tax?"

"Yes, sir."

"Whaddya say we go to bed and get some rest?" We stood up, and when I took his hand, he gave me a kiss that was anything but sleepy.

"What if I want something besides rest?" His voice sounded sandy, the way it got when he was horny.

I drew a couple circles on his chest. "You read my mind."

We stood there making out for a few minutes, while my tongue delved deep into his mouth and my right hand played with his dick. He sneaked his hand inside my pants too, and when I started to feel the early warnings of a coming blast, I broke the kiss and stepped back.

"Wanna be inside you."

He smiled shyly, as he often did at these moments. "I want you inside me."

"Right here?"

"Let's go to bed."

In the bedroom, we wasted no time getting our clothes off. On the bed, John pushed me back against the pillows and crawled down between my legs.

After half a minute, I tugged at his hair. "You gonna do anything down there or just stare at me all night?"

"Aw!" He slapped at my hand. "Can't I admire a work of art for a minute without being battered?"

"Just going kinda crazy up here." He looked at me, sporting a wicked smile, and I told him what was what. "You're just laying down there watching my dick go *thump, thump, thump* and all I feel is it bouncing away."

He reached out a finger and traced the bottom of my pulsing cock. I sucked in breath and thrust up into the air. "John, *please*!"

All at once, I was buried in his hot, wet mouth. I couldn't help but whimper, and he looked up at me again with his mouth well-stuffed, giving me the best eye smile you could imagine. I stroked his hair and lay back on the pillow, closing my eyes. He was using just the right amount of suction and I was twisting around some, really wanting to fuck his pretty mouth. As good as that would have been, I wanted something else even more, so after a moment, I patted his head and hesitantly pulled out. He crawled back up the bed.

"Didn't you like it? Was I doing something wrong?"

I brushed his nose with a knuckle. "You were doing everything right, babe, but I don't wanna come with you way down there. I want you to come with me."

He kissed me while he ground his hard meat into my thigh.

I backed out of the kiss and whispered. "I wanna be inside you, like I said."

He reached down and squeezed my cock, making me gasp at the tickle of precum oozing out of the slit.

"I want you inside me." He nipped at my ear lobe. "You belong inside me."

I flipped him on his back, and he spread his legs for me. I crawled between them, where I kissed his hard dick and traced his balls with my tongue. When I blew breath across his cock, he moaned softly.

"Hand me the lube?" I asked.

He pulled away a little as he twisted around to get it off the nightstand. "Lie down on your back," he said.

I lay back, a little nervous he might wanna fuck me, but we'd just discussed me being inside him. I was being silly, though. John was a total bottom, and I was a top. He'd never wanted it any other way. I guess if he ever really wanted to do it, I'd try, but we worked great the other way and I thought we should leave it alone.

John climbed on top of me and sat on my thighs. He looked hungry as he reached for my cock. I moaned from the pressure as he swirled on some lube, which felt like magic on my dick. I could've cum like that if he'd kept it up. He must have sensed the urgency because he took my hand and wrapped my grip firmly around the base of my cock.

"Hold there, but no jerking." He gave me the sweetest kiss before he sat up and squeezed some lube on his fingers. Raising up, he reached behind himself. Immediately, his muscles flexed and he squinted his eyes. When he grunted, I was jealous of his fingers, inside him already. I watched his face and held on to my dick while he got himself ready. Soon he was sweating into his messy hair, and the sight of him so worked up inflamed my already serious need.

"Don't hurt yourself, babe," I said.

He was panting lightly. "No worries. I can't wait longer anyway." He squinted again as he pulled his fingers out and sat back down solidly on my thighs. Holding on to my hips, he scooted forward, lifted up slightly, and trapped my cock under his ass. I moaned, throbbing and hard, as he peeked at me from under hooded eyelids.

"Want to fuck me now?" He moved a little, causing my dickhead to slide against his hole, and fanning my fire into an inferno. I twisted, trying to get lined up without using my hands.

"Get up on it," I gasped. "Ride me!"

He smiled as he scooted forward. Raising up again, he reached down and adjusted the angle, and my cockhead breached the tight ring of his butt. The heat inside him was intense, and the pressure was perfect. I willed myself not to thrust upward, knowing I had to let him get used to me. He rose slightly and lowered himself again. *Holy Jesus!* Suddenly, half my cock was trapped in that tight heat.

He started moving slowly. As he grunted and set a rhythm, I thrust upward, meeting his movements with my own. His mouth hung open, his eyes were half closed, and he moaned and grunted every time my cock touched his prostate.

"Good babe?" I asked, panting like a dog.

"God, yes! Don't stop, just fuck me."

We kept it up for a while. I'd get really close, or he would, then we'd stop everything but our smutty kisses. We both tried to make the moment last forever, and I loved how he pleasured himself on my cock. He kept adjusting the angle, finally holding my hands completely still as he used my dick as his own personal joystick.

After what felt like forever, his eyes shot open and he gasped. "Coming! Now!" he shouted, firing a wad of cum right past the side of my head. Another, right behind it, landed on my cheek with a loud splat. That had my balls drawing up, and with a mighty shout, I was there. My cock heaved, working heroically to pump every bit of life within me out into John. He kept shooting, over and over, crying out my name, and my own voice roared as my spurting refused to ease up.

Eventually, I wasn't coming anymore but was still in glory. John's face, racked with pleasure, told me he was in the same place. In slow motion, he crumpled over, both of us gasping for air. We were totally fucked out, and I never wanted the moment to end as we lay there, more one than two.

29

Sunday, December 22

Liam

The alarm went off at 7:30. We had a lot of driving to do that day and needed to get an early start. On the way to Stowe, we had to detour through Wainscott to see the family and exchange gifts. It was one hell of a detour, but we both thought it was worthwhile. After Wainscott, we'd have a whole ten days alone together, and while John didn't know it yet, with any kind of luck, we would drive back home as an engaged couple.

He was as excited as I'd ever seen him about a trip. He said he'd always wanted to see Stowe, but I think his excitement ran deeper than that. He wanted us to be alone together, too, and I suspected he was counting on this trip to clarify our future.

John turned over and put a hand on my chest. "I'm so happy, sweetheart. Being with you is the best thing that's ever happened to me."

"Me too," I said. "Nothing else comes close."

We lay there listening to a dog barking down the street while John caressed my chin. "Really, Liam, this is like a dream. It's going to be the best Christmas ever, because I'm with you."

I gave him a happy kiss. "I agree. This is our first Christmas together, and I can't wait to have a hundred more." I pinched his nipple and smiled when he yelped.

He chuckled. "Only a hundred more? Do I hear two hundred?" He moved fast and nipped one of my nipples, drawing a considerably bigger yelp than I'd gotten out of him.

After a quick breakfast, I packed all our luggage into the car except the one bag John was still fiddling with in the bedroom. Then I sat in front of morning TV, feeling impatient but staying quiet. I would not be that guy who harassed his boyfriend for taking longer.

Finally, John walked into the room carrying his overnight bag. "I'm all ready. Sorry I took so long."

I switched off the TV, stood up, and winked at him. "I was wondering if you fell asleep again"

"Oh, you!" He swatted my arm. "I'll have you know, I packed a special bit of love into that overnighter. Good things take a while."

Stealing the bag from him, I made a show of testing its weight. "It does feel heavy." I gave him a quick peck. "Can't wait to get that special love."

John

We talked most of the way to Long Island, and eventually put on a playlist of Christmas music. I thought about the ring I'd packed in my bag before we left. I'd decided to propose while we were in Vermont, and I was pretty confident he would say yes. *Fingers crossed.*

Our brief time with the family would be good. Andie was cooking a big holiday dinner tonight, and we were going to open gifts tomorrow morning. The day after tomorrow, Christmas Eve, Liam and I would drive on up to Stowe.

Snow began falling about an hour out of Wainscott, more than a flurry but less than a snowstorm. Southerner that I was, I'd never gotten used to the snow, which I found magical. Nevertheless, snow mixed with cars made me nervous, so I invoked my backseat driver's license and urged Liam to be careful.

"*You're* telling *me* to be careful?" He flashed an incredulous grin. "Just be glad *I'm* driving. Remember two weeks ago when it was snowing, and you drove to school? It's a wonder we escaped with our lives, and that only a little bit of the paint from your car is on that tree."

I couldn't let him get away with that, so I called him the pet name he secretly loved but acted like he didn't. "*Sugar Plum*, that was all a plan. I skidded into that tree because I wanted to hear you scream."

"Didn't scream. Yelled!" He tried to look offended, but his toothy smile gave him away. "Regardless, I'm driving now, so we're in safe hands."

It was snowing hard by the time we arrived, and Chris came out to help us carry our things inside. In addition to our luggage, we'd brought food and supplies for Stowe. Since the temperature was freezing, we couldn't leave it all in the car.

Liam and I settled into our usual room near the kitchen before we ventured into the living room, where Andie had laid out enough snacks to feed an army. As soon as I was in the doorway, I stopped in my tracks, bedazzled by some of the most beautiful holiday decorations I'd ever seen.

Liam squeezed my hand and turned me to face him. "Merry Christmas, John. Ain't Mom the best?" The kiss he gave me was even more splendid than the Christmas tree, and he kept at it until my bones had all melted. He pointed upward when he finally pulled away, and I saw that we stood under a giant bundle of mistletoe.

"Glad my boys haven't gotten shy all of a sudden." Vonnie dashed across the room for hugs. "That's the best kiss this house has seen since the last time you two were here."

"Eat, guys," Andie commanded. "It's only three thirty and dinner isn't for hours yet."

Liam

I ALMOST TOOK John aside and proposed that afternoon. He sat in Mom's living room having a great time, talking to her and my sisters as if they'd known each other all their lives. It wasn't just that they all got along; they really loved each other, which made me love all of them even more. John was already a Macadam, and I had to convince him to make it legal.

After a while, he followed Mom into the kitchen. I got up to go too, but he told me to sit back down and enjoy visiting with everyone. Mom tried to tell John to stay, but he was determined to help her. After a little while, I heard them laughing and carrying on in the kitchen, having their own grand time.

Once, when the cider got the best of me and I had to go to the bathroom, I couldn't resist dropping by the kitchen to take a look. I stopped in the hallway just outside, amazed by what I saw. It was like synchronized swimming, except it was synchronized cooking. Mom had gone all out the way she always does, and both of them were busy as bees, working on different things, moving in a strange and beautiful dance. Unable to wipe the grin off my face, I turned around and walked away, the scene filed away in my mind to enjoy for years to come.

While I was in the bathroom, Chris went to the fridge in the garage and snagged us some beers. My sisters and I showed our geeky side by hauling out Scrabble, the official family game, for a bitter battle. Chris played but wasn't quite in our league. Later, as we sat on the sofas by the fire, John came into the room and hugged me from the back. "Having fun, sweetie?"

I twisted around and looked up into gorgeous blue eyes. "So much fun, and I know you did, too. I saw."

"It was great." His eyes glowed with excitement. "We're pretty much finished in there, so Andie said you should mix some martinis and she'll be right in to join us."

I went to the liquor cabinet and rummaged around for the good stuff before taking a poll for dirty or clean. Of course, given that crowd, dirty won, with the deciding vote cast by Andie Macadam herself.

"Just in time for preprandial libations, I'm glad to see," she said. "Put in some olive juice, Liam."

John and Chris laughed, and Cait rolled her eyes. "Mom! Who says 'preprandial libations?' Have you been reading those English murder mysteries again?"

Mom kept a straight face. "No, I've been watching *Masterpiece Theatre*."

I mixed three parts vodka, one-half part vermouth, one-half part olive juice, and a few dashes of orange bitters, and everyone loved the result. We discussed our plans for the next morning while we drank two martinis apiece. John sat next to me, leaning on my shoulder, and at one point took out his phone and let out a big whoop. "Sorry to drag this thing out, but I just remembered they started posting 1L grades today."

"Good news?" Mom was always great at stating the obvious.

"Three grades in, so far. I got As in Crim, Con Law, and R&W."

Applause and cheers accompanied his big grin, and I gave him a kiss after I told him how proud I was of him.

"Congratulations, John," Mom said. "That is outstanding." She was sitting on John's other side and took him in her arms for a big hug.

"Hey Mom, I make lots of As, too," I joked, putting on my best offended look. "Where are my hugs? Have I been replaced?"

Her eyes twinkled at me over John's shoulder. "Not replaced, son. Augmented."

We changed for dinner, and John was exquisite in gray wool pants, a white shirt, and the sapphire blue cashmere sweater I'd given him for Christmas last year. The sweater did magic things for his eyes, just as I knew it would way back then.

Mom outdid herself with dinner. We had a roast goose with all the trimmings, and dessert was a yule log. She made one every year and created it completely by hand, even the meringue mushrooms. After a cheese course, accompanied by a delicious Port wine, Chris invited John and me to join him outside for a cigar. We went out there with him, though neither of us was interested in smoking.

The snow was coming down harder than ever. It was thick across the yard and the street was buried. John was looking so forward to getting up to Stowe, and I didn't want to disappoint him, but it looked like we might have to stay an extra day. If it wasn't safe, it wasn't safe, and he would understand that. We'd leave when we could.

JOHN

I WOKE about seven o'clock needing to go to the bathroom. While I was up, I walked to the window, wondering if the snow had stopped. A massive wall of white confronted me after I pulled back the drapes, and snow was still falling. I thought about how eager Liam was to get us to Stowe, but if it wasn't safe to go that day, we shouldn't.

His warm, muscular arms folded around me as soon as I got back into bed. Something hard poked into the back of my thigh, and soon it started moving. I laughed and twisted around to find a smiling, beautiful man with sleepy eyes.

"Another hour's sleep?" I asked. "Then whatever you want."

He nodded, and I turned back over so he could wrap me up as his little spoon.

After another hour, I woke again to find him sitting on the bed next to me, looking serious. "I need you to listen to me."

I nodded as I skimmed the inside of his arm with my fingertips.

"There's a huge snow outside and it's still coming down. I just checked the weather on my phone, and I'm afraid we won't make it to Vermont today." He wrinkled his forehead more than it already had been. "I'm sorry, I know how much—"

"Shh." I put two fingers across his lips. "One question."

He nodded.

"Will we be together today?" Rhetorical, obviously.

He smiled and nodded again.

"Then everything's fine. As long as we're together, the rest is gravy."

LIAM

The metamorphosis was complete. Just as the snow had transformed the everyday world into an enchanted place, time and circumstance had transformed our love into an enchanted thing. John and I were imperfect individuals, but the love that bound us was flawless. I knew what I was going to do.

First, I luxuriated in having my back and hair washed in the shower, and in John's sweet kisses after he rinsed the suds from my face. As I washed him, I marveled that his body was mine to touch. In that shower, I realized that the reverence and affection John and I showed for one another transcended anything sexual. It was spiritual.

After we dried off, he asked me what I was wearing to breakfast, and I pretended to think carefully. "Gonna wear flannel PJ bottoms and a thermal," I said. "Hey, you know those burgundy plaid bottoms of yours?"

He cocked his head. "The ones you put in my suitcase?"

"Yes. Wear those?"

He wrinkled his nose. "They're getting kind of ratty."

I ran a finger across his cheek. "Wear them, please?"

"Okay."

"And that pink thermal?" I said.

He cocked his head again, farther than before. "It's older than the flannel bottoms."

That time, I couldn't keep my lips off his cheek. "Please wear it, John. For me?"

"Sure," he said, then squinted his eyes. "This is exactly what I wore—"

I chuckled, nervous but happy. "I know. I brought mine too." I pulled on blue plaid PJ bottoms and a beige thermal. "I wanted us to have exactly the same things we wore on our first trip together, last Thanksgiving."

That earned me such a big kiss that I wondered if we

should skip breakfast, but John broke away. "Let's go eat, I'm starved."

I patted the comforting shape of the box in my pocket and followed him out of the room.

In the dining room, Mom was drinking coffee while she read something on her iPad, and Vonnie sat looking out the window, sipping hot chocolate.

"Good morning." Mom used a hand to indicate all the food on the table. "I hope you're hungry."

"Starved," John answered. "I always get so hungry here."

"Everything smells great," I said, and kissed her cheek.

John took a seat across the table from Mom, and I sat down beside him.

She poured coffee for us. "I'm afraid you won't be leaving today. They're saying the entire eastern part of the state is snowed in and the roads are closed."

"It's okay," I said. "We already know."

John smiled. "We're happy here, if it's all right with you."

"If it's all right? I'm thrilled to have you here. I know you want to get up to Vermont, but please stay as long as you can."

John nodded and asked Vonnie if she'd slept well.

"I slept *barely* okay. No thanks to you guys."

I shook my head and didn't even look at her. "You're full of it."

"Just kidding," she said, turning her chair back to the table. "It was actually Cait and Chris—"

Mom put down her iPad. "Siobhan Macadam! No more!"

"Okay, okay," Vonnie said, wearing a smirk. "Pass the eggs, please."

We talked about all the little things families think of around a table. Vonnie was telling us about a dog she might adopt when Cait and Chris came down. I chuckled a bit when I realized they really did look worse for wear. *God, do John and I look that way?* A quick glance in his direction reassured me that we didn't, or at least he didn't.

"Was it as cold down here last night as it was upstairs?" Cait asked. "We thought we'd never get warm."

Vonnie couldn't help herself and laughed out loud. Mom cleared her throat, looking stern. "I have an assignment for you, Siobhan Macadam. I want a boyfriend—or girlfriend, whatever —here with you next year. You have made fun long enough, and it's time for you to settle down."

Vonnie's eyes shot open and she started sputtering. "But.... Mom, I... I can't...." She scoffed. "I can't just wave a magic wand and...."

Seeing Vonnie truly flustered was a rarity, and when Mom started laughing, we all joined in.

Vonnie huffed and rolled her eyes. "Okay, you had me. I'll be good."

Mom took a sip of coffee and looked across the table. "I have an idea, John, if you're interested. I need to make more cinnamon rolls for the next few days, and I remember last year when you asked me to teach you how. Since you're going to be here today, it would be fun to do it together if you want to."

John beamed at her while he struggled to swallow the eggs he was eating. "I'd love to! They're great, and I have such a good time cooking with you."

Mom never let any of *us* help with the cinnamon rolls. It made me remember the day before, when I'd realized that John was already a Macadam. When we left Syracuse, I had a definite plan in mind for Stowe, but sometimes you realize that the right thing to do is different from what you've planned, and you need to go with it.

I gulped as I stood, and everyone looked over while I pushed my chair out of the way. John flared his dimples for me, and I stared into his gorgeous deep blue eyes. "John William

Lawrence...." I choked up. He turned his head to the side, and I tried again. "John...." *Easy, Liam. Just go slow.*

I had his full attention, along with everyone else's, and I gulped again. *Deep breath.* "John, last year at Thanksgiving, in this room, you did a very brave thing. You made me feel like the most important man in the world, and you still do, every day. Now it's my turn to be brave."

Reaching into my pocket, I took out the box I'd put there in the bedroom and sank down beside him onto one knee. He looked confused for a minute and then a little panicky as realization dawned. "Liam, I...."

I shook my head slowly, grinning so widely I couldn't say a word. Everyone was watching, all eyes huge. "We've been through a lot, you and me, good times and bad. You put up with me, which means you put up with a lot." *Breathe!*

"Oh, honey—" That would be Mom, immediately shushing herself with a hand across her mouth.

John's eyes were wet, glimmering in the morning light that streamed in through the windows. "You are my treasure, John, my life's treasure. You make me feel alive, like no matter what, things will be okay as long as we're together." *Keep breathing. You don't want to pass out before you ask him.* "You said it this morning, as long as we're together, the rest is gravy."

John made a guttural sound and put his hands over his mouth. I had a flash of worry, but his amazing eyes told me to keep going. "You changed me for the better on the first day we met. I fell in love with you hard and fast." I stopped to swallow, and the room was so quiet that I heard my shirt rustle from the slight movement. "If I've learned anything during the last year, it's that I can't live worth a damn without you, but I live the best life on earth *with* you. I don't ever want to be without you again."

John moved his hands from his mouth, and although his

eyes were full of tears, he was grinning at me. Peripherally, I saw tears streaming down my mother and sisters' faces, and Chris's mouth hung open. *You're almost there. Only a few more words.*

"John, my love, would you please do me the honor, the favor... give me the privilege...."

I held the blue box up in front of him, opening the lid so he could see the ring. "Will you marry me?"

He sat frozen and blinking hard as tears spilled out onto his cheeks. Something was wrong. *Surely he's not going to say no.*

"Marry me?" I asked again.

He roused himself and yelled, "Wait! Just wait." Then he got up and fled the room.

I couldn't believe it. I was down on one knee, and the man I'd just publicly begged to marry me had run out of the room. I registered confusion on the faces around the table, but in a few seconds, I heard John in the kitchen, running back. It sounded like he bounced off something, and then he rushed back into the room. His face was flushed and his eyes were wild.

"I'm sorry I ran out! I had to get something out of my bag."

Unbelievably, he pushed his chair out of the way and got down on one knee, too, right in front of me. His face was still wet, and his dimples were huge as he held up another box, this one burgundy. The lid was open, and another ring was inside.

He tried to talk but couldn't get anything out, so we were both just kneeling there, holding rings in each other's faces, wearing the most hopeful expressions you've ever seen.

He kept trying to clear his throat and finally was able to croak some words out. "Liam. Oh God...." He started laughing despite the tears that were still coursing down his cheeks. "I love you so much. You make me unbelievably happy. You're the love of my life."

I wore the grin of the redeemed.

He sobbed, and I wondered how anybody could sob and laugh at the same time. "I was going to do this in Vermont." He put his free hand over his heart and huffed for air. "I was going to ask you up there, but you beat me to it. And I'm so glad because... *oh*... this is so right."

Tears cut off his voice, and I realized I'd only thought he was beautiful up until then. He looked hopeful and frazzled and happy and dazed, his hair was a little kerflooey, a lopsided grin lit up his face, and his tears created stunning blue prisms in his eyes. *And those dimples*, they were deeper than ever.

I got that he was saying yes in the most beautiful way possible, and I was crying too, but trying in vain not to show it because I wanted to be strong for him. *Ha!* We were both on the floor, desperately in love with each other, and neither of us was able to form a word.

After a moment, he took a shuddering breath and cleared his throat again. "Liam.... Yes! I want to be your husband more than anything else." He held up his left hand and I took my cue, removing the ring from my box and pushing it onto his finger. He looked between me and his hand in amazement, as if he couldn't believe it was real. After a moment, he took the other ring from its box, and I held up my left hand. Grinning at me, he slid it onto my finger.

He chewed his lip for a few seconds. "I love you, Liam."

"And I love you, John."

Wordlessly, we stood up and I moved in, kissing him, cradling him like the prize he was, enjoying the way his tongue moved softly against mine. Finally remembering where we were, I backed off and looked at my fiancé in wonder. It was about then that I heard sniffles and looked around to find a table full of women wiping their eyes with their napkins.

Chris was the first to react. "Awesome! *Jesus*, guys!" He started laughing, jumped out of his chair, and ran around the table, where he grabbed John and me into a triple hug. "Congratulations, you two, this is so great! I love you guys!"

The women were beginning to stand, the shock on their faces slowly giving way to glee. One by one, they came over and hugged John and me, crying and laughing in that way I hadn't realized was possible before this morning. Vonnie squealed while she and John jumped up and down, and Mom had me by the shoulders.

"Liam," she said, still sniffling, "I am *so* happy for you. This is a great day in the Macadam family. I'd say I wish your father were here to see this, but he is, and he's thrilled for you, son."

"Oh, Mom, I—" Now she had me crying again.

"You've grown up into a splendid young man. You deserve the very best, and I believe you've found it."

John

After a while, Liam and I started for our room but somehow ended up in the living room instead, cuddled on a sofa by the fire. He'd caught me completely unawares. For some reason, I thought he was waiting for me to propose.

Opening Christmas gifts had been forgotten for the moment, and everyone else was in the kitchen doing the breakfast dishes.

"Wanna go to our room, Punkin?" he whispered, kissing my ear.

"I do, but can we wait a little while? This feels so good, and I want to enjoy sitting here with you."

We sat for a few more minutes. "Liam?" I finally asked.

"Mm?"

"It really happened, right? I wasn't dreaming?"

I loved his happy laugh. "Yes, it really happened. You haven't changed your mind, have you?"

"No way. But could we get married today? I don't want to wait."

"Sure, if you want to. But with all the snow, I don't know if we can find—"

"No!" Our heads jerked around as Vonnie entered the room. "You can't get married today because you will not cheat us all out of a proper wedding."

"Vonnie," Liam said, "if John wants.... I mean, we don't necessarily need—"

"Yes, you do, we all do. You've earned the right to stand up in front of your loved ones, and anyone else you want, and say vows to each other."

"But—"

"Think of me. I need it, too." Her expression was intense. "I deserve to be your best woman and have my faith restored in the possibility of love."

"You're right," he told her, but she was on a roll.

"Think of Mom. She's already in there talking about your wedding, and how she hopes you'll have it here. She'd never forgive you if you eloped. She'd be so disappointed if you didn't—"

"Okay, okay," Liam said, standing and holding up his hands in surrender. "We get it. We were just thinking out loud, anyway."

"Okay, then." She walked around in front of Liam. "Remember when we were teenagers and promised to be each other's best person?"

They grabbed each other, and I marveled at the love I felt for my new family.

Chris and Cait came in after a moment, followed by Andie. "I called the bakery up near the school," Andie said, "and they're open. The family lives upstairs over the shop, you know. Why don't we all go for a walk in the snow and buy some bread? Then you and I can make cinnamon rolls, John."

I nodded, still grinning from watching Liam and Vonnie. "Sounds great."

"Why don't we wait until this evening to open presents," Cait said. "We've had a lot of excitement today already."

We all agreed, and Liam and I went to our room to change.

Liam

I WAS PRACTICALLY JUMPING up and down. "Engaged! Frickin' engaged! We're gonna get married, John!" I was bouncing at the knees.

"Yes, we are, and the sooner the better."

He threw his arms around my neck, and I gave him a little kiss. "I think we need to celebrate."

He smiled while he rested his hands on my chest. "Why, Mr. Macadam. Do you mean what I think you mean?"

"Probably, Dr. Lawrence." I paused and nodded. "I probably do."

He grimaced a little. "Now? I thought we were getting changed for a walk with the family."

I pulled him in tight. "We're getting married for all kinds of reasons, and great sex is only one of them, but I think we deserve a little postproposal love. They'll wait for us. They understand." I couldn't delay another second, and I laid a big one on him.

He pulled back after a moment, wearing a grin that was no less than lascivious. "I think we deserve it, too." He turned his head a little to the side. "And as special as this day is, you'd better leave me very well-fucked."

John

Liam kissed me before I could say anything else, and it was hot and desperate. We made our way to the bed and spent a few minutes making out and getting our clothes off. When we were naked, he crawled on top of me and I spread my legs for him. I moaned while he kissed my throat and lightly stroked my cock, and when I trailed my hand down his belly, I found him hard and sticky. He groaned lustily when I closed my hand around his dick.

Finding his mouth, I tempted him into a smutty kiss while we wiggled against each other. My need quickly snowballed and I pulled away long enough to plead for what I wanted. "Fuck me, please."

"Gotta get you ready first." He reached across me to the nightstand and leaned back again as he clicked the lube bottle open. Slick fingers entered me, and he played with me until I was almost mad with lust. "Ride me?"

He groaned as I straddled him, and we both cried out as I slid down his hot, swollen cock, knowing I wouldn't last long.

I rode him hard. Soon his eyes were bulging, and his forehead was slick with sweat. "You're a great cowboy!"

"You're... an amazing... bull." I laughed as much as I could, considering how hard I was squirming around, finding the angles that pushed his dick hardest into my prostate. "Feels... so good," I whined. "Love you."

His face, already very red, turned almost purple. "*Dammit!* Ride me harder."

Our pace quickened and the steady hum of electricity that had been buzzing in my stomach spread to my balls. The stretch was delicious as his hard cock plunged up into me, harder and harder. He was rolling his head back and forth, sucking breath through the "O" of his mouth, and when I slammed down extra hard, his eyes flew open. "Oh, fuck!" he practically screamed.

He erupted inside me, and I loved the feeling of his hot spurts of cum, filling me up. "Yes! *Fuck!*" I hung right on the precipice, riding him as hard as I could, not quite there. He shoved into me again and that did it. I shot long streaks across his belly, one of them making it all the way to his forehead.

When I collapsed beside him, I quickly wiggled into the crook of his shoulder. "That was *so* good," I mumbled.

He chuckled softly. "You've got good aim, that's for sure." I glanced over in time to see him using the edge of the sheet to wipe my cum off his face.

Liam

An hour later, we were showered and dressed for a walk to the bakery, and John was still smiling.

I raised my eyebrows. "You said I'd better leave you well-fucked. Is it safe to assume I succeeded?"

"Oh yes," he said, and followed that up with a little grimace. "I may be walking with a limp for a day or two."

I snickered. "Limping, eh? I did good, then."

He huffed indignantly. "Don't laugh." Picking a sock up off the floor, he threw it at me.

I chortled louder. "So *that's* how you want to play it?"

I grabbed a couple socks and some undies from the floor where we'd tossed them before, and we threw clothing back and forth until I jumped him and dug my fingers into his ribs, making him squawk. "Yeah, that's it," I said, holding on tight and tickling him harder. "Squeal like a little girl!"

By the time we made it to the living room, everyone had already gone to the bakery and was back. Mom was waiting for John, ready to make cinnamon rolls.

After they went into the kitchen, the rest of us sat around talking. Eventually, Chris and I decided to play video games and have some drinks. During a bathroom break, I sneaked to the kitchen door and caught sight of Mom and my future husband working with dough and talking about Christmas in the 80s. They didn't know I was there, and I pulled back so I could still see them while I listened.

They talked about things like Jordache jeans, Members Only jackets, and Atari video games. John said that in the late 80s, he got his first computer for Christmas, a Macintosh Plus. She remembered them, and they laughed, saying that those computers didn't even come with a hard drive.

Mom asked John what he thought the best thing was that came from the 80s and he answered before he had time to blink. "Liam Sean Macadam, hands down. You have no idea, Andie. I was lost, my life was in shambles, and I saw this incredible guy across the room at law school orientation. He changed my life." He paused for a second. "How did you choose his name?"

Mom stopped kneading and looked at John, her expression quizzical. "Liam was his grandfather's name, and Sean was his great-grandfather. Why?"

John smiled. "I've always been interested in names, and I looked his up. It's the perfect name for him, *Liam Sean—Strong Protector, God's Gracious Gift*. That's what he is for me, no doubt."

Holy shit! I'd just fallen even more deeply in love with John, as impossible as that seemed. I was lost in my thoughts when I felt an arm around my shoulder.

"Dude, I wondered where you went," Chris said. "Let's go in and steal some cinnamon sugar."

About an hour later, Chris and I were locked in another video battle when John came into the room. "All right guys, time to rejoin the family." John took my game controller out of my hands, and I didn't even care that I died on-screen because the warm lips on mine were very much alive.

Soon we all had drinks in hand and enjoyed the late afternoon. Mom eventually raided the freezer and gave us leftover lasagna for dinner. Chris, John, and I chose a beautiful Barolo to go with it, and Mom insisted on making a toast before we ate.

"I'll always remember this as Liam and John's Christmas," she began. "You shared a beautiful thing with us today, and we are all thrilled for you. The first time you came home together, I knew things were special between you two. The last year, full of love, drama, and redemption, has convinced me that you were made for each other."

"Here, here," Vonnie said.

Mom smiled and went on. "I'm very glad the two of you finally realized it, as well. You've already been through more than some couples go through in a lifetime—"

"And you put us through it, too," Cait said, smirking.

"Cait!" Mom glared at her and then looked around the room, taking all of us in. "Yes, it was an ordeal for everyone because we love you so much, and we were hoping against hope that things would work out. Now, we can thank God that they have." She raised her glass, and everyone else did, too. "To John and Liam, we wish you every happiness, and we're overjoyed that yours has proven to be *no brief affair*."

"No brief affair," the family echoed.

30

Liam

It was the twenty-sixth before John and I were able to get out of Wainscott. The drive to Stowe was about seven hours in normal weather, and we'd planned to leave early because I wanted to get the driving done in the daylight before everything refroze. Everyone in the house got up to see us off.

"Liam and I are so glad we stayed," John said, after we all hugged goodbye. "This was what a family holiday is supposed to be like."

Mom kept going back and forth between John and me, giving us hugs. "I'm so happy you stayed. Don't forget, you're coming here for MLK weekend so we can talk about the wedding."

"I can't wait," John said. "And thanks for inviting my sister. She really wants to be part of things, and Liam and I are going to need all the help we can get navigating through all the bullshit."

Mom shot a hand to her heart. "Language, John William

Lawrence!" She was smiling at John, and his grin told me he realized he'd officially arrived as her new son.

"We gotta shape him up so he's not such a shitty son!" I said, shaking my head. "That language sucks."

Chris tried hard, but unsuccessfully, not to laugh. "For sure," he said. "What an asshole, using language like that."

Everyone broke up, and Mom shook her head. "You're all going to have to shape up. Dear God, now I've ended up with three sons to keep in line."

Chris reminded John and me that we'd agreed to visit him and Cait in the City for Super Bowl weekend. "Our new place has plenty of room, as long as you're willing to sleep standing up."

"We won't forget, dude," I promised. "We'll be there."

Cait gave me a hug. "You better not bail. We'll drive up to Syracuse and impose on you guys there if you do."

"Anytime," John said, glancing at his watch. "All of you are welcome there whenever you can come."

We finally managed to get in the car and drive away, and soon we relaxed into a peaceful silence. Vonnie had given John a book by his favorite mystery author, and he read that for a while. Eventually, he found some Christmas music on his phone and Bluetoothed it through the speakers.

He drank some coffee out of a thermos Mom sent along with us, and after I had some, he screwed the top back on and settled in his seat. "What are we going to do about names? I want to be a Macadam."

"Well...." I thought about it. "I'd kind of like to be a Lawrence. Let's just go the double-name route."

"Exactly what I was thinking. So, Lawrence-Macadam, or Macadam-Lawrence?"

I chuckled. "Whichever. We have time to figure that out."

"I'm sorry." He grinned like a little kid. "My mind is racing about everything."

I nodded. "Mine too. When are we going to do it? The wedding."

He wrinkled his brow for a minute and shrugged. "I guess we have to confer with our families, and we need to think about our own schedules. Cait and Chris are getting married in June. You're going to be working at McBurnie all summer and we'll be in the City. We have to think about it carefully."

"Not to worry, we'll figure something out." I winked at him. "As long as we're together, the rest is gravy."

John

We made excellent time and got to Stowe midafternoon. Our first stop was a grocery store to pick up some perishables, and from there we went to the realtor's office to get the key to the cabin. I didn't know what to expect because Liam had refused to show me any pictures of the place, but I was impressed when we drove up. It was a log cabin all right, but much larger and more elegant than I'd imagined. Snow surrounded the two-story structure, but the driveway, walkway, and front porch had been cleared.

We gathered as many of our provisions as we could carry and went inside, where I was blown away. The furniture was rustic bordering on elegant, with leather upholstery and light pinewood tables. A high cathedral ceiling with wide beams soared over a combination living-dining room that spanned the width of the cabin, and a two-story-high stone fireplace dominated the space. Behind the living room was a modern, well-equipped kitchen that opened onto a comfy TV room, and off to the side was a small bathroom.

Both bedrooms were upstairs. The master bedroom was larger and had another stone fireplace. French doors opened onto a balcony overlooking the mountains. I went out there and saw that the first-floor deck extended past the back of the house, with the hot tub situated so you could sit there and take in the view.

Liam joined me on the balcony. "Did I do okay?"

I turned toward him, shaking my head in awe. "It's glorious, the cabin *and* the scenery. You've outdone yourself."

After a few moments admiring the snow-covered vista, we went back downstairs to bring in the rest of our things. Once that was accomplished, we built a fire in the living room and cuddled on the sofa beside it for an hour.

"You hungry?" Liam asked, after we'd taken a nap.

I wiggled farther into his embrace. "I don't really want to move, but my stomach is complaining. Put on some music while I start cooking?"

I sautéed some chopped fennel and broiled a fish we'd bought in the village, and Liam made a spinach and walnut salad and opened a bottle of Chardonnay. We had ice cream for dessert.

Liam found candles in the sideboard, which cast a romantic glow around the beautiful room. Outdoor lights had come on when it got dark, and the reflections and shadows from the snowy exterior played through the windows. After we ate, we went back to the fire until the embers died down and Liam asked if I was ready for bed. We walked upstairs, holding each other close.

We got ready quickly and climbed into the king-sized poster bed. "C'mere," he said, wrapping me up in his arms. We held each other for a while, nibbling and licking at each other's throats and lips. When one of his hands slid down to my ass, I was glad I still went to the gym and suffered through all those squats. His other hand was behind my head, and he pulled me toward him for more soft kisses. Lip brushings, noses rubbing, and murmurs of affection were followed by a nose bump and giggles. Soft kisses escalated to hungry ones, and soon we were exploring each other's bodies.

A few minutes later, we had our cocks in each other's hands, both moaning pleasure into the other's mouth. He stopped jerking me and broke our kiss. "I need to be inside you so much I'm shaking."

I glanced at his hand, and he really was. "Get me ready." I gazed into his beautiful eyes and thought out loud. "I wish I could get pregnant and have your baby."

He picked up the lube and nipped my nose before heading below. "Don't know if that's in the cards, but we can sure give it our best shot."

Liam

I woke up later, still lying halfway across John, who was unconscious. I'd fucked him from behind, and he totally came apart. It made me feel amazing when he lost it like that. We'd always had a great sex life, and I'd long before lost count of the incredible orgasms we'd shared, but that night's could have been the best yet. Our incendiary, no-holds-barred love for each other found its expression in legendary sex.

John moaned when I shifted off of him. "That was incredible, Liam. Was it okay for you?"

"You know goddamn well it blew my fucking mind!" I said. "You're everything."

John

We talked into the night, thrilled to be fiancés. I wondered how much of the change we felt was in our minds. Promising to marry changed our expectations, but how much did it alter the reality of how we felt about each other? I eventually realized that our promises really had changed our feelings, deepened them. Words and promises are powerful, and things between us were different—better—precisely because our words and promises *had* changed our outlook.

I might have fallen half asleep while thinking such profound thoughts because the next thing I knew, I was twisting around, screaming. Liam was tickling me! He tickled, and I laughed, and he laughed, and I tickled him back. We wrestled as long as we could, which was not very long. We were both too worn out.

"Time to sleep, babe," he said, and gave me a long kiss.

There was something especially beautiful in Liam's eyes when we broke for air, and he smiled at me. I spent a moment basking in that warmth before I settled down. "I love you, my fiancé. More than I ever dreamt I could love anyone."

We turned on our sides, my back to Liam's front, and I pulled his arm across my chest.

He kissed the side of my throat. "I might have dreamed about it once or twice when we were apart, but those fantasies were so lame compared to the real thing." He stroked my belly for a moment. "Hey, you think we can dream together tonight?"

"I wouldn't have it any other way. See you there, my Sugar Plum."

THANK YOU

Thank you for reading *No Brief Affair*. We're very grateful for your support and hope you enjoyed the story.

Please leave a review on Amazon. Reviews don't have to be long, and they do so much to help the authors and other readers.

BOOKS BY RYAN TAYLOR & JOSHUA HARWOOD

Macadam Universe

No Brief Affair (Beyond Courtship Book One)

Legally Bound (Beyond Courtship Book Two)

The Chrismukkah Crisis: A Holiday Romance

What He Really Needs

Too Close to the Flame

Bethesda Barracudas Hockey

Nice Catching You

The New Next One

Fire in the Ice

Ice Angels

Ice Devils

ABOUT THE AUTHORS

Ryan Taylor and Joshua Harwood met in law school and were married in 2017. They live in a suburb of Washington, DC, and share their home with a big, cuddly German shepherd. Ryan and Josh love to travel, and hockey is practically a religion in their house. Ryan also enjoys swimming, and Josh likes to putter in the garden whenever he can. They began writing to celebrate the romance they were so lucky to find with each other, and the sharing soon developed into a passion for telling stories about love between out and proud men. You can contact Ryan and Josh through their website at

www.ryanandjoshth.com.

Made in United States
North Haven, CT
08 November 2024